PRAISE FOR K~~~ O9-AIF-598

904-224-2694

"Nobody can capture the essence of Americana heart and soul quite as well as Kathleen Kane."

—*Affaire de Coeur*

"Kathleen Kane infuses her novels with the wonderful sense of warmth and sweetness that makes you feel toasty right down to your toes."

—*Romantic Times*

THIS TIME FOR KEEPS

"Wondrous romance that will leave you longing for more. Ms. Kane's extraordinary talents shine."

—*Romantic Times*

"A lively plot of all-out seduction with Kane's witty dialogue and fine portrayal of the headstrong, hot-to-trot heroine and the equally stubborn cowboy."

—*Publishers Weekly*

STILL CLOSE TO HEAVEN

"Warmhearted, funny, delightful, and memorable, STILL CLOSE TO HEAVEN is a novel to savor and cherish. Ms. Kane's innovative tale shows us how a small ripple in one's life can widen, altering the course of one's destiny forever. Readers will cheer, laugh out loud, and shed more than one tear while Rachel and Jackson travel the course to their destiny. Bravo, Ms. Kane! A keeper."

—*Romantic Times*

"Ms. Kane has crafted a story filled with tenderness and danger, heartache and smiles—and a story that will make you wish for a ghost of your own."

—*Painted Rock Reviews*

More . . .

"Unique, endearing characters grab hold of your heart-strings and never let go. A magical romance to treasure time and again."

—*Rendezvous*

A POCKETFUL OF PARADISE

"Ms. Kane is an expert at breathing life into her characters . . . a sweet and spicy romance, sprinkled with inspiration and hope."

—*Romance Forever*

"Kane once again displays her remarkable talent for unusual, poignant plots and captivating characters."

—*Publishers Weekly*

"A beautiful, sensitive, humorous, uplifting story."

—*Romantic Times*

"A gloriously inventive love story with a spectacular plot."

—*Rendezvous*

"Will leave tears in your eyes and gladness in your heart."

—*CompuServe Romance Reviews*

"Ms. Kane writes with a rare sensitivity that thoroughly draws you into the story . . . A POCKETFUL OF PARADISE has humor in all the right places yet is jam-packed with heart-wrenching emotion. You'll need a few tissues before you're finished with this uplifting story. I loved every word and I'm off to find the rest of her work. Very, very highly recommended."

—*Under the Covers Book Reviews*

ST. MARTIN'S PAPERBACKS TITLES
BY KATHLEEN KANE

A Pocketful of Paradise
Still Close to Heaven
This Time For Keeps
Dreamweaver

Exellent

Dreamweaver

good book

KATHLEEN KANE

St. Martin's Paperbacks

NOTE: If you purchased this book without a cover you should be aware that this book is stolen property. It was reported as "unsold and destroyed" to the publisher, and neither the author nor the publisher has received any payment for this "stripped book."

DREAMWEAVER

Copyright © 1998 by Kathleen Kane.

All rights reserved. No part of this book may be used or reproduced in any manner whatsoever without written permission except in the case of brief quotations embodied in critical articles or reviews. For information address St. Martin's Press, 175 Fifth Avenue, New York, NY 10010.

ISBN: 0-312-96808-6

Printed in the United States of America

St. Martin's Paperbacks edition / December 1998

St. Martin's Paperbacks are published by St. Martin's Press, 175 Fifth Avenue, New York, NY 10010.

10 9 8 7 6 5 4 3 2 1

To my mother-in-law, Mary Ann Child, for the years of laughter and love we've shared. For the Sicilian cooking lessons, for being a terrific Nana, and for always being on my side instead of your son's. All of your daughters-in-law feel lucky to have you and blessed to call you a friend.

And to the memory of my late father-in-law, Dan Child. A kind, funny, thoughtful man whose love knew no limits and who left us years too early.

PROLOGUE

In this world," Gideon said, his deep voice thundering across the heavens, "there is a place for everything. Even nightmares."

"But he was such a *little* boy," Meara Simon countered, and three of her colleagues took hasty steps backward, distancing themselves from her and the risky stand she took against the Dream Master.

She could admit to a touch of nervousness. But no Simon had ever run from a fight and she wasn't about to be the first. If her knees were more solid than spirit, everyone in the vast chamber would no doubt hear them knocking together.

Gideon's black eyes flashed. "It's not your duty to decide who gets what kind of dreams, Meara," he declared, and to his credit, didn't raise his voice again. But then, he didn't have to.

Every soul in the area was already quaking.

"I simply don't understand why you're so upset," Meara went on, determined not to give in to her perfectly natural impulse to run and hide. "It was just one dream, after all. And he was so tired."

Gideon glowered at her for what seemed an eternity before shaking his head in apparent disgust. "He was *supposed* to be tired."

"Well, now," Meara answered quickly, both hands at what used to be nicely rounded hips—and now, were no more than her soul's echo of her former body. "That makes no sense a'tall."

Someone behind her gasped and Gideon's dark brows drew together. But she sailed right past the warning signs. If she was going to be judged, then by thunder, she would at least speak up in her own defense.

"A growing boy needs his sleep, for pity's sake. *Everyone* knows that. I should think you'd be grateful to me rather than roaring like a lion with a thorn in its paw."

Another gasp, from farther away this time. Really. She would have thought that *someone* would speak up for her and brave the Dream Master's legendary impatience.

"Roaring?" Gideon repeated, clearly incredulous.

"Aye," she told him, snapping him a nod that sent the echoes of long, curly red hair flying into her face. "Roaring you are and roaring I say."

"You have been here for only—" The Dream Master broke off to consult a record book that looked thick enough to hold every thought ever entertained. "*One* century," he went on a moment later, "and in that time, you've defied me, disobeyed me, and in general, created more confusion in the Dream World than has been seen since time began."

She'd only done what she thought right—and wasn't that all that was asked of any soul? Still, she permitted herself a small smile. After all, it wouldn't do to be too proud. Hadn't her own dear mother, may she rest in peace, always told her that one day, she would make herself known? And hadn't she only had to follow her dear father's advice to do it? How many times, Meara wondered, had her father intoned, "A little revolution now and again is good for every living thing"?

"Meara Simon," Gideon proclaimed, bringing her out of her pleasant thoughts, "this time you've gone too far.

Charges will be heard against you at Sunrise."

"Charges?" she whispered, beginning to feel just the faintest twinge of uneasiness. Perhaps she'd gone a bit too far with her revolution. But—what could Gideon do to her? He couldn't very well have her shot. She'd already been shot. One hundred and two years before.

A smattering of hushed voices swirled around her and for the first time since leaving her earthly life behind, Meara felt utterly and completely . . . alone.

Gideon's tight, angry features gave her no comfort as he finished. "You may present your defense, and then a judgement will be handed down."

In the next instant, he was gone.

Most of the other Dream Weavers began to drift off, apparently content to know that *they* weren't the ones having to face Gideon's anger. Meara looked slowly around the nearly empty chamber and paused when her gaze landed on one friendly face.

Daisy hadn't been there long, not more than twenty years or so, but in that time, she'd proven herself a true friend, despite her rather . . . well, *coarse* manner.

With a bold suggestion of a sway in her hips, Daisy crossed the space between them, smoothing her hands down her deeply cut bodice, then giving her formidable breasts a push upward.

"Well, honey," the other woman said with a shake of her head. "You've cooked your goose good and proper now."

"I don't see what all the fuss is about." It was just one little dream, Meara thought.

"Don't guess Gideon cares if you see or not," Daisy said. "But I been askin' around and I figure the best thing for you to do is skedaddle outa here for a little bit."

"Skedaddle?" Meara frowned slightly.

"Vamoose," Daisy clarified. "Take off. Get on your pony and ride."

"I don't have a pony." Meara pointed out what she

would have thought was a fairly obvious fact.

"I mean, get out of town. Let 'ol Gideon get his six-guns back in their holsters."

"Six-guns?"

"We got no time for this," Daisy said and headed for the nearest exit, dragging Meara along behind her. "No man is gonna stand still and let a little bitty thing like you show him up. Best thing for this here situation is for you to get your butt out of sight and keep it there."

If she could have, Meara would have blushed. Instead, she tried to keep up with the spirit who was once, according to Daisy, the owner of the best damn cathouse in Bear Creek, Texas.

Although why cats deserved a home of their own was a puzzle to Meara.

"Where can I go?" she asked when her friend finally came to a sudden halt.

"Honey," Daisy assured her with a grin, "I got just the place."

A few earthly heartbeats later, Meara vanished in a blink of light.

Daisy smiled thoughtfully. Maybe she should have warned the little thing that she had a few surprises headed her way. Was it really fair to send the girl into hiding without telling her everything?

A minute later, Daisy shook her head. No, it had to be this way.

If Meara had known the whole truth, she might not have gone.

CHAPTER ONE

It ain't right, *nor* fittin'."

"Leave it alone," Conner James grumbled and sank deeper into the cushions of his favorite chair. He flicked a quick, irritated glance at Grub Taylor, housekeeper/cook/thorn in his side.

"Man your age," the older man went on, warming to his familiar theme, "with nothin' to show for livin'. No wife. No young'uns."

Conner reached out one hand for the glass of whiskey resting nearby, took a sip, then interrupted Grub's sermon. "I've got this ranch, don't I?"

Unimpressed, Grub snorted. "Yeah, and you've had it for two whole years and still livin' in it alone."

"If I was alone," Conner shot back, a rumble of temper coloring his tone, "I wouldn't be having to listen to you harpin' on me to get married, now would I?"

That statement bought him a moment's peace. Conner looked at the older man and silently admitted something he would never own up to out loud. He was glad to have the old coot around. Even if he did have to hear Grub's opinion on absolutely everything.

Darn near bald but for one or two strands of iron gray

hair that he insisted on combing across the top of his gleaming pate, Grub boasted snow-white whisker stubble that rose and fell on his lined, weathered face like fresh powder on mountain crevices. But the man's keen black eyes were as sharp as ever and his thin, wiry body was stronger than a man of sixty-eight had a right to expect.

They'd been together a long time and Conner was downright fond of the old cuss. But what he didn't know about women could fill Lake Tahoe basin.

"We been through this, Grub."

"Let's do 'er again." The older man set his jaw in a line that clearly said he was ready and willing to fight.

Conner shook his head. "No woman in her right mind is gonna want to marry a man like me."

"What the hell's wrong with you?" Grub demanded. "You got a nice place. You're young. Not too stupid. And you ain't stop-a-train-ugly."

Conner scowled, took another long drink of whiskey and felt the fire spread throughout his chest. Despite Grub's notions, Conner knew good and well that no decent woman would ever marry the son of a whore and a gambler.

But he didn't care.

He'd been alone most of his life—but for Grub—and he'd gotten along just fine. When he wanted a woman, he found a good-sized town and bought one for the evening. A simple, honest transaction. No feelings or emotions involved. No disappointments or broken promises.

Grub mumbled something and Conner sighed. Whenever his old friend had some comment he was sure no one else would agree with, he had a habit of muttering that comment—just loud enough to drive a body crazy wondering what he said. "What was that?"

"I *said*, you're talkin' like a fool."

Conner laughed shortly, stretched his long legs out and crossed his booted feet at the ankle. Closing his eyes, he balanced his whiskey glass on his chest and decided to ignore Grub and try for a little peace and quiet.

That hope was shattered in the next instant when a crashing thud sounded from upstairs.

Conner's eyes flew open and he shot a quick look at the hall and stairway, half expecting to find the shingled roof lying across the scarred wood floors.

"What the hell was that?" Grub demanded.

"Sounds like the whole damn place is falling in," Conner shouted as he set his glass aside. He raced for the stairs and the second story beyond. Blast it, he should have fixed the dang roof before building that new corral. But he'd wanted to take care of important things first. And his small string of horses was the most important thing in the world to him at the moment.

He took the steps two at a time, his long legs carrying him far faster than poor Grub could manage. Absently, he heard the older man's footsteps pounding heavily on the stairs behind him, but didn't slow his pace to wait for him.

The long hallway stretched out in front of him. The frayed, threadbare carpet runner snaking along the marred oak flooring masked his steps slightly as he hurried down the hall toward a series of smaller sounds; muffled crashes and a tinkle of broken glass echoed in the big old house.

He hardly paused before the closed door to his bedroom. Grabbing the brass doorknob, he twisted it and gave the door a push. Stepping across the threshold, he stopped dead.

It looked as though a twister had set down in the middle of his room. Through the roof. A wide, gaping hole displayed the deep blue sky and Conner stared for a long, stunned minute as threads of clouds drifted past the opening. "Damn it," he muttered before turning his gaze on what was left of his room. The mattress on his four-poster bed now lay drunkenly half on the floor, its supporting slats broken beneath it. A side table lay on end, the contents of its single drawer scattered across the faded Oriental rug. The globe hurricane lamp that had once rested on that table lay smashed into fragments and the smell of lamp oil permeated the room. Even the curtains hung askew on the windows.

How the hell had this happened? he wondered. And why now? Didn't he have enough to worry about without picking up after some rogue tornado?

Behind him, Conner heard Grub breathing heavy from his run up the stairs. "What—" Puff, "—in tarnation—" Pant, "—is goin' on?"

"Looks like some blamed twister dropped in."

"A twister?" Grub repeated, astonished, as he took in the mess. "Here?"

"You got a better explanation?" Conner snapped in disgust and kicked at a shard of glass that lay winking at him in a patch of late afternoon sunshine.

"Here now," an indignant female voice shouted from behind the torn, dark green draperies hanging from one of the bed's four posts. "There's no need to be slicin' me into ribbons. Haven't I only just survived bein' crushed by this great bed of yours?"

A woman?

What the devil was going on around here? Conner stomped farther into the room and looked around the end of the bed. His gaze landed on a redheaded female, sitting on his floor with her skirt hiked up above the knees of extremely shapely legs. "Who the hell are you?" he demanded.

She didn't even blink those huge green eyes of hers, she simply looked him up and down, then said, "There's no need to shout. My hearing's quite unaffected by my upset, thank you very much for asking after me health." Pushing a mass of wild red hair back off her face, she went on in a rush of words. "Meara Simon's my name," she said. "Though why you should be carin' about such a thing when it's clear to any who have eyes . . ." She paused knowingly as she tugged her skirt down over her legs. ". . . and who haven't been struck blind for lookin' where they've no right, that I'm in need of a bit of assistance, is beyond my understandin' at the moment."

Amazing female. She actually looked offended.

"You're Irish," he said lamely.

"My, but you're a quick one," she snapped, her green eyes glinting dangerously. "Just what is your name, then?"

"Conner James," he told her.

"Conner, is it?" She gave him a brief smile that dazzled him. "Then you've a bit of the Irish in you as well. I should have noticed straight off, what with your black Irish good looks starin' me in the face . . . but . . ." She sighed and looked around her. "What with all that's happened an' all . . ."

He didn't want to be dazzled by her, so he ignored the odd lurch of his heartbeat, threw his hands wide, and demanded, "What exactly *did* happen?"

She frowned at him. "Isn't that what I'm tryin' to understand myself?"

Her emotions were like quicksilver. Anger, pleasure, and confusion streaked across her features in dramatic shifts of expression.

"Look, lady," he said tightly, determined to get to the bottom of this despite her tendency to wander off the subject. "This is my house and *my* bedroom you've destroyed."

"Aye, well, I'm sorry about that," she offered lamely. "Though I can't imagine how . . ."

"Just tell me how the hell you got into my room."

"As you've no doubt noticed," she answered, with a quick glance at the yawning hole in the ceiling, "through the roof." She frowned uncertainly. "I suppose."

"Don't you know?" he asked and threw a glance himself at the hole, as if expecting to find a clue to this mess.

"Well now, if I knew the answers to everything, I could

apply for the Almighty's job, now couldn't I?"

She had the nerve to look insulted. Behind him, Conner heard Grub's muffled laughter. He was glad *somebody* was enjoying all of this.

All right, maybe it wasn't her fault she'd crashed through his roof. But he'd be damned if he was going to let her make him feel as though his house had been in her way.

Scowling, he looked from her to the roof and back again. He'd heard of wagons being sucked up by twisters and plopped down again, sometimes miles away. Once or twice, he'd even heard people talk about cows that had survived a ride in a tornado. But damn it, Conner had *never* heard tell of a person living through such a thing.

And, as far as he knew, there hadn't been a tornado seen in Nevada in . . . ever.

But what other explanation was there? Women didn't just fall from the sky.

"Now," the redhead said, capturing his attention completely. She blew a stubborn red curl out of her eyes and held out one hand toward him. When he didn't take it immediately, she shook it for emphasis. "Will ya be be givin' me a hand or do ya expect me to crawl up out of this mess on me own?"

He grabbed hold of her hand and pulled with all the delicacy of a man snatching a trout from a river.

Meara flew off the floor and smacked right into the hard, broad wall of his chest. A white-hot bolt of something too exciting for words streaked through her, but before she could try to identify it, he released her and her knees buckled. Instantly, he grabbed hold of her again and this time, didn't let go, a fact for which she was grateful.

Now that's odd, she thought, looking down at her legs. Why did her limbs feel so weak and trembly? And at the same time, she had a sense of heaviness about her as well. As though her body was somehow . . . *wrong*. Too clumsy and large by half. She frowned thoughtfully. Oh, she wasn't well a'tall.

His long fingers bit into the flesh of her upper arms and she felt as though his touch was the only thing holding her in place. Tipping her head back, she stared up at him. Blast if he wasn't a big one, though. Her neck was getting a crick in it already and she hadn't begun to look her fill of him.

Thick black hair was swept back from a high, intelligent forehead, yet one wavy lock refused to be tamed and fell forward to hang just above an arched black eyebrow. Eyes as blue as the lakes of Kerry glared down at her, and his fine, generous mouth was tightened into a grim slash across his well-cut features.

Well, what right did he have to be so bloody angry? But for some bits and pieces of furniture, he was hale and hearty. Which was more than she could say for herself as an assortment of aches and pains began to make themselves known.

Heat from his hands settled into her bones and something inside her swirled into a flutter momentarily and stunned her to her toes. Blood rushed into her cheeks and her heartbeat thundered in her chest.

"Aren't you as handsome as the devil himself," she muttered, not even realizing she'd spoken aloud until she heard the older man behind him sputter into laughter.

He practically growled at her. "The devil and me have more in common than looks, lady," he said, clearly determined to ignore his friend's amusement. "Now that you're on your feet," he went on in a voice as deep and dark as a well on a black night, "why don't you tell me who the hell you are and what you're doing in my house."

Her eyebrows lifted and she looked at the older man. " 'Handsome is as handsome does,' my mother used to

say. Well, apparently, this boyo's handsome only goes
skin deep."

Grub snickered.

"If you're through insulting me," Conner grumbled
through tightly compressed lips, "answer my questions."

"I've already told ya," she said, turning her gaze back
to Conner. "My name's Meara Simon. As for what I'm
doin' here . . ." She scowled at the sudden and total
blankness welling up in her mind. "I'm afraid I've no
idea."

"What?" He let go of her abruptly.

She swayed and teetered for a long, breathless minute,
then locked her knees and willed herself to stay upright.

"I don't know why I'm here," she said, glancing
around the room as if looking to find answers hidden
there somewhere. "Or how I came to be here. Do you?"

"Would I ask you if I did?" he bellowed, and she
winced at his tone.

"How'm I to know the answer to that?" she fired right
back. "I've only just seen ya, haven't I?" Rubbing at the
spot on her forehead directly between her eyes, she muttered, "You could be as honest as the Pope or as crooked
as a hunchback for all I know."

Grub laughed out loud.

Conner exhaled in a rush of frustration.

She knew just how he felt. Sweet Saint Bridget, she
thought, if she could just lift the curtain of fog clouding
her mind, surely she could think her way out of this kettle
of fish she'd landed in. Idly, she reached around and
rubbed at the aching soreness in her behind. However
she'd gotten there, 'twas obvious to her at least, that
she'd landed square on her bottom.

A shift of emotions crossed Conner's face until at last,
she spied a bit of concern. Perhaps he wasn't all bad after
all, Meara told herself.

"It was a twister, wasn't it?" he asked, his voice less
hostile than a moment before.

"Twister?" she repeated.

"A tornado."

She frowned up at him. "Now what in blue blazes is a tornado?"

He stared at her as if she was speaking Gaelic, which she knew she wasn't because she wasn't sure she remembered how to speak Gaelic at all. Oh, this was a fine mess indeed, she thought, disgusted.

"A tornado," he said, and clearly his patience was at its end, "is a big wind. Strong enough to lift farm wagons into the air and drop them miles from where they started."

"Holy Mother," she whispered and crossed herself hurriedly. "And ya think I've been sucked up by one of these great winds and tossed into your fine house?"

"It's the only thing that fits," he said, lifting his gaze to look at the huge, wide hole in the ceiling. He inhaled sharply and blew it out again.

" 'Tis a miracle I'm alive," she said and immediately began patting herself down, just to make sure she had all of her parts and that they were in working order.

Turning his deep blue gaze back to her, he asked, "Are you all right? Did you break any bones?"

She sniffed and shot him a narrowed look. " 'Tis high time you think to ask *that* question." His eyebrows lifted, but she went right on. "And as for this *tornado* of yours . . . if that's what brought me here, you've no right to be blamin' *me* for fallin' through a roof that was apparently no stronger than two sticks an' a prayer."

The whiskered man behind him gave up all pretense of smothering his laughter, and Meara sent him a broad smile in appreciation.

Conner "Handsome Devil" James inclined his head slightly, one corner of his mouth tilting in a suggestion of a smile. "You're right. It wasn't your fault. Are you hurt?"

Well now, he was much more agreeable when he

wasn't shouting. But then, she liked a good shouting match as much as the next Irishman, too.

She ran her hands up and down her body, then shook both legs and arms for good measure, just to be sure. She seemed to be sound of limb, but she couldn't help wondering why her own body should feel so . . . strange. Different. Wrong. 'Twas as if she'd no notion of how to move or stand. She felt burdened by the heavy weight of her limbs and the clothing she wore.

'Twas all so very odd.

"Are you hurt?" Conner repeated, less patiently than before.

"No," she said softly, her mind racing with question after question. "I don't think so."

"That's something, I guess," he muttered, with another look at his precious roof.

"Very gracious of you, I'm sure."

Grub muffled another snort of laughter and Conner shot him a disgusted look.

Turning to look at the more pleasant of the two men, Meara said to Grub, "If it wouldn't be too much bother, do ya think I might have a cup of tea?"

CHAPTER TWO

"Well, perfect," Conner muttered and pushed both hands through his hair. Tea. That's all she had to say? Anger simmered in the pit of his stomach and colored his voice as he said, "Yeah, let's have some tea while I figure out how to keep rain from coming in through the roof and drowning me in my sleep."

One red-gold eyebrow lifted into a high arch. Meara gave the soft blue sky and wispy white clouds a long, thorough look, then said, "There'll be no rain this day."

Conner laughed shortly. "Obviously you're new around here. This high in the mountains, the weather can change its mind quicker than a fickle woman with two beaux."

"Mountains, is it?" Meara breathed quietly. "With snow, do ya think?"

"Hopefully not tonight," Conner said pointedly, deliberately ignoring the gleam of excitement in her eyes.

"Ah," she sighed and nodded solemnly.

Conner slanted a look at Grub. The older man shrugged and shifted an uncomfortable glance at the woman.

"You're a wise man," she told Conner and gave his forearm a friendly pat. " 'Tis best to be prepared for fair or foul weather. After all, as me father used to say,

'There's no need to fear the wind if your haystacks are tied down.' "

He thought about that one for a long minute or two, then shook his head. "It's not haystacks I'm worried about," he told her. Casting a quick look at Grub, he said, "Go make her some tea. I'm going up on the roof. Find out just how bad it is."

Grub chuckled and Conner shot him a glare that could have felled a grizzly at a hundred paces. The old coot's grin never wavered. Damned if he wasn't enjoying himself.

"I'm no expert," Meara said, her tone thoughtful, "at least, I don't think I am. But if you'd like my opinion, I'd say the roof's ruined."

Grub chuckled again and Conner gritted his teeth. He didn't see a damn thing funny in any of this. Meara's green eyes were on him and when he looked her way, he felt himself near falling into the cool, spring freshness of her gaze.

And with that ridiculous notion rattling around inside his head, he turned on his heel and left the room.

Outside, Conner spared a quick glance at the men working in the corral. One of the men stood in the center of the enclosure, with a yearling mare on a short halter rope, trotting her in tight circles, easing her into the idea of wearing a bridle and reins.

But it was to the men outside the corral, leaning on the fence that he called. "Hobart!" When a tall, lanky man turned in his direction, Conner yelled, "Get the ladder out of the barn and bring it over to the side of the house, will you?"

"Yessir, boss."

"Problem?" the man beside Hobart shouted.

"You could say that."

Conner turned and headed to the far side of the split-log house. A couple of minutes later, he heard someone walking up beside him. He glanced at his foreman,

Tucker Hanks. "Did you hear anything a bit ago?"

The man's sharp blue eyes narrowed. "Like what?"

Hell, if he'd heard a crash, the man wouldn't be asking what kind of sound they were talking about. "Like somebody falling through a roof."

Tucker tipped his sweat-stained hat to the back of his head and stared at him. "Huh?"

Conner jerked his head toward the house. "A few minutes ago, a woman fell right through the damn roof and landed in my bedroom."

"A *woman*?" Tucker's long, thoughtful face broke into a wide grin. "I always did say you was a lucky man, boss."

Yeah. Lucky. "And you always were loco," Conner muttered.

Tucker chuckled.

An instant later, Hobart arrived, balancing a wooden ladder across one narrow, bony shoulder. He eased it into position against the side of the house, then stood back, wiping his forehead with the sleeve of his shirt. He looked from one man to the other before asking, "What's goin' on?"

Conner ignored him and started climbing, but he heard Tucker answer, "Seems like somebody dropped a female right into the boss's lap."

"No foolin'?" Hobart asked around a slow whistle. "Who is she?"

"Don't know," Tucker admitted.

"Is she pretty?"

"Ain't got a look at her yet."

Conner shook his head and muttered darkly to himself. Pretty. Is that the only thing they wanted to know? Well, hell yes, she was pretty. Instantly, an image of long red hair and brilliant green eyes filled his mind. All right, she was more than pretty. Beautiful, really. But that didn't mean a damn thing, did it? He wanted to know who the hell she was, how she came to fly through his roof, and how she was going to get back to wherever she came from.

Stepping off the top rung onto the steeply pitched roof, Conner scrambled toward the gaping hole, his boots sliding on the wood shingles, his fingers grabbing for purchase. When he was finally in position and looking down into the mess that was his room, he admitted that Meara had been right. The roof *was* ruined.

Of course, he'd known that before he'd climbed up to the damn roof. When you can look through your ceiling and see the sky, there's a big problem.

Disgusted, he eased his way back to the ladder and started down, only half listening to the conversation between the two men below him.

"I never heard the like," Hobart said, clearly awestruck. "Imagine that. Women fallin' right outa the sky. Heck, it's gettin' so a man ain't safe nowhere."

Tucker chuckled. "Most men wouldn't mind a pretty female landin' on 'em, Hobart."

"Don't even know if she *is* pretty. 'Sides, the pretty ones is always the most trouble."

Conner scowled to himself. Hobart was right. Pretty women were trouble. And he had a feeling that Meara was going to be more than her fair share's worth.

"You want you some peace," Hobart was saying, "find you a ugly woman. She'll be so damn grateful, she'll settle right in and not give you a minute's worry." He inhaled deeply and released it on a sigh. "Course, even a ugly woman's too much trouble for me."

"Hobart," Tucker said on a laugh, "you spend too much time with those horses."

Only half listening, Conner jumped to the ground, then looked at the men and nodded grimly. "Tucker, you and Hobart get on up there and nail down some planks over that hole. Tomorrow, you can start the reshingling."

"I ain't much good high up, boss," Hobart reminded him.

Tucker snorted. "Nor on the ground, if it comes to it."

Conner shook his head. It was true, Hobart wasn't much for work. In fact, he'd never met a man with a wider lazy streak. But the man was a genius with horses. Getting him to do anything outside a corral, though, was a chore and a half. "I need that roof fixed before the next rain," Conner said tightly. "You two are gonna do it."

Tucker nodded.

Hobart sighed, then asked, "How you figure that female ended up fallin' through your roof, boss?"

Conner looked up at the roof and shook his head. "I don't know. Twister, maybe?"

"Pickin' up people and layin' 'em down again?" Tucker asked no one in particular. "Never heard of that before."

"Me neither," Conner allowed. "But nothing else makes sense."

Slowly, Conner turned and walked around to the front of his house, leaving the two men to their work. For one brief moment, he forgot all about Meara Simon as he gazed at the sturdy structure in front of him.

It still gave him a thrill of pride to know the place belonged to him. Made of rough-hewn logs felled on the property, it stood two stories high with gabled windows on the second floor. There was a stone fireplace in the main room on the ground floor, tall enough for a man to stand up straight in, and from the second-story windows, he had a clear view of the surrounding forests and most of Lake Tahoe.

The outside could stand some cleaning up, he thought as his gaze moved over the straggly weeds poking through the gaps in the steps and along the front wall. Hell, the inside could too, for that matter, but the logs were sound. And there was a wide front porch just right for sitting back in the evening, enjoying the end of a day. Of course, he was still too busy trying to get the ranch up and running to be able to lounge around much. But one day, he would. One day he'd sit down there and admire all he'd accomplished. He'd show everyone who ever said he was no good.

He smiled to himself at the image in his mind, then frowned as the future faded into the reality of today. Conner shoved his hands into his pants pockets and braced his legs wide apart, as if readying for a fight. Hell, he had no time for this. He had to concentrate. On building this ranch into the best damned horse-breeding outfit in the country.

Then he'd have everything he'd ever dreamed of. And, a voice whispered from the back of his mind, you'll still be alone.

Well, he argued silently, what was the alternative to being alone? Married?

What in the hell would he do with a wife?

But wasn't having a family all tied in with having a home? He wasn't sure of that, either. Conner snorted a choked laugh. The only thing he *was* sure of was that he finally had a place of his own and the only way he would leave it was feet first, stretched out in a box.

Shaking off thoughts of a future still too distant to worry about, with a critical eye, he looked at the home he'd won in a high-stakes card game. Looking for signs of twister damage. But there didn't seem to be a thing. Damned odd tornado, he told himself. Blow in, drop a woman, and blow out? All without a sound or rustle of wind against the glass panes? His gaze shifted, drifting over the familiar landscape of his ranch. Not a rock out of place.

Frowning, he started back around the side of the main house and stopped dead a minute later. He hadn't noticed this before. Must have been too busy concentrating on damage to the house. A huge, heavy limb from one of the giant pines that ringed the ranch house lay on the ground. He walked to it, knelt down and examined the torn bark and eerily white inside of the tree branch. It had been torn from the tree. Ripped, like something a spoiled child would do to a doll.

Glancing up, he quickly found the injured pine, marked with a wide slash of white against its dark trunk. His sharp eyes looked it up and down until he'd convinced himself it looked safe enough. He sure didn't want the rest of the damn thing falling down and taking a bigger chunk of his house with it.

He got to his feet, shaking his head, then twisted around to look at the damage to his house. Somehow, the damned branch must have been slammed into the roof. That's one hell of a wind. But that didn't explain how an Irish girl had landed in his house.

If there had been a tornado, he would have heard it. Wouldn't he? You don't just get a rogue wind strong enough to lift a woman and throw her through a roof without so much as some kind of warning.

So if it wasn't a twister . . . how in the hell had she ended up in his house?

"Thought you said ya wanted some tea?" Grub asked, taking hold of Meara's arm only to be shaken off a moment later.

"Aye," she said softly, pressing her nose to the window pane, "I do, I do." She watched as himself, Conner James walked along the side of the house until he was out of her sight. Meara braced her hands on the windowsill and pressed closer against the glass, but she couldn't see Conner anymore. Oddly disappointed, she shifted her gaze to a wide line of blue beyond the tall pines standing like soldiers at attention. "Would that be a lake?"

He leaned in close, squinted over her shoulder and said, " 'Course it's a lake."

"Ah, lovely," she said with a smile. "And what would you call it?"

Grub swivelled his head to stare at her. "Tahoe," he told her, in an odd, strained voice. "You mean to tell me you don't know this place at all? Don't even know Tahoe?"

A tremor of uneasiness swept through her. It was a hard thing, this ugly blankness in her mind. Why couldn't she remember? "An odd name for a lake, don't you think?"

"It's Indian."

Meara looked at him. Indian?

"Means 'Big Water.' "

She shifted uncomfortably as he stared at her with questioning, gray eyes. She could almost hear him wondering about her and couldn't really blame him. So, she wasn't about to ask him what "Indian" meant. Inhaling sharply, Meara tried to focus her mind. Tried to bring up one little fact about herself. One tiny hint as to who she was and how she'd come to be there.

But there was nothing.

She shivered slightly and swallowed past a sudden knot of fear clogging her throat. But for her name, she knew nothing of herself. What had happened to her? And how could she fix it?

"You ain't all right, little girl," Grub said softly. "Are ya?"

No, she thought. No sympathy. Tears stung the backs of her eyes, but she willed them away. If he felt sorry for her now, she would join him, and crying would serve no purpose a'tall. That much she knew instinctively. Squaring her shoulders, she stared out the window, unwilling to meet Grub's concerned gaze.

"No," she finally said. "I don't think I am."

"Well," he said giving her shoulder an awkward pat, "don't you go frettin'. We'll figure out where ya belong. Sooner or later."

"And until then?" she whispered almost to herself.

"Don't go worryin' about that now," he said.

But she *had* to worry, didn't she? Stepping back from the window, Meara noticed her handprints on the gritty windowsill, then glanced at her hands. Her fear receded in a burst of disgust. Clucking her tongue, she brushed her palms together thoroughly. Imagine letting lovely wood like that get covered in dirt and smudges.

"Mother of Saint Bridget," she muttered. "Do you people not own a dust cloth?"

Grub muttered something she didn't quite catch, then pulled the curtains down to hide the prints left in the dust. "I can't do everything, ya know. This here's a big house. And I ain't as spry as I used to be."

And hadn't been for quite awhile, Meara mused as her gaze drifted over the dustballs gathered in the corners and the dull glint reflecting off a grimy mirror hanging nearby. It was a grand big house, but a blind woman could see that without care, it would soon fall apart from the inside out.

'Twas clear to her that these two men desperately needed help around this cavernous place. Suddenly, she felt better. She might not know who she was yet, but she knew how to earn her keep until she could find out.

After all, it didn't take much of a memory to take a broom and cloth to a place, did it?

Conner found them in the kitchen, the woman perched on a stool near the fire and Grub busying himself at the stove. Before she noticed him, Conner took the opportunity to study her.

Wild, curly red hair fell about her slumped shoulders in soft waves that tempted a man to run his fingers through it. Her profile was turned to him and in the firelight, he noticed the dusting of pale gold freckles dancing across her nose and cheeks. She crossed her arms under her full, lush breasts and something inside Conner shifted, tightened, in response.

Damn everything, he didn't need this kind of distraction. Cursing his own reaction, he fought it down and reminded himself of the important questions.

Where had she come from? Where was her family? Her people? And what the hell was he supposed to do with her?

He stepped into the room and she turned her head to look at him. Briefly, he lost himself in the deep, pure green of her eyes. Then, she straightened up slowly, squaring her shoulders. She lifted her chin and kept her gaze locked with his as he crossed the room.

With a nod at Grub, Conner pulled a bench out from under the long pine table and sat down across from her. "We need to figure out what to do about you," he said bluntly.

She blinked, pushed her hair back from her face and shot a quick look at Grub's back. Then she seemed to gather her courage and wrap it around herself like a warm blanket before saying, "As to that, I've an idea that might serve us all well."

Suspicious, he cocked his head and waited. Since his old friend hadn't looked him in the eye yet, Conner had a feeling that she and Grub were in this together.

"I'd like to work for you," she said, then added, "for awhile, anyway."

"Work for me?" Whose idea was this? he wondered. He threw a quick look at Grub, but the man still hadn't turned around. If anything, he seemed to be paying quite a bit of attention to the pot of chili on the stove.

"Aye. I happened to notice your house is in need of a good scrubbing." Getting to her feet, Meara stood straight as an arrow and said, "I'll clean and wash and do whatever Grub might be needin' help with. And all you'll owe me is a room and meals."

He shot another look at the man, who refused to look at him. "Grub takes care of the house and the cooking," he said, stalling for time. Time to think. To plan.

"And a fine hand he is in the kitchen, I'll wager," she said quickly. "But the layers of dust on your fine things would be enough for any man to build a nice-sized cottage for himself."

"A cottage?"

"Aye," she said, explaining. "A wee small house."

He sighed. "I know what a cottage is."

"Well, of course ya do," she said. "Who's sayin' ya don't?"

"You just—"

"Of course," she went on, shifting her gaze to roam about the well-appointed kitchen, "a cottage would not be so grand as the home you have here. But then again, a cottage is a cozy thing, don't you think?"

This conversation was pulling wide of its mark. "I never gave it a thought."

"If that isn't just like a man," she said and gave him a small, knowing smile. "If he's fed and warm, he'll think no more about his surroundings then an old lame dog."

"A lame dog." Now he didn't even remember what they had been talking about.

"But then, 'tis a woman's job to fix the home and run it properly, don't ya think?" She nodded her head sharply, sending a tumble of curls into a dance around her shoulders.

"I—"

"By this time tomorrow," she interrupted neatly, "I promise ya your things will have a shine on them that would do the angels proud."

Conner just looked at her. Now that she'd finally quieted, he couldn't think of a damn thing to say.

"I'm a fierce worker," she assured him as if he was doubting her. "And I don't eat much. A crust or two will do me." She finally stopped then and watched him. Waiting.

It felt as though an iron band was squeezing his chest. For all of her brave talk, he could see clearly what this little speech had cost her. She had pride. That was plain in the way she kept her chin tilted defiantly even while practically begging for a job. And she was afraid. He saw her fear in how she held herself ramrod stiff. But most telling were her hands, locked together in front of her waist, gripping each other until her knuckles whitened.

Damn it, he didn't want to be saddled with her. He had his own life, such as it was. Yet, he felt himself softening toward her.

"What about your home?" he asked. "You probably have people looking for you. A husband. Family."

Her gaze shifted from his and she stared unseeing at the far wall. For a long moment, she said nothing, then finally, "I don't think so." She inhaled slowly, deeply, shaking her head as she did. "Surely if I had a husband, I couldn't forget him. But even if I have, until I find where I belong, I need a place to stay. And work to hold me." At last, she turned her green eyes back to his. "If you've no need of me, I'll just go along and find someone else. Somewhere else."

Damn. Conner looked again to Grub and wasn't surprised to find the man glaring at him as if daring him to get rid of her. Shifting his gaze back to the woman waiting for his decision, Conner knew that he couldn't just turn her out and wish her good luck. As much as he might want to.

He'd been in just her position too many times. Broke, no place to stay. Nowhere to go. Sure, there might be someone out looking for her. But for right now, she had no one. No one but him. Damn it.

"All right," he said and noticed when her stance relaxed just a bit. "For now. But tomorrow, we go to town. Take you to the doctor. See if he can help you remember anything."

"Town?" Grub asked. "You?"

"Yeah, me," he countered and pushed up from the table. "No call to sound so surprised. I've been to town before. Twice."

"In two years."

"I still remember where it is," he snapped. What difference did it make if he hardly ever left the ranch?

"You sure?" Grub asked. "I could maybe get one of the boys to show you the way."

"Thanks."

"I'm sure I could find it on my own," Meara offered.

"I know where the town is," he said, and heard his voice getting louder with every word.

"I should think you would," Meara said, one golden red eyebrow lifting into a high arch. " 'Tis your town, after all."

Grub snorted and mumbled something Conner couldn't catch, and he had a feeling it was just as well. He was through talking about going or not going into High Timber.

He'd never been a man to make friends easy. And as a rule, he steered clear of most folks. But to get his life back, he'd take Meara Simon to town.

And pray like hell that someone there recognized her.

CHAPTER THREE

A long night with very little sleep left Conner with a pounding headache and eyeballs that felt like red-hot lumps of coal in his skull.

In the eerie half-light of the hour just before dawn, he gave up on the idea of rest and pushed himself to a sitting position. Scowling at his surroundings, he tried to tell himself that he hadn't slept because the damned mattress in the guest room was lumpier than a bowl of Grub's winter oatmeal.

But, since it hadn't been so long ago that he'd spent his nights in a bedroll spread out on rocky ground with only the stars for a roof, even *he* didn't believe that lie.

It was *her* fault.

That small woman who'd shown up out of nowhere just in time to toss his life into chaos.

Scraping both palms across his face, Connor rubbed away the last traces of sleeplessness, then threw the quilt aside and swung his legs off the bed. If he wasn't going to sleep any, he might as well get dressed. The sooner they got to town, the sooner he could find out where Meara really belonged.

Only as he reached for his jeans, tossed carelessly over a nearby armchair, did he notice the incredible aroma spiralling up the stairs from the kitchen.

Cinnamon.

He sniffed experimentally, just to be sure.

His mouth watered and his stomach growled in anticipation. Whatever Grub was cooking smelled a helluva lot better than the usual coffee and fried eggs.

Hurriedly, he got dressed and headed for the stairs.

"Well, this is *good*," Grub said, taking another hefty bite of the warm, cinnamon apples in front of him.

"I told ya it would be, didn't I?" Meara countered with a smile. She used a towel to cover her hand before grabbing the coffee pot, then she poured the older man a cup full of the strong, black liquid. Wrinkling her nose as the aroma rose up in a cloud of steam, she said, "I don't understand how you can wash down my apples with this awful stuff."

Around a mouthful, Grub told her, "A man needs his coffee in these parts, little girl. And Conner likes his brew to be thick as mud and strong enough to crawl down his gullet under its own steam."

Meara shook her head as she set the coffee pot back down on the brick hearth near the fire.

"What I don't get is how come you cooked these apples in a pot over the fire? Why didn't ya use the stove?"

She frowned thoughtfully and threw the cast-iron stove a black look. She had tried for nearly an hour to figure out how to start a blaze in the unholy thing. But finally, she'd given up and turned to an iron kettle hanging over the fire on a blackened swing arm. 'Twas certainly a good bit easier to deal with an open hearth than it was to make sense of drawers and handles and chimney pipes that climbed the wall and disappeared into the ceiling.

To Grub though, she said only, "It seemed much quicker to build a fire in the hearth than in that great iron monster. And the blaze is a cheerful thing in the morning."

"You're a pistol, girl," Grub told her as he reached for his coffee cup and took a sip.

"A pistol?" Should she be insulted or pleased?

"Yep." He nodded to himself. "Just look at ya," he went on, waving his free hand at her. "Up before the birds, cookin' up a storm, and half the kitchen cleaner than it was the day it was built."

"Idle hands, you know," she began to say, but Grub cut her off neatly.

"I ain't sayin' that I couldn't have shined up that old brass lamp just as good as you, but I *am* sayin', you're mighty damned fast for such a little thing."

She gave a quick look at the hanging brass lamp overhead. It glimmered and shone in the flickering light of its burning wicks and Meara smiled, pleased with the results of her efforts. She'd been up and busy for hours already.

Anything to avoid the strange, almost frightening dreams that had haunted her sleep. She didn't remember much of them. Flashes of images, no more. A big room. Lots of people. The urge to run. Hide. And a deep, hard voice that rang like a death knell and seemed directed right at her.

She'd awoken in a cold sweat with her stomach churning as she gasped for air. Unwilling to trust sleeping after that, she'd simply set to work. Meara's gaze moved around the room, and she admitted to herself that her promise to have the whole house gleaming by today might have been a bit overstated. She'd been cleaning the kitchen for hours and had yet to make a dent in it.

But then hadn't her dear mother often said that one man alone was a crime, but two men alone were enough to ruin a perfectly good house?

Surely it would take her more than one day to repair the neglect done to this place.

"Grub?" Conner's voice came from the hall. "What have you got cookin' in there?"

Meara spun around to face the door and lifted both

hands to smooth her tangle of hair into submission. Then she tightened the strings of the apron protecting the only clothes she owned and waited for her new employer.

She told herself she was merely anxious to make a good impression on the man giving her a job and a home, however temporary. But the lie was a hard one to believe when even the sound of his voice sent ripples of goose-flesh streaming up and down her arms.

He stepped into the kitchen and the smile on his face faded a bit when he saw Grub sitting at the table and Meara herself standing in front of the roaring fire.

"What's this?"

"Set down," Grub told him and waved a spoon in his direction. "This little gal made up some cinnamon apples that'll set your insides to shouting, 'Hallelujah!' "

Slowly, he turned his gaze from the old man to the woman standing beside him. Her face flushed from the heat of the fire, her cheeks were rosy, and a few damp tendrils clung to her forehead. Grub's apron was wrapped twice around her narrow middle and the strings were tied in a lopsided bow just below her breasts.

She looked young and lovely and altogether way too much of a distraction. Tearing his gaze away from the mystery woman, he took a seat at the table and thanked her when she poured him a cup of coffee.

Grub swivelled around on the bench, dipped up a portion of apples from the gently bubbling pot, then slid the bowl across the table to Conner.

Sniffing, he inhaled the aroma of cinammon and spices before picking up a spoon and having a taste. Flavor exploded in his mouth. Tart and sweet at the same time, the long-simmered apples nearly melted without his having to chew them at all. Maybe having her here won't be so bad, he thought. For awhile, anyway.

Both eyebrows lifted as he raised his gaze to hers. "This is great," he said and grinned as he spooned up another bite. "The boys're gonna love this."

Her pleased smile dimmed just a bit. "Boys?"

He nodded. "The men who work for me. They'll be along for their breakfast anytime now."

"There's more of you?" she asked, giving a look at the door as if expecting a crowd to storm the room.

"Yeah," he said. "Can't work a ranch alone." How much had she forgotten? he wondered. Anyone who had lived in the west would know that there were usually a dozen or more ranch hands working a place. And as soon as he could afford it, he'd be hiring more himself.

"How many?" She asked.

"Five more, besides Grub and me."

"I didn't know," she muttered and turned to stir the half-empty pot. "There's not enough. I didn't think . . ." She shook her head. "I'll have to make something else."

Conner watched her fidget with the cooking ladle, her expression suddenly worried, and he heard himself speak up. "Cooking's not your job, Meara. It's Grub's."

"Oh," she said, "but I like to cook, so it's no bother. I only just wish that I'd known . . ."

"Don't you fret over them boys in the bunkhouse," Grub said. He pushed up from the table and sent Conner a scowl. "Most of 'em would eat a boiled saddle if you put enough hot sauce on it." He gave her shoulder a pat before moving around the kitchen gathering up supplies for the fried eggs and ham steaks he'd cook the boys. "I'll take care of that bunch, don't you worry."

Conner just looked at the old coot. Usually grumpy as a hungry grizzly first thing in the morning, Grub was fussing over Meara like an old hen with its last chick.

"I'll do better tomorrow," Meara said and slipped into Grub's now vacant seat.

Conner's eyes met hers and he felt a tug come from deep within him. Something in those forest-green eyes of hers touched him in places he'd never been aware of before. And he wasn't at all sure he liked it.

Damn it, he'd learned a long time ago that tender feelings weren't for the likes of him. Some men were born for hearth and home. Others, like him, were born for a hard world, to be walked through alone. And the sooner a man realized just which kind he was, the better.

No, there was no wife and family in his future and when he needed a woman, he took himself to town. He wasn't about to start entertaining any fond notions about this woman. No matter how green her eyes were or how tempting her figure.

"When you goin' to town?" Grub asked, snatching at Conner's attention.

Town. To see the doctor. To try and locate Meara's people. He tore his gaze from hers and studied instead the inky blackness of his coffee. "A couple of hours," he said, then drained the contents of his cup. "Want to give the chesnut mare a workout first. I'm tryin' her with a bridle this morning."

Grub snorted. "That animal ain't about to let you get anywhere near her. Meanest female I ever seen. Outside a couple I cain't mention in polite company," he added with a wink at Meara.

"You have horses?" she asked.

Almost reluctantly, Conner looked at her again. Her eyes widened until he could see the whites clearly around the brilliant splashes of emerald. "Yeah. That's what I do. Catch mustangs, break 'em, and sell 'em."

"Mustangs?" she echoed, her voice just a bit fainter than a moment before.

"Wild horses," he explained. His brow furrowed as he looked at her. The healthy flush of pink in her cheeks had paled to a snowy white. Her freckles stood out in stark relief, looking like gold dust sprinkled on a field of snow.

"You're afraid of horses?" he asked.

Immediately, she stiffened and lifted her chin a notch. "I'm not afraid," she lied and not very well. "But I don't like them. Great, smelly beasts, too large by half and most of them with an evil temper."

"That mare surely has a temper. Mean as the devil," Grub commented, but no one was listening.

"It's plain you haven't been around many horses," Conner said and stood up. "And that means you haven't been out west for long."

She stared at him, waiting for an explanation.

He took a breath and told himself that this was a good sign. Not too many pilgrims were arriving at Lake Tahoe these days. People fresh from the east would be the centers of attention in the little town of High Timber. Local folks would remember newcomers. Especially if they talked with an accent. And if he couldn't find anyone there who knew her, he'd haul her over to Virginia City in a few days. Talk to the sheriff. Get him to look for her family.

"What makes here so different from somewhere else?" she asked.

Grub snorted a chuckle, but Conner ignored him. "Back east, a man can take a carriage or walk most anyplace he has a mind. Out here, you need horses. To help with the work. To get from one place to the next, when towns might be a week's ride apart." He walked around the edge of the table, plucked his hat off a peg by the back door, and settled it on his head. "If you and your family are fresh from the east, somebody in town will know where to find your folks."

"And if they don't?"

He looked down into those eyes again, even though he knew it was a mistake. Conner inhaled sharply. "Then we'll keep looking until we find something." He grabbed the doorknob, turned it, and pulled. Over his shoulder, he said, "Be ready to go in two hours."

Then he closed the door on those eyes.

*   *   *

Two hours wasn't long enough to make much of a dent in the cleaning of this fine house, she told herself. But it was plenty of time to get started. She walked through the main room and paused to admire the lovely river stones used to build the fireplace. It was a huge thing. Meara wagered that she could stand inside the hearth and not even bump her head on the overhead stones.

Black, dusty andirons stood to one side of the empty hearth, and a heavy layer of ashes lay in the grate. She shook her head. On either side of the chimney were shelves, holding all manner of books. Meara sucked in a breath in admiration. Conner James must be a wealthy man to own such treasures, she thought wistfully.

Slowly, her gaze wandered around the room, taking in the dustballs beneath the sideboard and the coating of dirt atop the fine tables standing alongside the long, red settee and the overstuffed chairs. Clucking her tongue, she turned her back on the main room and headed off down the hall, to explore the rest of the first floor.

She matched her steps to the muffled thud of hammers pounding against wood as some of Conner's men repaired the hole in the roof. Rubbing her backside in memory of her drop into this place, she opened the first door she came to.

Poking her head inside, she found a linen closet, stuffed to the gills with towels and sheets and blankets. So much, she thought. Surely no one here had to suffer the cold of winter. Then there was a storeroom, with boxes and barrels holding supplies that on further inspection proved to be flour and sugar and what seemed to be a mountain of ammunition. 'Twas as if Conner James was preparing for war.

But with who, she'd no idea.

Leaving the storeroom, she went along to the end of the hall and opened the last door. An office, she guessed, for there was a desk littered with papers sitting in the very center of things. An overflowing wastebasket was tumbled onto its side, and the dirt on the outside of the one window was such that it looked like evening despite the fact that the sun was shining outside.

With a sniff of disgust, Meara pushed her sleeves up and dug into the work. An hour later, she had straightened the papers on Conner's desk, thrown out what was on the floor, and rubbed away what looked like years of grime from the windows and the furniture. There were still the rugs to see to, but she wasn't a miracle worker, after all.

Pleased with her efforts, she took a step back from Conner's desk, then reached forward and tweaked one of the leaves of the ivy plant she'd set at the very corner. Shining green leaves spilled over the top of a lovely white china bowl with small, painted pink rosebuds encircling it.

She smiled to herself. Just grand. A bit of life in this musty old place will do him a world of good, she thought.

"What are you doing in here?" Conner demanded from the doorway.

"Jesus, Mary, and Joseph," she shouted, clutching at her heart as she whirled around to face him.

He stood, legs wide apart, arms crossed over his chest, and glared at her as though she'd just shot his favorite horse. "I asked what you were doing in my office," he repeated, the words even harsher the second time.

"As anyone can see," she snapped, not liking his tone in the slightest, "I've cleaned it. Though to do a through job, more than likely, I'd need years."

He stomped into the room past her, and made straight for the desk. Thumbing through the neat stacks of papers, he muttered something under his breath.

"What was that?" she asked.

"I don't want you in here disturbing things," he said.

"But you've hired me to do the cleaning," she reminded him, feeling her own temper spurt to life inside her.

"Not in here."

"Ah, become accustomed to the dirt, have ya?" she asked. For the love of heaven, she'd slaved like a serf for an hour and *this* was the thanks she got? "And I suppose you've named all of the little dustballs I unthinkingly swept up. Think of them as family, do ya?"

He turned to look at her. He wasn't amused. "Just take care of the rest of the house, all right? And leave me in peace here?"

"Fine," she sniffed. "All you need do is ask, ya know. I don't have the second sight." Frowning, she wondered aloud, "At least, I don't think I do."

He exhaled impatiently and said, "I've got some work to do in here. Be ready for town in an hour."

"Yes, your lordship." She gave a clumsy, halfhearted curtsy, but reasoned that his behavior didn't merit a real one anyway.

"And take this with you," he said as she started to leave.

Meara turned around and found him holding out the white china bowl containing the sprig of ivy. "But I potted it for ya," she said, reluctant to take it. " 'Twill cheer you up in this gloomy place."

He shook the bowl and the ivy leaves trembled as pebbles of dirt spilled onto the filthy rug. "I don't need cheering up," he told her, "and this is in my way."

"So I see," she said, eyebrows lifting into high arches on her forehead. "You've got to have room for the dust to grow again."

He frowned at her.

Meara glowered at him and took the china bowl between both hands. Handsome he may be, she told herself firmly, but he had a nasty temperament that no doubt explained why he was still a single man, unattached at his advanced age.

"I'll be ready in an hour," she told him as she headed for the doorway. And she hoped to heaven they'd find someone in that blasted town who knew who she was.

The sooner she got away from this unreasonable man, the better off they'd all be.

Meara turned her head this way and that, looking at each side of the tiny town, not wanting to miss a thing. She didn't even mind sitting beside Conner, though she was in no mood for talking.

The road was narrow. It didn't look wide enough for two carriages to pass each other, and when a wagon came lumbering up from the other direction, she held her breath and tightened her grip on the wooden edge of the buckboard they were riding in, sure a horrible crash was coming. But Conner didn't even flinch. He stared straight ahead, his gaze never wavering, and when the other wagon passed them by, Meara relaxed slightly and returned to her staring.

A small town, to be sure, yet there were a dozen or more shops strung out along the narrow road. Buildings hunched at the roadside, leaning against each other as if for support. They reminded her of drunk old men leaving a pub, trusting in their fellows to hold them upright. Wooden frames looked time-tested and weathered. Long strips of paint had peeled up, leaving great patches of bare wood behind.

The signs intrigued her, both because she realized that she could read them and because of their names. Haberdasher. Mercantile. Feed and Grain. Emporium. Now there was a grand name, she thought. Far too grand to be splashed across a storefront that looked as though it was ready to fall down in a stiff wind.

"Seem familiar to you?" Conner asked, and she jumped, startled at the sound of his voice. He hadn't spoken a word to her on the journey out from the ranch.

"No," she said, half turning to give him a quick glance.

She felt disappointment rise up in her as she admitted quietly, "It doesn't."

His mouth tightened a bit and he reached up to pull the brim of his hat down lower over his eyes. "Take your time," he told her. "Look around good. Try."

"Of course I'll try," she snapped. "Do ya think I like knowing nothing about who I am or where I came from?" Or having to stay where I'm so clearly not wanted, she added silently.

He shot her a look from the corner of his eye. "No, I suppose not."

She jerked him a nod, then turned her gaze back to the street and the people wandering its length. Faces. Dozens of faces. And none of them familiar. Meara tried to study them all.

The hard-eyed man in dusty clothes leaning against a porch post. The short, busy woman, herding three children along in front of her. The fat man, sitting on a chair situated in the dirt in front of a barber shop. A tall, lovely woman in a red-spangled dress with a blue feather in her snow-white hair.

Meara caught herself staring, but couldn't seem to help it. The woman looked dazzling even from a distance, and though Meara couldn't make out her features, she had the impression that the woman was smiling at her. Then in the next instant, she lifted one hand in a brief wave and Meara grabbed hold of Conner's arm.

"Look!" she said hurriedly, pointing. "Who is that?"

"Where?"

"Over there. The woman in red."

Conner shifted his gaze in the direction she indicated and frowned. "What woman?"

Now Meara frowned. The woman was gone. She looked up and down both sides of the street, but there was no sign of the lovely creature. "I don't understand," she whispered, more to herself than to him. "She was only just there."

"Well," he pointed out unnecessarily, "she's not now. Did you know her?"

"No," she said with a shake of her head. "But I thought I saw her wave to me."

"Then she knew you."

"Perhaps."

"What'd she look like?"

"Tall. White hair. Lovely, sparkling red dress."

One black eyebrow lifted. "A red dress?"

"Aye."

He studied her thoughtfully for a long minute, then said, "Keep your eyes open. Maybe you'll see her again. Or something else that will nudge your memory."

Meara did as he asked, but aside from that one woman, there was nothing. No sense of belonging. No sharp tug of recognition. She was a stranger still.

When Conner pulled his contraption to a stop in front of a whitewashed, one-story building, he wrapped the reins around a brake handle, then turned to her. Nodding at the building, he said, "This is Doc Sorenson's. We'll start here. Let him look you over, make sure you're all right."

"I feel fine," she told him and slanted the doctor's office a wary look. She might not remember much about her life or how she'd come to be at Conner's ranch, but Meara knew she didn't like the idea of a strange man "looking her over."

Conner jumped down from the high bench seat, walked around the back end of the buckboard, and over to her. He held up both hands to help her down, but Meara didn't move.

His hands dropped to his sides as he stared up at her. "What's wrong?"

"I don't want to see your doctor," she said, and hated knowing that she sounded like a whiny child. Then she glanced past him to the building beyond and stiffened her spine. "I said I feel fine. There's no need for your man to go pokin' and proddin' me."

Conner pushed his hat back further on his head and glared at her. "You fell through a roof, Meara."

"And landed on me behind, not my head, thanks very much."

"We'll let the doctor tell us that."

Outraged, her eyebrows shot up on her forehead. "No stranger's going to be looking at my . . . *self* that closely, I can tell ya that much right this minute."

"Meara," Conner said, his voice low and hard, "either you get down off that damned buckboard and walk to the doctor . . ." He paused.

"Or?"

"Or I pick you up and carry you in there myself."

A woman passing along the walkway behind him, turned startled eyes on Conner and hurried past.

To avoid other curious ears, Meara leaned toward him to say, "I'm a grown woman, Conner James. I'll decide if I need a doctor or not."

"True and false," he said grimly.

"And what does that mean?"

"You're a grown woman all right," he told her, reaching up to grab her around the waist, "but you get no say in this doctor visit." Before the words were completely out of his mouth, he'd snatched her from the wagon. Cradling her in his arms, pinned to his chest, he glared down at her. "You *will* see the doctor."

"You great oaf," she protested hotly while shoving at his rock-hard chest for all she was worth, "you're a bully and a brute. Put me down."

"As soon as we're inside," he told her and turned for the building behind him.

Chuckles drifted to her, and Meara turned her head to see that they'd attracted quite a crowd. Four or five men stood in a half circle, watching them with all of the appreciation they would have given a stage play. And as much as she wanted to go on fighting the fool carrying her, Meara wasn't going to put on more of a show than she already had.

She crossed her arms over her breasts, closed her eyes to the laughing faces, and promised herself to get even with the man causing her such humiliation.

Henry Sorenson pushed his spectacles higher on the bridge of his nose, tilted Meara's face into the direct sunlight streaming through the shining glass windows, and studied her eyes carefully. For the second time.

"Well?" Conner James's voice came from the corner, where he'd insisted on staying throughout the examination.

"As I told you before," Henry said, shooting the man a quick look, "I can see nothing wrong."

Meara pulled her chin from his grasp so that she could send a sneer toward the man in the corner. Brave woman, Henry thought. Conner James's expression was hard and tight. He didn't look like a man who liked being pushed. Or argued with.

Of course Henry couldn't be sure. He'd only seen James once or twice since the man had moved into the territory two years before. He almost never came to town, and when he did, he conducted his business and left again. There was no visiting around town. No trying to make friends. Which wouldn't have been easy anyway, what with Robert Carlisle bad-mouthing the man every chance he got.

But Conner's steering clear of town only served the local gossiping harpies. The sharp-tongued biddies of High Timber spent most of their time wondering about the tall, good-looking man and the rest of their time repeating Carlisle's stories about him and swearing it was gospel.

"Then why can't she remember a damn thing?" Conner demanded.

"I don't know," Henry admitted as he ran his fingers over Meara's scalp, checking for any bumps or bruises.

"You're a doctor," Conner reminded him. "You're supposed to know these things."

Henry smiled sadly. "Unfortunately, in medicine, the one thing we're sure of is how much we don't know."

The other man pushed up from his chair and came to stand beside him.

"Then what good are you?"

"For the love of Saint Bridget." Meara turned on the surly man, jerking her head out from under Henry's questing fingers. "Can't ya see the doctor's only trying to help? 'Twas your idea to come here, and now you've only insults for the man?"

Henry ducked his head to hide a smile.

Conner took a long, deep breath, shifted his gaze from Meara's, and asked, "When will she get her memory back?"

Henry shrugged. "Hard to say. Since we don't know how or when she lost it, there's no telling when or *if* it will return."

"If?" Conner and Meara both repeated that word at the same time.

Helplessly, Henry took a step back from them and lifted both hands in a shrug. "I'm sorry I don't have answers for you. But I just don't know." Turning to Conner, he asked, "Are you sure she fell through a roof?"

"There's a hole in my ceiling just her size," the man assured him.

"Strange," Henry admitted softly. "No cuts. No bruises that I can see. It just doesn't make sense."

"That much I knew already," Conner said.

"Have ya finished with me, doctor?"

"Hmm?" Henry's gaze flicked to the pretty redhead. "Yes. Again, I'm sorry, but there's nothing I can do but advise patience."

"Patience." Conner repeated the word as if it was a foreign language.

Henry wasn't surprised. Conner James didn't strike him as the patient sort.

"I thank ya for your time then," Meara said and held out her hand to him.

Henry took her smaller hand in his and gave it a gentle squeeze. "I'll keep my ears open. See if I hear anything about people looking for you."

She nodded stiffly, but he could see the disappointment glittering in her eyes.

Conner fished in his pants pocket and came up with two coins he handed to Henry. "Thanks," he grumbled, then took Meara's elbow and steered her toward the door.

Outside, he turned left and led her down the uneven boardwalk. The toe of her shoe caught on a lifted plank and she stumbled. Conner tightened his grip until she righted herself.

She shot him a quick smile of thanks, then spoiled it by saying, "I told ya I was fine, didn't I?"

"Now we know for sure."

"But we don't know anything more."

True, he thought grimly. Damn it, he'd been secretly hoping for some sort of miracle. He'd imagined the doctor examining her, saying, "Here's the problem," and fixing it on the spot. He should have known better. Miracles just didn't happen. At least, not for men like him.

He wasn't sure, but he had a feeling that Heaven reserved its special powers for saints, not sinners like himself.

Glancing down at the woman on his left, Conner felt impatience rise up inside him and he hated himself for it. What right did *he* have to be upset about this? It was *her* memories that had been stolen. Her life that was in darkness.

She must have felt his gaze on her, because she swivelled her head to look up at him. A glimmer of something he couldn't quite identify shone in her eyes.

"I'm sorry I near bit your head off in there," she said.

He frowned, remembering, then nodded. "Doesn't matter." Guiding her around a small cluster of men standing outside the saloon, Conner tipped his hat to a woman who darted past him.

"But you needn't worry," Meara went on, in time to the tapping of their heels against the plank sidewalk. "I won't be stayin' on at your ranch forever."

Conner stopped dead on the boardwalk and his grip on her elbow tightened. "What do you mean?"

She shrugged indifferently, but her eyes swam with emotion. "You heard the doctor. He doesn't even know if my memory *will* come back. Ever."

"He doesn't know it won't, either."

"True enough," she admitted, ducking her head to avoid looking at him.

Conner caught her chin in his hand and tilted her head back until she was forced to meet his gaze. Now he recognized the emotions filling her eyes. He'd seen them often enough in a mirror to know them well.

Fear. Worry.

His stomach clenched and an invisible band tightened around his chest again. For most of his life, he'd lived with those two companions. He'd buried them time and again only to have them rear their heads and come charging back into his life to take over.

Well, he'd finally beaten them back. In the last few years, he'd actually made a start on never having to face those two emotions again. Seeing them now, in her eyes, brought it all back.

The loneliness.

The desperation.

And the lies you told yourself to pretend differently.

He couldn't let her face those things alone. He hardly knew her, yet seeing his past in her eyes, bound them together, however he might wish it to be otherwise.

"You've got a job at the ranch, Meara," he heard himself say and waited for the clouds to lift from her features. "For as long as you need it."

CHAPTER FOUR

A cowbell hung over the door jumped and clanged a discordant note as they entered the grandly named Emporium.

Meara moved forward slowly, her gaze darting about the cluttered room, taking in everything. Stacks of clothing lined neat shelves that covered one wall. A long table, fitted with small slats of wood to divide it into sections, was littered with hair ribbons and a small mountain of wool, already carded, combed, dyed, and spun into great balls of yarn. And in so many colors, too! Her palms itched suddenly and she had the almost overwhelming urge to find a pair of knitting needles.

She smiled to herself as she realized there was one more piece of information about herself. She knew how to knit.

Letting her gaze wander further, she saw a few dozen books alongside a row of glass candy jars. Gloves, shirts, and socks filled a tower of shelves, and there were huge barrels, filled with all manner of foodstuffs. Along the narrow, gleaming countertop sat small, glass-covered cases containing rings, brooches, pocket watches, and hair combs.

And nothing in the place seemed the slightest bit familiar. Frowning to herself, Meara admitted that not only didn't she know *this* store in particular, she felt as though it was the first time she'd ever seen a store anything like this.

A curl of worry started in the pit of her stomach as she looked from the ladies' dresses to the men's hats, hung on pegs lining the wall above the shelves. Surely, she thought, she would have at least some memory of these things. Why would everything seem so odd. So completely foreign?

Even the yarn she'd admired a moment ago didn't seem . . . *right*.

She rubbed her forehead between her eyes and told herself that she should stop trying so hard. Maybe if she would only calm herself, her memories would return. Nodding thoughtfully, she decided to stop trying to delve into the shadows of her mind. Instead, she would simply go about her business each day. She would work and shut off worrisome thoughts that did her not a spit of good anyway.

Conner walked right behind her and she felt a rush of gratitude spring forth inside her. He wasn't going to throw her out of his house. So she had a place to stay. And a job to keep her hands busy no matter what else happened.

And at least, his face was one she knew.

For now, she decided, that would have to be enough.

Decision made, she walked across the store, taking comfort in the sound of Conner's heavy footsteps behind her.

Behind the counter sat a man so thin Meara thought she could count his bones through his skin. Wide, brown eyes looked them over as they neared, and then the skeleton spoke.

"Help yourselves," he said, and lifted one hand as if it weighed the world. "Look about, find what you need, then bring it on up here." He sighed. "My woman'll add it all up for you."

"What woman?" Meara glanced at her surroundings but didn't see another soul.

"Dora's back yonder." He waved that bony hand toward a door on his right. "In the storeroom, fussin' over something or other. Never did know a body with more gallop in them than my Dora. She wouldn't know slow down if she fell on it, poor thing. Gonna work herself to a early grave."

Meara bit her tongue from telling the man that if he was worried about his wife, mayhaps he should get up off his backside and help. But then again, by the look of him, the man was deathly ill. Perhaps he hadn't the strength to do more than sit and watch his life whirl by. Although she didn't much care for the way he'd said "my woman," much as he would have said "my dog" or horse or shoes, for that matter.

"Morning, Higgins," Conner said from just behind her.

The man narrowed his gaze, as if finally recognizing his customer, then asked, "How is it you're here? Is it a year gone by already?"

"A year?" Meara glanced up and behind her. Then she remembered he and Grub talking and how Conner'd only been to the town twice in the two years he'd lived here. Odd for a man to be so much alone. Why, the men she'd known in her life wouldn't stay away from a tavern longer than a night or two at the most.

She frowned at that fuzzy thought and wondered how she could be so sure of it, yet remember no particulars.

"Not quite," Conner answered, shifting his feet on the polished floor. "Need a few things anyway, though."

Like a king, Mr. Higgins inclined his head. "Don't let me keep you."

Conner nodded and moved off to his right, pulling Meara along behind him. He came to a stop in front of a row of women's dresses, hanging lifelessly from pegs tapped into the wall.

She looked from them to him and asked, "What?"

He rubbed his jaw, glanced at her, then away again. "Get yourself some clothes, Meara. You're going to need more than you've got."

Her gaze dropped instantly to the only set of clothes she owned. Admittedly, her yellow shirt and black skirt didn't look fresh as a morning's wash, but she wasn't about to take charity, either.

"These'll do," she said stiffly.

He looked at her long and hard for minute, then said. "It's not charity."

She blinked at his ability to read her mind so well.

"You're working for me now, I'll take the clothes out of your pay."

"You're only paying me room and board."

"I'll give you a raise."

"I don't need them." Stubbornly, she kept her gaze locked with his. Wasn't it bad enough she must carry the taste of gratitude on her tongue? She wouldn't be asking for more than she needed. She could take care of herself. As soon as her faculties returned.

"You do, unless you're ready to clean the house in your shimmy," he pointed out.

"Shimmy?" Even the word sounded strange.

He sighed and looked uncomfortable. "Your underwear."

Her eyebrows lifted. Now that didn't make any sense a'tall. "Why would a body want to wear clothes *under* clothes?"

He stared at her as if she had just sprouted horns. Leaning toward her, he shot an uneasy glance over his shoulder as if to make sure Mr. Higgins hadn't sneaked up on them, then whispered, "You mean you're not—"

She drew her head back and stared at him. "I've already told you, these are all the clothes I have."

His eyes closed briefly as he straightened up. Shaking

his head, he muttered, "I'm going to try to forget you said that."

Impatient now, he reached out, plucked a yellow, flower-sprigged dress off a peg, and thrust it at her. "Here. Now pick out a couple more."

Meara held the gown up in front of her and had to smile. The blasted thing was big enough for a family. Its hem lay on the floor in a puddle of material and the waist was large enough to fit around the middle of one of his blasted horses.

"It won't fit," she told him in a vast understatement.

Grumbling, he rummaged through the others until he found a few smaller ones. Clenching them tightly in one fist, he shoved them at her.

Meara hung up the big dress and studied the others. With a nip and a tuck here and there, they would fit her, she thought, though it still went against the grain to be accepting such things from a man she hardly knew.

But he had turned away from her to look over a pile of white cotton clothing. Jerking his head toward it, he told her. "Get yourself some of those, too."

She took the two steps to stand beside him and looked down at the lace-edged, fragile-looking clothing. Picking up the top garment, she stuck her hand inside it and noted that she could nearly see right through the thing. "Now why would a body bother to wear a thing no thicker than this? It won't be very warm."

She thought she heard him groan, but she couldn't be sure.

His features tightened slightly and a muscle in his jaw began to twitch. "That's the underwear I was talking about."

Her lips pursed and she stared at her hand through the fragile fabric. "Why would a body bother with it? 'Tis hardly there a'tall."

She heard him muttering again, but couldn't understand a word.

"We'll get them anyway."

Meara shook her head. Hardheaded, he was.

"You'll need a coat, too."

"No."

He slowly turned his head. His deep blue eyes locked with hers, and Meara felt that small thread of awareness spiralling through her insides again. Odd, that. She didn't ever remember feeling *that* before now, either. And a feeling that pleasant she was sure she'd remember, no matter how many other memories disappeared.

"What do you mean, no?" he said quietly, keeping his voice low enough to avoid being overheard.

"I mean," she said, just as quietly, "I'll accept the dresses, and even"—she pointed to the white lace garments—"these underclothes, though I still don't understand the reasons for them. But I'll not have you spending any more money on me. 'Tisn't proper."

"Proper?" He bent down until their faces were only a breath apart. But Meara didn't back up. She met him glare for glare. Stubborn she might be, but she had a line she would not go past.

"Aye," she told him.

"You can stand there and tell me you're not wearing underwear and then talk about being proper?"

Perhaps he had a small point there, she conceded. What a woman wore on her body was no man's business but her husband's. " 'Twas a mistake," she said.

"This whole thing is a mistake," he reminded her.

"True enough, but a woman cannot feel beholden to a man she's not married to." She held up one hand to let him know she wasn't finished. "And in the best marriages, she won't be beholden to *him*, either."

"You're not beholden," he said, and his voice was as tight as a drum. "I've already told you, I'll take it out of your pay."

The cowbell over the door clanged out a warning as someone else entered the store. Meara backed up from the entrance a bit, to keep their little conversation private. As she had known he would, Conner kept pace with her.

She looked past his broad shoulder to the room beyond and noticed a big woman holding a small girl by the hand. Thankfully, the two of them went right on up to the counter. Meara heard Mr. Higgins giving his new customer the same speech he'd given them.

"I can't afford to buy this myself," she told Conner when she felt it was safe to speak again.

"I'm going to pay you."

"Even so, if I'm to take care of myself, I've no business spending money I've yet to earn on clothes I don't want to wear."

He reached up, snatched his hat off and pushed the fingers of his left hand through his hair. Settling the hat back into place, he whispered. "You are the most infuriating, frustrating woman I have ever met."

"Be that as it may," she hissed, "I'll be taking no charity from you or anyone else for that matter."

"It's not charity!"

"Then we're back to me spending my money, which I don't want to do, even if I had some, which I don't."

He inhaled sharply and blew it out in a gust. His mouth worked furiously as if he was fighting valiantly to keep back words just itching to spew. A slow tide of angry red color began to creep its way up his neck and cheeks and the vein in his throat began to throb.

Meara lifted her chin even higher and straightened her shoulders as if expecting a blow. His next words added starch to her spine.

"Consider the dresses and things a gift, then."

She watched him for a long minute, then shook her head.

"Jesus, woman, what's wrong with a *gift*?"

"Perhaps nothing," she said, her gaze staying with his.

"But I remember my mother telling me, 'Take gifts with a sigh, most men give to be paid.' "

He drew his head back as if she'd slapped him. "I'm not asking you for a damned thing, Meara," he assured her. "And whether you want them or not, you're having those clothes."

"But—"

"If you have to, consider them a gift to me."

"And how's that?" she demanded hotly.

"Trust me," he said in a hush, "I'll sleep better knowing that you're wearing underwear."

Now it was her turn to feel the hot sting of blood rushing into her cheeks. She swallowed heavily and cleared her throat before saying, "Perhaps 'twould be best if you weren't thinking about me a'tall."

"No doubt it would," he told her grimly. "All I have to do is figure out how to do that."

A spurt of pleasure shot through her veins. Ridiculous, she knew, to be embarrassed and then excited by the selfsame thought. But there it was.

Before she could say another word, he turned around and took a step toward the counter. But it was just one step before he swung back to look at her in astonishment.

"What?" she asked. "What is it, man?"

"You said you remembered your *mother* giving you that advice."

"Aye . . ." She waited for him to go on and then the same thing that had occurred to him, struck her full in the face. "I remembered!"

"But what else do you remember?" he prodded. "Think, Meara. Think hard."

She tried. Clutching her new clothes to her bosom, she squeezed her eyes shut and searched her mind for any other clues. The smallest idea. The tiniest flicker of memory.

But there was nothing. How she had pulled that piece of her past from her brain, she had no idea. But however she had done it, she wasn't going to be doing it again. Not today at any rate.

After several minutes of fruitless attempts to recall more about herself, Meara opened her eyes to look at the man watching her.

"Well?" he asked.

"There's no more," she said on a sigh she hadn't felt building. "It's as though my mind was wrapped in a dark cloth that's slowly unwinding. There's no pulling at it, you see. I'll simply have to wait until the wrappings fall away on their own."

He straightened up and nodded, giving her a small smile. But Meara saw the frustration in his eyes and knew it was mirrored in her own.

"At least I remembered *something*," she said after a long minute.

"Yeah," he said and took her arm to lead her back up the aisle to the front counter. "It's a start, I guess."

Dora Higgins was at her post waiting for them when they approached. A short woman, round as her husband was thin, energy pulsed around her in waves. Even standing beside the brass and copper cash register, she fairly bounced with the need to be moving, doing.

She smiled at Meara and gave Conner a slow, careful look. "So did you find everything you needed?" she asked as Meara laid her selections on the highly varnished counter.

"That I did," Meara told her. "You've a lovely store here. So many wonderful things." Her gaze drifted to one side where the lovely yarn stood waiting to be knitted into clothing. Meara ran a finger over the closest skein.

"Such colors," she murmured. "I've never seen the like." At least, she didn't remember seeing yellows and blues and greens and reds in such true, vibrant shades. She reached out and picked up two pair of polished wooden knitting needles and ran her fingers over their smooth surfaces.

Meara smiled softly. She knew how to knit. She could feel it. And with these needles and some yarn, she would be able to make a few things. Not only for herself to wear, but for Conner and Grub as well. Perhaps to lessen the load of indebtedness she felt bowing down her shoulders.

"How kind of you to say so," Dora said, and plucked a sharpened pencil from behind one ear. Then she reached up and smoothed her perfectly groomed silver-frosted hair in its knot atop her head. "I do try to keep abreast of fashions and all," she sighed and began listing Meara's purchases in a neat ledger. "But being so far from the big cities, it isn't always easy."

"I'm sure," Meara said and felt rather than saw Conner move up beside her.

As if reading her mind again, he took the knitting needles from her and set them on the counter. Speaking directly to Dora, he said, "We'll take these too, and whatever yarn Meara wants."

She flicked him a glance, but he wasn't looking at her. This time though, she didn't offer him an argument over a purchase. This time, she would be able to pay him back just a bit for the kindnesses he was doing her.

As Meara began pulling out skein after skein of sky blue wool and setting them down in front of her, Dora said, "I don't believe I've seen you around town before this, my dear."

Ah well, Meara thought, so this woman too, didn't know her.

"Meara's . . . visiting me for awhile," Conner said into the silence. "She's waiting for her family to arrive. I don't suppose you've heard of any newcomers here lately? Irish ones?"

"No," Dora said with a slow shake of her head. "But I'll be sure to keep both ears open."

"Is that you, Mr. James?" a female voice, high and thin

splintered the conversation and all heads turned in her direction.

The big woman with the little girl. Meara laid the last skein of yarn on the counter and studied the woman as she made her way up the aisle. She moved like a ship under sail. Effortlessly, letting nothing stand in her path, she dragged her daughter behind her until the girl's small feet were scurrying to keep up.

Meara frowned and instinctively wanted to scoop the child up into her arms to give her rest.

"It is," the woman said, her tone slicing through the sudden, awkward silence in the store. "It *is* you, though how you have the gall to show your face in this town is beyond me."

"Mrs. Carlisle," Conner muttered, inclining his head.

"Now, Hester," Dora tried to interrupt, but the big woman wasn't going to be hushed.

"I said to Isabelle"—she shook the child's hand— "*there's* the man who stole your home, my dear, and forced you to give up your pony to live in a tiny house in town."

Meara looked up at Conner. His features tight, he looked as though he would rather be anywhere but where he was at the moment. And what did this woman mean? How had Conner *stolen* her home?

One stray lock of dark brown hair fell across Hester's forehead and danced in front of her nose, making her eyes cross occasionally as she tried to look around it. Finally, she reached up with pudgy fingers and took hold of it, tucking it up beneath the brim of a silly hat with a stuffed canary sitting ungainly on the brim.

"Why, my husband will be appalled to know that I've run into you. I don't know how you can show your face here."

"It's the only face I've got," Conner said thinly, his mouth barely moving.

"Hester," Dora put in quickly, "why don't you go and

do your shopping? When I've finished with Conner here, I'll be right with you."

The big woman smiled, but it never got close to her eyes. "I'll do that," she said, then added, "as soon as I find out who this young woman is."

Her gaze landed on Meara and she almost shivered, fighting down an incredible urge to cross herself. Black eyes, sharp, assessing, looked her over and found her wanting.

Conner, despite the anger simmering off him in waves, did the gentlemanly thing. "Mrs. Hester Carlisle, this is Meara Simon, my housekeeper."

"Well, well," Hester said with a knowing smirk. "I can't say I'm not surprised. A man like you. Alone. No wonder you'd prefer a pretty little thing to that old claim-jumper you deposited in *my* kitchen."

Meara's temper flared. She knew exactly what the old biddy was thinking. It was plain in her expression that she believed the only housekeeping Meara did for Conner was in his bedroom. She pulled in a deep breath, but Conner spoke up first.

"Grub's still working for me," he said, more politely than the woman deserved. "And Meara's a big help to him."

That strand of hair untucked itself from Hester's hat and slid down to dangle over her nose again. She blew at it. "I'm sure she is," Hester noted, letting her gaze slide dismissively over Meara. "She looks as though she would be . . . useful."

Again, Meara's temper blazed and this time, she had her chance to speak. Smiling sweetly, she said, "I can clean most anything"—she paused for effect—"save a dirty mind."

Hester's night-black eyes narrowed at the unexpected hit.

Conner snorted a choked laugh, and Eli Higgins let his loose, threatening to shake down the rafters.

"Why you cheap little Irish—"

Meara moved in a step.

"Hester," Dora Higgins piped up, "perhaps it would be better if you conducted your business later."

"You're telling *me* to leave?" she hissed.

"Of course not, Hester," Dora soothed. "But . . ."

"It's all right," Conner interrupted. "We're just leaving."

Conner called up every ounce of self-control and used it to keep his temper in check. Hester Carlisle and her husband Robert had been after him for two years. They'd done everything they could to blacken his name and make living in High Timber impossible.

Not that he could blame them entirely. After all, if *he* had lost his home in a high-stakes poker game, he might have a hard time being kind to the man who'd won it.

He'd put up with Hester's snide comments and gossipy tongue. And no matter how bad it had gotten, he'd never before been tempted to hit a woman. Not even Hester. Until now. Watching her shoot arrows into Meara had him ready to toss the old bitch into the pickle barrel. Despite the fact that Meara seemed able to handle her own in a cat fight, the best thing to do was to get out of that store before he gave in to his urge.

"Mrs. Higgins?" he asked, turning his gaze on the storekeeper. "Have you tallied up what I owe you?"

"Hmm?" She jumped, startled. "Oh, of course. That's eight dollars and seventy-three cents, Mr. James. Shall I put it on your bill?"

"That's fine, thanks." Then he took Meara's arm and turned for the door. "Good day." And in an afterthought added, "Good day, Mrs. Carlisle."

The door hadn't even swung closed behind them when Eli Higgins spoke up. "One of these days here, Hester," he said, "somebody's gonna put a fist right in that big mouth of yours."

Hester gasped, outraged.

"And," he went on, unmoved by her distress, "if I didn't have me such a bad back, I'd get up and do it myself.   ·

They walked all over High Timber. Stopping in each store they passed. Conner asked if there were any new folks around and was told that no one had come through since that bunch of Mormons in late spring.

No one knew Meara. No one had heard anything about a missing woman. There was no sign of any newly arrived Irishmen, and after two hours of trying, even he was willing to admit that this was getting them nowhere.

"What now?" Meara asked as they stopped alongside the buckboard.

He tipped his hat back and stared over her head at the distance. Hell, he didn't know what to do next. According to that doctor, her memory would either show up or it wouldn't, an opinion which made Conner wonder why the man had had to go to medical school at all.

"Conner?" she asked, and he tore his gaze from the horizon to look down at her. Amazingly enough, she was smiling. Though what she had to smile about was beyond him.

"Since no one seems to be looking for me," she said with a shake of her head, "shall we go back to that ranch of yours so I can . . ." She tapped her chin with the tip of a finger. "How did you put it? Be a lot of help to Grub?"

He frowned as a new ripple of anger washed through him. "I'm sorry about her. It's me she's mad at."

"And why should you be apologizin' for the likes of her?" she demanded, hands at her hips.

"Since it was only because of me she said anything to you at all."

"Ah no," she told him. "It's nothin' to do with you. Women like her enjoy bein' spiteful. Vinegar is as sweet to them as sugar is to most others. I've met her kind before this."

He found himself smiling. "Have you?" he asked. "Where?"

She blinked, paused, and after a thoughtful moment or two, shrugged. "I don't have the slightest idea," she admitted.

Conner looked into those green eyes that seemed to call to him. "I almost envy you," he said softly, letting his gaze move on, to drift over her face and her figure before coming back to meet her eyes again.

"Mother of Saint Bridget," she exclaimed. "Why would you be envyin' me?"

"You can't remember your past," he said. "And sometimes, I think that would be more blessing than curse."

"Ah no, Conner," Meara said, reaching for his hand. "To lose your memory is to lose pieces of yourself. Pieces that together add up to the whole of you."

Amazing. She was, quite simply, amazing.

Placing both hands at her incredibly tiny waist, he grabbed her and lifted her up into the buckboard. Her skirt got twisted around her leg, showing him a delectable few inches of bare, creamy-white skin. Instantly, his blood burst into flame inside him.

He battled the sudden, ferocious blast of desire until he felt comfortable enough to speak. Then he only looked at her and said, "Sometimes, Meara, the pieces don't add up to make a whole person."

CHAPTER FIVE

Two days later, Meara stood outside in the late afternoon sunshine, beating at the rugs hanging on a rope she'd stretched between the main house and the bunkhouse. She took a good grip on the cane beater and swung again, blinking at the cloud of dust that rose up and seemed to settle right down on top of her.

She sneezed violently and shook her head.

She should be more upset, she knew.

No one in town had known her. No one was looking for her. It was as though she belonged nowhere and to nobody. A lonely situation if ever there was one. To add to that, she worried still about the woman she'd seen in town. The woman in the red dress. The woman Conner *hadn't* seen.

She gave the rug another vicious slap and told herself that maybe she hadn't lost her memory. Maybe she'd lost her mind. If that were true, she should definitely be more upset, than she was. And yet . . .

If no one was looking for her, then she wouldn't have to leave this place. And she wasn't ready to leave. Not just yet.

Meara stretched and glanced around the ranch yard. A few of the men were working with Conner in the corral. It gave Meara the shivers to watch the wild mustang they'd cornered rear up and slash its hooves at the men, but none of them seemed the least bothered.

Mechanically, she went back to her task, swinging the tightly woven cane switch over and over again at the dust-ridden rugs. This was a mindless task. One in which her brain was free to wander as it would. Naturally, her thoughts kept returning to Conner.

His tense stance as Mrs. Carlisle had jabbed at him with her spear-point tongue. His insistence that Meara have the dresses. His protective hand on her shoulder. And the hard, warm strength of his hands at her waist as he lifted her into the buckboard.

She closed her eyes and remembered the instant when Conner's gaze had locked on her legs, bared by an up-drawn skirt. Once again, a sizzle of something hot and sweet and completely wonderful jolted along her spine to settle in the pit of her stomach.

Meara opened her eyes again, bit her lip and beat the rugs even harder. This felt familiar, at least. The ache in her shoulders, the swing of her right arm as she worked, the tightness in her back.

These sensations she understood. The other . . . was confusing as well as exciting.

Setting the beater aside, she took down the rugs, one after the other. Smiling to herself, Meara thought she could be sure of one thing at least. She'd done her job this day and every day since landing here. The house was beginning to take on the look of a home well loved. The bricks on the hearths had been scrubbed, that great monster of a stove had been blacked, the brass lamps polished, and the windowpanes sparkled.

Feeling just a bit prideful, she hurried into the house.

"Boss," Tucker Hanks said slowly from his seat on the fence, "you don't watch what you're doin', that mare'll kill ya."

Conner flicked him a quick look, then returned his

concentration to the animal he held on a long tether. Hanks was right. He'd been distracted watching Meara at the clothesline she'd rigged. But was it his fault that she looked so damned good doing everyday tasks?

He turned slowly in the center of the corral, trying to ease the mare into a trot. But the horse, just like every other female he seemed to be meeting lately, refused to cooperate.

"You got any better ideas on how to work her?" he called out.

"Nope," Hanks answered and squinted around a curl of smoke drifting up from the cigarette clamped between his lips. He watched his boss try again to make the mustang heel to the tether and had to admire the man's pure cussed stubbornness.

Conner cursed the mare and Tucker smiled to himself. It wasn't the horse botherin' the boss. It was that little Irish whirlwind who had every man on the place scurrying to clean and pick up after himself.

"Catch her, will you, Hanks?" Conner asked as he began to loop up the tether.

Tucker trotted to the mare and grabbed hold of the leather bridle. Naturally, the mostly wild horse turned its head real quick and tried to take a bite out of him.

He laughed and jumped back. If Conner ever managed to break her, this mare would be a prize. Plenty of spirit and not an ounce of give up in her.

Coming up beside him, Conner said almost the same thing. "Once she allows a saddle on her, this mare'll be the best on the place."

"*If* she allows a saddle," Tucker said.

"She will," Conner swore solemnly. "Even if it kills both of us."

"You're a stubborn man, boss."

"Yeah, so I've been told." Conner shifted his gaze away, handed the lead rope to Tucker, and turned for the house.

* * *

He found Meara in the main room. She didn't see him at first, so he paused in the open doorway to look around the changed room. Late sunshine poured in through the gleaming windowpanes, laying down bright patches of gold across the freshly cleaned rugs and the polished tables. The place smelled of beeswax and nearly shouted at a man to take his shoes off before stepping inside.

Hell, she'd done amazing things in a few short days. His gaze wandered over everything and rested briefly on the white china pot holding the ivy plant. It was still sitting on the mantle over the fireplace, where he'd put it after discovering it back in his office earlier that morning.

Conner smiled to himself. Good. At least she hadn't tried to sneak it back again.

Then he turned his head to look at Meara and his breath hitched in his chest. On all fours beside the blood-red leather sofa, she was pushing at the rug she'd just cleaned, trying to get the corners to lay right. Softly singing to herself, she was completely unaware of him. His gaze locked on the curve of her behind as her backside moved and swayed delectably with her movements.

Conner's body tightened painfully and he told himself to look away. To say something. To let her know he was there. But he didn't.

Mouth dry, he only half heard the words to her song, something about an Irish highwayman on the moors with a blunderbuss.

Absently, he found himself wondering if she was wearing the new underthings they'd bought a couple of days ago. He swallowed back a groan as his insides burst into flame. His hands itched to reach out and grab her. Hold her. Turn her in his arms and kiss her until neither of them could draw a breath.

Stunned at the force of his response to her, Conner

inhaled sharply, deeply, then deliberately cleared his throat.

Meara shrieked instantly, turned, and looked at him over her shoulder. Shaking her head, she smiled and gave a half laugh. "You scared the life out me," she told him.

"Sorry. I didn't mean to," he said, trying to get control of his raging heartbeat.

"I'll live," she said and pushed herself to her feet. She arched her back slowly, easing out the kinks in her muscles.

Conner bit back another groan as his gaze dropped to the swell of her bosom, straining now against the fabric of her old yellow shirt. "Where's Grub?" he asked, when he found his voice again.

"He isn't back yet."

Conner scowled. How long could it take to buy a few more chickens? But, knowing Grub, the old coot had probably stopped at the saloon for a few drinks and there was no telling when he'd be getting back.

"I just came in for some coffee," he said at last, turning back for the kitchen.

"Well," Meara answered as she hurried after him, "sit yourself down then, I'll get you a cup."

"I can serve myself, Meara." His tone was a bit sharper than he'd intended it to be but there was no taking it back. "It's not your job."

"As you say, your lordship," she snapped as they stepped into the kitchen.

"Quit calling me that."

"Then stop giving me orders as if you were the Pope himself."

Conner inhaled and sighed the air out again in frustration. "I only said I'd serve myself."

"Aye, with royalty in your tone." Her eyebrows lifted slightly and she waved him into a chair before hustling about the kitchen. "This is part of my job," she told him. "Before he left, Grub showed me how to use this monster of a stove and told me to keep a pot of coffee going on it all day." As she talked, she pulled a cup from a shelf, picked up a towel, then lifted the coffee pot and poured it. Setting the pot down on the back of the stove, she turned for the table, shaking her head. "Though how any of you can drink this stuff, I don't understand. Even the smell of it's enough to curl your hair."

He glanced at her unruly, tangled mane and smiled as she handed him the cup. "And have you been sniffing the coffee?"

A brief moment passed before she grinned and lifted one hand to smooth back a single long, curly strand. Tucking it into the haphazard braid she'd fashioned to keep her hair out of her way, she shrugged. "My father used to say that curly hair was a gift from the angels. Though it often seems more curse than gift."

He stared at her for a long minute, then asked, "Your father?"

"Aye," she replied with a grin that slowly dissolved as she realized what she had said. "Oh my."

"The other day you remembered your mother."

"And now me father."

"Do you remember their names?"

She frowned. "No."

"What they look like?"

"No."

"Where they are?"

"No." Clearly frustrated, she paced the kitchen floor. Her bare feet slapped against the wood as she muttered furiously to herself. "Why can't I remember?" she asked of no one in particular. "Why do I pull these bits and pieces from my mind instead of the whole?"

"Meara . . ." He shouldn't have said anything. He shouldn't have prodded her with questions that would only frustrate her. Pushing up from the table, he crossed the floor to her side and grabbed hold of her shoulders when she would have kept pacing.

" 'Tis maddening, this," she told him in an understatement.

A swell of admiration for her filled him. He couldn't imagine what it would be like to have lost such a huge part of yourself. To have no memory. No past. No present.

To someone like him, it might not have mattered. His recollections rarely brought him comfort. There were damn few pleasant memories scattered in his past. In fact, he'd spent a good amount of time *trying* to forget the last twenty years of his life.

But for Meara, he knew, it was painful. He saw it in her eyes, heard it in her voice. What must it feel like, he wondered, to actually *crave* a link to the past?

He lifted one hand to brush her hair back from her face. As he did, his fingertips dusted across her ivory skin, sending bright sparks of sensation skittering through his bloodstream. He tried desperately to ignore it.

"Don't worry," he said. "We'll find your people. Your memory will come back."

"When?" she demanded, her voice thick with emotion. "Even the doctor didn't know for sure."

"It's already coming back," he said softly, letting his gaze slowly move over her features.

"Aye, in bits and pieces."

"It's better than nothing."

"I suppose."

"You're as stubborn as I am," he said, hoping to coax a smile from her. It worked.

"There's no need to be insultin'," she said with a sniff. Then she studied his face for a long moment before adding, "You're a kind man, Conner James."

He let go of her instantly. "No," he assured her and took a step back. "I'm not."

She laughed, and the sound hung in the air like the melody of a song you can't forget.

"You should see your face," she told him. "Kindness isn't a sin, you know."

"In my world it was," he answered darkly.

"That makes no sense, Conner."

"It makes perfect sense, Meara."

She shook her head, not understanding. And Conner didn't know how he could make her see. Or if he should try. Then she took a step closer and laid one hand on his forearm. Her touch sent jagged edges of heat slicing through him and he knew he had to make her see at least a part of who he was.

For her sake as well as his own.

"In the places where I've lived my life, kindness was a weakness," he said, his voice tight and hard with the memories flooding him. "And a weakness was something to be taken advantage of. The weak don't survive there long. And I survived, Meara. More than survived. I took what I learned and it got me this ranch."

"What are you talkin' about?"

His gaze locked with hers, he went on, his voice hard, deep. "You haven't asked me about the woman we met in the store the other day."

"The harpy, ya mean?"

A brief, humorless smile lifted one corner of his mouth. "Yeah. But she's got a right, I guess."

"How's that?"

He turned his head to one side and let his gaze slide over the room. "This place used to be her home."

"What?" Meara asked and he heard the surprise in her voice.

"I won it from her husband in a high-stakes card game. A man fool enough to bet it on three Kings and a pair of nines. When I showed him my straight flush, he begged me not to take the place from him. Well," he said on a deep breath, "here I stand. That should tell you that I'm not a kind man."

She didn't say anything.

"When begging didn't work, he accused me of cheating. I didn't," he added, not knowing whether she'd believe him or not. "But Robert Carlisle's been badmouthing me around town ever since."

He watched her eyes, waiting for her to acknowledge what he already knew. That he was a selfish bastard.

Instead, the foolish woman shook her head again and even gave him a sad smile.

"So you're to be blamed for winning a ranch away from a man feebleminded enough to risk his home on a game of chance?" She tightened her grip on his arm and continued. "Because he begged for mercy when he lost, you think you should have returned it to him?"

Conner scowled at her. "A *kind* man would have."

"Ha!"

His gaze narrowed as he stared at her smiling face.

"An even bigger fool would have given this glorious place back to a man who clearly had no love for it. 'Tis easy enough to wager your home if you don't care about it."

"You don't understand," he said, and wondered how in the hell she'd missed the point of his story.

"No, Conner," she told him. " 'Tis *you* who doesn't understand. Let me ask you a question."

He nodded, took a deep breath and waited.

"The next time you're playing a game of cards, would you consider wagering this ranch of yours?"

"Never."

"Not even if it meant a chance to win piles of gold?"

He shook his head.

"Well then, there you are."

"Where?"

"You're a man who loves his home, Conner." She patted his arm gently. "No matter how you came to be master of this place, 'tis yours and you'll hang on to it, come heaven or hell."

"So?" She was so far from his original point now, he

had no idea of how to get back where he'd started.

"So," Meara said with another slow smile, "you're not so evil a man as you'd have me think."

"Meara." He inhaled sharply and blew it out of his lungs in a rush. "You're not listening to me."

"Oh, but I am. You're just not makin' any sense."

"I took the man's home from him."

"You won it from a fool."

"I wouldn't give it back." His voice rose to a near shout.

"And why should ya?" she yelled back at him, spots of color staining her cheeks.

"Can't you see I'm trying to warn you away from me?" he muttered, reaching out and grabbing her shoulders with both hands.

"So you're tryin' to save me?"

"Yes, damn it!"

"And would an evil man be so kind, do ya think?"

He didn't know. He didn't care, either. All he knew for sure was that his blood was pumping through his veins and his heartbeat was thundering in his ears. Staring down into the green eyes that tugged at his soul, he surrendered to the inevitable, bent his head and kissed her.

Her gasp of surprise quickly shifted into a soft sigh. And that sigh died abruptly when Conner broke the kiss almost before it started and took a step back. He looked over her head at the door and the yard beyond.

"Damn," he muttered.

"What is it?" she asked, wanting him to start kissing her again.

Conner looked down into her eyes and lifted one hand to stroke her cheek. "It's Grub. He's back."

"Mother of Saint Bridget," she whispered and lifted one hand to smooth her hair. She could hardly believe that she'd been kissing Conner only a moment before. What would she have said if Grub had strolled into the kitchen and found them like that? A flush of embarrassment rose up in her cheeks.

The door opened.

"Ah, Grub," she said, too brightly. " 'Tis nice to see you home safe."

The older man paused on the threshold, his gaze drifting from one of them to the other. He hadn't seen a pair of such guilty faces since the night the town sheriff and his deputy were caught with their pants down, literally, when the local cathouse went up in flames.

"What's been goin' on in here?" he asked, his gaze shifting to Conner. The man he thought of as a son shrugged and shook his head.

"Did ya get the chickens?" Meara asked breathlessly.

"Yeah," Grub said. "They're outside, on the wagon."

"Lovely," she exclaimed. "I'll just go have a look, shall I?"

That said, she darted past him, her bare feet hardly touching the floor in her haste. She was out the door in a flash of movement, leaving the two men alone in the room.

Grub studied Conner for a long, thoughtful minute before saying softly. "That's a decent girl yonder."

Conner's gaze narrowed, but Grub had known him too long and too well to back down from it. Finally, the younger man relented.

"I know that," Conner said, his gaze straying to the window and beyond that, to Meara.

"Well, you just keep on rememberin' that," Grub said in a voice he'd used on the other man when he was a boy of fifteen. "If you got an itch, you go get it scratched at Ida's place in town."

Several moments ticked by before Conner spoke again.

"What if it's not that kind of an itch? What if it goes deeper than that?"

Grub studied him and slowly shook his head. "Then that'd be different, wouldn't it?"

Yeah, it would, Conner thought as he watched Meara climb into the back of the buckboard to examine the chickens in their wooden crates.

Very different.

He was still watching her that evening, as they sat in the main room before a roaring fire. Grub, asleep in his chair, snored just loud enough to be annoying and the soft, repetitive clack of Meara's knitting needless was almost soothing. She hardly looked at what she was doing, he noticed. Though her fingers flew at her task, she mostly stared into the fire, daydreaming.

Firelight played on her red-gold hair as it lay loose around her shoulders and brought a soft glow to her creamy skin. A wistful smile curved her lips, and one of her feet tapped gently on the carpet as if in time to an inner song only she could hear.

She looked up at him then and smiled, and Conner instantly lowered his gaze to his book. He'd already tried to read the same page three times and was making no headway at all.

Unable to concentrate around her, he stood up, setting his book down on a nearby table.

"Off to bed?" Meara asked.

Don't think about bed, either, he told himself sternly. "No," he said. "Thought I'd go into the office. Get some paperwork done."

She smiled at him and something tightened around his heart. Jesus, what was happening to him?

"Shall I wake Grub?"

The older man continued to snore, undisturbed by their conversation.

"Wake him when you go up," Conner said and started walking.

"G'night, then," she called as he left the room without another word.

The office, he thought. Close the door. Concentrate.

Forget about her hair. Her skin. Her voice. Her eyes. Like a man running from the hounds of hell, he quickened his pace, entered his office, and closed the door firmly behind him.

Then suddenly, he laughed at the foolishness of it all. What the hell was wrong with him? No woman had ever affected him this way. Shaking his head, he determinedly brushed away thoughts of Meara and headed for his desk.

He took two steps and stopped dead.

The rose-painted, white china ivy pot was back. Perched on the edge of his desk.

And it was as if Meara was in the room with him.

CHAPTER SIX

He dreamed that night of the old days. The days spent travelling with his father from town to town, city to city, always in search of the next poker game. The next chance at the fortune that always seemed just out of reach.

Shifting uncomfortably in his sleep, Conner unwillingly drifted deeper into a past he longed to forget.

At thirteen, he was near man-sized and caught the eye of a few of the younger whores in the saloon. But his gaze was locked on a poker table. Five men sat hunched over their cards, their expressions carefully blank, their suspicious gazes constantly flicking to their opponents.

A bubble of hope lifted in Conner's chest as he watched his father gather a handful of chips and toss them carelessly into the pot. Maybe this time, the boy told himself. Maybe this time it would be different. Maybe his father's luck would finally change.

Then one of the other players laughed triumphantly, displayed his winning hand face-up on the table, and gleefully raked in the pile of chips. Chairs scraped against the scarred wooden floor. Stubs of cigars were ground out in disgust as the players dis-banded, each of them heading off into the night.

All but one.

Conner's gaze never left his father's lined, pale features. Once a handsome man, Trevor James's good looks had dissolved in a mixture of alcohol and hopelessness. He'd spent most of his adult life chasing the elusive Lady Luck, always just one step behind the fortune he never tired of talking about.

Conner had been with him only the last three years and already, he had learned a great deal. He now knew exactly what he didn't want out of life. He knew that travelling from one saloon to the next, relying on the kindness of whores for free meals, wasn't the way he wanted to live. He was tired of being looked down on by town boys his own age. He wanted to go to school. He wanted a home.

And one day, he would have it all. One day, he would find a way to be somebody.

Detatched from the scene and yet somehow still a part of it, Conner watched the boy he had been and wished again that he could just let go of the past once and for all.

"Then why don't ya?" Meara asked as she drifted toward him.

"Why are you here?" he asked.

"Your dream called me, Conner. You must want me here."

"No, I don't even want to be here."

Swirls of mist rose up around them, blanketing the saloon and other painful memories beneath a soft, gray shroud. Conner looked down at her, los-ing himself in her eyes.

"What was that place, Conner?" she asked.

"The world where I grew up," he told her.

"Why do you hate it so?"

"Because it was ugly. And dirty. And so damned empty."

She reached up and touched his face gently. He closed his eyes and swore he felt that touch sink into his soul.

"Then why do you dream about it?" she wondered aloud.

He caught her hand in his and held it pressed to his cheek. "I don't want to. It won't leave me."

"Because you won't look at it, Conner."

"I lived it. I don't want or need to look at it again."

"But you do," she said, with a slow shake of her head. "You have to look at it and see it for what it really was."

"Don't you think I know what it was?" he asked and the grayness around them trembled. "I've spent most of my life trying to forget it."

"But it's what made you who you are. How can you forget?"

"I have to," he whispered and held her hand tighter when he felt her begin to fade from his touch. "Otherwise I'll never be more than the boy I was."

"Foolish man," she said, even as her image began to shimmer and dissolve into the surrounding mist. "Without the boy you were, you couldn't be more."

"Don't go, Meara," he said, suddenly feeling very alone in the enveloping clouds of the dream world.

He woke up in a lurch. Thirty-five years old and still those dreams rattled him to the bone.

Sitting straight up in bed, he rubbed one hand over his face, wiping away beads of sweat from his forehead. Swinging his legs off the side of the bed, Conner braced his elbows on his knees and cupped his face in his hands.

Now he couldn't keep away from her even in his sleep.

Meara woke up abruptly and lay in the dark, staring up at the ceiling and the pattern of moonlight scattered across the overhead beams. Her heartbeat thudded painfully in her chest and her breathing was labored.

Had she been dreaming about Conner or had he been dreaming about her? So strange. It had felt so real.

Of course it wasn't, she told herself and rubbed her eyes tiredly. She'd dreamed of Conner because he had kissed her. And she had kissed him back, Meara admitted silently.

Something hot and slow and sweet spiralled through her body at the memory. If she tried, she could almost taste his mouth on hers. Feel the strength of his arms as he held her to him. Shaking her head on the pillow, she told herself not to try. It should never have happened. She still wasn't sure how it had.

But until she knew for sure that she wasn't another man's wife—or someone's mother—she couldn't allow herself to be drawn to Conner James. No matter the temptation.

As she tried to push all thoughts of that kiss to one side, Meara found herself remembering the dream instead. In her mind's eye, she saw the young Conner, thin and frightened, and heard again Conner the man, denying his past, running from it.

Too, Meara recalled the heavy gray mist that had swirled around her and Conner. It had seemed somehow comforting and yet dangerous. Something niggled at the back of her mind. Something . . . important. Familiar. But as hard as she tried, she couldn't quite grab hold of the elusive thought.

She shivered slightly as a sudden, overpowering sense of cold settled over her. Had she left the window open before she went to bed? Darting out from under the quilt, she crossed the wood floor quickly, her bare feet stinging on the icy surface.

But the window was closed.

And in the next breath, the cold was gone.

Still rubbing her arms with both hands, Meara stood stock-still in the moon-drenched darkness, trying to understand what was happening. A chill that had nothing to do with the temperature of the room crawled along her spine. More mysteries? she mused. More unanswered questions? Hadn't she enough to wonder about already?

Her mind busy with too many thoughts to allow sleep, Meara crossed the room to the wardrobe on the far wall. She opened the door, reached inside and pulled out one of her new dresses.

If she was very quiet, she could go to the kitchen and get to work. Let the men in this house sleep. As for her, she needed to keep both mind and hands busy.

Already, she felt at home in this big house. As if she'd lived there for years. She had no need of a candle to find her way, the sprinkle of moondust was more than enough light to see by. As she hit the bottom of the stairs, she stopped.

Hands at her hips, she scowled at the white china ivy pot, sitting on the narrow table along the back of the sofa. "Stubborn man," she muttered darkly. "He must have taken the time to move it before going to bed." Shaking her head, she hurried forward, grabbed up the pot and walked down the long hallway to his office. "Well, he's not the only one who can move a plant," she said to herself and set the china bowl on the top shelf of a row of bookcases.

Then smiling, she left the office, headed straight for the kitchen. Moving around the room barefoot, she began gathering the things she would need to make sweet buns for breakfast. When Meara checked the pantry, though, she realized she'd be needing eggs if she wanted to make anything a'tall.

Slipping outside, she hurried to the chicken coop, beyond the bunkhouse. In the still quiet of the night, sounds carried easily. Over the soft sigh of her own breath, she heard the heavy, yet muted stampings of the horses in the barn. She kept a wide distance between herself and the animals Conner thought so highly of.

Night birds called to each other, and in the distance, a lone animal howled, sounding like a lost soul. At that thought, Meara crossed herself nervously and quickened her steps. Not that she was afraid, mind you, but there was no sense in wandering about in the dark when a wild animal might swoop down on you at any moment.

Tiny rocks prodded at the soles of her feet, and she winced, wishing she'd taken the time to go upstairs for her boots. She slipped past the bunkhouse and frowned at the chorus of snores drifting into the night air. How did any of them get a wink of sleep? she wondered absently. Even as that thought presented itself though, a new sound rose up. Soft. Sad. Someone was playing a fiddle. Meara stared at the darkened building as she listened to the mysterious musician coax out a lovely tune that seemed to float atop the rumblings rising from the sleeping men.

But she had no time to spend woolgathering in the night. The chicken coop loomed ahead, a darker splotch of black silhouetted against the night. She'd forgotten something to carry the eggs in, but decided to simply cradle a few of them in her gathered-up skirt. She set her hand on the latch and paused when she heard a faint rustling sound from within.

Another shiver raced along her spine. What if there was a fox or a wolf—or worse—in there with the hens? She listened for another moment or two, straining her ears to catch the slightest sound. But there was nothing.

Silliness, she thought. If there were a fox in there, the hens would be all aflutter, sending up a screech that would have wakened even those in that noisy bunkhouse.

She lifted the latch and stepped inside, securing the door behind her. A few quick eggs, she told herself. Just a few, then she'd be off for the house like there were wings on her feet.

Whispering gently to the hens perched on their straw-covered roosts, she began the gather. But as she slipped her hand beneath the second hen, she heard that sound again. Now that she was closer though, she recognized it as the soft brush of cloth on wood.

Not some*thing*, then.

Some*one*.

Gathering the threads of her fast unravelling courage, she said quietly, "Who's there?"

Nothing.

Meara swallowed past a hard knot of fear and brazened the intruder out. "I know you're in here," she said. "Speak up and I won't harm ya."

A moment passed, then a small voice came from the far end of the coop. "I ain't scared of you. You're just a girl."

Pent-up breath left her in a rush, and she felt the near giddy sensation of relief pouring through her bloodstream. A child. 'Twas only a child. Laughing at her own wild imagination, she tried to keep her voice steady as she said, "Step into the moonlight, then. Let's have a look at ya."

She waited while the boy decided whether or not to cooperate and was finally rewarded when he came out from hiding and moved into a patch of silvery light.

Scrawny was the first word that came to mind. The torn, dirty clothing he wore hung on his bony frame, and even in the pitiful light, she could see shadows beneath his eyes. His hair stuck up at odd angles all over his head and his bare feet were filthy.

He couldn't have been more than eight or nine.

"Who might you be?" she asked.

He ran the back of his dirty hand beneath his nose. "Name's Luke Banyan."

"Well then, Luke, what're you doin' skulkin' around a chicken coop in the middle of the night?"

"I ain't sayin'."

Meara nodded slowly and reached beneath the closest hen for another egg. "You wouldn't be stealing eggs now, would ya?"

"You can't prove nothin'."

She hid a smile. Such brave talk from a boy near shivering with the cold and hunger. As she watched him, he eased closer to her, further from his hiding place where she was sure she could find several empty eggshells. Her heart went out to him, but she recognized the streak of pride and defiance in him and knew he wouldn't be thanking her for her pity. Instead, she made him an offer.

"You're right of course, and I've no cause to be callin' you a thief."

His pinched face tightened warily, and his gaze darted toward the door as if judging his chances of getting past her and making an escape.

"To apologize," she went on, smoothly stepping between him and the latched door, "I'll cook you some breakfast."

He cocked his head and looked at her suspiciously. "I ain't hungry."

"No," she said, "I can see you're a man who's not missed many meals, but 'twould make me feel better about this misunderstanding if you'd eat with me."

"I don't know," he said, clearly tempted by the idea of food he didn't have to snatch at. "I got places to go, you know. I got a job waitin' on me in town."

A job. Her heart twisted in her chest. Poor boyo. Where in heaven were his parents? His family? Why was one so young out wandering in the woods in the middle of the night looking as though no one had spared him a thought in years?

Meara pushed her concerns aside for the moment. Right now, she only wanted to get a hot meal into the child. There'd be time enough later for questions and answers.

"Then we'd best put a good foot under us, eh?" she said.

"You talk strange, lady."

"But I'm a good cook," she assured him. "Now, if you'll just help me gather up a few more eggs, we'll go inside and start the feast."

She turned her back on him then, concentrating on the roosting hens. She was giving him his chance to run and hoping the promise of food would be enough to make him stay. Meara released a breath when she felt him move up beside her.

As he reached under a chicken, he looked up at her. "What's a feast?"

She smiled at him. "You'll soon find that out, boyo."

Conner stepped into the kitchen and stopped so fast, Grub slammed into him from behind.

"What the hell's wrong with you, Conner?" the older man snapped and pushed past him, only to stop dead himself.

There at the table sat the dirtiest kid Grub had ever seen. Small, narrow face with sunken cheeks and hard, sharp eyes, the boy's hands were clean to his wrist, where the dirt started again, making it look as though he was wearing white gloves. His mouth full, he stared at the two men as if he was trying to decide which way to run.

"What in the Sam Hill . . . ?" Grub muttered just as Meara sailed into the room from the pantry. Her arms full of kindling wood, she nodded at the two of them.

"Good morning." Before another word was said, she dropped the wood into the basket near the stove, then moved to stand behind the kid. Laying one hand on the boy's shoulder, she looked first at Grub, then at Conner.

"As you can see, we've a guest this morning. His name is Luke Banyan."

Grub stared at her, not daring a glance at Conner. The woman really was a pistol.

"And what's Luke doing here?" Conner asked, his voice a low, dangerous grumble.

The kid pushed up from the table, sending Conner a glare that could have fried bacon, but Meara's hand on his shoulder shoved him back onto the bench. "He's on his way to town to find a job, and I invited him to have a meal with us."

"I ain't gonna take nothin' from him," Luke snarled, clearly reacting badly to the tone of Conner's voice.

"You aren't," Meara told him sharply. "You're taking it from me. Now eat up, while it's hot."

Still keeping one eye on both men, the kid picked up his spoon again and dug into a bowl of cinammon apple slices. Well, Grub was curious. But not curious enough to miss his chance at those apples. And if he didn't move quick, that skinny youngster might finish them off.

Muttering "Morning," to the boy, Grub took a seat opposite him and helped himself.

Conner didn't move. He simply turned his gaze on Meara and jerked his head in the direction of the main room behind him. Then he stepped aside and let her lead the way to where they might have a private conversation.

"What the hell were you thinking?" he asked before she'd even turned around to face him.

Then she did whirl around, the skirt of her new dress flaring out about her legs with her sharp movement. "I was thinking that if I didn't get some food into that child soon, he'd keel over from the hunger."

"Without so much as *telling* me first?"

"Do you begrudge a starving child a bit of food?"

"Of course not," he snapped, refusing to be put in the wrong. Her green eyes glittered dangerously, but he wouldn't be stopped by that warning sign, either.

This was *his* house. And *he* would be the one to decide who came and went. Wasn't it enough that he'd had a strange woman drop into his life unexpectedly? Wasn't it enough that his house didn't feel like his own anymore because of that woman?

Was he also supposed to stand still while she brought even *more* people into his home? Without even bothering to mention it to him?

His breath hitched as an image of the boy rose up in his mind. Dirty. Neglected. Suspicious eyes that looked at the world as if waiting for the next blow to fall. His jaw tightened and his hands closed into fists at his sides. At first glance of Luke, he had tumbled back into his own past. He'd seen himself in that boy and hadn't liked it one damn bit.

He'd come a long way from the rough-and-tumble life he'd known back then, and every goddamn day he made a conscious effort to forget it. But one look at that kid and it had all come rushing back at him.

"He's just a child, Conner," she said, her voice softening a bit. "Alone. And hungry."

Conner's guts twisted. He remembered that empty feeling all too well. And the fear that accompanied it. Fear that you'd never find enough food to fill the hunger. Fear that even if you did manage to eat today, there was still the next day to be faced.

And the next.

He gritted his teeth and ruthlessly shoved those memories away, down into the darkest corner of his mind. Where he hoped they would stay.

"I found him in the chicken coop," Meara was saying, forcing his attention back to her, "stealing eggs and eating them raw."

Conner winced as the taste of stolen eggs settled on his tongue. The slick slide of it into a stomach so empty a whole henhouse full of eggs wouldn't have been enough.

"I know what it is to be hungry," she told him and took a step closer.

So did he, but he wasn't going to tell her so.

"I know what it is to be cold and afraid," she went on.

More memories, flooding him. Drowning him in a past he couldn't seem to shake.

"I couldn't turn him away."

He looked down at her and read pity in her green eyes. He could have told her from experience that the kid wouldn't thank her for it. The only thing worse than being hungry was being beholden to those who fed you.

But at the same time, he knew that he wouldn't have turned the kid away, either.

Shaking his head, he said quietly, "I know. I guess it was just a surprise, walking in and seeing him sitting there."

She laughed softly. "It was a surprise for me, too, runnin' into him in the dark. Scared the life outa me."

Reluctantly, he smiled. How was she able to coax more smiling out of him than he'd done in the last ten years? Then something she'd said came back to him. "A minute ago, you said you remembered being hungry. And scared."

Meara blinked and looked away from him. "I did, didn't I?"

"Do you recall anything else?"

She thought for a moment, then shook her head slowly. "No. There's nothing now." Scowling to herself, she muttered, "Frustrating is what this is. Bits and pieces floating about in my mind and not enough to make the whole."

Conner took a step back from her. It was almost exactly what she'd said to him in his dream.

His confusion must not have shown on his face, because a moment later, she inhaled sharply and sighed. "Best not to think about that now," she said. "I've got people to feed, a boy to wash, a house to clean, and sweaters to knit."

"Sweaters?" he echoed lamely.

"Aye," she told him with a quick grin. "Great, wooly warm things you wear when 'tis cold." A moment later, she slipped past him, headed for the kitchen, but stopped when he asked, "What do you mean, a boy to wash? Didn't you say he was on his way to town? Something about a job?"

She gave him a look most people reserved for village idiots and stupid children. "Ah, Conner, you don't really believe the little devil is goin' after a job, do ya?"

He planted both hands on his hips and waited, sure she wasn't finished. She didn't disappoint him.

"And if he's going to be stayin' here and eatin' in my kitchen, he's going to be a sight cleaner than he is at the moment."

Then she was gone and Conner was left staring at an empty doorway.

The boy was staying?

And since when had the kitchen become *hers*?

A small fist clipped her on the chin and snapped her jaw shut, hard. Briefly, Meara saw brilliant stars flash in front of her eyes and was sure she'd knocked a tooth or two loose. But she didn't have time to worry about it at the moment.

"Here now!" she snapped and dragged the boy another foot or so toward the barrel of soapy water she'd set up in the kitchen. "Hit me again, and I'm liable to warm your backside for ya."

"You ain't my ma," Luke shouted in a surprisingly loud, high voice. "You cain't make me take no bath!"

Meara bent over, planted her bare feet on the wooden floor and heaved. For a small boy, he was surprisingly strong. "Aren't you ashamed?" she said. "A boy your age makin' such a to-do over a bit of water and soap."

"It ain't healthy, gettin' wet all over," he shouted, and grabbed hold of the table leg. "You tryin' to kill me?"

Meara blew a long curl of hair out of her eyes. "What's not healthy is the layer of grime on ya. I'll wager you haven't looked at the world from under water in a year or more."

He jerked his arm from her grasp and slithered away. Darting to the opposite side of the table, he began to sway back and forth, trying to judge which way she'd move so he could jump in the opposite direction.

"You're *goin'* in that tub, boyo," she said firmly, "if I have to sit on you to make sure you stay."

"It ain't decent. I tell ya," the boy shouted. "No dang female's gonna be givin' me no bath!"

"Luke boy," she tried reasoning with him. "You've enough dirt on you to plant a decent crop of potatoes."

He looked at her like she was crazy.

Clearly, reasoning with him wasn't going to work.

She made a quick move, which he countered just as quickly. Muttering under her breath, she called on Saint Bridget, Saint Patrick, and whatever other saints were hovering about doing nothing, to give her a hand with the boy.

"What in the hell is going on in here?" Conner shouted as he charged through the back door. "I can hear the shouting clean over to the corral."

"Keep her away from me, mister," Luke shouted, and made a break for the door. "She's plumb loco!"

Conner caught the kid's collar and dragged him to a stop. He held him at arm's length to avoid the swinging fists and feet. Looking at Meara, he demanded, "What are you trying to do to him?"

Straightening up, she lifted her chin, glanced from the filthy boy to the man holding him so effortlessly and said, "I'm trying to get him into that tub of water, there."

"And I ain't gettin' naked in front of no danged

woman," Luke shouted in a tone high enough to hurt Conner's ears.

He gave the boy a gentle shake, then looked at Meara in disgust. "No wonder he's screaming. No boy wants a woman to bathe him."

"Fine," she snapped. "*You* do it."

"Me?" Conner shouted, astonishment coloring his features.

Luke flashed her a triumphant smile. "See, lady, I don't need no bath."

"You stink to high heaven, boyo," Meara countered, with a look for him and a glare for Conner. "And if either of ya expects to be eatin' supper tonight, you'll be havin' a bath."

Conner looked down at the boy. Rings of dirt and grime covered the kid's neck and his hair was so filthy, it was impossible to tell what color it was. Added to that, he was just beginning to notice a distinct smell clinging to the kid.

"No supper, huh?" Conner muttered, trying not to take too deep a breath.

Luke turned a suddenly worried gaze up to him. "Hey, mister, you ain't gonna let her boss ya, are ya?"

"Boy," Conner said, with a wink for Meara, "first thing you've got to learn about women, is don't argue with 'em when there's supper at stake."

"I ain't hungry," Luke yelled and took another swing at the man holding him at bay so easily.

"Well I am." Conner told him, then shot a meaningful glance at Meara. "You can go now," he said. "And supper better be damned good.

In perfect understanding, she promised, "A veritable banquet for you and yours."

Then she sailed past the two of them, pausing only long enough to shoot Luke a triumphant look before heading out the back door, closing it behind her.

Briefly, Conner envied her her escape. Then, with the kid cussing a blue streak, he picked the boy up under one arm and marched for the tub.

CHAPTER SEVEN

Curses colored the air.

Meara stared at the kitchen door as though she could see through it to the battle beyond. Across the yard in the corral, several of the hands were making bets on who would give up first, Conner or the kid. And Grub just sat on the porch smoking a pipe, looking at peace with the world.

"How do you stand it?" she demanded, shooting him a glance, then returning her attention to the closed door.

"Stand what?" the man asked.

"Don't you want to get in there and help him?"

"Hell no." Grub chuckled around the stem of his pipe and lifted both feet to cross them on the porch rail. "I'm too old to fight a little devil like that one."

Blowing her hair out of her face, Meara shook her head as the sound of the boy's shouts got louder. "What manner of man is he that those shouts don't tear at his heart?"

Grub looked down, pulled his pipe from his mouth and studied the bowl as if looking for answers in the tiny curl of smoke lifting from it. Finally, he said, "He's a hard man. But a good one."

"How do you mean, hard?"

Grub heaved a sigh that seemed to come all the way

from the soles of his feet. Then he said. "You'll find most
men in these parts are hard ones. 'Leastwise, the survi-
vors are. The weak ones get weeded out. Almost like
nature culls 'em like you would a bad cow from a herd."
He smiled at her gently, and Meara guessed that her confusion was written plainly on her face. "Back east, a
weaker man can get along fine. He's got policemen to
look after him and lots of close neighbors to run to in
time of trouble. In the west, a man stands on his own
two feet. Most times, you can't find a lawman when you
need one and neighbors are mighty far afield. If you can't
watch out for yourself, you don't last long here."

Meara shivered. "Sounds like a lonely life."

"It can be." He let his gaze drift a moment over the
ranch yard, and a peaceful, contented expression crossed
his face. "But she's a good one, too. If you've got the
nerve to reach out and grab what you want and then
have the guts to fight to hang on to it." His gaze shot to
hers. "Conner does. Always has."

"You've known him a long time, then?"

One corner of Grub's mouth tilted slightly. "Longer
than I care to think. Knew his pa, too."

The shouting in the kitchen behind them quieted down
and all she heard for a moment or two was the vigorous
splashing of water spilling over the side of the tub. She
didn't want to think about what the kitchen was going
to look like when the battle was all over.

"What was he like?" she asked. "The father, I mean."
She wondered if she might learn more about the son by
knowing about the man who'd sired him.

Grub shook his head and pursed his lips as if he'd
bitten into something bitter. "Trevor James was a disap-
ponted man."

"Disappointed in what?"

Grub snorted. "Everything. Cards. Women. Durn fool
wouldn't have known a winner if it walked up and shot
him." Drifting into his memories, the man stared off into

the distance and went on. "Didn't even know he had a son till Conner's ma died when he was ten and sent the boy to him." A look of disgust clouded his features. "The jackass didn't even see what a gift the boy was. All he saw was more bad luck. Then ol' Trevor dragged Conner around after him from saloon to saloon for close to five years."

She tried to imagine a young Conner drifting from place to place, following behind a man who didn't want him. Briefly, she remembered the dream she'd had where she'd seen for herself the young Conner, lost and alone, waiting for a father who apparently hadn't cared.

Meara took a seat beside Grub and prodded, "What happened then?"

"Trevor tried to cheat the wrong man. Died over a poker table."

"Oh my," she whispered, seeing the scene in her mind's eye. "And Conner?"

"He was there. Fourteen he was then. Buried his pa, then took off."

"Alone? Where did he go?" she asked. "What did he do?"

"Don't know for sure," Grub told her and stuck his pipe stem back in his mouth. Gripping it with his teeth, he said tightly, "He won't talk about it, 'cept to say he joined the Army when the war broke out. Hell, I don't even know which side he fought on. Not that it matters a damn to me."

"War?" she whispered, furrowing her brow. There was a war? Why couldn't she remember something that important? As she tried to prod her memory, a vague, whisper-thin image rose up in her mind, then evaporated quickly, leaving behind only the suggestion of men in blood-red tunics astride powerful horses, charging down a hillside directly at her.

Frowning, she fought to coax more from her mind, but it was useless. The images were gone now as if they'd never been and she was left more confused than before.

A war. And Conner had fought in it. How old had he been at the time? She hoped not too young. She saw again the dream Conner, with his tired, old eyes and pinched expression. Her heart twisted and she wanted to reach back in time to comfort him. To be with him.

"Somethin' happened to him in that damned war," Grub was saying. "I seen it in his eyes from time to time. Same thing I seen in Hanks's eyes and a few others." Shaking his head again, he sighed heavily. "There's a blackness inside them. A hard, cold knot of something they ain't been able to get shed of. It's true what they say, y'know," he added quietly. "Old men plan wars. Young men fight 'em. And have to live with the after."

Though particular memories still eluded her, Meara's mind conjured up images of battlefields. Wounded and dying men and the terror that hung over them all. A chill raced along her spine as she imagined Conner among them. Surviving, but at what cost?

Grub's next words shattered her thoughts. "You don't remember the war, either?"

Instantly brought back to the porch and the sunshine scattered across the ranch yard, Meara frowned. "No. 'Tis maddening, this emptiness that crowds my mind."

Unexpectedly, he reached out and patted the top of her head. "It'll pass, little girl. Most things do."

Most do, she repeated silently. But what if this didn't? What if she was left with these holes in her memory forever? What if she never knew who she was or where she came from or if someone was waiting for her?

Was she to live her whole life in the waiting?

Wrapping her arms about herself, she recalled being held in the circle of Conner's arms. The feel of his mouth on hers. His breath dusting across her cheek.

Was she never to feel those things again? If she couldn't remember her past, how could she claim a future?

The back door flew open and crashed against the side of the house, splintering her thoughts.

Grumbling in disgust, Conner stepped through the doorway and down the three short steps to the dirt below. Only then did he turn to look at Meara and Grub.

Holding his hands out away from his soaking-wet body, he said, "The kid's clean. Finally. I gave him one of my shirts to wear until you two get him some decent clothes."

"What happened to what he was wearing?" Grub asked.

"I threw 'em in the fire," Conner told him flatly. "Nothin' more than rags."

Meara looked at his tight expression and the haunted shadows in his eyes and spoke up quickly. "I'll go into town. Buy him a few things, shall I?"

Conner shifted his gaze to the corral, but nodded stiffly. "Get him some shoes, too. It's coming on to winter. The boy can't go barefoot in the snow."

"I will," she promised to his back.

He didn't say another word, just stomped off toward the barn, apparently anxious to get back to work.

"A hard man," Meara whispered, remembering what Grub had said only a moment or two ago. Her gaze locked on his retreating form, she finished the thought. "But a good one."

At the Emporium, Meara piled the clothes she'd picked out on the counter. Two pairs of pants, two shirts, *underwear*—she shook her head—and shoes. She only hoped they fit the boy.

As she waited for Mrs. Higgins to finish with her other customer, Meara's gaze drifted over the well-stocked shelves until she spied a row of cans, several rolls of paper, and a tin bucket holding all manner of brushes.

Intrigued, Meara left her purchases on the counter and crossed the store. Paint. Can after can of paint. All different colors, judging by their labels. White. Red. Sunshine yellow. Lovely, she thought, and lifted that can to study it.

"James thinkin' about paintin' that place of his?" Eli Higgins called out from his perch behind the counter.

Meara spun around, still holding the paint can. Already, she could see the lovely yellow paint covering those dark brown halflogs inside the kitchen. Wouldn't it be a nice, warm thing to look upon during cold winter months? Like having a bit of summer in the room.

The more she thought about it, the more sure she was that Conner would have painted the rooms of his house if he had had the time. Naturally, the poor man had far too much work to do. So she would assume the task for him.

"Would you be havin' any more of this lovely yellow paint, Mr. Higgins?" she asked.

"Yeah." He inclined his head toward the storeroom door behind him. "In yonder, there's stacks of them cans. All different colors, though I can't say why. White should be enough for anybody. Too much color's hard on the eyes, I always say."

But she wasn't listening. Already, she was imagining the inside of the house. Yellow kitchen. Perhaps a nice blue in the main room. And red for what Grub called the "necessary" out back. Lovely, she told herself, and picked up a few of the brushes before heading back to the counter.

Dora Higgins finished with her other customer, smiled widely at Meara, and pulled a pencil out of her topknot to figure the bill. She started with the clothing piled on the counter. "A boy, eh?" she said. "They surely are hard on clothes. Relative of yours?"

"No," Meara said. "He's . . ." She really didn't want to say that she'd found him robbing the hen house. "Staying with Conner for a few days."

Dora shot her a quick look. "Who is he? From around here?"

"Dora," Eli spoke up from his customary chair. "Don't be so dang nosy." Clucking his tongue, he added, "What is it about you women, always gabbin' about one thing or another?"

The woman smiled at Meara before answering her husband. "And what is it about you men, always sticking your two cents into the pile?"

"Married man's lucky if he has two cents."

"Married man's just plain lucky if you ask me," Dora told him.

"I didn't," he shot back.

"Hush up, Eli, while I talk to Meara here." Dora turned back to her. "So, who is this boy?"

Meara read the paint can label as she answered, "He says his name is Luke Banyan and he looks half starved."

"Luke," Eli spoke up again, tipping his head back to stare at the ceiling as if looking for answers. "There was a boy come 'round here last week, called himself Luke. Enough dirt on him to plant a decent crop of corn."

Meara nodded and looked up, grinning. "That'd be him."

"We let him sweep out the storeroom for a meal," Dora put in, ignoring Eli's huff at her interruption. "And right after he ate, he disappeared. Haven't seen him since."

"He's a wily youngster," Eli said quickly before his wife could go on. "His kind generally are. And as footloose as a tumbleweed in a high wind. Don't you go gettin' attached to him now. He'll make out on his own and won't thank you for charity."

Meara looked at the man. "His kind? What do you mean, his kind?"

"Trail orphans," he said shortly, as if that explained everything.

Dora "tsk-tsked," shaking her head sadly.

"What exactly is a trail orphan?" Meara asked, her heart melting for the boy all over again.

Eli opened his mouth, but Dora spoke first. "Families travelling west? Accidents happen all the time. Parents are killed, and the children left to fend for themselves. Sadly, most of them die in the wilderness. Those who don't support themselves however they can."

"Woman," Eli's voice was snippy, "when I'm tellin' a story, don't you be steppin' into the middle of it."

"I only answered her question," Dora said and tore off a sheet of brown paper to wrap Meara's purchases.

"Isn't that what I was doing?" he demanded.

"Trail orphan," Meara whispered to herself, no longer listening to either of the Higginses as they threw themselves into a friendly argument.

She thought about the forests and the wild animals and the dangers facing one small boy and marvelled that he had survived so long on his own.

"Did I hear you say you wanted more of that paint?" Dora asked, demanding her attention.

"Yes," Meara said. "Can you add it to Conner's account?"

"Be a pleasure," Dora said as she led the way into the storeroom. "It's about time somebody took that man in hand and gave him a little shake. It ain't right for a body to tuck himself away on a ranch and not set foot in town but once a year."

"You women, can't stand to see a man find some peace."

"A man can't find peace. A woman's got to show it to him," Dora said, planting a quick kiss on top of her husband's bald head as she passed him.

Meara followed the storekeeper, but paid no attention to what she was saying. Instead, her mind whirled with questions. Conner, staying hidden on his ranch, hardly seeing the people around him. A boy alone, trying to survive a hostile world. A woman with no memories.

Was it Fate, she wondered, that had brought them all together on Conner's ranch?

A man with a past he wanted to forget, a woman with a past she couldn't remember, and a boy with no future?

As she left the Emporium and placed the last of her purchases into the short wooden bed of the buckboard, Meara shifted her gaze briefly to the line of nearby mountains. Their craggy peaks already dusted with snow, they reached toward a sky so brilliantly blue, it nearly pained her eyes to look at it. A sharp, cold wind raced down the narrow street, and she could have sworn she heard the dilapidated-looking buildings around her tremble in its wake.

She shivered slightly and shifted her gaze to the activity surrounding her. Early-afternoon crowds dotted the boardwalks and the dirt road. Horses tied to hitching posts stamped restively in place, and an overburdened wagon rolled down the street, its huge wheels creaking and groaning in protest.

Meara took it all in slowly, still somehow hoping for a spark of recognition to dawn on her. Surely there was someone, somewhere, who would know her. Who could help her to know herself.

As if in answer to her prayers, a familiar face suddenly appeared in the crowds. Meara inhaled sharply and held it, feeling her heartbeat quicken. 'Twas her. The woman in the red dress. Even at a distance, Meara recognized the pure white hair with the dark blue feather tucked rakishly on one side.

As she watched, frozen in place, the woman turned, looked directly at Meara and smiled as she would at a dear friend. Hope staggered into Meara's chest and she released the pent-up breath strangling her lungs. The woman knew her. She hadn't been imagining things the other day. The woman was real.

Meara felt herself smile in return even as her mind

struggled to identify the woman. She looked so familiar. So, *comforting*, somehow. As their gazes met and held, a sense of peace settled over Meara. A peace she hadn't known since tumbling through Conner's roof with no memory of how she'd happened to land there.

Hurry, she told herself and willed her feet to move. She had to catch up with the woman who was already turning away and moving off down the street. This was her chance. Perhaps her only chance to discover the truth about herself. To find out who she was and where she belonged.

So why wasn't she moving?

She looked down at her feet, half expecting to find her shoes had been nailed to the boardwalk beneath her. Everything in her mind urged her to chase after the woman. And yet apparently, her body was reluctant to take up the challenge.

Finally, she took one halting step and then another. What was it? she wondered. Why wasn't she running after her? Then the simple reason tumbled into her mind and once she acknowledged it, everything made perfect sense.

If the woman *did* know her, then Meara's past would no longer be a mystery. And there would be no excuse for her to stay on at Conner's ranch. She would have to leave. To go where she belonged.

And just the thought of that was enough to curdle her stomach like a pail of milk left too long in the sun.

Meara's gaze shot once more to the woman's back. Her red dress shimmered and sparkled in the afternoon sunlight. People streamed past her and around her. Meara squinted, trying not to lose sight of the woman. But the crowd swallowed her up and in moments it was as if she'd disappeared entirely, and Meara's chance was gone.

Foolishness this, she told herself. It did no one any good a'tall to go on pretending that her time with Conner wasn't going to come to an end. Wouldn't it have been better for all concerned if she had simply followed the woman and ended this situation now . . . before it was too late? Before her feelings for Conner deepened?

Or, she wondered bleakly, was it far too late already?

"I'm headin' up to the high country," Conner said tightly and snatched his coat off the wall peg closest to the kitchen door. "Take a look around."

"Uh-huh," Grub commented.

"What's that supposed to mean?" Conner demanded as he shrugged into the heavy, sheepskin-lined coat.

"Nothin'," the older man told him with a shrug. "Just that usually, you only ride the high timber when you got somethin' on your mind."

Conner gritted his teeth and glared at his old friend's back. He knew him too well. Conner did have plenty on his mind at the moment and the only thing that would help was a slow ride through the deeply forested north section of his land. There was a peace in the shaded depths of the pines that he'd never found anywhere else.

"That boy hit a little too close to home?" Grub asked, never lifting his gaze from the mound of bread dough he was kneading.

"Why should he?" Conner asked, despite knowing it was pointless to deny it.

"Kinda reminded me some of you at that age."

Tension coiled tightly in the pit of Conner's stomach. As it had since first laying eyes on that boy. The kid's wary eyes and lightning-quick reflexes reminded Conner far too much of himself the summer after his mother's death. He, too, had looked at the world through hostile eyes and had kept himself on guard against threatening situations. Always ready to move. To escape.

But he wasn't willing to admit to any such thing. Instead, he asked casually, "That so?"

Grub shot him one meaningful glance over his shoulder, then resumed his task. "Figured you might'a thought the same thing."

"You figured wrong." The lie tasted familiar. Like a once-favorite meal, untasted in years.

"If you say so."

Damn it, couldn't the old man see that he didn't want to remember those years spent with his father? Didn't he know that there were *no* pleasant memories from the years after his mother had died and left him to Trevor James's uneven care?

Hell, if anybody *should* know, it was Grub. He'd been there. He'd seen what kind of father Trevor James had been.

"Leave it alone, Grub."

The older man nodded.

A long, tension-filled silence stretched out between them for what seemed an eternity. Finally, gratefully realizing that the man was going to drop the subject, Conner asked, "Where's the boy now?"

Grub chuckled. "He wore himself out fightin' that bath. Fell asleep and ain't moved a hair since."

Conner nodded, glad for the reprieve before having to face his own past in that scrawny, distrustful young face again. Reaching behind him, he grasped the doorknob in a tight fist and turned it. Before he stepped out into the late afternoon sunshine, he muttered, "Feed him again when he wakes up."

As the door closed quietly behind Conner, Grub smiled to himself. All things happened for the best, he firmly believed. Maybe it was time for Conner to take a good hard look at his past, so he could finally bury it and look for the future he deserved.

CHAPTER EIGHT

Conner's horse stepped daintily into the deeply shadowed tree line. As the cool darkness poured over him, Conner shrugged deeper into his jacket and felt himself relax for the first time in days. Cold damned early this year, he thought, guiding his horse on a winding course through the pines. Of course, the fall sun couldn't warm things up this deep into the forest. Branches were so thick and heavy, only an occasional slice of sunlight pierced the canopy of trees, looking like golden spears tossed down by the angels from heaven.

He chuckled softly to himself. Angels. He was getting fanciful in his old age. But then again, he thought, if ever there was a place designed to prod the imagination, it was the forest.

The ground thickly carpeted by layers of fallen pine needles, his horse's hooves were muffled, barely disturbing a silence only accentuated by the soft rustle of small animals moving through the undergrowth all around him. Heavy afternoon lake mist, creeping up from Tahoe, snaked along the ground and through the trees like questing fingers. A pine cone dropped suddenly and sounded like a gunshot in the eerie quiet.

Reins held loosely in his left hand, Conner steered the gelding into the heart of the forest, where a man might convince himself he was alone in the world.

He glanced up at the ceiling of trees and thought, not for the first time, that there was almost a church-like feel to this place. And these woods were as close as he ever came to believing in a God. Hard not to, he reasoned, when looking at the years-old pines, towering skyward, and the mountain-fed streams and waterfalls. At least, he'd never known a man who could have designed something so beautiful.

As his horse plodded on, its hooves thumping against the forest floor, Conner's thoughts wandered. Directly to Meara. An unbidden image of the woman rose up in his mind. Clouds of red, curly hair dancing around her face. Deep green eyes that reminded him of the shadowy forest he now rode through. A quick smile that seemed to reach inside him delivering shafts of warmth to all of the dark, lonely corners of his soul.

Shaking his head, he tried to figure out just what had happened to his carefully laid out world. In less than two weeks, his home had been invaded, not just by her, but now by a boy who looked as though he hadn't eaten a decent meal in months. And who stirred unpleasant memories Conner had long struggled to bury.

He'd been living on his ranch for two years and but for the two neighbors whose land adjoined his, had kept to himself. He'd deliberately avoided going to town any more than absolutely necessary, and he wasn't a man to look for friendship. Now, because of Meara, he'd talked to more people in a couple of weeks than he had in the last two years.

The gelding snorted, twitched its ears, and Conner leaned forward to pat the big animal's neck. He cocked his head to listen, but when he didn't hear anything, he returned to the thoughts still rattling around in his mind.

He didn't want friends in town. And that was a good thing, because he certainly didn't have any. Carlisle had seen to that. Since losing his ranch to Conner, Robert

Carlisle had made it his mission in life to see to it that Conner never knew a happy day again. He'd discovered the secrets of Conner's past and told everyone in town. For months, no one would do business with him. The so-called "decent" folks in High Timber wanted nothing to do with the son of a whore and a gambler. But that hadn't surprised him any.

It had happened before. Too many times to count. Always the same. *Good* people never wanted a damn thing to do with his kind. And he'd long since stopped trying to be anything but what he was. Years ago, he'd almost convinced himself that people could change. That *he* could change. But it just wasn't so. It didn't matter that he owned his own ranch now. It didn't matter because the stink of saloons and bordellos clung to him, and he would never be rid of it.

But at least things had gotten a bit easier in High Timber. Most of the merchants now were willing to overlook his past in favor of his money, which had to make Carlisle crazy. Still, Conner wouldn't relax his guard, because a man like Robert Carlisle didn't get over losing. And from what Conner'd heard, the man's wife had made Carlisle's life a living hell ever since he'd lost the ranch.

The gelding lifted its head abruptly. Its ears twitched again and this time, Conner pulled him to a stop. In the cool afternoon air, the horse's breath clouded around its muzzle. Conner soothed the animal with whispered nonsense while at the same time, he strained to hear even the slightest sound. His right hand slid backward on his thigh until it rested comfortably on the stock of his holstered pistol.

He must be getting old and careless. Damn, he'd let thoughts of Meara crowd his mind so much, he hadn't even been paying attention to his surroundings. Which was a good way to get himself killed.

Not only were there bears roaming around, looking to

eat enough to get them through winter hibernation. The forest was a perfect place for an ambush. Not that he was expecting one, but then, the man who wasn't looking for trouble was usually the man who found it.

Muttering curses under his breath, Conner's hand tightened on his pistol stock. He drew the gun silently, making no more than a whisper of sound, and quietly thumbed the hammer back.

A rustle of pine needles sifted into the air and Conner's gaze narrowed as he turned to face the noise. Then he heard it. Another rider approaching. Calmly now, he kept his gaze locked in the direction of the sound.

Seconds ticked by. And then pine branches were pushed aside as an animal entered the small clearing. When Conner spotted the chestnut horse with a splash of white on its chest, he took a breath, eased the hammer of his gun down, and slipped it back into the holster.

Tucker Hanks.

When the man and horse cleared the line of trees, he called out, "Hey, boss, didn't know you were comin' up here today."

Conner shifted in the saddle, propped both hands on the saddle horn, and leaned forward slightly. "Hadn't planned on it. Needed to get away for a while."

Hanks's dark eyebrows lifted and there was a suggestion of a smile on his face. "Gettin' a mite crowded down there, ain't it?"

"Too damned crowded," Conner agreed, knowing that Hanks understood completely. Though they'd never talked about their backgrounds, Conner had the feeling that Tucker Hanks and he had a lot more in common than a way with horses.

"Course," Hanks went on, smiling, "bein' around that Irish woman is no trial. If she ain't the prettiest little thing I've ever seen . . ."

Jealousy reared up inside him with a hot, pulsing anger

and Conner had to fist his hands to keep from wrapping them around Tucker Hank's neck.

"Did you get down to the south fence line to check for breaks?" Conner asked as the man rode closer.

"Nah." Tucker's gaze slid from his to study the line of trees opposite. "Sent Hobart instead."

Reluctantly, Conner smiled. As long as Hanks wasn't talking about Meara, they'd get along fine. "Bet he was pleased."

Tucker grinned and tipped his hat back further on his head. "He left cussin' a blue streak, but he'll do the work." Tucker paused for a heartbeat or two, then added, "I hear that boy you got corralled on the ranch knows some cuss words that even Hobart ain't heard before."

Instantly, Conner's smile dimmed. From what he'd seen, the boy had earned the right to a bit of cussin' once in awhile. A twinge of pity erupted in his chest and strangled his effort to breathe. Conner knew better than anyone that the kid would be insulted by sympathy, yet he couldn't help himself. No kid should have to collect the kind of memories that undoubtedly haunted Luke Banyan waking and sleeping.

"What're you gonna do about that kid, boss?" Tucker asked.

Conner turned a weary eye on his foreman. "I don't have the slightest idea, Hanks," he admitted.

Life had been much easier when he was on his own. Responsible for no one and nothing. Now, there were way too many people crowding his life. And he didn't like it.

"Well," Tucker said, reaching into his shirt pocket for tobacco and papers, "I seen his kind before. He'll prob'ly take off as soon as he gets a couple of meals into him."

"Probably," Conner mused aloud and couldn't help wondering where the kid would go. What he would do. He scowled furiously at the realization that he actually *cared* what happened to the boy. Damn it, he didn't want to care. About Luke or Meara.

But it seemed he didn't have a choice about either of them. The caring had already started, and he didn't know how to stop it.

"I'm headin' back for the home ranch," Tucker said abruptly. "You comin'?"

"No," Conner said grimly. He needed a couple more hours on his own. To enjoy the quiet. To try and figure out how he was going to get his life back the way he wanted it. "I'll be up here awhile. Tell Grub I'll be there for supper."

Tucker's lips tightened around the end of his cigarette. Squinting through the smoke curling up around his features, he nodded, said, "Yessir, boss." Then he added, "Wonder if Miss Meara's cookin' tonight." Before Conner could say anything, the other man had wheeled his horse around to go back the way he'd come.

In seconds, Conner was alone again. Just the way he wanted it, he told himself, and tried to keep from thinking about Tucker Hanks smiling at Meara. He rode deeper into the forest, where shadows lengthened and the old growth was so thick, sunlight rarely reached the earth. Ancient pines stood shoulder to shoulder like silent soldiers at attention. Heavy trunks and limbs acted like a curtain, shutting out sound and light. Somewhere close by a fast stream chuckled over the smoothly polished stones lining its bed. A sigh of wind dusted through the trees, brushing at his hair as it passed.

He should feel peaceful, damn it!

He should be content.

Always before, these woods had fed his soul and eased his heart. Until today. Because today, he hadn't come to the forest alone. He'd carried the images of Luke and Meara with him.

And with his mind filled with thoughts of them, there would be no peace.

*   *   *

"She was here, in town again," Hester told her husband stiffly. "Her! Living in *my* house. With *him*. No better than they should be, either of them."

Robert Carlisle reread the same paragraph he'd already read three times and still couldn't concentrate. Ever since catching a glimpse of James's redheaded companion in town that afternoon, Hester had been like a woman possessed.

"Walking down the street as bold as brass!" Hester sniffed, crossed the room to her husband's side, and stood there, glaring at him until he lifted his gaze to hers. "This is *your* fault, Robert," she said for what had to be the thousandth time in the last two years. "If not for you, I would be sitting in my own front parlor right now, with my things about me." She turned her head slightly and sneered at the small set of rooms they now called home. "Instead, I'm living in this rat's nest while that tramp is painting my kitchen! *Painting*. Robert!"

Robert bit down hard on the inside of his cheek. Pain welled up in his mouth, and he welcomed it. Anything to distract him from Hester's tirade. Even if he did deserve it, which he doubted, since anyone with half a brain knew that the son of a gambler was no doubt a notorious cheat, he was damned tired of listening to Hester's daily complaints.

"I won't continue to live like this, Robert. Do you hear me? I'll go home first. Back to my father's house."

He glanced at the woman beside him and knew that if she left him, the money her wealthy father still sent them monthly would stop. He couldn't let that happen.

"I'll take care of everything, my dear," he said smoothly, his mind already turning over ideas.

"He ain't gonna like it," Grub warned, and Meara tossed him a quick look over her shoulder.

"He'll like it," she said, more to convince herself than

the older man. She took a step back and stared at the results of her afternoon's work. But for the white chinking between the logs, the kitchen walls were now painted.

Frowning, Meara admitted silently it didn't look quite as she'd imagined. Of course, the wood was so old and thirsty, it had drunk in the paint like a sponge soaking up water. It wasn't *her* fault that the blasted things had dried looking so uneven. Her gaze moved over the walls, determinedly skipping over the patches that looked more like orange dirt than the "sunshine yellow" she'd been promised.

Still and all, even with the spotty places, it was lovely and bright. So much more cheerful than the gloomy, smoke-stained logs. Besides, once it had dried completely, she'd paint it again. Surely another coat or two of paint would make the walls look less splotchy.

"Conner ain't the kind of man to take well to change," Grub warned, as he had since she'd returned from the store to find Conner gone off to the far reaches of the ranch.

Sighing now, Meara turned around to face the older man. He'd been howling like a banshee bringing bad news all afternoon. "No man *likes* change," she said, "unless he has years to plan for it. But as my mother used to say. 'You'll never plow a field by turning it over in your mind.' "

"Huh?"

She shook her head, then brushed back a lock of hair that fell from the scarf she'd wound around her head. "No matter," she said and scratched her nose with a paint-smeared hand. "Now, let's go and help young Luke, shall we?"

"No, ma'am," Grub said flatly. "I ain't gonna help you paint what don't need paintin'. You and that boy yonder can work yourselves into a frazzle if ya want." He crossed his arms over his chest and jerked his head at the wall. "This here is gonna make Conner mad enough to spit nails."

Meara scowled at him, but she refused to let her spirits dim. Why would the man be angry about something as innocent as this? No. Grub was wrong. She knew it as surely as she knew her own name.

Pausing, she thought about that for a long minute. With the sketchiness of her memory, perhaps that wasn't a very good example. Still, she looked about her one last time, admiring her handiwork and told herself that if the man hadn't the sense to be thankful for the lovely thing she'd done for him, well, that wouldn't be *her* fault, would it?

Leaving, Grub muttering all matter of dire predictions. Meara bustled out the back door into the late afternoon sun. As she scurried across the ranch yard toward the barn, she told herself that Conner would love what she'd done to his home. Why, he'd probably be so excited, he'd be speechless.

"Who in the hell painted the stalls in the barn?" Conner shouted as he stormed into the house two hours later.

Startled, Meara jumped, and spun around, still holding the long-handled spoon she'd been stirring the stew pot with. As she turned to face him, she watched his jaw drop and his eyes widen in disbelief.

Obviously stunned at the glorious sight before him, he moved in a slow circle, letting his gaze slide over the yellow and white striped walls as if he couldn't believe what he was seeing.

Meara smiled proudly. Like a mother with a brilliant child, she simply stood quietly to let others do the admiring. All of her hard work had been more than worth this moment. She only wished Grub was here in the room to see how wrong he'd been. But she could tell him later that his fears had been for naught.

Impatiently, she waited for Conner's thanks.

When he finally looked at her, though, he said only, "You painted the inside of the barn, didn't you? Of course. It had to be you. And you painted the house, too?"

She shrugged modestly. "Not the whole house yet, I'm afraid. That'll take some time yet. But aye. I did. With some help from Luke."

"Luke." He nodded. "Naturally," he said, and glanced at the walls again. She thought she saw him flinch as if in pain. "Who told you to paint?"

"No one," she assured him. " 'Twas my own idea. And isn't it lovely?" Taking a step closer to him, she laid one hand on his forearm and said. "Grub, silly man, insisted you'd be angry. But how could a body not be happy to be surrounded by such lovely color?" She looked around the room again herself, pleased that the paint seemed to look a bit more evenly distributed as it dried. She cocked her head slightly and wondered if it was just her imagination or was the lamplight really making the yellow seem more dazzling to the eye somehow. Meara sighed, well pleased with her afternoon's work. "So much brighter than those dark old logs."

He swallowed heavily. "Brighter. And the barn?" he asked, yanking off his hat to push one hand through his hair. "Half the stalls are painted blue."

"Aye well, we got a late start," Meara told him. "Luke tried to get as much done as he could, but he's only a boy, after all. And the poor lad was that tired, he's already had his supper and off to bed."

"So," he said calmly, "half of them are painted because he got tired."

"Aye."

"And they're blue."

"Sky blue, the can claims," Meara said. "Though I don't agree. I've never seen the sky that color. Have you?"

"No," Conner said and shook his head, rubbing one

hand across his jaw until his speech was garbled. "Not lately. A little too much purple in it for a sky."

"Exactly my thoughts," she said. "Though '*tis* lovely."

"Lovely." That was certainly one word for it, he thought grimly, still trying to forget the hideous shade of paint that now decorated his barn. God, when he'd first seen it, he'd wanted to murder whoever'd done it. But how was he expected to hang onto his mad, when faced with Meara's obvious joy in what she'd accomplished? "Whose idea was it to paint the stalls? Yours?"

"Ah no," she turned back to the stove, gave the stew another swish or two with the spoon, then set it down on a nearby plate. " 'Twas Luke's idea to use that paint on the barn."

"Ah . . ." He inhaled slowly, telling himself to be calm. After all, it was just paint. Hideous paint. But still, just paint. Besides, Conner thought as he looked at her, she was so damned pleased with herself. Her green eyes sparkled and the splash of rose on her cheeks only heightened the beauty of the face that already haunted his every waking moment. Hell, even the streak of yellow paint on her jawline, that she'd obviously overlooked when cleaning up, only added to her charms.

Then she started talking again, and he silently warned himself to pay attention or he might find himself painted blue before morning.

In a confidential tone, she said, "Actually, I'd thought to use that lovely blue in the big room, where we could all admire it on an evening."

She thought she saw him shudder, but since the fire was roaring and there wasn't a chill to be found in the room, she must have been mistaken.

"Didn't you think to ask me if I *wanted* the walls painted?"

Meara's eyebrows lifted. His voice sounded odd. Choked, really, as though a cold was coming on. "No," she said. "It wouldn't have been a surprise then, would it? And we did surprise you, didn't we?"

He nodded, his gaze still drifting occasionally to the yellow walls. "Oh, you surprised me all right."

" 'Twas our way of thanking you. A gift as it were, for letting me—as well as Luke, stay here for a time."

"A gift?"

She frowned now. He really did sound dreadful. Shaking her head, she hurried to him and drew him to the table. Pushing him down onto one of the benches, she felt his forehead with the palm of her hand and was relieved to note that he didn't have a fever.

"What are you doing now?" he asked, ducking out from under her ministrations.

"You don't sound well at all, Conner," she told him and headed for the stove. Snatching up the kettle, she walked to the pump, filled it with fresh water, then carried it back to the stove. Setting it down on the fire, she reached onto a high shelf for a cup, then turned to look at him. "I'll just fix you a nice cup of tea."

"Tea?" He stared at her as if she'd just offered him a nice hot drink of hemlock.

" 'Tisn't poisonous, y'know," she said with a smile.

"I don't want any tea," he muttered, his gaze once again flicking to the muddy, brownish-yellow walls. Briefly, he remembered the room as it had looked only that morning. Now, not only was it a hideous shade of yellow, but there were splotches of dark and light, and whole sections that looked as though she'd barely touched them with a paint brush.

Still, he hadn't received a "gift" in years. Not since before his mother died when he was a boy. Meara and Luke had gone to a lot of trouble just for the pleasure of surprising him. He imagined the slight boy exhausting himself painting half the stalls in the barn. Unexpectedly, his throat tightened and it felt as though a hard fist took a grip on his heart.

Conner looked around the kitchen and brought up the image of Meara, standing on chairs to reach the highest logs with her paintbrush. And no matter how awful the place looked, he knew how much work had gone into the painting. How much effort.

For him.

They'd done it all for him. It was a humbling experience, he realized. To be cared for.

All right, he could live with the paint job, he supposed, but he had to know one thing. "Why does it look so . . ."

"Uneven?"

As good a description as any, he guessed. "All right."

"I think I should buy more paint. These dratted logs soaked up the first coat like a thirsty man with his first ale at the end of Lent."

Conner swivelled his head to give her a long, slow look. A chill of foreboding swept over him. "*More* paint?"

She laughed, and the sound lifted into the air and settled over him like a warm, cozy blanket on a cold, harsh night.

Blast it.

"Of course more paint, man. This is a big house. We've hardly begun." Clucking her tongue, she hurried back to the stove and began to make him the cup of tea he'd already told her he didn't want. "Ah, Conner, I'm thinkin' you won't know this place when I've finished with it."

That's what he was thinking, too.

CHAPTER NINE

First thing in the morning, he found the china pot back in his office. This time sitting square in the middle of his desk. Like a challenge.

A challenge he accepted. Grabbing up the pot, Conner carried the damn ivy plant back to the main room. Muttering to himself, he finally set it atop a massive walnut bookcase on the far wall. Then he took a step backward and nodded to himself. Blasted woman thought she could win every battle just because he hadn't said anything about her painting his house? Granted, moving an ivy plant wasn't much of a victory, but at this point, Conner would take the small win and be grateful.

The stink of fresh paint had escaped the kitchen to stink up the air in the great room as well. As he headed outside, he told himself that the smell was enough to drive any man toward fresh air.

Needing to be busy, he turned one of the mares loose in the corral and set to work.

Later, after putting the animal through its paces, Conner grabbed hold of the horse's bridle and pulled her head down far enough to scratch between her ears. He grinned as the big animal all but purred, moving against his hand and snorting in pleasure.

He'd spent the morning working in the corral, since he

couldn't stand being inside the barn any more than he could the house for longer than a few minutes. Meara and Luke were bound and determined to finish painting the stalls, and even the horses seemed eager to be outside, away from the smell.

As he continued to scratch the bay mare's head, Conner glanced around at the ranch yard. A couple of the hands were working in the paddock, breaking a few more of the mustangs. The rest of them, including Tucker Hanks, were out on the range.

In fact, to look at the place, no one would guess that anything had changed. On the surface—except for the freshly painted areas—Conner's ranch looked just as it had a couple of weeks ago. But appearances were deceiving. Looking back now, Conner thought of the days before Meara and Luke had arrived and wondered why he'd never seen how empty his so-called "peace" had really been.

Sure, life had been quieter without the two of them. But strangely enough, it was getting harder to remember a time when they weren't around.

Beneath his hands, the mare shifted, bringing him back from his mental wanderings. Sucking in a deep gulp of air, Conner warned himself not to start caring. Sooner or later, they would find Meara's people and she would leave him. And Luke would no doubt skedaddle as soon as he'd put a few square meals under his belt.

Pretty soon, Conner would be on his own again. Just him, Grub, and the hands working for him. He scowled thoughtfully and wondered why that thought didn't make him happy.

"Hey, mister," Luke called from behind him.

Conner half turned to look as the boy climbed up on the corral fence behind him and straddled the top rail. Blue paint dotted his face, and even his pale blond hair was splashed with that strange shade of purple/blue. But aside from the paint smears, the kid looked healthier, stronger than he had just a day or two before.

Amazing the difference some new clothes, a bath, and a couple of decent meals could make. Yet his young features still bore the same, carefully guarded expression Conner had seen the first time he'd laid eyes on the kid. And his too-knowing, too-old blue eyes looked as if he was waiting for the world to cave in on him again.

Conner knew that feeling. All too well.

"What is it?" he asked, his tone gruffer than he'd intended.

If possible, the boy's features tightened even further. "Meara said to tell ya that we're all done paintin' them stalls."

Conner nodded and didn't even bother trying to dredge up the mental image of what it must look like in his barn. He'd have to face it soon enough as it was.

"Looks like you got more paint on you than my barn," he said instead.

Luke's gaze dropped to the front of his new shirt where streaks of blue slashed across the once-white fabric. He brushed at the smears with both hands, but only succeeded in spreading the still-wet paint into a wider pattern. His eyes widened in dismay and his cheeks paled.

Swallowing hard past a knot of regret lodged in his throat, the boy looked up, his worried gaze clashing with Conner's steady stare. "I didn't mean to," he said, despite the slight tremor in his chin.

Conner caught the flash of fear in the boy's eyes and his heart did an unexpected lurch. "Don't expect you did," he said.

Cocking his head to one side, Luke watched the big man carefully, waiting for signs of a building temper. But there weren't any. "I aim to pay you for these clothes, anyway," he finally said.

The man nodded, stared at him thoughtfully for a long minute, then said, "You do that," before turning around to stroke the mare's neck.

That was it? No yelling? No quick, fierce slap across his ears? No cussing?

Luke's jaw worked as he fought to keep his bottom lip from quivering. It was a trick, he told himself. The man was just trying to get him to relax some. *Then*, he'd try to give Luke a good whipping for ruining his clothes.

Well, he wouldn't be whipped again. He'd run away so fast, that fella wouldn't be able to lay a hand on him. Not that he didn't deserve it.

To his shame, Luke felt the sting of tears fill his eyes. Heck, he couldn't remember the last time he'd had a new shirt. And he'd wrecked it. The worst part was, he hadn't even noticed the paint on his fine new duds. He'd been too busy working. Trying to earn his keep so nobody would tell him to leave.

He didn't want to run away. He wanted to stay.

Forever.

It was nice here at the ranch. Nobody shouting at him. Plenty to eat. A bed to sleep in. Blankets when he got cold.

And then there was the horses.

Luke sniffed, ran one hand under the tip of his nose, and looked out over the corral and the paddock beyond. Mares, stallions, and geldings wandered around their separate enclosures, their sleek hides glistening in the midday sun.

They were so beautiful it almost hurt to look at 'em.

"If you're finished in the barn, you could give me a hand here," Conner said quietly.

Luke's gaze snapped to the man's broad back. Had he been talking to *him*? Tightening his hold on the top rail of the fence, Luke concentrated on the bite of the wood digging into his palms. "Doing what?" he asked, not that he cared. He'd be willing to do just about anything to stay at the ranch. At least for a while longer. Until the man started in hitting him.

Still rubbing the animal's neck, Conner said, "This

mare's pregnant, and she's getting fat and lazy."

Blond eyebrows arched high on Luke's forehead. His gaze fell to the mare's belly, looking for signs of a baby. But she didn't look especially fat to him.

"She needs some exercise without carrying anybody too heavy," Conner went on, tossing him a glance over his shoulder. "How about it?"

A bubble of excitement swelled in Luke's chest, making it suddenly hard to breathe. He fought against it, because he'd already learned that disappointment usually followed on the heels of happiness. Still, the thought of actually riding that beautiful horse was almost too much to bear.

His hands tingled and his mouth went dry. His breath hitched in his chest.

"Well?" Conner prodded him with another quick look. "Are you going to help me or not?"

Worry wrestled with desire. Luke wanted to sit atop that mare more than he wanted his next breath. But what if he made a mistake? What if he did something wrong? Then he'd get hit, he reasoned. But as much as he feared another beating, the chance to ride that beautiful horse was too grand to give up.

"I reckon I can," Luke finally managed to say. He didn't want to sound too pleased. Too eager. Then the man would change his mind and Luke would never know what it was like to sit on top of that mare.

Quickly, he jumped off the fence and onto the ground. Sun-warmed dirt pushed between his toes as he hurried to Conner's side.

The animal was even prettier close up. Her red-brown hair looked all shiny and soft. So close, he thought. He lifted one hand to stroke the mare's side, but thought better of it and let his hand drop again before actually touching the animal. Wouldn't do to let the man see how much he wanted to ride that horse.

He'd learned a long time ago that there wasn't anything a man liked better than to slap down a kid's dreams.

"How old are you, boy?" Conner asked suddenly. "Six? Seven?"

Outraged, Luke straightened his shoulders, lifted his chin, and squinted up at the tall man. "I ain't no infant. I'm close on to ten."

"How close?" Conner asked, his eyes narrowing.

To be honest, Luke wasn't exactly sure. Time seemed to have drifted past since his pa died in that mudslide a year—or was it two years—ago. But if Conner thought he was too young, he wouldn't get on that horse. Clearing his throat, Luke told the man, "Close enough to ride this here horse."

The man's lips twitched slightly. "Suppose you show me how good a cowboy you are, then."

Before Luke knew what was happening, the man grabbed him around the middle and swung him up onto the horse's broad back. The mare's sun-warmed coat felt good beneath him. Better than he'd ever dreamed. He inhaled sharply and looked down. At the man. The ground. He was so high up, he figured he could probably just reach on up and touch the sky if he had a mind to.

"How's she feel?" the man asked.

Wonderful, he thought, but said only, "Not bad."

Conner ducked his head to hide a smile. Tough little bastard, he thought as he looked up again into wide, blue eyes. The kid clearly loved being up on that horse, but would probably rather be tortured by Apaches than admit to it.

"I'm gonna just walk her around the corral," he said. "You hang on."

"Yessir," the boy whispered and briefly stroked the mare's neck.

Conner started walking, leading the gentle horse around the edges of the enclosure. Her heavy steps thudded behind him and he could feel the boy's excitement shimmering in the air.

Damn. A couple of weeks ago, he'd been a happy man. Nobody around to bother him or expect anything from him. His life had been pretty much perfect. Now, he had a woman who couldn't remember a damn thing about herself driving him loco and a kid with shadows in his eyes making him remember too much about himself.

So why the hell was he enjoying himself? he wondered.

Conner ran one hand across the back of his neck. How in the hell had everything gotten so damned complicated so damned fast?

The lingering scent of fresh paint hovered in the barn and Meara quickstepped down the center aisle, headed for outside and fresh air.

Of course, to be honest, it wasn't only the smell of paint driving her out. It was being so close to the big animals whose stalls lined the aisle. Her long red hair fluttering around her shoulders, she kept a wary eye on the horses on either side of her. Big heads poked over the stall doors, they watched her with their deceptively gentle brown eyes.

She wasn't fooled.

Wispy threads of memories floated in her mind like feathers in the wind, and as hard as she tried to reach them, they danced away from her just as quickly. And still, she was left with the impression of snorting horses racing toward her, their breath clouds of steam in the cold air. She heard the thunder of their hooves on the rocky ground. Heard the men atop them shouting as they swung long, gleaming swords over their heads in wide arcs. She felt overpowering fear build inside her chest as she looked desperately for a place—*anyplace*—to hide and found none. A brief glimpse of an older man's eyes filled her mind instantly, and she read the sorrow clouding their deep green depths.

And then the wisps were gone, leaving her shaken and more afraid than before.

Here, in Conner's barn, the great beasts seemed to be reaching for her, their lips pulled back to expose large, dangerous-looking teeth. One on her right side lunged forward suddenly, straining its neck toward her. Meara squeaked a protest and instinctively stepped back.

Her breath caught in her chest as she realized her mistake. She'd backed right into another of them. Meara froze in place. She couldn't have moved if her skirt was afire. Terror snaked through her as the beast behind her snuffled at her hair. Hot breath dusted her neck just before the horse rested its great head on her shoulder.

Meara groaned deeply and her eyes widened until she thought they might pop from her head. Mouth dry, throat closed tight, she heard its deep, even breathing rumble in her ear.

From the corner of her eye, she glanced at the chestnut-brown muzzle so close to her face.

The big animal didn't move. Truthfully, the blasted thing looked quite comfortable with her as a pillow. And to be truthful, now that Meara's initial fright had passed, the weight of its head was almost . . . comforting.

This beast wasn't roaring and snorting. Its hooves weren't slicing grooves in the earth in its haste to rend her limb from limb. She inhaled slowly, forcing air into her lungs.

Across the aisle from her, another horse snorted and shook its head, mane flying. That animal looked far less congenial, so she kept her distance. But her new friend seemed unconcerned, and Meara tamped down the flash of fear that had reared in her chest. Slowly, cautiously, she lifted one hand to touch the gentle horse's nose. Soft. Smooth and warm. She smiled as, like an overgrown dog, the horse moved its head against her hand, looking for affection.

Chuckling quietly, Meara stepped away from the stall

door and turned to look at the surprisingly docile animal. Mild brown eyes, a sleekly chiseled head, and a rust-brown mane.

"Why," Meara said softly, astonishment in her voice, "you're lovely, aren't you? And not nearly so frightening as I'd thought."

The horse's head bobbed, as if agreeing with her.

Meara grinned and tossed a quick look over her shoulder at the far less friendly beast behind her. Just because she was willing to like one horse, didn't mean she was ready to trust all of them. Turning back to the first animal, she said, "I hope you like your pretty new home," and looked down the aisle at the bright blue stall doors.

"Still an' all," she went on, "we'll need a sight more paint to finish the job." Her gaze lifted to the hay rick above and the beamed roof overhead that. "An ocean of paint might do," she said, tired just thinking about the hard work ahead of her.

But, 'twas better to keep mind and hands busy than to dwell on the mystery that had become her life.

A trickle of unease rippled through her. Mysteries. She half turned toward the open double doors leading to the ranch yard. She stood in deep shadow, staring into brilliant sunshine that lay splashed across the yard. A wry smile curved her mouth briefly. Shadow and sun. Past and future. Mystery and truth.

She walked toward the light in slow, measured steps. Her mind danced with images that floated and twisted like dancers moving to silent music. Bits and pieces swirled together and apart again, reminding her all too well of the dreams that continued to mar her sleep at night. Meara scowled and concentrated, trying to snatch at even one of the elusive pictures in her mind. But the harder she tried, the more ephemeral those images became. It was like trying to grab a handful of smoke.

Frustration simmered inside her. How was she to move on with the rest of her life? How was she to know what to do? Where to go? If she couldn't remember where she'd been?

She shivered as she stepped into the yard. It wasn't cold making her shake, though. It was the not knowing. The uncertainty. How much longer could she stay at Conner's ranch, pretending she belonged there?

"That's not bad," Conner said, and Meara turned toward the sound of his voice.

Her gaze swept over him, as it did far too often. Long legs, encased in that worn, blue fabric called jeans. Narrow waist, wide shoulders, and the beaten-looking hat he seemed never to be without. Her heartbeat skittered uncertainly and Meara forced herself to remember that she had no place here. And no claim to the man who sent jagged points of heat darting through her bloodstream with just a look.

Moving to the corral fence, she watched as Conner helped Luke get down off one of the horses. The boy's expression shifted quickly from pleasure to feigned disinterest, and Meara's heart broke for him. Was he so afraid of being happy?

"Don't pull so hard on the reins next time," Conner was saying. "Her mouth is tender. You'll hurt her without even trying."

"I didn't mean to hurt her," the boy said quickly and took a quick step back from Conner.

"I said you *could* hurt her," Conner said and moved toward the boy, who ducked, covering his head with his hands.

Meara muffled a gasp as she realized the child was expecting a beating. But before she could speak, Conner went down on one knee and gently pulled the boy's hands down to his sides.

"Hey," Conner said, so quietly Meara had to strain to hear him. "You don't have to be afraid here," he went on, and Meara thought she heard a slight tremor in his voice.

Luke risked a quick glance at the man in front of him and she saw the wariness of a trapped animal flicker over his small features.

"I ain't scared. I been hit before," he muttered.

"I know," Conner said quietly.

Sudden tears filled Meara's eyes and she blinked them back hurriedly. How had he known? She'd thought the child to be merely hungry and alone. How had Conner guessed at the truth? And how had she missed it?

The boy's head came up and he glared at Conner. "You saw, didn't ya? When you made me take that bath."

Saw? she wondered. Saw what?

"Yeah, I saw." A well-deep sadness colored Conner's voice, and the boy responded sharply.

"Well, nobody's hit me since pa died and I aim to keep it that way."

Even from a distance, Meara could see Conner's jaw tighten at the boy's words. She wanted to race into the corral, gather the child to her bosom, and hold him until his injured heart could heal. But at the same time, she had a feeling that what Conner and Luke were saying to each other was too important to interrupt.

"It's a hard thing," Conner said quietly, "to have your own pa whale the tar out of you."

Luke eyed him suspiciously. "You too?"

Conner nodded briefly. "Until I got big enough to hit him back. But then he died, and I didn't have to think about it anymore."

"How old were ya?" Luke asked.

"Almost fifteen."

The boy nodded thoughtfully. "As near as I can figure, I'm about nine. Not so close to ten as I told ya."

"Close enough," Conner conceded.

The man's soft voice must have angered the boy because his voice came out harsh and tight as he said, "I don't need you feelin' sorry for me, mister."

"Who said I was feelin' sorry for you?"

Luke's eyes narrowed dangerously. "And I ain't scared, neither. You want to hit me, you can, 'cause I can't get away with you holdin' onto me like this."

Immediately, Conner released him and Meara took a step toward them, afraid the boy would bolt. Apparently, Conner shared her fear, because he spoke up quickly, stopping the boy in the middle of a quick turn.

"I won't stop you if you want to leave," he said, and Luke half turned to look at him. "But if you decide you want to stay, I give you my word nobody here will raise a hand to you."

She could see the boy wanted to believe, and it broke her heart to know that he was afraid to trust Conner.

It was as if the world took a breath and held it for the length of time it took for Luke to speak again.

"How do I know you're tellin' the truth?"

Conner shook his head. "There's no way to be sure, boy. You'll just have to trust me."

For a moment Meara thought the boy would give in to his obvious desire to stay. But as she watched, Luke took a deep breath and shook his head firmly.

"I 'spect I'd best be movin' on," he said reluctantly.

"You interested in a job?" Conner asked quickly.

Luke cocked his head at the change of subject, squinted, and stared up at him. "Doin' what?"

"Exercising this mare every day," Conner told him as he stroked the horse's neck with his long fingered hands.

Meara smiled as Luke's eyes widened and a flash of excitement he couldn't smother shot across them.

"Every day?" the boy repeated.

"Every day," Conner told him, then warned sternly, "but you've got to take care of her, too. Rub her down, give her fresh hay and water."

"I could do all that," Luke assured him with a nod hard enough to send his hair flying into his face.

"Of course," Conner added, "if you'd rather go off and find some other job. I'll understand."

The boy tried to hide his pleasure, but couldn't quite manage it. "No," he said, trying desperately to sound casual. "I reckon I could stay around here awhile longer."

"If you're sure . . ."

"I'll do a good job," Luke assured Conner.

"I expect you will," Conner told him. "And you'll get paid for good work. How's a dollar a week sound?"

"A *whole* dollar?"

"Yep."

Luke straightened up, squared his thin shoulders, and said, "I reckon I can do that, mister. You won't be sorry."

"I trust you," Conner told him, and handed over the reins.

The boy blinked and closed his fingers over the leather straps as gently as he would over the golden key to Heaven's gates.

"Why don't you get started now?" Conner suggested. "You'll find the curry comb and brushes in the tack room."

Luke nodded and started for the barn, leading the mare with tender, crooning words.

Meara's chest hurt, her heart was so full. Conner swiveled his head to watch the boy walk away, and when he caught sight of her, he stiffened as though he'd been caught doing something shameful.

What manner of man was this? she wondered, not for the first time. He'd just given a child a bit of pride and confidence. He'd taken away the boy's fear, yet he acted like a man caught with his hand in the poor box.

Luke, headed for the barn, didn't even see Meara, so intent was he on talking to the mare and hurrying about his new job.

Conner pulled his hat brim down lower over his eyes

as he turned away from her and started across the corral. She started after him instantly. Bustling through the open gate, she ran after Conner, still not sure what she would say when she caught him. All she knew was she had to talk to him. To look into his eyes.

But his long legs covered more territory than she could even at a run, so she finally called, "Will you not stand still for a moment, Conner?"

He paused, then said over his shoulder, "I've got work to do, Meara."

"As do I," she called right back, never slowing her pace. At last, she caught up to him at the far fence and grabbed his elbow.

Reluctantly it seemed, he turned to face her. "What is it?"

Meara looked up into his eyes and saw, of all things, embarassment. Foolish man. Was he ashamed to have been seen doing a kindness for the boy? She shook her head as her gaze locked with his. Before he could say a word, she reached up, took his face between her palms and drew his head down to hers. Looking deeply into his eyes, she whispered, "You're a kind man, Conner James."

He took her hands in his and pulled them down. Her breath caught at the rush of warmth that flooded from his hands to hers and into every corner of her body. But if he too, felt that warmth, he did a good job of hiding it.

"No one's ever called me kind, Meara," he said, a warning note in his voice. "Don't make that mistake."

"And are ya tryin' to warn me off now for me own safety?" she asked, her head cocked to one side.

"Someone should."

"Then that would be a kindness again, wouldn't it?" she countered quickly, a laugh bubbling up from her chest.

"Damn it, Meara. Don't you have work to do?"

"Oh, aye, and I'll be gettin' to it in a minute." Swallowing back a smile she knew would only irritate him further, she asked, "Why is it, do ya think, you're so worried about doing a small kindness for a boy?"

"I'm not *worried* about anything," he snapped, releasing her hands. "Except maybe having to stand here all day instead of finishing my work."

She clucked her tongue at him, missing the touch of his hand as she would a nice fire on a cold night. " 'Tisn't a weakness, you know," she said softly. "Being kind, I mean."

"You're making a mistake, Meara." Those deep blue eyes of his stared at her.

She reached up and cupped his cheek with one hand. " 'Tis no mistake. I saw what you did for Luke."

He took her hand again, his fingers wrapping around hers in a strong, firm grip. "I didn't *do* anything for him. I offered him a job."

She wasn't fooled. Hadn't she seen him in this blasted corral every day, patiently walking the mare in circles himself? Meara smiled knowingly, ignoring the hard mask of his face. "And have you broken your leg?"

"What?"

"Your leg." She glanced down at his two perfectly normal limbs, then back up to his eyes again. "You walk that horse yourself, Conner. You treat the beast as though she was made of the finest glass. I was wondering why you'd be needing to hire someone for the task."

He inhaled sharply and lifted his gaze to the distant horizon behind her. "I'm a busy man."

"And a kind one," she put in, wiggling her fingers against his palm, relishing the feel of his hand on hers.

"I needed someone to do a job. He was right for it."

"Oh aye," she said, her smile blossoming just a bit. "I can see that. He must be the only trained person for miles. How fortunate you were to find a near-starved boy to walk your precious horse for you."

His lips tightened even further, but he returned his gaze to hers, giving her a glare that should have set her hair on fire.

It didn't.

"Don't make something out of nothing," he told her, squeezing her hand more tightly.

Her breath caught as heat pulsed through her. He must have finally felt it, too, because he stopped and stared at her as though struck by lightning. Something flickered in his eyes. Something she couldn't quite identify. Something that settled deep in the pit of her stomach, before sending spirals of a strange, achy sensations to even the tips of her fingers.

"I'll say it again," she whispered, when she found her voice. "You're a kind man." Then, giving into an impulse she couldn't deny, she went up on her toes to kiss him. He didn't back away. He simply stood stock-still, as if he didn't trust himself to move.

Meara brushed her lips across his, and the effects of that short contact shot right down to her toes. She swayed against him as her knees buckled in response to the quivering of her limbs. Conner released her hand to catch her about the waist. She felt the imprint of his fingertips right through the fabric of her dress.

Stunned speechless, she stared up at him and saw that those eyes of his were no longer angry. But as she watched, the dark blue depths filled with shadows that tightened a fist around her heart and lungs, making it difficult to draw a breath.

Not wanting to see regret shining down on her, Meara closed her eyes and, emboldened, she kissed him again, a bit harder and longer this time, wanting to feel that shock of sensation once more.

Then he pulled her to him, pressing her body to his, wrapping his arms around her, and holding her tightly. Every inch of her skin felt as though she was on fire. She burned. She yearned for something she couldn't identify.

Her breasts pressed to his chest, she felt the thundering of his heart and knew that whatever he might say, he, too, was experiencing the overwhelming sensations swamping her.

Suddenly, he groaned and bent his head to the kiss, angling his mouth over hers. His breath dusted across her cheeks. Meara's hands slid to the back of his neck and she held on for dear life. What she had felt when she kissed him was dwarfed by what she felt now that he was kissing her back. Every limb in her body was as flimsy as meadow grass. And yet at the same time, she felt energized, more alive than she'd ever been before.

His tongue parted her lips and swept into her warmth with the determination of an invading army. She sighed into his mouth, reeling with the white-hot sensations pouring through her. She wanted him to kiss her like this forever. To never be parted from him.

Her mind spun like a whirlwind and brilliant splashes of color exploded behind her closed eyes. Eagerly, she returned his caresses, her tongue entwining with his and stroking until each of them went a little mad.

His arms tightened even further around her and she felt as though she couldn't draw enough air into her lungs. But she didn't care. This kiss, this moment, was worth any price.

And then it was over and he was releasing her, stepping back, shaking his head like a man coming up from under water for the last time.

A long moment passed. Meara struggled to stay upright. Reaching out with her right hand, she grabbed hold of the top rail of the fence and dug her short nails into the wood. She fought to draw air into her still-quivering body. When she looked up into his deep blue eyes, she shivered again.

"I told you, Meara," he grumbled, obviously disgusted with himself. "I'm not a kind man. But I *am* a man, and there's only so much temptation I can stand."

"Temptation, is it?" she repeated quietly as she met his gaze steadily.

"Yes, temptation," he snapped. He kept his voice low and took a step toward her. She held her ground, refusing to back away. "You stand there looking at me with those beautiful green eyes of yours and tell me I'm *kind*? You kiss me and expect me to do nothing?"

"I didn't expect anything of you," she told him, keeping her voice calm despite the thread of temper beginning to unravel inside her.

"Exactly." He threw his hands wide, then let them fall to his sides again. "You can't kiss a man and expect him to do nothing about it."

"But I've only just said—" she started, but he cut her off.

"If you don't want to be kissed, stay the hell away from me," he warned, then set both hands on the top rail of the fence and leaped over it. Clear of the corral, he marched across the ranch yard toward the bunkhouse.

Well now, she thought. Here was a problem. To avoid being kissed, she was to stay away from him. But, since she'd liked being kissed very much, she was in no hurry to avoid it in the future. So that meant she'd have to stay close to the man indeed.

Her gaze shifted to follow his progress as he walked straight past the bunkhouse and on toward the fenced pasture. She lifted one hand to touch her lips, where the taste of him still lingered. As her heartbeat slowly steadied again, Meara's thoughts returned briefly to the problem she'd been thinking about before kissing Conner.

The problem of who she was. And where she came from.

If she was to be kissing one man, she'd best make certain she wasn't promised or—Saint Bridget protect her— *married* to another. There was no more time to be wasting, hoping that someone, somewhere, would hear something about her.

'Twas time she took her problem in hand herself. First thing in the morning, she'd set about finding the truth to her past. *Then* she could think about her future.

After all, as her mother used to say, "You must crack the nuts before you can eat the kernel."

CHAPTER TEN

Small arms fire.

Conner ducked behind a hedge, propped the barrel of his rifle on an outcropping of rock and tried to see past the roiling gray clouds of gunsmoke into the battle, raging only a few feet from him.

Someone nearby screamed, and he jerked his head to the right, peering into the dense foliage, squinting against the sting of smoke and the thundering blasts from the artillery on the hill behind him. He couldn't see a damn thing. Nothing. There was only fog and noise. It was as if he was alone in this hellhole. As if the screams and shouts of the dying and terrified were nothing more than echoes of what had once been and he alone had been trapped here. To relive it over and over again. To taste the coppery tang of his own fear. To feel sweat running into his eyes, blurring with the tears brought on by the haze of smoke that never lifted.

A shadow crossed in front of him. A man. Which side? What color was the uniform? What damned difference did it make? Beneath the caked-on mud covering the blue or the gray, was just another man, beaten down by too many years of war and too much death.

He looked down the barrel of his rifle, his gaze locking on the tiny front sight. He concentrated, wanting to be ready to shoot if someone suddenly appeared out of that gray nightmare.

"Conner?"

Meara? he thought. Here?

Lifting his head, he looked around wildly, desperate to find her before someone else did.

"Conner, what is this place?" Meara stepped out of the grayness, and walked toward him, her plain white nightgown billowing out around her like an angel's wings. But there were no angels on a battlefield. There was only the gate to hell and the men streaming through it.

She turned her head toward the roar of artillery and her red-gold hair swung out in a brilliant rainbow of color. A mortar shell exploded behind her, outlining her in a white light so bright it hurt him to look at it. In the distance, screams rose and fell like waves on an ocean of pain.

The sharp crack of rifle fire erupted again. Bullets flew across the field where Meara stood, the distinctive whine of their passing terrifying Conner into action.

He leaped up from behind the rock and rushed forward. The tug of bullets tore at the fabric of his uniform. Fear for Meara prodded him on. He grabbed her, then tumbled back into the small niche of safety he'd found. He landed atop her and lay, looking down into wide, surprised green eyes. "What are you doing here?" he demanded, feeling his voice scrape against a throat raw from too little water and too much shouting.

"You wanted me here," she said softly, and her

sweet breath brushed his face, even as she reached up to caress his cheek.

Conner turned into her touch, relishing the soft, cool brush of her skin on his. Like a balm to his seared soul, he drank in her presence. Silently, he thanked the same gods who had ignored his existence until now for sending her to him. But she was in danger, damn it.

"I don't want you here, Meara. You could be hurt. Killed." Another bullet whizzed past his head, and he ducked, bringing his face to within a breath of hers.

"Ah, Conner, don't you see? 'Tisn't real. None of this."

Another scream, and water splashed into the air when a mortar landed in the pond just ahead of him. As the war rained down on them, he shook his head, "It's real, Meara. I know this place."

"Aye, you did once," she said, lifting one hand to smooth his sweat-dampened hair back from his forehead. "But now, 'tis only a dream."

A dream? He shifted slightly, to look out into the gray mists still hovering over the field of battle. As he watched, the gunsmoke parted as if an invisible hand had swept it aside. Men, in both colors, lay on the grassy ground. Dead and dying, they littered the earth like fallen leaves, with none of the glory granted by an autumn day.

No more crashing of the big cannons. No more rifle fire. No more screams. It was as if the world had come to a shuddering stop.

Slowly, cautiously, Conner sat up, drawing her with him, holding her hand tightly, to keep himself anchored to this sudden silence.

On their feet, they stood together, looking out over the carnage of Conner's memories. He felt her hand in his. The warmth. The pulse of life amidst *all of the death and destruction, and clung to it.*

"Ah, Conner," she whispered, as if in a church, "such terrible dreams."

He shook his head. As hideous as the war had been, it was in the past. And not even remembering it could be as dreadful as living it had been.

"It's been years since I've dreamed about it," he said, keeping his voice as quiet as hers. "Why now? Why with you?"

"I can't answer that for you," she said, tipping her head back to stare at him.

The battlefield faded around them, drifting into and becoming a part of the very smoke and fog that had defined it. And the two of them were left alone in a void of color and sound.

"Meara," he said and pulled her closer to him until her pristine white nightgown was pressed against his muddy, bloodstained uniform, "stay with me."

She lifted both arms to wind them about his neck. Going up on her toes, she held him tightly. "I'm here now, Conner. For whatever reason. I'm here now."

It wasn't the answer he needed or wanted. But it was all he had and he took it. Bending his head, he covered her mouth with his, tasting her, breathing in the fresh, clean scent of her, banishing the last of his nightmare in the beauty of her.

Their mouths met and scorched his soul with a fire that seemed to have been waiting for its chance to explode into flame. Hungrily, he parted her lips, his tongue darting inside her warmth. She opened to him, stroking his tongue with her own, sending him hurtling toward the edge of completion. It wasn't enough. It would never be enough, Conner realized. He needed her as he'd never needed anyone in his life. And though that sudden, over-

whelming knowledge terrified him, he refused to question it now. Be this dream or reality, he didn't want to waste a moment of it in worries about a future still too tenuous to see.

He held her tightly, loathe to let her go. So soft, so small, and yet she anchored him to a world apart from the ugliness of his memories. His arms wound around her, holding her to him with an iron strength. And when his lungs clamored for air, he pulled back, breaking the kiss, yet still, he didn't release her. Bending his head, Conner rested his cheek against hers and closed his eyes to the void surrounding them. The only important thing in his world at the moment was Meara. Her breath warm on his neck, her heartbeat steady against him, her small, sure hands splayed on his back.

When she kissed his throat, then laid her head on his chest, Conner felt the threads of his life begin to unravel. How had she come to be so important to him? How had she slipped past the barriers he'd hidden his heart behind for years?

"Meara," he whispered, and she pulled back in his arms to look up at him. "Meara, what's happening?"

She smiled and shook her head gently. "Does it matter?"

A moment's hesitation, and then, "No," he said softly. "God help me, it doesn't matter. As long as you're here with me, nothing else matters."

"Ah, Conner," she said on a sigh, then, even as he stared at her helplessly, she slipped further into the colorless void that surrounded him.

"No!" he shouted into the vast and utter stillness, and he knew he was alone again.

Meara woke up with a start, her body tingling, her breathing short and sharp. She closed her eyes instantly against the moon-drenched darkness of her room and tried to return to Conner. Every inch of her body hummed with a need she'd never been aware of before. How was it possible that a dream could be so real? *Feel* so real?

And whose dream was it? she wondered. Hers? Or Conner's?

Minutes passed before she was willing to admit that her time with Conner was over. She opened her eyes and stared up at the ceiling, watching the play of shadows dance across the beams. Uncomfortable, she shifted position on the feather mattress, hoping to ease the ache she felt building deep within her. But it didn't help.

Because she could still feel Conner's arms around her, she squeezed her eyes tightly shut to savor the lingering sensation. How was it a dream could feel so real? Seem so natural?

She frowned suddenly as she remembered the rest of the dream. Nightmare, really. The battlefield. The weariness in Conner's eyes. Poor man, to be haunted by such memories. And what kind of woman was she to be thinking only of her own pleasure at his hands than of the torment he must endure when thoughts of his past plagued him?

She ran one hand up the front of her body, skimming lightly across her breasts, their nipples still upright and trembling from the imagined caresses of Conner James. A remnant of pleasure rippled along her spine, but Meara knew that only Conner's touch could ignite the fire she'd felt too briefly.

And the chances of a wide-awake Conner indulging in such a thing were as good as a drinker's to give up the ale.

Conner woke with a start, heart hammering in his chest, sweat pooling beneath him on the sheets, his body hard and aching. He forced a long, deep gulp of air into heaving lungs and rubbed his face with both hands.

"Jesus," he whispered into the darkness. So real. It had all been so real. The war. He inhaled and almost smelled the sharp sting of gunpowder. And Meara. He could still taste her on his lips.

What was happening? he asked himself. Was he losing his mind? He must be, he thought. Why else would Meara be appearing in long-buried dreams of battle-fields?

He threw one arm across his eyes and concentrated on steadying his heart, calming himself. Anything, to keep from remembering the rest of the dream and how good— how *right* she had felt in his arms.

At breakfast the next morning, Conner was bleary-eyed from lack of sleep and feeling as cheerful as a rattler caught in a sack.

He stomped into the kitchen, ignored Grub, grabbed a cup, and poured himself some coffee. He took a long drink of the thick, black brew before risking speech. His gaze shot around the kitchen, and he winced at the still-splotchy yellow paint. Thanks to Meara, it was too damn bright in here even when the sun wasn't up yet. But then, thanks to Meara, he wasn't getting any sleep, either, so maybe the painted walls only looked bad to him. At the thought of her, he turned his gaze on the older man kneading bread dough at the table.

"Where's Meara?"

Grub flicked him a glance. "Gone."

His next sip of coffee stuck in his throat, and Conner coughed until tears filled his eyes. Then he slammed the cup down onto the table, not even noticing the hot liquid that sloshed onto his hand. "What do you mean, gone?"

Grub ducked his head to hide a small smile. Just as he'd hoped and suspected, Conner cared for the girl.

Even the notion of Meara leaving had him jumping out of his socks.

"Went into High Timber."

Conner's tense position relaxed a bit. "Why so early?"

Now Grub looked up at the man he loved like a son. "Took Luke with her. Wanted to get him started in school."

"School? Who the hell told her to do that?"

"Nobody had to tell her nothin'. Everybody knows a child needs schoolin'." He sent a deadly look at Conner. "Heck, *you* shoulda thought of it."

Immediately, Conner's back went up. Grub could see it in him and he wanted to shake him for it. Here the damn fool had a chance at having a family for the first time since he was a boy and he was too stupid to see it. Was the man going to pretend that Meara and Luke meant nothing to him? Was he going to stand still and let the two of them slip away from him?

Conner took a sip of coffee before saying. "How does she know the boy's going to stay long enough to even *go* to school?" He rubbed his eyes, then the back of his neck. "The kid's a drifter. He'll be moving on again. You'll see."

Grub slapped the mound of bread dough down onto a flour-covered cloth and pounded his fist into the middle of it. Flashing Conner a quick look, he snapped, "When are *you* going to see?"

Conner took another swallow of coffee, then slammed the half-full cup down onto the table. "I'm in no kind of mood for this today, old man."

"Old man, is it?" Grub straightened up and balled his dough-covered hands into fists. "You think you can take this old man on, you just come ahead, boy."

Crazy. The whole world had gone crazy. It wasn't just him, Conner thought, though that brought little consolation. And he was way too tired to be dealing with whatever Grub had stuck in his craw. "What the hell's wrong with you?"

Grub shook a fist at him, and flecks of dough dropped from his hand to litter the oilcloth-covered table top. "You can ask me that when you stand there pretendin' you don't give a good goddamn about Luke or Meara?"

Something inside him closed off and shut down. His gaze locked on the older man, he said tightly, "You don't know what I feel."

"Boy, I've known you most of your life, through good times and bad and I ain't never once been ashamed of ya. Until now."

Grub's gray eyes raked him up and down, dismissing him in disgust. Conner started stalking the kitchen, suddenly too churned up to stand still.

"I seen the looks passin' between you and her," Grub went on, his voice softening only slightly. "Hell, a man'd have to be blind to miss 'em."

"Doesn't matter," Conner muttered on his second pass around the close confines of the kitchen.

"Boy, it's all that *does* matter, when you get right down to it."

Conner stopped dead and stared at him through haunted, sleep-deprived eyes. "You don't know a damn thing about it."

"I know love when I see it."

Conner laughed harshly and the sound scraped his throat raw. "*Love?* Jesus. Grub, just because I want a woman in my bed doesn't mean I love her."

"You damn fool."

Conner's guts twisted and his throat tightened so it was hard to draw a breath. Love. Hell, what did he know about love? All he knew for sure was that he wanted her more with every passing day. That he looked forward to seeing her. To hearing her voice. Even to finding that damned ivy plant in his office.

God damn it, he couldn't even imagine living without

her. Was that love? Or was it just the road to insanity?

Tired right down to his bones, he simply didn't have the heart to fight with Grub any longer. Changing the subject, he asked, "Which horse did she take to town?"

Grub's lips twitched slightly before he said. "She didn't. That's why she left so early. Her and the boy's walkin'."

"Walking?" Conner headed for his jacket on the peg by the door. "Hell, it'll take her two hours to walk into town."

"Where you goin'?" Grub asked as he opened the back door.

"Where the hell do ya think?" Conner muttered. "To find her and Luke."

When the door slammed behind him. Grub grinned to himself and tucked into the bread dough again. The boy may not know it yet, he thought with a contented sigh, but he was sure enough in love.

Luke looked as bright and shiny as a new penny, Meara thought as she left him sitting in the front row of desks. Hair clean and combed, face scrubbed, clothes fresh and ironed, the picture was only marred by his bare feet, dusty from their walk. But she hadn't been able to convince him to wear the shoes Conner'd bought him.

At the rear of the small schoolhouse, Meara paused before joining Conner outside for one last look at "her" boy. He sat straight in his seat, his gaze locked on the long, narrow face of his teacher. Meara glanced at the stick-thin man sitting behind his desk with the air of a king addressing his subjects. She didn't much care for his manner, stiff and unfriendly when she'd ushered Luke into his class. But, she thought, he must be a fine teacher, what with the row of books lining one wall and a grand big map of the world tacked up on the wall opposite. And the children had all looked to be fascinated with the man, never taking their eyes from him once and sitting so still and straight in their chairs.

She nodded to herself, slipped through the doors, and walked down the steps to where Conner sat waiting in the buckboard. Meara still didn't know what had prompted him to follow them, but she was grateful. 'Twas a much longer walk to town than she'd thought at first, and when she'd spied Conner coming up behind them, she'd been that happy to see him.

"Is he all set?" Conner asked as she stepped up and into the wagon.

"Aye," she said with another look at the schoolhouse. "Though he's not pleased to be there a'tall."

Conner chuckled and picked up the reins. Propping one boot up on the kickboard in front of him, he said, "I know just how he feels. Always hated going to school myself. But Ma was a terror for schooling."

Meara turned her head to smile up at him. "Tell me about her." she said.

Abruptly, the smile on Conner's face dissolved and he shot her a quick look from the corner of his eye. "Tell you what?"

"What was she like?" Meara asked. "Kind? Funny? Beautiful?" She managed to keep from adding that she wanted to know everything about him. That she longed to be a part of his life.

Small crowds of early-morning shoppers strolled past the buckboard. The town of High Timber was only just waking up. Along the boardwalk lining both sides of the street, merchants were busy, sweeping yesterday's dust from the walkway to make room for today's.

Conner stared off into the distance, letting the reins fall lax in his hands. Frowning slightly as if trying to dredge up long buried memories, he finally said, "She was pretty, I guess. Died when I was ten. Sent me to live with my father."

His frown deepened, and Meara remembered everything Grub had told her about his father. She knew instinctively that he wouldn't want to talk about Trevor James, so she asked instead, "But what was she like? Your mother, I mean."

His fingers tightened around the reins suddenly. He dipped his head, then lifted it again until he could look at her. "What was she like?"

Meara braced herself at the tone in his voice. Harsh, pain-filled.

"She was a good woman who fell in love with the wrong man and paid for it the rest of her life." As he spoke, his gaze shifted until he was staring off down the street as if his life depended on his concentration.

Meara laid one hand on his arm. Though it pained her to prod him further, her instincts told her to continue. To let him lance this boil he carried on his soul. To let old poisons out. "How d'ya mean, she paid for it?"

Conner took a deep breath and then let the words rush from him in a torrent. "She fell in love with my father. A gambler, who left town as soon as the cards went cold. After he was gone, she found out she was carrying me." His jaw tightened and Meara's hand closed over his arm in silent support. "Her family threw her out, so she followed after him. Whatever she was expecting he'd do for her, she was disappointed. She caught up to him in Texas. He told her he wouldn't marry her, he'd no use for a wife and kid. So she got a job. The only job she *could* get."

Conner swivelled his head to stare at her and she looked deeply into his blue eyes, hoping to tell him without words that whatever he was about to say would change nothing.

He licked his lips and his gaze skittered from hers. "She became a whore. *He* made her one."

Meara held her breath and waited for him to finish.

"She raised me in a bordello until I was ten. Made sure

I went to school and church and that I always had clothes to wear and plenty to eat."

Risking a comment, Meara said, "She was a good woman, then." Admiration for the woman rose up in Meara. Abandoned, with no family to turn to, Conner's mother had chosen a life of shame for herself, to see that her son would have better.

"Didn't you hear me?" he asked tightly. "I said she was a whore. She laid down with men for money."

"To take care of her son the only way she knew how."

A muscle in his jaw twitched as he nodded and his fingers tightened even further on the reins. "The only mean thing she ever did was to die and send me to him. But there was no one else," he said with a shrug Meara knew had cost him. "I stayed with the bastard almost four years. Then he died and I went out on my own."

"You and Grub."

He smiled fondly. "Yeah, there was Grub, too. Off and on over the years, we'd meet up. Then after the war, I ran into him and he just stuck around."

Smiling, Meara realized that he didn't even realize that he and Grub had stayed together to form a family they both needed.

"You're a lucky man, Conner," she said and gave his arm a pat.

Now he looked at her in astonishment. "Lucky?"

"Aye," she said with a firm nod. "You've known love and friendship. You've made yourself a home." She shrugged. "Lucky."

"You know," he said, his gaze drifting slowly over her features, "when most people find out I come from gamblers and whores, they're shocked. Disgusted. Hell, there are folks in High Timber who still cross the street when they see me coming." He frowned thoughtfully. "Carlisle found out about my folks after I won the ranch. He made it his business to tell everybody else. For awhile there," he added softly, "no one in town would do business with me. They figured the son of a gambler had to have cheated to win that ranch away from a fine, upstanding citizen like Carlisle." He shook his head. "That's why I don't come to town much. Figure if they don't see me a lot, they'll forget who I am."

"Ah, Conner . . ."

He turned to look at her and one side of his mouth tilted into a slight smile. "Should have figured you'd surprise me."

One red-gold eyebrow lifted. She rearranged her skirt and smiled at him. "Aye, ya should. Or hadn't ya noticed yet that I'm not most people?"

His smile grew and creased his handsome features. "Yeah. I've noticed."

Her stomach fluttered and Meara took a few fast, shallow breaths. What the man could do to her insides with just a look was downright sinful. And even as her heartbeat quickened, she reminded herself of the decision she'd made only the day before. With that in mind, she asked suddenly, "Conner, would ya mind taking me to Virginia City?"

His smile faded. "Why?"

"I've got to know," she said. " 'Tis time. 'Tis my memories I'm needin'. My past. My life."

"Maybe you'll find something you'd rather not remember," he said quietly. "Meara, I know better than most that memories are not always good ones."

She leaned in close to him, and Conner held his breath. The scent of her hair enveloped him, and the earnest plea in her eyes stabbed him to the soul.

"Conner, do ya not see that the only way out of this murky puzzle I'm in is to find the answers to my questions? Good or bad, I must *know*."

And good or bad, he told himself, he had to be with her. If she needed him he would be there. And if they found nothing, he would take her home again with him. Back to the ranch. Where she belonged.

That thought settled into his brain and for the first time, didn't terrify him.

After a long moment, he nodded grimly. "All right. We go to Virginia City."

She gave him a smile that warmed every corner of his heart, then shifted on the narrow bench seat to look straight ahead—to whatever she might find.

CHAPTER ELEVEN

Just outside town, Conner yawned, and an instant later, Meara repeated the action.

"Didn't get much sleep," he said shortly.

"Nor did I," Meara said, and instantly the dream images rose up in her mind to taunt her again. Blast and hellfire, she'd almost succeeded in forgetting about them.

"Bad dreams?" he asked.

"Not bad," she corrected in what she considered to be an understatement. "Just . . ." She glanced sideways at his profile. "Unsettling."

He shifted on the seat. "What'd you dream about?" he asked.

There wasn't much she could tell him without embarrassing the both of them. So she said only, "All I remember is a battlefield."

He stiffened slightly. "A battlefield?"

"Aye."

"And nothing else?" His voice sounded thick. Choked. As if he couldn't find moisture in his mouth.

"Mainly that," she told him, and mentally banished the memory of the dream kiss. 'Twould do her no good to go tormenting herself with that image.

"I dreamed of battlefields, too," he said after a long moment.

Her ears rang. The morning call of birds fell away, and she could no longer hear the heavy thump of the horse's hooves against the rocky ground or the squeak of the wooden wheels. Her stomach pitched and her heartbeat skittered. Was it possible? she wondered, and then told herself no. It wasn't. And even if it was possible that somehow, they had shared a dream, it had nothin' to do with the business at hand.

'Twas only a dream.

No more.

"Quite a coincidence," she said at last. "Don't ya think?"

"Yeah," he muttered. "A coincidence." Then, as if reading her mind and her reluctance to talk about the dream further, he slapped the reins over the black horse's back and set a lively pace for Virginia City.

The noise was enough to make a man with a hangover give up the drink.

A long, narrow street stretched out in front of them, with dozens of smaller, narrower streets splitting off of it. Meara could only stare helplessly at the crowds streaming on the boardwalks and slogging through the muddy road. Horses and carriages littered the roadway, with the occasional farm wagon jutting into the middle of the street.

For the last hour she and Conner had trudged up one side of the street and down another, poking their heads into shops and taverns, asking questions of anyone who would stand still long enough to listen.

And they'd learned nothing for their efforts.

Now, exhausted and disappointed, she waited outside the latest barroom for Conner to rejoin her. Her gaze moved over the buildings and she shook her head solemnly. Saloons, she thought. As far as the eye could see, saloons. And from every one of them came loud, discordant piano music. The notes tangled together in the middle of the street, creating a racket loud enough to wake the dead and have them screaming for peace.

Sandwiched between the rows of saloons were stores. Mercantile. Sweets. Bakery. Laundry. Feed and grain. Livery stable. Barber. In the distance, she saw tall buildings, some of them with crosses atop them, and others, grand, brick and stone structures.

Every last one of the businesses was so full of customers, the people were spilling out into the road. But no one seemed to mind. Above the din of the pianos came the muffled roar of conversations. Friends shouting to one another, children laughing and calling out, dogs barking.

She'd had such hopes when they'd first arrived. She'd thought surely in that mass of people, there'd be *someone* who recognized her. Or who knew of her family, if she had one.

But not a soul had stepped forward.

It was as if Meara had been born the moment she'd fallen through Conner's roof.

"Giving up?" he asked quietly as he stepped up beside her, only to move aside as a well-dressed matron shoved past him.

Meara's head snapped up. "Giving up? Are you mad, man? We've been all over this town and there's no one who knows me."

"So you've decided to quit."

She tightened her jaw slightly. " 'Tis not quitting to admit when you're beaten."

"Sure it is. You're only beaten if you get knocked down and *stay* down."

Her foot tapped in a rapid-fire rhythm against the plank walk. "So you don't want to admit there's nothin' here for me, is that it?"

"All I'm saying is that we haven't tried everyone." He smiled at her, blast him. "We can go to the sheriff."

"The sheriff."

"Yeah. Hell, we probably should have started there," Conner mused aloud. "He'll know if there's anybody around here looking for you."

A ray of hope pierced her breast, like the brightest beam of sunlight slanting through a freshly cleaned window. "The sheriff, then."

He inclined his head in the proper direction and started off, Meara right on his heels.

"Nope," Sheriff John Jacobs said as he shook his head and scratched a jaw that hadn't been shaved in a week or more. "Can't say that I know of anybody missing a woman."

Beside him, Conner sensed Meara's disappointment. He knew she'd been counting on finding out something about her past today. And he'd been half afraid that she would too. All he'd been able to imagine was some strange man running up to them, calling her name, arms open wide.

But as the hours passed and they were no closer to solving the mystery of Meara Simon, he'd found himself relaxing. Despite goading her into continuing their search, he'd been hoping they wouldn't find anything. Yet at the same time, he wanted to feel that he'd done what he could to help her. Though he didn't know what he might have done if that imagined stranger had shown up to sweep her into his arms. Just the thought of that was enough to send a cold chill snaking along his spine.

It had taken every last ounce of his nerve to come to the sheriff. Because all he really wanted to do was cart Meara back to the ranch and keep her tucked away safely. That way, no other man could show up making a claim on her.

Damn it, Conner wasn't ready to give her up. He didn't know if he'd *ever* be ready. And *there* was a disturbing thought.

"There's no one new in town?" Meara asked, and Conner kept his gaze locked on the tired-looking sheriff.

A weary smile crossed the man's face briefly. "New?" he repeated, with another shake of his head. "Ma'am, there's so many new people hittin' town everyday, even the new ones ain't new anymore."

"But surely—" she started.

The sheriff held up one hand. Shrugging his shoulders, he said, "I'll keep my ears open. Keep a special watch for Irish folks, but that's about all I can do."

Conner felt his insides slowly unwind from their tight coil. Hearing the sheriff say that their chances of finding Meara's folks were slim was like icing on a nice slab of cake.

"Can't you talk to people?" Meara asked, and Conner scowled at the desperation in her voice. Was she so unhappy at the ranch? Was she so eager to get away from him?

"Lady . . ." The sheriff leaned back in his chair and propped both booted feet on the edge of his desk, crossing them at the ankles. "I got two deputies. One of 'em just got married, and he's off to Denver on a wedding trip. And the other got himself shot the other night in a barroom brawl.

"I'm just one man here for awhile with a hell—excuse me, ma'am—heck of a lot of people to ride herd on." He held both hands out as if to prove how helpless he was in the face of such a challenge. "There's only so much I can do, ma'am. I purely am sorry."

Conner saw acceptance settle on her features. "Thanks, Sheriff," he said, when Meara didn't speak for a long minute. "Guess we'll be going, then." He headed for the door, with Meara following. She stopped alongside him and turned her head toward the man at the cluttered desk.

"Thank you very much for your help," she said, and

the sheriff got slowly to his feet, as if the movement cost him his last ounce of energy.

"Wasn't much help," he said. "And I know it. But I'll get word to the ranch if anything does come across my desk."

She nodded stiffly and stepped outside. Conner joined her on the boardwalk. Meara looked up at him and gave him a wan smile.

Damn it, he should be shot for being so pleased about something that obviously grieved her. But he couldn't help the way he felt, could he? Was it wrong to hope that she would stop looking for a place to belong and realize she already had that place?

With him.

"How about we go get something to eat before heading home?" he asked abruptly, a bit worried about the direction his thoughts were taking.

"Home," she repeated, letting her gaze sweep across the faces of the strangers milling by them. " 'Tis a lovely word, don't you think?"

"Never really thought about it before," he admitted. And why should he have? He hadn't had a home since he was ten years old and his mother died, leaving him to go and live with a father he barely knew.

And his father hadn't been the kind of man to have a home. Just a horse and a deck of cards, that's all that Trevor James had ever wanted or needed. Even his own son hadn't been more to him than a burden grudgingly carried.

He closed his mind to the past and the long-buried misery of never belonging. Never having a place to call his own or people who gave a damn whether he came or went.

Home.

Conner looked down at the woman beside him. He studied her profile for a long, silent minute and realized something that worried him. Owning a ranch hadn't given him a home.

The damn place had become a home the day Meara dropped through the roof.

Meara squinted against the thick smoke wafting over the bustling city as she and Conner walked up hill on one of the narrow tracks jutting from the main street.

Houses crammed together behind storefronts that hosted dozens of people running to and fro. To her right, smoke poured from the giant stacks of the silver mines, and the roar of the engines made a body wish for the gift of deafness.

"How do they stand it?" she asked, and Conner tilted his head to one side to better hear her. "The noise and the dirt. 'Tis dreadful."

"Most of 'em come for the chance to get rich," he said and straightarmed a drunk weaving his way into their path. "But the only ones getting rich around here are the saloon keepers."

So it would seem, she thought, and wrinkled her nose as yet another drunk staggered past her. Almost every few feet there was another saloon. With names like The Lazy Dog, Last Ditch, Silver Slipper, they drew men like bees to honey.

"Virginia City's got more than one hundred saloons and only four churches," Conner pointed out and took her hand to help her as the hill became steeper. "Now you understand why the sheriff said he couldn't be much help."

"Aye," she said, "I do." 'Twould be a miracle indeed to find someone you knew in a crowd this size.

At the Comstock Cafe, Conner pushed the door open and led the way inside. Meara, thankful that the noise level had dropped a bit, sighed in relief as she gazed around the crowded place.

"Over there," Conner said, and tugged at her hand as

he started through the mob of people toward a table at the rear.

When they were seated, Meara shook her head and looked around her in stupefied amazement. It was all so busy. So different from the quiet peace of the ranch. Strange, but exciting.

"Like it?" Conner asked, leaning his elbows on the table.

Meara turned her head to smile at him. "Aye," she said. " 'Tis grand, Conner."

A waitress, looking as though she could fall asleep on her feet, appeared at their table then, with a pad and pencil. Conner ordered for both of them.

"Steak, potatoes, coffee for me, and tea for the lady."

"It'll be awhile," the woman said and pushed a stray lock of dark hair behind her ear.

"We have time," he told her, before turning to Meara as the woman walked off, headed back to the kitchen. "I'm sorry you didn't find anything today."

"Aye, well," she said, leaning forward so he could hear her over the babble of voices rising and falling around them. "I've decided to stop worryin' over the lack of memory in this brain of mine."

"Really. Why?"

She glanced at a fat man to her left, whose booming laugh was enough to shatter glass. Then she shifted her gaze back to Conner. "We've done all we could and still found nothing. Perhaps I'm not meant to remember. Perhaps my past is a thing best forgotten."

Conner's heart twisted. Despite her words, he knew how badly she wanted to know who she was and where she'd come from. But for the first time, he had to wonder if maybe she had a point. Maybe it was better if she *didn't* remember. Maybe she was running from something. Or someone. Maybe her past was too painful to remember.

"You don't have to have a past to have a future," he said.

"Don't you?"

He reached for her hand, and she almost gasped at the tingling, warm contact of his flesh against hers. "Meara," he said, taking a deep breath. She prepared herself for bad news. His features looked tight, uncomfortable, which couldn't bode well for her.

Was he finally going to ask her to leave the ranch? After all, her staying at his house had been meant as only a temporary arrangement. He must have decided that he'd been indulgent long enough.

"Meara," he said again, and her insides twisted into knots as she waited for the blow to fall. Where would she go? What would she do? "I want you to stay at the ranch," he finished.

She stared at him for the length of several sluggish heartbeats. Clearly, he took her silence for regret, because he spoke up again quickly.

"There's no reason for you to go," he said. "Things have been working pretty well. You do a good job. Grub needed the help whether he'd admit it or not, and there's Luke to think about, too."

"Luke?"

"Sure. The kid needs somebody looking after him."

She nodded and breathed slowly, shallowly. "And what about you, Conner? Do you need me, too?"

His expression shifted. He glanced at the crowded room as if assuring himself that no one was going to overhear him and then turned back to her. Locking his blue eyes with hers, he squeezed her fingers tightly. "I want you to stay."

Meara looked at their joined hands and told herself it was something. He hadn't said he needed her, but he *did* want her. Surely that was a start. To what, she didn't know. But at least, he wasn't asking her to leave.

Leaving him would have broken her heart.

"So will you?" he prompted.

"Aye," she whispered, lifting her gaze to his again. "I'll stay. For now."

He smiled at her, and she noted the flash of relief in his deep blue eyes.

"Well, well, well." A deep, loud voice spoke up from beside their table, shattering the spell that had hovered between them. "Aren't you going to introduce me to your friend?"

Conner tensed visibly and swivelled his head to glare up at the man watching them. Tall, though not so tall as Conner, the man had iron-gray hair, neatly combed, and a sweeping moustache that disguised, but didn't quite cover, his thin, mean lips. Icy gray eyes stared down at them, and Meara noted there were few laugh lines at their corners. He wore a fancy suit with a gold watch chain draped across the front of his plaid vest.

Directly behind him stood Hester Carlisle, her sharp black gaze drilling holes into Meara's forehead.

"There she is," Hester whispered. "The harlot living in my house."

Conner stiffened, slanted a glance at Meara, and watched as her face paled, then flushed scarlet.

"Not for much longer," Robert Carlisle assured his wife.

"What do you want, Carlisle?" Conner said through gritted teeth.

"What's rightfully mine," the other man said tightly. "And I'll have it, too."

"You lost it. Bet that ranch on a hand of cards and lost."

"You cheated me."

Conner pushed his chair back, its legs scraping against the scarred wooden floor. Standing up, he faced Carlisle squarely. "That's a lie."

The other man's gray eyes narrowed thoughtfully as he took a safe step backward. He wanted to fight, that was clear. But he also wanted to win and knew he couldn't. So he settled for saying, "You and your tramp are on borrowed time, James. I'll have my ranch back yet, you mark my words."

"Mister," Conner said, "this is between you and me. You say one more word about Meara and I'll tear the hide right off your bones and feed it to the wolves."

Carlisle practically jumped backward, bumping into his wife, which sent her stumbling into a table, where she lost her balance and fell to land on the lap of a very slender man who groaned loudly in pain.

Ignoring his wife's predicament, Carlisle's eyes widened, then narrowed again instantly. Conner knew the look in those eyes. The man was deciding whether to fight for his pride or run for his life. At the moment, Conner didn't much care which one the man chose.

Robert Carlisle wanted to fight, that was clear. But he also wanted to win and knew he couldn't. So he left, stopping only long enough to pull his overweight wife off the man slowly turning blue in the face.

The moment the front door closed behind them, the crowd turned back to their meals and conversation as if nothing had happened. Anger still pounding through him, Conner dropped to his seat and looked at Meara, half expecting her to be horrified by his behavior.

Instead, she grinned as she sat down beside him. Then she reached out, took one of his fists in her hands, and squeezed. "Well done," she said.

And Conner felt an unfamiliar rush of pride.

At supper, Luke had been quiet. Too quiet, to Meara's way of thinking. "He said nothing about school, ya know," she said.

Conner looked up from the rifle he was cleaning to smile at her briefly. "He didn't want to go. Not surprising he don't want to talk about it."

Meara shook her head and set her knitting aside. The

sweater she was making for Conner was coming along nicely, but her heart wasn't in the work this night. Instead, she kept remembering Luke's solemn little face at the end of his first school day. Shouldn't he have been pleased just a bit? she wondered. Meeting children his own age. Learning new things?

She stared into the fire and concentrated on the flames licking and snapping at the logs in the hearth. With Grub in the bunkhouse enjoying a game of poker with the hands and Luke already upstairs, she and Conner had the great room to themselves. She should have been enjoying this time alone with him, but her mind was too filled with the memory of the shadows in Luke's eyes.

"Settling in isn't easy," Conner said as if reading her mind. "But he'll be all right."

"Aye," she told him. "I'm sure you're right. 'Tis only that he's such a little boy."

As soon as those words left her mouth, she stopped and cocked her head. They sounded familiar, somehow. As though she'd said them before in another time, another place. Frowning, she concentrated, trying desperately to remember what child she'd been talking about then? Her own? No. One hand dropped to her flat belly and she told herself that she would definitely remember if she'd ever borne a child.

But then, who had she been talking about? What child had she been trying to protect? Fog swirled in her mind, lifting slightly at the edges to give her a peek at the huge room she'd seen once in her dreams. Thousands of people wandered throughout the chamber, talking in whispers as a tall, dark-haired man stepped up onto a platform, lifted his arms and said . . .

"Meara." Conner's voice splintered the memory into a million jagged shards, none of which connected with another. "What is it? Are you remembering something?"

Frustrated, she jumped up from her chair and stood

staring down at him. "Do ya know what it is to try and try and never be able to grab ahold of what's closest to ya?"

"No," he said and stood up.

"I keep seeing bits and pieces of a place I've no knowledge of. There are people there. Lots of them. And only this moment, I saw a man."

Conner's features froze over like a lake in winter. "What man?"

"I don't *know*," she cried, frustration mounting inside her. "I only know that I know him, but I don't know *how* I know him."

Conner walked to her side. Taking her shoulders with both hands, his fingertips dug into her flesh. Even through the fabric of her flower-sprigged yellow dress, Meara felt the stinging warmth of him flow deep into her bones.

"Is he your husband?" he asked, his voice raw.

"I don't think so," she whispered.

"But you're not sure."

"No, I'm not. But he wasn't *with* me. He was standing at the front of a great room, preparing to talk to hundreds of people." She closed her eyes, trying to bring the images back into focus. "I can't see his face clearly, no matter how I try."

"Stop trying," he snapped, and her eyes flew open again.

"What?"

"I said stop trying, Meara." His gaze moved over her features like a dying man drinking in his last look at life. "See me. Only see me."

Then he dipped his head for a brief kiss that left her body thundering for more. When he pulled his head back to look at her again, he lifted one hand to stroke the line of her jaw. She trembled at his touch and felt those tremors rock her to her soul. "Conner," she whispered, "what's happening here?"

"I'm not sure," he said and let his hands drop to his sides. "Hell, I'm not sure of anything anymore."

A half hour later, Conner left his office, carrying the white china bowl. Shaking his head, he smiled to himself and admitted that he was enjoying this little game he and Meara had going. In fact, every time he went into his office now, he found himself looking for this blasted ivy plant.

Just as daily, he found himself looking for a glimpse of her. How had all of this happened? And so quickly. A month ago, he hadn't known she existed. Now, he couldn't imagine his life without her.

Taking the china bowl into the main room, he set it down on the table beside the chair where, across the cushion, a half-knitted sweater lay. He picked it up and smoothed his fingertips across the intricate stitches woven into the soft wool.

Her memory was certainly a tricky thing. She didn't know where she came from, but she knew how to knit. She didn't know if she had family, but she knew her name. She couldn't remember her parents, but she rattled off their favorite sayings without a blink.

And she had turned his world upside down in a matter of weeks. On that thought, Conner laid the sweater down again and headed for the stairs.

"Luke?" Meara asked as she pushed the boy's bedroom door open.

"Come on in."

She stepped inside and saw Luke, sitting on the floor at the edge of his bed, polishing the new shoes he never wore. He looked up at her, and blond hair fell down into his eyes. Meara reached down and brushed it back, clucking her tongue. "Maybe we'll get that mop of yours cut when we go to town tomorrow, eh?"

He shook his head. "Nah. Conner don't get his hair cut. It's all long in the back and sticks out over his shirt." Abruptly, he turned to show her the back of his head. "Is mine that long yet?"

Meara smiled. "Not yet, you've a ways to go."

Luke nodded and bent his head to his task again.

"Do ya know," Meara said, "I think those are the shiniest shoes I've ever seen." She picked up one of them and wasn't the least bit surprised to be able to see herself in the high gloss.

"Pretty, ain't they?" Luke whispered, and held the one he was working on out to admire.

"Aye, they are," she said with a glance at his blue-tinged bare feet. "But you should be wearin' them. Your poor toes look cold enough to drop off."

He glanced at them. "Nah. I ain't cold."

Stubborn boy, she thought and sat down on the floor opposite him. Reaching out, she caught one of his hands in hers. "Luke, darlin'," she asked quietly, "why won't you wear the shoes? Is it because you think of them as charity?"

The boy set his newly polished shoe carefully onto the rug and lifted its mate. Drawing the cloth across the toe of the shoe, he shined it while he answered. "No, that ain't it. Conner's payin' me now, so it ain't charity."

"Then why?"

He paused, laid the shoe in his lap, and looked up at her through the fall of blond hair. Just a brief glance, then he lowered his gaze to the precious shoes again. When he spoke his voice was almost lost in the quiet of the room. Meara strained to hear him.

"I never had me no new shoes before," he said, running the tip of one finger across the soft brown leather. "Pa, he never was much good for workin'. Didn't have much cash money, and what he did have, he lost at the saloon most times. He said it'd be a waste, buyin' me shoes, since I kept on growin'. Costs enough to feed a youngster these days, let alone buyin' him shoes he's only gonna grow out of before he wears 'em out."

Meara's mouth tightened, to keep back the curses she wanted to hurl at the man who'd so neglected his boy.

Luke looked up at her and smiled briefly. "If I wear 'em, they're gonna git all dirty and maybe ruined." He shook his head. "I like 'em just like they are."

"Ah, darlin'," she whispered, and smoothed her hand across the top of his head.

"I don't mind cold feet," Luke said, his voice a bit louder now. "I'm used to it. So I'll just keep my shoes right here. Where they'll be safe."

Meara nodded and pulled him into a long, reassuring hug.

Conner stepped back from the open doorway and squinted against the stinging in his eyes. Swallowing heavily, he choked back the emotion crowding his throat. He should have asked why the boy never wore his shoes. But no, he'd been so intent on teaching the kid what to do on a ranch and answering all of the boy's questions that he'd never thought about it.

Leave it to Meara to get to the heart of a problem.

He watched silently as she held the boy and rocked him, giving him the comfort any kid should have a right to expect. And what that kid in particular had probably never known. He knew better than anyone what kind of life that boy had had before coming to this ranch. Conner had seen the old scars on his narrow back when he'd bathed Luke that first day. Yet whatever the kid had been through hadn't ruined his nature. That was a good boy. With a good heart.

And in the time he'd been here, Luke had soaked up the love Meara offered freely like drought-stricken land with a fresh rain.

Abruptly, Conner turned away from the tender scene

in front of him. A boy shouldn't have to be so damn grateful for a pair of shoes, he thought, and promised himself to get the kid another pair. Soon.

One to wear and one to keep safe.

As Conner would keep that boy and Meara safe.

CHAPTER TWELVE

Robert Carlisle pushed through the batwing doors and stepped into the saloon. Clouds of smoke hovered over the heads of the men sitting at tables sprinkled around the room. The clack of poker chips softly underscored the muttered conversations. The tinny music from a nickelodeon in the far corner added its own discordant noise into the melee.

Walking into the crowd, Carlisle shoved his way through the mob of men until he reached the bar. He glared at the bartender's back and shouted, trying to get the man's attention. But the barman was busy, arguing with another customer at the end of the bar. That customer's voice rang out loudly, demanding service and offering to work for a drink.

Carlisle smiled as an idea formed in his mind. A moment later, he wormed his way through the men at the bar until he was standing beside the thirsty customer. Slapping two coins onto the bar, Carlisle ordered two drinks. One for himself. And one for the man who was giving him a grateful smile.

Meara couldn't sleep.

She'd been lying in bed for hours and every time she closed her eyes, those fractured bits of memories rose up in her mind, pushing aside all chance for rest.

At last, she quit trying. Pushing up from the bed, she walked across the room. Her long, white cotton nightgown dusted across the tops of her toes, and she had to kick at the hem as she hurried her steps. Maybe all she needed was a little fresh air and a walk around the ranch yard in the moonlight. Reaching into the wardrobe, she pulled out the old coat Grub had given her and shoved her arms into the sleeves. Then she made for the door and stepped quietly into the hall.

Shadows greeted her.

From the room beside hers came the unmistakable sounds of Grub's rumbling snore. She smiled to herself, then shot a look at Conner's closed door opposite. Not a sound came from his room, and she wondered if he was having another dream. A dream she couldn't join because she couldn't fall asleep. Then an image reared up in her mind of Conner, stretched out on his bed. Her stomach jittered as her mind painted a vision of his bare chest beneath a sheet that slid farther and farther along his naked body.

Meara shook her head, gulped in a breath, and headed for the stairs. She needed the cool night air now more than ever. But she came to an abrupt stop when she heard a sound coming from Luke's bedroom.

Moving closer to the door, she cocked her head to listen. The sound came again and this time, her heart twisted uncomfortably in her chest. He was whimpering.

Without giving it another thought, Meara grabbed the cut-glass doorknob and turned it, opening the door on Luke's moon-washed bedroom. The terrible, soft cries were louder now and tore at her heart like knives. In the shadowy light, she moved toward the bed where Luke lay, the blankets tossed to the floor by his wild, frantic movements.

Meara picked up the rose-flowered quilt and spread it over the boy only to have him kick it aside again.

"No, don't," Luke whispered. "I promise, I won't do it no more. I promise, Pa."

"Shh . . ." Meara whispered, and eased down beside him on the edge of the mattress. Every instinct she possessed demanded that she soothe this child, ease his terror.

"I swear, Pa," Luke muttered, and flinched in his sleep. "I swear."

" 'Tis all right, Luke," Meara said softly, reaching out to smooth his sweat dampened hair back from his brow. "You're safe. Safe."

He moaned quietly, and a tear rolled down his pale cheek and soaked into the pillow beneath his head.

Meara frowned and eased even closer. Running the palm of her hand across his face, she tried to comfort him, to let him know that all was well. That she would protect him from whatever night monsters were visiting him.

And then she was in his dream, watching him hide and duck away from blows being delivered by an angry man with a thick belt in his beefy hands. Madness filled the huge man's eyes as he wielded that belt like a whip, biting into the child's flesh again and again.

Darkness swirled around the pair.

Luke saw her and hope lit his eyes. "Meara," he cried, reaching for her with bloody arms, "help me."

Instantly, Meara gathered him close and placed herself between him and the beast of a man cursing him. Luke's father glared at her and drew back his belt again for another swipe.

She lifted her chin and shouted, "You've no power over this boy any longer. He's free of you."

In the next instant, the dream shifted, changed. Light crept into the darkness until the angry man and his belt disappeared and were replaced by a field of wildflowers beside a beautiful lake.

Slowly, Luke relaxed in her arms until at last, he sat

up and looked around him. His dream wounds healed, he stared up at her and asked, "Where are we?"

"Where you're safe," she told him, and leaned down to kiss his forehead.

"He won't find me?"

"Not here," she assured him, and smiled at the glorious sunshine sparkling on the ripples in the water.

"Ever?"

"Ever," she promised, turning her steady gaze back on the boy who so clearly wanted to believe. "You're safe now, Luke. He won't be hurting you again."

"My pa," he said simply.

Meara cursed inwardly at the man who had valued so little what God had given him.

"He's dead," Luke added, and burrowed closer to Meara, his thin arms wrapping around her waist. "And I'm glad. So that means I'm bad, huh?"

"Ah no, love" she told him, stroking his blond head and shielding him with all the love she could focus on him. Poor, wee thing. Feeling guilty because he was glad that evil man was dead, he continued to punish himself in his dreams. "You're only human. Of course you're glad the beatings have stopped."

"But I keep dreaming about him." Luke's voice was muffled by her nightgown. "So it's like he's still alive."

Heart aching for the boy who'd suffered too much in his short life, Meara took his head in her hands and turned his face up to hers. Solemnly, she told him, "He's only alive in your mind, Luke. And then only if you give him the power to hurt you still."

Eyes awash with tears that silvered his cheeks in the sunlight, Luke asked, "Will he stay gone now that you sent him away?"

She smoothed that too-long hair back again and smiled at him. "He will if that's what you want."

"It is. I don't want to see him anymore."

"Then he won't be back."

A long minute passed before the little boy drew in a deep, shuddering breath and gave her a tremulous smile. "Thanks, Meara," he said softly.

"Ah, darlin'," she said, " 'tisn't me you have to thank. You conquered your own fears. You sent the man from your dreams by reaching out to me."

He gave her another hard hug, then took a step back from her, swiping his eyes with the backs of his hands. "What am I supposed to do now?"

She grinned at him. Inclining her head toward the lake, she said, "I think I see a fishing pole over there."

Sure enough, there, beneath the shade of a giant oak, lay a pail of bait and a cane pole, just waiting for a boy to while away a day.

Luke raced off through the field of wildflowers, their gentle stems swaying with his passing. When he was settled beneath that tree, Meara found herself back in the shadowy confines of Luke's bedroom, staring down at a peacefully sleeping boy.

Rising, Meara covered him with the quilt again, and this time, rather than kicking it off in a blind panic, he tucked it up under his chin and snuggled his head down deeper into the feather pillow.

Smiling to herself, her mind still filled with the strange visions she'd had, Meara left the room, quietly closing the door behind her.

Outside, in the pale glow of the moon, she wandered barefoot across the yard, still trying to make sense of what she'd experienced. She'd been *in* Luke's dream with him.

Just as she had been in Conner's.

Pebbles bit into the tender flesh of her feet, but she paid them no mind. Her thoughts were too busy to take note of the small, nagging pains.

A shiver raced along her spine as she tried to understand what was happening to her. How could she enter other people's dreams? And was it real? Or was she losing her mind?

As she passed the darkened building where Conner's ranch hands slept, the soft, sweet strains of a fiddle being played rose up in the night. Meara paused to listen, her gaze fastened on the bunkhouse and the musician within. The tune sounded like fairy wings in the air. So light, so soft, as though it wasn't really there at all.

Finally, she continued her walk, her steps moving to the rhythm of the music following her on the still, night air. As she lost herself in the sweet melody, confusing thoughts and problems slipped from her mind.

Silently, she swayed to the tune filling the night. She went up on her toes, lifted the hem of her nightgown and danced and twirled her way across the rest of the yard. Her steps were feather-light and kept time with the slow sweep of the music she heard now from a distance.

Night dampness clung to the hem of her nightgown as she passed along the edge of the knee high meadow grass. Moonlight studded the yard with long shadows and odd patterns of light. She raised her gaze toward heaven and watched the stars swirl around in circles above her head while she danced, arms spread wide, relishing the night and her keen sense of being alive to enjoy it.

She didn't hear him approach.

So caught up was she in her dance, Meara didn't know Conner was there until he caught her in his arms and pulled her close to him.

She gasped in surprise, then relaxed again as he led her in a dance. He didn't speak, only looked into her eyes and spun with her in time to the music. Meara stared up at him, her gaze locked on his face as they moved in the moonlight, locked together, aware only of each other.

A soft night breeze sighed past them, but Meara didn't even feel its chill. Pressed close to Conner's chest, she was filled with a warmth that lit her soul with an ancient fire.

His eyes shone in the moonlight as he watched her, his

gaze never wavering. He held her gently, as if she were the most fragile piece of blown glass, and yet the strength in his arms sent tremors coursing through her bloodstream. Conner moved gracefully, leading her into wide circles and tight patterns across the yard. The music drifted through the night, and it was as if they were the only two people in the world. A world of silvery shadows and whisper-soft breezes, a world where the moon and a wide blanket of stars were all the company they needed. The mooncast night enveloped them in a cool, dark embrace, and everything else they might have needed, they found in each other's eyes.

But at last, the music ended, its final note piercing the stillness and hanging for a breathless moment before dissolving as if it had never been.

They stopped, but Conner made no move to release her. Her hand warm in his, she concentrated on the feel of his arm wrapped around her waist and the glorious sensation of his tall, muscular frame pressed close to her.

His gaze moved over her face almost solemnly. She felt the heat of it warm her soul.

"Where did you come from?" she asked, when she couldn't endure the hushed silence another moment.

"The barn," he said, his left hand splaying open along her spine. "Had to check on one of the mares. It's close to her time."

She shivered, feeling the imprint of each of his fingertips like the tiniest of fires, igniting her skin, setting her soul aflame.

"I couldn't sleep," she said lamely. "I thought a walk might help."

"Or a dance?" His mouth curved into a smile that touched her in ways she'd never expected.

Embarrassment heated her cheeks and she hoped he couldn't see it in the moonlight. Gazing up at him, Meara felt her blood stir into life. So many things he made her feel, she thought. So many wonderful things.

"I heard the music and 'twas so lovely, I couldn't help myself."

"Hobart often plays late at night. Says it helps him settle in." He stared at her for what seemed forever before adding, "I never enjoyed his playing more than tonight."

Shamelessly, she felt herself leaning toward him and was helpless to stop.

"Meara," he said as he released her hand to cup her face in his palm.

"Yes?"

"Nothing," he said, with a slow shake of his head. "I just like the sound of your name."

Sweet Saint Bridget, she thought, either help me withstand this man's touch or turn your back so you won't have to see my fall.

Then Conner bent his head to hers, hesitated briefly to study her eyes for what seemed a small eternity, and then dusted her mouth with a kiss more promise than substance. After too brief a time, he pulled his head back to look at her again. His eyes glittered in the moonlight and Meara's heartbeat thudded painfully in response to the emotions she read in those blue depths.

She blinked rapidly and prayed for breath.

His thumb traced the line of her lips with a gentle caress that sent ribbons of awareness snaking through her limbs. Mouth dry, she licked her lips, and the tip of her tongue touched his thumb. He inhaled sharply as if he'd been burned.

"Jesus, Meara," he whispered, "what are you doing to me?"

"No more than you've done to me," she answered, her voice a harsh, strained whisper.

He nodded thoughtfully and smoothed the pad of his thumb across her mouth again. She sighed and held perfectly still, imprinting the memory of his touch on her mind. She wanted to never forget this spellbound moment in time. She wanted to always be able to pull this night from the pages of her life and experience it again.

She wanted this moment to stretch into eternity and beyond.

And then he bent his head to claim her with a soul-searing kiss, and eternity no longer mattered. Nothing beyond this man and this moment mattered to her. Meara gave herself up to him. To his touch. His mouth on hers, his hands moving over her body, pulling her tightly to him, pressing his length to hers as if he could draw her inside him and hold her forever.

His tongue parted her lips, and at his first intimate caress, Meara sighed heavily and leaned into him. Wrapping her arms around his neck, she held on tightly, pulling his head down more firmly to hers.

He seemed to sense her hunger, and it fed his own. His arms became like iron bands around her. He tasted her depths, stroked her tongue with his, and groaned when her sighs brushed his cheek.

Conner couldn't hold her tightly enough. He couldn't invade her mouth deeply enough. He tasted her, explored her, and when she moaned gently, felt his body harden painfully. He ached to be buried inside her. To have her damp heat surround him. To lose himself in the magic that was Meara Simon.

She pressed into him, and he felt her hardened nipples brush across his chest. He lifted her off her feet; her bare toes moved against his shins. So small, he thought, even as he took her mouth more deeply. So small and soft. Supporting her with one strong arm, he moved his right hand around to cup her breast. The moment his fingers found her rigid nipple, she groaned aloud, shifting her body in his grip to give him access.

Tearing his mouth from hers, he sucked in a gulp of air, then turned his attentions to the line of her throat. She groaned again, louder this time, and one small corner of his brain was still rational enough to know that they couldn't be doing this out in the open, where anyone might look out a window and see them.

Jaw tight, he swung her into his arms and headed for the closest building that offered privacy. The barn. His long legs skirted the yard in a few quick steps. Even as he hurried though, Meara's mouth was trained on his neck and her lips and teeth moved over his skin like tiny branding irons, leaving a trail of singed flesh in their wake.

Inside the barn, he turned left quickly and headed for the tack room. His breathing hard and fast, his heart hammered in his chest. His body ached with a throbbing need, and his jeans strained tight across his manhood.

"Conner," she whispered brokenly, and her breath brushed across the base of his throat, teasing his blood into a boil. "Touch me there again. Just once."

He bit back a groan as he stepped into the tiny, enclosed tack room. "Not just once, Meara," he whispered, making the words a solemn vow. "Never just once."

Then he set her down on the narrow cot kept there for when the men were sitting up nights with a sick horse. She reached for his face, her hands smoothing over his jaw, cheekbones, and tracing lightly over the bridge of his nose and the contours of his mouth.

He turned his face into her hands, one after the other and kissed the palms, then lifted his own hands to cover her breasts. He cupped their fullness, his thumbs stroking back and forth across the rigid nipples, drawing her fine cotton nightgown over the sensitive tips until she was leaning into him, head thrown back, pushing her breasts into his touch.

It wasn't enough.

He had to taste her. Touch her. Explore her warmth with nothing between them but their own sighs. Conner felt just a little mad. As if the magic of the night had cast a spell over them both, hurtling them toward what had been inevitable since the first day of her arrival.

She scooted forward on the cot, toward him, into him. He knelt between her legs and she parted them further in her eagerness to be nearer to him.

Moonlight speared through the tiny window behind him, illuminating her in an otherworldly glow. The white of her nightgown shimmered in the silvery light, and her face seemed paler, softer, as if it was lit from within, like fine alabaster he'd once seen.

"Meara," he said on a groan, as her tongue darted out to lick dry lips.

"Oh aye, Conner," she whispered, twisting gently in his grasp. " 'Tis wonderful, this. I feel . . . I feel . . ." Her voice trailed off into nothingness, leaving only her soft gasps and moans to fill a strained silence.

His fingers tweaked at her nipples, tugging gently until she shivered with a need she didn't understand. He watched her face, saw the pleasure streak across her features and the wonder fill her eyes until she stared at him blankly, lost in a new world of sensation.

And suddenly, his own aching desire seemed less important to him than hers. That realization stunned him even as he shifted, turning, drawing her into his arms until he sat on the floor, his back braced against the cot, Meara in his lap.

"Why've you stopped?" she asked, focusing her passion-glazed eyes on his face. "Dear heaven, Conner, why've you stopped?"

Hell if he knew, Conner thought. She could have been his. He knew it. He could have taken her there, on a cot, in the barn of all places, and he hadn't. His body screamed with the agony of frustrated desire, and yet he knew he wouldn't take her like that. She deserved better from him..From anyone.

"Dear Saint Patrick," she muttered, dropping her head forward to rest against his shoulder. "My insides are as jittery as if there were bats in there, flappin' their wings like mad."

"I know," he told her and planted a kiss on top of her head.

"Then do somethin' about it, man," she groaned tightly. "You can't light a fire and then walk away. Can you?"

He couldn't walk now if there was a gun in his back, but he didn't say so.

"No," he said, looking down into those incredible green eyes of hers. He might spend another night in an agony of unfulfilled passion, but there was no reason to sentence Meara to that. The aching need she was feeling now was his fault. He'd pushed them both too close to the edge, and now there was a penance to pay. But this night, he'd pay it himself.

"I'll tend your fire, Meara," he said softly, even as his right hand swept down her leg and under the hem of her nightgown.

"Conner!" Eyes wide in shock, she demanded, "What d'ya think you're doin' man?" Her hands batted at him ineffectually while she tried to draw her knees up to her chest in instinctive protection.

"I'm going to send those bats in your belly somewhere else, Meara," he told her in a quiet, gentle tone just before he pressed his mouth to hers, stifling any further protest.

She moaned beneath him, her legs relaxing, her hands coming up to encircle his neck. He felt her surrender and moved to ease the ache he knew she was feeling. Up the length of her leg, across the inside of her thigh to the soft tangle of hair at her center.

Meara jumped in his arms and tried to scoot back, but his grip on her was tighter than the bonds of the church on a sinner.

No one had ever touched her so intimately before. She knew that instinctively despite a sketchy memory. This, she would have remembered. This, could not have been forgotten.

His fingertips brushed her most private spot, and spirals of pleasure danced in her veins. She sighed. Her body felt fluid, liquid. A dampness flowed from her in response to his touch, but she had no time for embarrassment.

He dipped one finger inside her and Meara's eyes flew open at the gentle invasion. She looked up into his gaze and saw tender understanding on his features as he slipped a second finger into her depths and pressed lightly on the walls of her womanhood.

Someone groaned and it was a moment before she realized that the sound had come from her. Her legs parted farther, almost of their own accord, inviting him deeper, closer. His fingers moved in and out of her body with a rhythm so like a heartbeat, she felt as if he was bringing life to long-dead limbs. And as his wonderful fingers teased her from within, his thumb began to stroke at a spot that was suddenly so sensitive, each touch sent jagged shards of sensation shooting throughout her body.

She couldn't lay still. She had to move. She had to reach something. What it was, she wasn't sure, but it was close. So close. Hovering just out of her grasp. Her hips rocked against his hand. She planted her feet on the floor and arched her body in time to his movements.

Someone whimpered, and again, she didn't realize at first that it was her own voice she was hearing. Meara didn't care, though. Nothing mattered except the touch of his hands and the incredible feelings growing and blossoming in her depths.

Vaguely, she heard him talking to her, whispering to her, encouraging her to "come with him." And at the moment, she would have gone anywhere he would lead. As long as he would promise to never stop touching her. To make these feelings go on forever and beyond.

And then even those half-formed thoughts scattered beneath the building need inside. She felt as though she was running up a steep hill. Her sides ached from the harsh breathing. Her limbs felt watery, without substance. And still, she climbed, hands outstretched, body taut as a bow.

Until at last, someone, she thought it was her, screamed as she reached the peak of the mountain only to find it was a cliff just before she eagerly jumped over the edge.

Conner held her gently while her body shimmered its release, and when at last she lay still again, he smoothed her nightgown modestly down over her legs. He prepared himself for the embarrassment he knew she would undergo now that the magic was over. She'd probably want to run off to her room and he'd have to let her go. Though his arms already ached at the thought of the emptiness she would leave behind.

Meara curled up into him, her face wreathed by a satisfied smile that surprised him. "By the Cross, Conner," she whispered, "I've never known such a feeling. My legs are wobbly, and even my toes are tingling."

A few more minutes, he figured, before she started thinking rationally and regretting the liberties she'd allowed him. Conner stared down into her eyes and felt the now familiar sensation of slipping into their cool, dark depths and wondered when it had happened that she had come to mean so much to him.

"Conner?" she whispered, shifting to sit upon his lap.

Here it comes, he thought, regret already stabbing through him. He wished it didn't have to be so. But he knew she'd now pull away from him and hide inside her own sense of shame. He took a breath, and released it before saying, "What is it?"

Meara tossed her hair back across her shoulders, looked deeply into his eyes and asked, "Can we do that again?"

Conner didn't know why he was surprised. Meara was unlike any woman he'd ever met. Naturally she wouldn't react as he'd expect.

"No," he said reluctantly, "we can't."

"Whyever not?"

"Because I'm not going to make love to you in a barn."

She shivered and her forest-green eyes looked suddenly darker. "Does it matter so much where we are? Are there rules about this kind of thing?"

Lord, she wasn't making this any easier. He wanted her more than he'd ever wanted anything in his life. If he gave in to the urges stampeding through him at the moment, he'd throw her down on the cot and bury himself so deeply inside her warmth that nothing and no one would ever be able to separate them.

But he wouldn't. Not like this. No, when they finally made love—and they damn well would—it would be something they would both remember forever. And blast it, a cot within whispering distance of a stable full of horses was *not* going to be part of that memory.

He tightened his arms around her and stood up, cradling her to his chest as he headed for the doorway.

"What are you doing?"

"Taking you to your bed," he said tightly.

Amazingly, she burrowed her head into the crook of his neck and kissed the base of his throat. "Ah yes, we'll be more comfortable there."

Conner's body hardened further—something he would have thought impossible a few minutes ago. "You're going to your bed. I'm going to mine."

"What?"

"It's better this way, Meara," he said and congratulated himself silently on squeezing the words out of a dry throat.

She pulled back from him as far as she was able and stared up at him in astonishment. "Better, is it?" Then she shoved futilely at his chest. "And you're the one to be decidin', I suppose, what's best and what's not." She shoved at him again. "Put me down, you great oaf."

He only held her more firmly and hurried his steps

across the yard. Keeping his voice low, he said, "As soon as we're inside, I'll put you down."

Of all the high-handed men! Furious, Meara grabbed the front of his shirt and, through the fabric, a fistful of chest hair, and yanked.

He stopped short and abruptly dropped her to her feet. "That hurt," he snarled.

"As it was meant to," she snapped, her voice an angry hush, mindful of the sleeping people nearby she'd no wish to wake.

"What the hell's wrong with you?" he demanded.

She looked up at him, his features hard in the moonlight. "I was just after thinking about the mistakes a woman can make."

Conner rubbed one hand across the back of his neck. "I knew you'd feel this way."

"Ah . . . and which way is that?" she asked, tossing her hair over her shoulder in an obvious huff.

"That what we did was a mistake."

"I didn't say that."

"That's why," Conner went on, ignoring her outburst, "we're not doing anything else tonight, Meara. When we make love, I want you to have a clear head, not one already clouded by passion."

Meara stared at him, eyes wide, mouth open in astonishment. "*When* we make love, is it? As sure of yourself as all that, are ya?"

He opened his mouth to speak, but she cut him off.

"So, you think your touch is so masterful that it wiped away me brain, leaving me nothing but a slobbering heap ready to lay me down at your feet?"

This wasn't going at all as he'd expected. "That's not what I said."

"As good as," she countered, tossing her hair back over her shoulder again, fighting with the breeze rising from the lake. "I'll have ya know Meara Simon is no woman to be trifled with! If you aren't the prize of all prizes," she muttered darkly.

"I'm doing this for you," he reminded her. Although he was discovering that doing the gentlemanly thing wasn't as fine a notion as he'd been told.

"And now you're waitin' for me thanks, is that it?"

"I didn't say that, either."

"You've said more than enough this night, Conner," she snapped, one bare foot tapping frantically against the dirt. Shaking her head, she went on muttering to herself. "If that's not just like a man—speak his piece and expect the rest of the world to agree quietly and go away."

"Meara . . ."

"Enough!" she snapped, holding one hand high. Then, she set her hands at her hips and leaned in toward him. "Do ya know, Conner, another of my mother's sayings has just come to my poor, addled mind as I look at you," she said, raking her gaze up and down the length of him.

She looked furious, so he braced himself, arms crossed over his chest. "What is it this time?"

Meara lifted her chin, locked her gaze with his, and quietly said, "Do not mistake a goat's beard for a fine stallion's tail."

That said, she spun about on her bare feet, stomped to the house, and let herself inside. Conner, alone in the moonlight, was left to wonder whether she'd just called him a goat's face or a horse's ass.

CHAPTER THIRTEEN

Meara stood with Luke outside the schoolhouse and watched as the other children hurried up the front steps. But Luke was dawdling.

"You'd best be gettin' on in there now," Meara told him, running one hand across his hair to smooth it into place. "You don't want to be late."

He shot a sideways glance at the whitewashed building, then squinted up at her. "I was thinkin' maybe I ought not to go today. I should maybe stay at the ranch. Be a help to Conner." He looked down at the new pair of shoes he was wearing. "Got to pay him back for these here extra shoes."

Meara shook her head slightly. The boy had a powerful streak of pride in him. "I told you, Luke, Conner said 'twas his mistake only buying you one pair of shoes. He said every man needs at least two. One for good and one for working."

He tipped his head back to look at her again. "You sure?"

"I am."

"Well, that must be right then," he allowed, although his expression said clearly this made no sense to him.

Silently, Meara gave thanks that it was Conner James the boy had landed with. No matter how angry she might be at him right now, she had to admit he was a good man. And after all, "As the old cock crows, the young cock learns." With Conner around to see to him, Luke Banyan would grow into a a fine man.

"Now off with ya," she told him, giving him a soft swat on the behind to get him moving. "There'll be plenty of work left to do on the ranch when you get home."

"Yes'm," Luke mumbled, and with his head hanging, he shuffled up the steps and into the schoolhouse like a condemned man climbing the gallows.

The door had no sooner closed behind him when Meara turned for the buckboard she'd driven into town. Truly, she was becoming quite a hand at driving herself. So long as she didn't have to bother with the horse.

"Good morning," a deep voice came from nearby, and Meara half turned in response.

Robert Carlisle strode up to her side, the gold watch chain stretched across his belly winking in the early morning sun.

She'd not had much sleep the night before, lying awake thinking of Conner and all of the other things she should have said to him, so she was in no mood to be dealing with the likes of Robert Carlisle. "Good morning," she replied and turned back to the buckboard. Setting one foot on the hub of the giant wheel, she pulled herself up onto the bench seat and gathered the reins.

"I wanted to apologize for my behavior the other afternoon in Virginia City," Carlisle said, leaning one hand on the front kickboard.

Meara looked at him askance. The words were right, but the expression on his face belied them. There was no hangdog look about him. No trace of regret or contrition. So what was he up to, then?

"You still know nothing about your past, I understand?"

She frowned at him. "Now how would you be knowing that?"

He shrugged. "Small towns, Miss Simon—or may I call you Meara? I'm afraid there are very few secrets kept in a place this size."

Meara frowned and tried to look away from his eyes. But they seemed to hold hers. Much as a snake's would hold a rabbit's.

He reached further across the kickboard and gave her knee a pat.

Meara shivered and shifted further away.

"I've told everyone in town, you know," he went on, "that I was wrong to suspect you of being a kept woman."

She only stared at him.

He smiled and she shivered again, as though someone had stepped on her grave. "I'm sure it's all perfectly innocent," Carlisle added, "and I've told *everyone* that the—unsavory rumors, shall we say, about a pretty young woman living on a ranch with seven men and a boy are simply not true."

She looked into his pale eyes and found emptiness. This then explained why even Mrs. Higgins at the Mercantile was less than friendly with her this morning. Suddenly, Meara felt the stares of unseen townspeople boring into her back. And the knowledge that only the night before she'd behaved as brazenly as this spalpeen was suggesting didn't make her sit any easier.

But she'd not give him the satisfaction of seeing her squirm. Meara finally found her tongue. "You've a black heart and a mind to match, Mr. Carlisle," she said, and tightened her grip on the reins. "Mind you don't 'apologize' to Conner in the same fashion as you have me. You'll find him, I think, not so forgiving as I."

With that, she smacked the reins over the horse's broad back. The buckboard lurched away, Carlisle jumping for safety.

* * *

Later that afternoon, Luke was a bundle of energy. He helped the ranch hands as they worked one of the mustangs in the corral and went about his chores with a spring in his step and a look to his face that said his burdens had been lifted.

Meara paused on her way to the house and balanced a basketful of clean laundry on her hip. Shielding her eyes with her free hand, she looked at the boy, perched on the top rail of the fence and smiled to herself.

"What's got into him today?"

She stiffened slightly as Conner's voice came from directly behind her. Since the night before, when she'd run for the house, leaving him alone in the night, Meara had done her utmost to avoid him and had been surprisingly successful. But then, she had a feeling her success was due partly to the fact that he was trying to avoid her, as well.

Which had made it easy to keep from telling him about her encounter with Robert Carlisle.

He took the basket from her and rather than fight him for it like a child, she let it go.

"That kid's been on my heels for hours," Conner commented. "This is the first time all afternoon I haven't turned around and felt him run into me. He's talked my ear off and badgered the men until they're near ready to gag him. And he's shown off his new 'work' shoes at least a dozen times."

She smiled. "He's happy to be out of school and proud to bustin' of those shoes."

"Yeah, I know. He told me," Conner said, stepping up beside her, his gaze, too, locked on the boy across the wide yard. "But it's more than that. There's no shadows under his eyes today. Kid always looked like he was ready to drop. But today, he's got more get-up in him than most of the men."

True, she thought, and realized that she hadn't even

noticed the difference in the boy until that moment. And she was fairly certain of what had caused the change.

"Sleep," she said softly.

"Huh?"

She shot Conner a quick look from the corner of her eye. "He was finally able to sleep last night. For the first time in Heaven knows how long."

"What are you talkin' about?"

"He's been plagued with nightmares. I heard him last night, whimpering in his sleep."

Conner set the basket of laundry down onto the sparse grass, then straightened up and looked at her. "Nightmares?"

"Terrible ones," she said softly, still looking at Luke's back. "His father, beating him with a thick belt while he cowered, helplessly trying to duck the blows."

His voice tight, Conner said, "When I bathed him that first day, I saw the scars. I asked him about 'em and he wouldn't talk to me. Wouldn't say where they came from." Conner lifted one shoulder in a half shrug. "Until that time in the corral."

She remembered that day well.

"How'd you get him to tell you about the beatings?" Conner asked.

Without thinking, she answered him truthfully. "He didn't."

"Well then, how'd you know about it?"

"I saw it happening. In his dream."

Conner moved to stand in front of her, blocking her view of Luke and practically forcing her to look at him, instead. "You saw his dream?"

She flushed. She felt the heat of it sting her neck and cheeks as the color rushed beneath her skin. "Aye, I did."

"How?"

"I don't know," she snapped, shaking her head. "I was comforting him and suddenly I was there. With him."

His gaze narrowed. "Been in any other dreams lately?"

She met his stare and nodded. "A few."

He inhaled sharply. "Then it did happen," he muttered, more to himself than to her.

"Aye, it did."

"How the hell did you get in my dreams? And how can you remember them if they *are* my dreams?"

"I don't know," she snapped. "Do you not see that I've no idea how this is happening?"

He grabbed her shoulders, his fingers biting into the flesh of her arms. But what he would have said, she'd never know, for at that moment, Tucker Hanks rode into the yard at a high gallop and drew his horse to a stop near them.

"Trouble, boss," he said, jerking his head in the direction of the main gate where a stranger was climbing awkwardly off a horse. Tucker, too, stepped down before continuing. "Met this fella a mile or so back." He shot a quick, sympathetic look at Meara before turning back to Conner. "Says he's got business here."

Meara swallowed hard. The foreman was rarely without a smile, and the shadowed worry in his eyes now was enough to let her know that her world was about to shatter.

"What kind of business?" Conner asked, and watched as the stranger turned in a slow circle, his gaze raking across the buildings and the ranch yard before coming to a stop on Meara. A curl of foreboding slithered up Conner's spine.

"Personal, he says." Tucker shook his head and looked like he wanted to spit.

"Meara, darlin'!" the stranger shouted and broke into a long-legged run across the yard.

"What in heaven?" she muttered, moving closer to Conner's side as the man drew near.

"Do you know him?" Conner asked quickly.

"I've never seen him before this," she answered.

"Meara, me own sweet love," the stranger yelled as he

grabbed at her only to be stopped by Conner stepping in front of her. The man gave her a shamefaced look and shook his head slowly. "Have ya no hug of welcome for me?"

Meara's ears were ringing and her throat felt as dry as the road to hell. She felt the stares of every person on the ranch as she peeked around from behind Conner's broad back to ask, "And why would I be welcomin' you?"

The stranger's shock of dark auburn hair fell across his forehead as he yanked off a well-worn cap and clenched it between two huge, freckled hands. His features were pale and well-defined. Two sapphire-blue eyes looked at her sadly and his full lips twisted into a grimace of disappointment.

"Then 'tis true," he said at last, with another slow shake of his shaggy head. "What I heard in your fine little village a short time ago. Your mind is gone."

Taking umbrage at this, despite the misgiving blossoming within her, Meara stepped out from behind Conner and snapped, "Me mind is right where it's supposed to be," she told him. "As am I."

"Ya belong with me, love," he told her firmly.

"And who might *you* be?" she demanded, though she feared she knew what his answer was going to be.

"Well now," he said with a tilt of his lips, "I *might* be Peter the Apostle. But I *am* Mick Reilly." When no one spoke, he added, "Your husband."

Her world *did* shatter. She heard the jagged pieces of it hit the earth around her feet. Her brain swam, her stomach churned, and she fought down a rising tide of hysteria.

Here it was then. What she'd been waiting for. Her past had arrived and with it, a profound sense of loss. A husband. But she'd been so sure there was no man in her life before Conner. Blindly, she glanced down at her left hand. No ring rested there, nor was there a paler circle of flesh to indicate there had *ever* been a ring. And yet, here was himself, Mick Reilly, claiming her as his own and she with no way to disprove him.

Meara swayed into Conner, and he caught her instinctively, though he wasn't sure his legs would support either of them. Damn it, he hadn't expected this. It had been weeks with no word. Not a hint of a family—a husband searching for her. He'd about convinced himself that they would never learn the secrets in Meara's past.

A cold fist squeezed his heart and a heaviness filled his soul. Briefly, he considered picking her up, throwing her on a horse, and riding off with her. This was a big country and Conner knew more hideouts and tucked-away valleys than most men could dream of. He could take Meara where no one would ever find them again.

But it wouldn't be good enough. Conner knew Meara well enough to know that she'd never leave with him if she thought she was legally bound to another. He would just have to find some way out of this mess. He just needed to think. To plan.

But there was no time now because Mick Reilly's gaze was shifting to meet his.

"And you'll be the fella I heard about in town," the Irishman said softly, dangerously. "Conner James, is it?"

He stiffened, as if readying for a fight. "It is."

The interloper's sharp blue eyes swept the ranch yard, taking in Tucker Hanks, whose perpetually smiling face was now frozen into a mask of displeasure, the men walking toward them from the corral and finally, the boy who'd protectively planted himself in front of Meara. Looking back at Conner, Reilly said, "I've seen your kind before, boyo. You with your money and your fine homes."

Conner said quietly, "You know nothing about me."

"Do ya make a habit of sullyin' other men's wives?" Reilly asked. "Or is it only mine you've ruined?"

In less time than it took to think about it, Conner's fist plowed into Reilly's square jaw. His auburn head snapped back, but like an oak in a high wind, the man swayed slightly, but didn't fall. Watching Conner speculatively, he rubbed his jaw with one hand, then tossed his cap to the ground and lifted both fists, a smile on his broad face.

"Stop it," Meara yelled, stepping past Luke and ignoring the interested onlookers surrounding them. She deliberately stepped between the two men and glared at first one, then the other of them. "You'll stop this now, the both of ya."

"Keep out of this, Meara," Conner said tightly, wanting nothing more than to take another shot at felling the man threatening everything he had come to hold dear.

"Aye darlin'," Mick told her. "Do as your fancy man says. This won't take long."

"Fancy man?" Meara smacked the Irishman's chest with the flat of her hand. "You keep a civil tongue in that head of yours. And don't be tellin' me what to do, either of ya," she said, a thread of steel in her voice. "Fightin's not going to get the answers I want to hear, so there'll be none of it."

"Mind your tongue, woman!" Mick bellowed, and Conner tensed in response.

"You're no husband of mine," she snapped quickly, "if ya think I'm one to be ordered about like a dog."

"Meara, step back," Conner said.

"Yeah, Miss Meara," Tucker added as he and Hobart stepped in close behind their boss. "We can take care of this right now."

Grub quietly drew Luke to one side, out of harm's way.

"So that's how it's to be, eh?" Reilly asked, his gaze shooting to the men flanked behind his opponent. "First you use me wife and next, you'll have me set upon by your hired thugs?"

Meara flashed a quick look at Conner and saw his lips tighten into a grim slash of anger. A muscle in his jaw twitched dangerously as he glanced at his men.

"Keep out of this," he said tightly. "All of you. This is between me and Reilly here."

Judging from the murderous expression on Conner's face, Meara knew that if these men fought, only one of them would be walking away from the battle. And though she appreciated Conner's wanting to defend her, she needed to know the truth about Mick Reilly and whatever he could tell her of her past.

"You're all wrong," Meara spoke up into the tense silence. "This is between the three of us. And before there's a fist thrown, there'll be some talking."

Conner looked from her to the man who was claiming her and felt his insides tighten into a mass of knots. Damn it, he wouldn't lose her like this. With no warning. With no goodbye. If it was the last thing he did, he'd keep her at the ranch. With him.

But what if she was really married to Reilly? his mind whispered. What then? Would any of them have a choice in what to do?

He banished the idea as soon as it formed. He'd worry about that when he had to. For now, he too wanted to hear what Reilly had to say. And he wanted to know how a man could lose a wife like Meara and not bother searching for her.

"Let's go inside," he said quietly, keeping a wary eye on Mick Reilly.

"Aye," the other man agreed. "Let's have this finished and done so me wife and I can be on our way."

Conner's hands fisted helplessly at his sides. How could he let her go with this man? Hell. How could he let her go at all?

He kept those thoughts to himself and stepped aside to let Meara lead the way into the kitchen, taking care to be the one behind her. For as long as he was able, he'd keep Mick Reilly as far from her as possible.

*   *   *

Meara stared at the burly man sitting at the table with all the ease of the Pope himself and tried desperately to find some sense of recognition for him. But there was nothing. No bits and pieces. No tantalizing swirl of memory to try and grab onto. 'Twas as if she was seeing him for the first time.

But that couldn't be true. Why would a man pretend to be a husband when most men ran from marriage like scalded dogs?

She took a seat at the side of the table and realized that this was the first time since she'd come into this house that she didn't feel at her ease.

She also realized that this could be the last time she would sit in this homey kitchen. That thought brought a pang of regret so sharp it sliced her insides and she wanted to weep for it.

How could she leave, though, with a man she didn't know? How could she go and sleep in a stranger's bed when her heart told her that she belonged with Conner? On the other hand, how could she stay where her heart demanded if in the eyes of the law *and* the Church, she was another man's wife?

Her head hurt.

Mick Reilly slurped at his tea, grabbed up a slice of fresh bread and took a huge bite. As he chewed, he looked around him at the still-splotchy walls.

" 'Tis a fine place you've landed in, Meara darlin'," he said.

"Stop callin' me darlin'."

He winked at her. "As you say, me love."

Meara blew out a breath that sent one long curl flying up to the top of her head.

Conner pushed his chair back, the legs screeching loudly against the floor. "If you're her husband where the hell have you been for the last few weeks?" he demanded. "Why weren't you searching for Meara?"

"I'll ask the questions, Conner," she said and placed

both hands on the table top in front of her. Reilly shot Conner a victorious glance that faded when she ordered, "Answer his question, boyo."

Mick took another slurp then set his cup down before saying, "I've had a bit of trouble here lately, love. A small misunderstanding with the local constabulary."

"The law?" Conner asked.

"Aye," Mick said without bothering to look at the man. "In a small town a day or two's ride from here. There was a fight, and bein' the new man in town, I was blamed." He shook his head like a man burdened with the world's troubles. "But isn't that always the way, then? A poor Irishman tryin' to make his way . . ."

"So you were in jail," Conner said.

"Aye." Reilly leaned back in his chair and stretched his legs out ahead of him.

"Well, that's a fine thing," Meara snapped, and moved her feet away from the man's muddy boots.

"As soon as they let me go, I looked for ya, love," Mick was saying and even snaked one hand out, trying to take hers in his. Meara moved away. He frowned and sighed. "But ya weren't at the camp we'd made and no one had seen a sign of ya."

"And where was this camp?" Conner demanded shortly.

Mick smiled at him. "I don't rightly recall. 'Tis such a big country, and I'm but a poor Irishman lost in its wilds."

"You don't believe him," Conner asked, his gaze locked on Meara, "do you?"

Lord knew she didn't want to, but all she said was, "It *is* a big country, Conner."

Mick smiled again. " 'Ta, love."

"So you're saying she wandered off," Conner said, moving to stand directly behind Meara.

"Either that," Mick said with a pointed glance at him, "or you took her."

Conner surged toward him, but Meara grabbed his fist and held on.

"He took me nowhere," Meara said flatly. "I fell through his roof and landed here all on me own."

Reilly's dark eyebrows lifted into high arches. "Through the roof, is it? And how did you manage that?"

"Don't you want to know if your *wife* was hurt?" Conner asked.

Reilly cleared his throat. "Can't I see for meself that she's as fine as a spring rain?"

"This is ridiculous," Conner snapped. "Why the hell are you here and who the hell are you?"

"I'm her husband," Mick countered. "Just who are you?"

"Someone who cares a damn sight more for her than *you* do," Conner shouted.

"When were we married?" Meara demanded, shouting to be heard over the both of them.

With a last sneer at Conner, Mick turned his charm on Meara. "Weren't we married the minute we set foot off the boat from Galway?" he said. "Near two years ago now, saints be praised."

"Two years," Meara murmured, and felt Conner squeeze her hand briefly. Two years of her life spent with this man? Why didn't she remember? Why couldn't she at least have a smidgen of an image of the man she'd slept with and lived with for two long years? Sweet Saint Bridget, she'd been with Conner a few weeks only and yet she remembered nearly every moment she'd spent with him.

About Mick Reilly, though, there was nothing save the gray fog she was all too accustomed to.

"We're supposed to take your word for that, are we?" Conner snarled his question at the man, and even Meara felt the tightly coiled rage humming through him. "You say you were married two years ago, and I say, 'Oh, well then, that's fine, take her and I wish you well'? Is that what's supposed to happen here?"

"Why would I lie?" He shrugged and smiled.

"Indeed," Meara wondered aloud. "Why would ya?"

It might have been her imagination, but she thought she saw Mick's complexion flush a bit. As if he were uneasy about something. But then the moment was gone and he was standing up.

"Enough of this, darlin'. Let's be on our way."

"She's not going anywhere with you," Conner muttered.

"You'd try to keep a man from his wife?" Reilly countered.

"We don't know she's your wife."

"Haven't I just said as much?"

"Not good enough," Conner said shortly.

"Then it's back to fists, is it?" Reilly asked with a grin before spitting into his hand and rubbing his palms together. "As you wish, Yank. I've nothing against taking a minute or two to teach you the way of things."

"Conner," Meara said and turned her back on Reilly, effectively dismissing him.

"No," Conner said, sparing a quick glance at the man behind her. "I'm not going to believe him just because he says it's so. I won't let you leave with a man we know nothing about."

"You know all you need to know, boyo," Reilly told him.

"Not by half," Conner told him tightly.

Meara laid one hand on his arm and looked up at him. "If what he's sayin' is true . . ."

"Where's his proof?" Conner demanded. "If you're married, he'll have a license and a certificate. *Something* to back him up."

"But . . ." She bit down on her bottom lip, and Conner's insides tightened as he fought to convince her to stay with him.

"For all we know," he said, "this bastard's heard about us looking for your family and is just trying to get some money out of me."

"Here now!" Mick shouted.

"But, Conner," Meara said as if the other man hadn't spoken. "What if he is telling the truth?"

"Do you think he is?"

"I don't know."

"Do you remember him?" He had to ask and hope like hell that she'd recalled nothing of Mick Reilly.

"No," she said quickly with a shake of her head. "Not a bit."

Conner released a pent-up breath and nodded. Then he asked the only important question here and held his breath, waiting for the answer. "Do you want to go with him?"

She glanced over her shoulder at the man who would claim her, then turned back to look at him again. "No, 'tis the truth, I don't."

"Then you're not going anywhere," Conner said with quiet determination.

"It's not your business, Yank," Reilly blustered.

Conner stared him down, not budging an inch. "You'll need proof before Meara goes anywhere with you, Reilly."

"Proof?" The man stepped out from behind the table and walked toward them. "You have the proof of my word, and that's all you'll be gettin' from me."

"It's not enough," Conner ground out.

"We'll see what your village sheriff thinks about you keepin' another man's wife."

"Guess we will at that." Conner folded his arms across his chest and braced his feet wide apart. "You'll find that western sheriffs don't think kindly of men who try to take advantage of women."

To Meara, Reilly said, "Come with me, darlin'. Don't make me force ya."

"You'll force me nowhere, Mick Reilly," she said calmly, though Conner felt her tremble beside him. That tremor only steeled Conner's resolve. He wouldn't be handing her over to some stranger. Not while there was a breath left in his body.

"We'll see about that as well, then," Reilly said and strode to the door, his muddy boots leaving clumps of dirt in his wake. He opened the door and paused for one last look at the two people. "You've not seen the last of me," he promised.

Reilly had no sooner closed the door behind him than it swung wide again. Luke raced into the kitchen. He paused, shot a look at Conner, then skirted past him, and headed straight for Meara. She staggered slightly as the boy wrapped his arms around her waist and held on tight. "Grub says that fella come to take you away," he whispered fiercely, strengthening his grip on her. "You ain't leavin', are ya, Meara?" Luke asked, his voice muffled against her dress.

Meara's heart broke at the shuddering grip the boy had on her. She looked from the boy's bent head to Conner's clear blue gaze. In his eyes, she read the stark emptiness she knew was reflected in her own. She wanted to reassure the boy, to promise she would never leave. But she couldn't give him that. Instead, she stroked Luke's hair gently, and said only, "I'm not leavin' yet, darlin'. Not today, anyway."

At that last, Conner's jaw tightened again, but there was nothing she could do about it. After all, if there was proof that Mick Reilly was her husband, she'd have little choice in the matter. She'd have to leave this place and go off with a man who meant nothing to her, while leaving the one man who made her heart sing with just a look.

Slowly, Grub and the ranch hands stepped into the kitchen. Tucker nodded at Meara grimly, then looked at Conner. "You want me to follow him, boss?"

"Yeah," Conner said and pointed at one of the other men. "And take Tommy with you. See where Reilly goes, who he talks to, and bring me word."

"Yessir," Tucker said with a sharp nod. Before he turned to leave, he paused and smiled at Meara. "Don't you worry, ma'am, the boss'll get this all straightened out."

She forced a smile because she could see that they were all doing their best. But Meara's insides were cold and she was afraid she'd never be warm again.

CHAPTER FOURTEEN

A few hours later, Tucker Hanks rode into the yard and went straight for the corral where Conner was working one of the mares. Instantly, Conner walked to meet him.

"Where'd he go?"

Tucker took his hat off and wiped sweat from his brow with his shirt sleeve. "He's stayin' in a room over the saloon. Didn't see him talk to nobody. Just sat down at a table in the corner with a bottle and a glass."

Grimly, Conner nodded. It would have been too easy to find out anything this early. "Where's Tommy?"

Tucker gave him a half smile. "Left him sittin' in the alley alongside the saloon. He's lookin' through a dirty window, wishin' he was inside with a beer."

"Good. Keep watchin' him."

"Whatever you say, boss," Tucker said, then added, "But what exactly are you hopin' to find?"

"I don't know," Conner told him and shifted his gaze to look up at the stand of pines on the mountain behind them. Usually, just looking at the dark green splash of color backed by the brilliant blue sky calmed him down. Not today. "There's got to be something, though. A man doesn't just lose a woman like Meara."

"Hell no," Tucker agreed. "If she was mine, I'd tie a

bell around her neck just so's I'd always know where she was."

Conner laughed shortly despite the emptiness yawning open inside him. "Tuck," he said, "you ever tie a bell around a woman like Meara and she'll hang you with it."

Tucker gave a long, low whistle, then smiled wickedly. "I figure the hangin' just might be worth it."

"You're right there," Conner said and knew it for the truth. *Anything* was worth having Meara a part of his life. Absolutely anything.

Uncomfortable with the harsh, pained expression on his employer's face, Tucker looked away. "I'll, uh, get on back to town. Spell Tommy."

"Yeah," Conner said grimly. "If you need a couple more of the boys to trade off with you, send word."

"Yessir." Tucker swung aboard his mount, gathered up the reins, then looked down at Conner briefly. "Don't worry boss. Reilly won't be able to change the part in his hair without us knowin' about it."

Conner nodded and stared after his foreman long after the dust had settled behind him.

Late that night, Conner was exhausted. He'd worked himself and the men harder than usual all afternoon in an attempt to keep from thinking. It hadn't worked.

His mind raced constantly with visions there was no escaping. Again and again, he saw Meara leaving the ranch, her tears streaking her cheeks as Mick Reilly dragged her away. Or worse, the images of Mick Reilly running his big freckled hands over Meara's body.

Viciously, he rubbed his hands over his face, wishing he could wipe away his thoughts as easily. But there was no peace to be found. Moving through the dark, quiet ranch house, Conner walked straight down the long hall to his office. Flopping down onto his leather chair, he lifted his legs to the corner of his desk and crossed his booted ankles. He reached up, yanked off his hat, tossed it at a wall peg, and missed, the hat falling to the floor. He let it lay and turned his gaze to the cluttered desktop. He knew there was paperwork to be done, but he didn't know if he could summon the heart to deal with it. Wearily, he dropped his legs to the floor, grabbed up a match from a dish beside the kerosene lamp and lit it. The tiny flame sputtered into life and as he reached for the chimney on the lamp, he paused, his gaze landing on the ivy plant in its white china bowl.

It was back again.

No matter how many times he carried it out of his office, Meara only returned it. He had even begun to like the look of the blasted plant, though tomorrow, he would move it again just so she could bring it back.

Tomorrow.

He stared at the waxy, shiny green leaves and wondered how many more tomorrows he and Meara had together. He continued to stare at the damn plant until the match he held burned down to heat up his fingers. Then he jumped up, waved it out and tossed the dead match onto the desktop.

Together.

He and Meara.

Meara.

Invading his life. His dreams. Meara crowding his mind until he could think of nothing else but her. And now he might very well be about to lose her forever. Surrendering to an impulse, he walked out of the office to the foot of the stairs. Gripping the polished, gleaming newel post, he stared up into the darkness of the second floor, letting her image rise up in his brain.

Meara laughing. Smiling. Kissing him. Opening her body to him and convulsing in his arms as satisfaction rippled through her.

His body hard and unyielding, he climbed the stairs quietly and walked down the length of the hall until he was outside her bedroom. He laid the flat of his hand on the door and looked down at the glass doorknob.

Emotions crowded inside his heart and mind, each of them appearing and disappearing so quickly, he hardly had time to identify them before a new one had taken its place. He wanted her more than ever—*needed* her more than he ever had before.

And he couldn't have her. Not now. Not when she must be feeling overwhelmed by the events of the day. Not when neither of them knew if she was another man's wife.

Everything within him roared into denial at that thought. He wouldn't believe it. Not unless Reilly presented some proof that he couldn't ignore. Meara couldn't belong to another man. Not when Conner was only just realizing how very much she meant to him.

He let his hand fall from the door panel as he took a hard step back. Then quickly, before his resolve disappeared, he went to his own room.

Meara sat in the darkness, breath held, gaze locked on her bedroom door. She'd heard him approach. She'd sensed him pause. Now, she waited.

She yearned for him. She wanted nothing more than to be held by him, cradled against his broad chest with his strong arms wrapped protectively around her. Yet at the same time, she knew that once they were together, comfort would soon turn to something more. Something that she dare not even consider until she knew for sure if Mick Reilly was indeed her husband.

What a shameless thing she was, Meara thought, for wanting Conner so badly her body cried for his lack. She called on all the saints she could think of for the strength to resist him should he open her door. And yet a small corner of her heart silently prayed that the knob would turn and Conner would appear in the splash of moonlight.

Then she heard him walk away, and though she knew she should be relieved, it wasn't tears of joy raining down her face.

Mick Reilly had done his work well. It seemed he had spread his story from one end of Nevada to the other.

Within two days, they were the talk of the territory.

People from High Timber streamed to the ranch on one pretext or another. They looked at horses they had no interest in buying, dawdling for hours. Silently, they refused to leave until they'd at least caught a glimpse of the *Scarlet Woman* in their midst.

Meara felt herself flushing almost continuously. The men's gazes moved over her like dozens of pairs of hands. And the women looked at her as though she were a rabid dog that should be shot, but as it was so fascinating to observe, they weren't quite ready to kill it yet.

Shopkeepers had presented bills to Conner, demanding immediate payment, saying they'd no wish to do business with a man who would hold another's wife captive. Meara saw what it took for Conner to remain calm, to keep from hitting the very men he needed to do business with to survive. She listened to him explain the situation and saw that none of the townspeople were convinced.

For two years, they'd listened to Robert Carlisle insist Conner had cheated him out of his ranch. Now, there were some hinting that perhaps Carlisle had been right. After all, a man who uses another man's woman wouldn't be above cheating yet another man out of his home.

Meara felt Conner's frustration and shared it. If only she could remember something. Anything. But her mind remained a blank but for the knowledge that her presence might cost Conner the thing he held most dear.

Now, as she stepped down from the buckboard and adjusted Luke's collar before he went to school, Meara bit her lip as a woman passed her, holding her skirt to one side, as if brushing the hem against Meara would dirty the fabric.

It wasn't easy, remaining a lady when all and sundry thought you a whore.

She stiffened her spine and lifted her chin haughtily. She'd not give those peeping at her from behind their curtains the satisfaction of seeing her bowed and beaten. Which was exactly the reason she'd given Conner when he'd offered to have someone else drive Luke to school.

"Meara," Luke said for what had to be the thousandth time in the last two days, "you ain't really going nowhere with that fella, are ya?"

They'd seen no more of Mick Reilly at the ranch, so apparently, he had no "proof" of their marriage to show. And since she'd remembered nothing of the man in the last two days, she had no intention of taking his word for anything. So she could honestly answer, "No, love, I'm not."

"Good, 'cause I don't like him any," Luke said. "He's got mean eyes. They don't smile when his face does."

Truer words were never spoken.

"Don't you be worryin' over that now," Meara said. "You must do well in school, all right?"

"Do I hafta go?"

"Aye, ya do." She smiled to soften the sentence, but he knew it was no use to argue the point.

She watched him reluctantly shuffle off toward the schoolhouse and after he went inside, Meara turned for the shop closest to her. The bakery. But even as she started for the door, the proprietor slapped a "closed" sign in the window and turned the lock.

Meara sucked in a breath and felt like the pariah she was. Had it only been four days ago that she'd passed a few lovely minutes chatting with Agnes Weatherby in her bakery? And why was it people were always so willing to believe the worst in their neighbors?

Shaking her head sadly, Meara walked down the

boardwalk, her heels clicking against the wood planks. She tried to ignore the fact that no one wished her a good morning as she passed and none of the men tipped their hats to her. But she wouldn't allow them to beat her down. She'd done nothing wrong—that she knew of. And as for that one night with Conner in the barn . . . well, perhaps she shouldn't be thinking of that right now.

Steeling herself for what might be another dismissal. Meara stopped at the Mercantile and hesitantly pushed the door open. The bell over the door bounced and clanged. Several heads turned at the sound and almost as one, the women in the place sniffed and averted their gazes.

Before Meara had time to walk to the counter, the other customers in the shop had streamed out of the place as if running from a bad smell.

Dora Higgins's cheeks were dotted with bright splotches of red and she had a hard time looking Meara in the eye. Sad to think that here, too, she would be unwelcome. She'd begun to think of Dora as a friend. "Perhaps I'd better go."

Instantly, Dora blurted, "You'll do no such thing." She took a breath and went on through gritted teeth. "I'm sorry for how they acted, Meara. Sorry and mad. In fact, I'm so darn angry, I wish I could swear."

From his perch behind the counter, Eli told his wife comfortingly, "I'll do it for ya later."

Meara sighed inwardly in relief. So the high color on Dora's cheeks wasn't embarrassment, but fury. Somehow, she felt a bit better knowing she had at least *one* friend in town. Laying a slip of paper on the counter, she said, "I've a list here, if you don't mind . . ."

"Mind?" Dora asked and patted her hand briefly. "That's what we're here for, isn't that right, Eli?"

"Well," the skeletal man said, "we sure ain't here to have to listen to that bunch of harpies that just left. I'd thank ya for scarin' 'em off, Meara," he added, "if I wasn't so blamed tired."

"This is just terrible, all of it," Dora went on, measuring out white sugar into a brown paper sack. "I'm so ashamed of folks around here, I could just spit."

"I'll do that for ya, too," Eli assured her.

Meara smiled halfheartedly.

"It ain't Christian," Dora said huffily, "driving a man out of business this way."

"What?" Meara asked.

Eli shot her a fast look then said, "Now, Dora . . ."

"Don't you 'now, Dora' me," his wife said, sending him a glare that had him scooting to the far side of his chair. "This whole town should be ashamed of itself."

"Driving him out of business?" Meara asked. "Conner, you mean?"

"Of course." Dora folded the top down on the bag, then turned to shelves to fill the rest of Meara's order. Quickly, efficiently, she moved back and forth, setting tins and jars onto the counter. "No one but us will do business with him, you see."

"But how will that . . ." Meara was confused.

"A man has to be able to buy feed and grain for his animals. And he'll need the blacksmith from time to time."

"But surely—"

"He needs to be able to sell his horses, and no one from around here will be buying. And, too, this year, Conner'd planted a crop of wheat that he'd planned to mill and sell here in town." Dora shook her head. "Poor man. It's just not fittin' what folks around here are doing."

Meara'd had no idea. Conner had said nothing about any of this. "What about Virginia City?" she asked, looking from Dora to Eli and back again. "Couldn't he do business there instead?"

"In spring and summer, yes," Dora told her gently as

she boxed Meara's order. "But in the fall and winter, the passes are heavily snowed and usually closed. And without selling his crop and animals, I doubt he'll last until next spring."

Because of her, Meara thought. Though no one here was saying it out loud, this was all her fault. If she'd never come to Conner's ranch, he'd be fine. Now, because he was keeping her safe from a man neither of them trusted, his home was in danger.

She couldn't let this happen to him. She wouldn't stand by and watch him lose the only home he'd ever had. Not when she knew how much the ranch meant to him.

"Meara?" Dora asked. "You all right?"

"I will be," she answered softly, and reached for the box of supplies. Lifting it, she turned for the door, already planning what she would do to settle this matter.

Luke waited until Meara had turned around, then he scooted back down the school steps and dashed behind the edge of the building. He couldn't go in there and listen to that boney old man talk about kings and such when Meara might be going away. He had to do something. He had to help. Somehow.

Heading for the saloon, Luke kept to the backs of the buildings so no one would see him. All he had to do was find Tucker. Then he could help the foreman keep watch. He had to help. He couldn't lose Meara. She was the closest Luke had ever come to having a mother. His own ma had died birthing him, something his pa had never let him forget. And until coming to Conner James's ranch, Luke had never known what it was to have a female to fuss over you. He *liked* it when she ruffled his hair. He liked it when she came into his room at night and tucked the blankets up around his chin. Heck, he even liked it when she gave him the holy dickens about school.

The thought of losing her now brought a pain to his chest that frightened him something fierce.

Keeping low, Luke ran across the mouth of the alley between the livery and the blacksmith's place. The clang of a hammer on an anvil sounded out in the chilly air, and briefly Luke considered how warm and toasty it must be inside the blacksmith's shop. He imagined the roaring fire and the huge man in a leather apron using the bellows to stoke it even higher.

He shivered slightly and kept going, darting past the livery corral where several of the horses snorted and tossed their heads at his passing. When he heard voices, though, Luke stopped, curious. The storeroom door at the back of the saloon was open just a crack. From inside came the sounds of two men arguing.

Cautiously, Luke moved forward, straining to hear over the noise from the blacksmith. He scowled as he tried to place the voices, wishing the men would speak more loudly. Inching closer, Luke took each step with care. He imagined himself an Apache, stalking some careless buffalo hunter. The voices were clearer now. And familiar. Did he dare take the chance to race past the partially opened door to run for Tucker? Or should he stay put and learn what he could? What would an Apache do? He smiled to himself and scooted quietly closer. He held his breath and listened.

"Luke Banyan!"

A squeak of surprise edged from his throat and he jumped, throwing himself off balance enough to sprawl face-first into the dirt. Lifting his head, he turned to meet Meara's furious expression.

"Mornin', Meara."

"Mornin', indeed," she said, one foot tapping dangerously against the ground. "Why are you not in school where I left ya?"

Luke cocked his head toward the saloon, but as he'd feared, the voices were silent now. He'd never know who he'd been sneaking up on. Dad blast it anyway. Pushing himself to his feet, he brushed the dirt off the front of his shirt and pants, then tilted his head back to look at the woman waiting impatiently for an explanation.

"Aw, Meara . . ." he started.

" 'Tis a good thing for you I happened to spy you sneaking about back here," she said, cutting him off and reaching for his hand.

Luke kicked at the dirt as she started walking toward the schoolhouse. "I just wanted to go help Tucker," he said, knowing even as he said it that it wouldn't help.

"The best way for you to help is to stay in school," she snapped, marching up the steps, nearly dragging him in her wake.

Already dreading walking through those doors, Luke hung his head.

The teacher's monotone voice broke off at the interruption of Meara and Luke appearing at the back of the classroom. The children turned in their seats to stare at them, and Meara couldn't help wondering why those little faces looked so appalled.

"Please forgive us," Meara started to say.

"You're late," the teacher spoke directly to Luke, ignoring Meara's presence entirely.

"Aye, he is," she said, demanding the man's attention. "But 'twas my fault," Meara added, somehow feeling the need to protect Luke.

"He's old enough to arrive on time for school," the tall, thin man snapped as he waved Luke to his seat. Merely glancing at Meara, he said shortly, "If you'll excuse us, we are in the middle of a geography lesson."

"Oh, aye," Meara said, backing toward the door with a last glance at Luke, who kept his head bowed in supplication.

Outside, she listened briefly to the teacher's droning voice, then hurriedly went down the steps and crossed the street to where the buckboard sat waiting. As she put one foot on the wheel to climb up, she noticed Luke's lunch pail sitting on the floorboards. Shaking her head, she snatched it up and quickly went back to the school she'd just left. She could only imagine the teacher's reaction to yet another interruption.

When she opened the door and stepped inside, though, she stopped dead and gasped aloud.

At the front of the class, bent over the teacher's desk, was Luke, his face turned toward the blackboard, away from the eyes of the children about to bear witness to his beating. The teacher, his back to the class, stood to one side of Luke, holding a long, narrow stick upraised in his right hand.

In the second it took for Meara to see all of this and register it in her mind, that stick came down hard on Luke's behind. The boy's muffled cry shot straight to her heart and propelled her forward, swinging Luke's lunch pail like an avenging sword.

To think! She'd delivered her child into the hands of this . . . this . . . Sadly, Meara could think of no word bad enough for the man.

In her haste, she noticed nothing but the fact that the monster looming over her boy had raised his bloody damned stick for another blow. Shrieking her fury, Meara hurled the lunch pail at the man's head and had the satisfaction of seeing it meet its mark. He grunted, clasping one hand to the back of his head. The pail opened, spilling fried chicken and cookies onto the floor at the teacher's feet even while the man himself swivelled around.

Luke hadn't moved except to turn his face toward Meara. Tears of pain and humiliation silvered his cheeks and fed the fires of righteous indignation already licking at Meara's soul.

"Have you taken leave of your senses, madam?" the teacher cried, clearly furious as he swung his stick at her to make his point.

"I've only just regained them," Meara snapped, side-stepping him to grab Luke and hold him to her.

"You have no right to interfere," the man shouted, and his voice grated like fingernails running along a piece of slate.

"I've every right here," she told him, holding Luke while advancing on the man in front of her. " 'Tis you who have no right to strike this child. *Any* child."

"I've the right to discipline those in dire need of it," he said, refusing to back down.

"Discipline? Is that what you'd call it?"

Luke held onto her tightly and she wrapped one arm around his back protectively.

"I am in charge here, madam," the teacher said, waving that stick at her as if expecting her to cower as the children were.

" 'Tis a sad thing when a small man gets a bit of power."

"See here!"

"No," she cut him off. "*You* see. Luke won't be back to your bloody school. What you have to teach, he's in no need of learning. And," she added as she eyed that stick again, "if you wave that blasted thing at me again, I'll take it from ya and show you what it feels like to be 'disciplined.' "

He paled but for twin bright patches of red on his cheeks.

Dismissing him from her mind, Meara turned toward the other children, now staring at her as if she was the Holy Mother and Saint George the Dragon Slayer combined. "I've no right to tell you to go home," she said, shifting her gaze from one to the other of them as she spoke. "But when this day's done, tell your parents what this man's been doin' to ya. Spare him nothing. Do not fear that stick, for once your parents know what's been happening in this place, I've no doubt you'll never have to worry about feelin' the bite of it again."

As she and Luke marched back down the center aisle, there was a sprinkling of applause before the teacher called the class to order.

Moonlight dusted the fall of her hair as she said, "I don't think I've ever been so angry in me life."

Jaw tight, Conner nodded. Ever since that morning, when she'd brought Luke home from school and told him about what the teacher had been up to, Conner had had to fight the urge to go back to town and plow his fist into the man's scholarly face.

"I wish I'd been there with you," he said now.

Bracing her arms on the corral fence, she turned her head to look at him. "I'm glad you weren't."

He blinked in surprise. "Why?"

"Because then I wouldn't have discovered what I did in the Mercantile."

"What are you talking about?"

"I think ya know."

Conner looked away from her suddenly too-knowing eyes. Yeah, he knew what she was talking about. He'd already had two people cancel their plans to buy some of his horses. And the bills that had been delivered for payment in the last couple of days had seriously emptied his cash reserves.

"Why didn't ya tell me?" she whispered. "Why didn't ya let on that my bein' here might cause ya to lose your home?"

Because, Conner thought, if he *had* told her, she might have left. But he didn't say that. "It doesn't matter."

She laid one hand on his arm and waited until he turned to face her. "Of course it matters, man. 'Tis your home we're talkin' about here. I won't be the cause of you losin' it."

Conner looked down at her hand on his arm, then lifted his gaze until he was staring into the green eyes that had captivated him from the first moment he'd seen them.

"I've thought it out," Meara said before he could speak. "I'll be leavin'. Tomorrow."

Everything around him stopped short. The world stopped spinning. The moon stopped shining. Night sounds faded away until he was caught in a heavy web of silence. He pulled in a deep breath, fighting past the strangling knot that had lodged in his throat. She meant what she said. He could see the determination in her eyes and suddenly, he grabbed her, as if he could hold her here. With him.

"Conner," she said, "don't ya see? 'Tis the only way."

His fingers bit into the flesh of her shoulders. His voice came out raw and harsh. "Don't *you* see?" he said, words rushing from him. "I don't give a good goddamn if this place burns to the ground. If you're not here, it's not worth a damn to me."

"No, Conner." She shook her head, and he watched moonlight dazzle on the curls that trembled with the motion. "If I'm not here, you'll have your home. And there'll still be Grub. And Luke."

"No," he ground out, already feeling the emptiness of her absence reaching out to him. "Without you, there's nothing. God help me, I don't even care anymore if you're another man's wife, Meara. I need you. Stay here. With me."

"Conner." Her voice broke on his name and even in the dim light, he saw her eyes fill with tears. "I want nothing more than to be with you, but I won't be the means of destroying you, either."

"Don't you understand?" he asked, lowering his head toward hers. "If you leave me, *you'll* destroy me. Nothing else can."

CHAPTER FIFTEEN

His words cut to the heart of her. She saw the truth of them in his eyes and realized in that instant just how much she'd come to love this man. And how much she wanted to be with him.

Meara watched as he came nearer, closer. His mouth just a breath away from hers, she told herself to stop him. To not let this happen. It wasn't proper. It wasn't right—especially if she really was a married woman.

But despite the voices in her mind clamoring for her attention, she leaned into him, sure of only one thing. For this moment, this night, she belonged in his arms.

Since the moment she'd crashed through his roof, confusion had ruled her world. The one stable point in her life had been this man. Even in her dreams, she was drawn to him and he to her.

There had to be a reason for that connection. Perhaps she had been meant to stumble into his life with no memory of a past so that she could build a future here. With him. Unencumbered by what had gone before.

Briefly, Mick Reilly's features leaped to mind, but she squashed the image and concentrated on Conner. As far as she knew, Meara had never loved before, but she recognized the emotion when she felt it.

Then his mouth covered hers, and she gave herself up

to the magic flooding through her. It was as if a thousand candles had been lit inside her. She glowed with a warmth that continued to spread until her entire body felt awash with light and heat.

"Come with me," he said softly when he broke the kiss.

"Where?" she asked, although she knew it didn't matter. She would have gone with him anywhere.

"Inside," Conner whispered and ran the tips of his fingers along her cheek.

"Aye," Meara agreed. "Inside it is."

Together they crossed the moonwashed yard and entered the house like sneakthieves. Tiptoeing across the hall and up the stairs, moving through the darkness with quiet assurance. When they stopped outside Meara's bedroom door though, Conner asked, "Are you sure?"

She reached behind her, turned the knob and opened the door into her lamplit room. "Oh, aye, Conner," she told him. "I've never been more sure of meself than I am at this moment."

He pulled her into his arms. Meara wound her arms around his neck and held on as if he meant her life or death. Conner closed the door quietly, then crossed the floor to the bed. Gently, he set her down onto the mattress and leaned over her.

Burying his face in the curve of her neck, he dropped feathery light kisses on her skin, and she shivered in response.

"God help me, Meara," he said, his voice muffled against the warmth of her throat, "I need you so much, I ache with the wanting."

Her insides trembled and she realized a sense of power she'd never before known. To be able to bring this strong, stubborn man to his knees was a heady thing. She moved her right hand to the tiny seed pearl buttons that started at the neck of her dress and slowly pushed them free. His gaze followed her progress and she felt the heat of his stare like a hot poker laid against her skin.

When the last one was freed, she shrugged the material off, leaving her breasts exposed to Conner's hungry gaze. He sucked in a breath of air and smiled faintly. "I thought you were wearing that underwear we bought."

She shook her head and her hair fell wild and free across her shoulders to curl at the tips of her hardened nipples.

He groaned tightly as he pushed her gown further down her arms. The night air kissed her skin, sending a chill along her spine. And then Conner touched her flesh and warmth exploded within her.

She held her breath as his fingertips glided across her skin with the tenderest of caresses. They smoothed along the top of her breast and then circled beneath, cupping her, testing her fullness in his palm. His thumb brushed across her rigid nipple, and she gasped at the resulting lightning-like bolt of sensation.

"Conner, love," she whispered, "your touch is magic."

"No, Meara," he assured her, "*you* are the magic." Then he bent his head and took her hard, rosy pink nipple into his mouth.

"Sweet heaven," she said on a sigh. "I'd no idea . . . none."

He smiled against her. She felt him. His tongue stroked her sensitive flesh, toying with the tip of her nipple until she swayed unsteadily into him. His hands took her around her waist, sharing his strength with her, holding her so that he might taste her more fully.

The edges of his teeth scraped against her flesh and a new tendril of sensation began only to intensify as he took her more firmly into his mouth and suckled her.

Stars exploded behind her eyes. Brilliant stars, in bright colors that shimmered in her mind with wild abandon. She gasped his name and clung to him, her fingers digging into his shoulders even as she arched into him, instinctively searching for more. Again and again, his mouth and tongue drew on her, pulling at the very corners of her soul. She felt his suckling to the tips of her toes and knew what it was to be loved by a man.

And still, she wanted more.

"Conner," she whispered again, tipping her head to watch him at her breast.

"Hmmm?" he answered without taking his mouth from her.

Meara smoothed her hand over the back of his head, relishing the feel of his clean, too-long hair beneath her fingers. Holding him to her, lest he try to move away. "Did ya know that I have two of those?"

He pulled back from her, and she wanted to weep at his loss. But he straightened up, grinned at her, and said in a hush, "All in good time."

Then he kissed her, and as his mouth covered hers, he reached down, took the hem of her dress in both hands, and lifted it. He broke their kiss only long enough to pull the gown up and over her head. He tossed it to the floor and looked his fill of her.

Maybe she should have been embarrassed, Meara couldn't help thinking. But in truth, she was proud. Proud of her body and the light that came into his eyes when he looked at her. A small, completely shameless part of her wished heartily that she'd left more than one lamp burning so that there would be a brighter light filling the room.

After a moment, she reached for his shirt and unbuttoned the first two buttons. But her hands were eager and clumsy and she was taking far too much time at her task.

Conner did the rest simply by yanking the edges of his shirt apart, sending buttons skittering to the far corners of the room.

Meara smiled, despite the sudden knot of nervousness in the pit of her stomach. When he pulled his shirt off and tossed it down beside her now-forgotten dress, though, her nervousness vanished in the need to touch him as he had touched her.

She ran the flat of her palms over his chest, silently marvelling at his broad, muscular frame. Her fingers dusted lightly across his flat nipples and he sucked in air, giving her a burst of pleasure to know that he, too, felt wonder when they were touched.

Conner took a step back from the bed, took off his boots, then undressed completely, letting his jeans fall on the growing pile of discarded clothing. Her eyes widened slightly as she looked at the hard, thick, man strength of him, but then he was laying her down on the cool, fresh sheets and aligning himself alongside her.

And she didn't have time to think. Or worry.

His hands roamed over her body, exploring and caressing every square inch of her skin. She felt more alive than she ever had as his fingers left a trail of heat wherever he touched her. Up the length of her legs, along the inside of her thighs, and Meara tensed, waiting for the intense pleasure she'd experienced only the night before. But he didn't touch her there. Instead, he turned her over on the mattress until she lay on her chest, her face turned to one side on the pillow.

Again, his hands explored her as his mouth and tongue followed their lead. Feather-light kisses adorned the column of her spine and the rounded contours of her behind. She lifted her backside and shifted, aching, needing more.

But Conner was in no hurry. He kissed the length of her, drawing his tongue over her legs and nipping at her skin with his teeth until she was whimpering into her pillow with the building ache inside her.

"Sweet heaven, Conner," she said, muffling a groan into the feather pillow, "can ya not see you're torturing me?"

"I see it, Meara," he whispered, working his way back

up her body until his words brushed against the back of her neck. "And I'm enjoying it."

"You're an evil man," she said as he flipped her over again and dipped his head to her breast.

"And you're glad of it."

His mouth closed around her nipple and as he suckled her, more fiercely this time, she whispered, "Aye, Lord help me, I *am*."

He chuckled and his breath brushed across the dampness on her nipple. Then he turned his attention to her other breast and in moments stoked the fire within her to a raging inferno. Alternating between her breasts, he let his right hand slide down her body. Over her ribcage, across her abdomen, to the small triangle of curls he'd touched so expertly the night before.

"Conner," she groaned tightly as he covered her with his palm. Meara planted her feet on the bed and lifted her hips into him. Pressure. She felt it rising inside her and did what she could to help herself. Rocking against his hand, she searched for the road to the pleasure she knew was waiting for her. "Love a duck, man, help me."

He lifted his head from her breast and looked down into her eyes. She stared at him, his features tight, drawn, as he steered them deeper into the well of passion.

Meara reached for him, threading her fingers through his hair, pulling his face down to hers for a kiss she needed as much as her next breath. Her lips parted for him and when their tongues met in a tangle of desire, her heartbeat thundered in her ears, rolling on and on, like a frenzied drumbeat.

He tore his face from hers then and shifted to plant kisses along her throat. The scrape of his whiskers against her skin only added a new sensation to those already churning within her.

"Meara," he said, his voice low and hushed, "I feel like I've waited my whole life to find you."

"And I you," she told him breathlessly.

"You're so beautiful," he murmured, and began to move on her, sliding his body along hers, kissing her, tasting her as he moved lower and lower.

She felt beautiful. In that one, glorious moment, she fet like the most beautiful woman in the world.

Meara reached for him, but he avoided her grasping hands neatly until he was kneeling between her legs. She watched him, her breath laboring in her chest, her own heartbeat the only sound she could hear. Meara felt her breath catch as he lifted her hips from the mattress, cupping her behind in his palms.

"Conner," she whispered, a little anxious, despite the desire rocketing around inside her. "What are you up to?"

"Loving you, Meara," he said, and kept his gaze locked with hers as he lowered his mouth to cover her.

She gasped aloud, curled her fingers into the sheets beneath her and instinctively arched her hips higher. Meara watched him, amazed and stunned at the force of her response to this intimate caress.

His tongue dipped into her warmth, delving deeply, slowly, sliding over her flesh with a slick heat. His fingers kneaded her behind as he tasted her thoroughly. His breath brushed over her most sensitive spot a moment before his tongue teased her there as well.

Meara grabbed a pillow and stuffed the corner of it against her mouth to muffle a scream she could feel coming. Dragging in air through her nose, she gave herself over to his ministrations. His tongue dipped inside her again before moving to concentrate on the one small spot that held all the sensations in the world.

He suckled her here, as well, and Meara felt the last of her mind slipping away and knew she wouldn't miss it. Not so long as she could feel the way she did at that moment. And then she was on that steeply pitched road again. Running, running toward the explosive end to her torture. Eagerly she reached for it, and when the first wave of completion struck her, Meara almost sobbed with the joy of it. Biting down on the corner of the pillow, she squeezed her eyes closed and rode the tiny ripples of satisfaction until her body was nearly humming.

Conner held her steadily as a powerful climax roared through her, then, before her trembling had ended, he moved to cover her, pushing slowly inside her. When he met a barrier keeping him from claiming her fully, Conner stopped.

"What is it?" she whispered brokenly.

Every muscle screaming for control, he held himself perfectly still within her. Looking down into her eyes, he said softly, "You're a virgin, Meara."

She blinked up at him through dazed eyes. "A virgin, did ya say?"

"Yeah."

"How can ya be sure?"

He groaned tightly. "Trust me. I'm sure."

Her breath exploded from her. "Then, Mick Reilly . . ."

"Lied," Conner finished for her.

"So I'm not married to him."

"Or anyone," Conner said, dipping his head to claim a brief, hard kiss.

She smiled up at him. Tentatively at first, that smile blossomed into a grin. "Then love me freely, Conner darlin'. There's no law in the land to stop us."

His body pressed deeper into hers and her eyes widened at the invasion. Again, Conner stopped, giving her time to adjust to his presence. God, it felt perfect to be inside her. To be held by the warmth of her and surrounded by her. And, if he was to be honest, at least with himself, to know that he was the first man to love her—and he wanted to be the last, as well.

Conner's jaw clenched with his effort to be still. To wait until she was ready for him to go on. He looked down into pleasure-streaked green eyes and knew this waiting was the hardest thing he'd ever had to do in his life.

At last, though, she lifted both hands and slid them up his shoulders. Just the feel of her soft, gentle palms skimming over his flesh was almost enough to make him lose a control he'd always prided himself on.

"Conner," she said on a sigh, " 'tis better than I'd hoped."

He groaned and bent his head, resting his forehead against hers. "Jesus, Meara," he said tightly, "you unman me."

"Sweet Mother," she countered, running her hands up and down his back, "I hope not."

Conner chuckled and lifted his head again to look at her. A mischievous light gleamed in her eyes and tilted her smile at a devilish angle.

Her hips lifted into his and the friction of that movement coursed through him. And still, he didn't move.

"Conner, love," she told him, "I'm fine and I want to know the rest. All of it."

Moving one hand to sweep her sweat-dampened hair back from her brow, Conner nodded and left a kiss on her forehead. Then, bracing himself on his hands, he drove himself home. She arched against him and a moment later, lifted her hips to beckon him into the dance.

She was so much more than he'd ever hoped to find. He lost himself again and again in the heart of her. Meara lifted her legs to wrap them about his hips, pulling him closer, deeper. When his control was frayed and his aching desire at its highest pitch, he surrendered control and emptied himself inside her, safe with the knowledge that all he would ever need, he held in his arms.

In the soft, warm cozy world inhabited by just the two of them, Meara snuggled in close to Conner and sighed when his arms came around her. He wanted to squeeze her tightly, mold her to him so that she could never be separated from him.

"Conner," she whispered.

"Hmmm?"

"What you said before . . ." She tipped her head back on his shoulder to look up at him. "About my bein' a virgin?"

"Yeah." His voice was harsh, it was colored with the confused frustration he felt deeply within.

"Why would Mick Reilly lie about bein' my husband?"

"I don't know . . . *yet*," Conner admitted. "All I'm sure of is that a woman married for two years would *not* be a virgin."

"I wouldn't think so," she agreed, and laid her head back down on his chest, directly over his still-thundering heart. As she drifted into sleep, Conner promised himself and her that he would get to the bottom of Mick Reilly's lies and find some way of proving to the townspeople just what kind of woman Meara really was.

Cuddled into Conner's side, Meara fell asleep, entering the dream world almost immediately. She walked what seemed miles, and couldn't seem to find her way past the gray, misty barriers that surrounded her. She searched for Conner, expecting to find him, and when she didn't, her heart wept.

She shifted in her sleep, mumbling softly, calling his name, and still, she was alone in the grayness.

Someone called her name, and she hurried toward the sound, thinking, Conner. At last. As she came closer to the source, though, she realized it was a woman's voice she was following. A woman she knew.

Her mind whirling, she tried to identify that voice while at the same time, something inside her told her to wake up. Wake up quickly before everything was ruined. Listening to her own instincts, she turned away and ran back the way she'd come. Back to wakefulness. Back to Conner and the safety of his arms around her. Back to the life she'd built for herself.

"Meara, wait," the voice called.

But she couldn't. Wouldn't. Heart racing, pulse pounding, she jolted awake, sitting up in the bed, and tried to draw air into heaving lungs.

"Meara," Conner asked quietly, pushing himself up to sit beside her. "What is it? What's wrong?"

She turned to him, burrowing in close, relishing the warmth of his skin, the strength in his arms, and the steady, comforting beat of his heart. She shook her head, wordless. Unable to explain the fear that still gripped her, she simply held onto him as if her life depended on it. And suddenly, she thought perhaps it did.

"Nightmare?" he asked, running his hands up and down her body in slow, rhythmic strokes.

All right, yes, she thought and nodded into his shoulder. She didn't know *what* had frightened her, but she could feel the force of that fear even now.

He eased back down onto the pillows, drawing her with him, holding her to his chest. Conner kissed the top of her head before whispering, "They say there's a reason for everything, y'know. Even nightmares."

Meara's eyes flew open.

Her breath caught.

She stared blankly at the wall opposite as her mind twisted and turned. She knew that phrase. She'd heard it before. Recently. But where? Who had said it?

And why didn't her mind want to remember?

"Go to sleep, Meara," he said softly, and she tried to concentrate solely on his voice.

"I don't want to," she admitted, moving in closer to him.

"You can't stay awake all night," he said, and she

heard the smile in his voice. "If you do, how will we dream together?"

Meara tipped her head back to look up at him. "How does that happen?" she asked. "Doesn't it frighten you?"

"I don't know," he answered. "And no, it doesn't." His arms tightened around her, his thumbs moving back and forth over her skin. "I admit, it's a strange thing and I can't explain it. But scare me? No."

"It does me, a bit," she admitted. Not the dreams themselves, of course. There was nothing to be feared from Conner. She knew that. Yet the very idea that she could enter another person's dreams was somehow a terrifying thing.

He was quiet for several minutes, their breathing the only sound in the darkness. But finally, he said, "Look at it like a gift, Meara. Even when we're asleep, we can be together."

She nodded against him, still not completely convinced.

Meara heard the smile in his voice when he said, "I'll hold you until you fall asleep. Then I'll head back to my room."

Of course, he couldn't stay there with her. She knew that. And yet, she wasn't ready for him to leave. Doubted that she ever would be. Stretching one arm across his chest, she held onto him as she would a floating log in a raging river and slowly closed her eyes.

"Sleep, Meara," he whispered, then added. "I'll see you in my dreams."

This time, there was no voice calling her from a distance. This time, when Meara slipped into the Dream World, there was someone waiting for her.

"Are you enjoying yourself, Meara?" the woman asked.

"What do you mean?" Meara asked. It was the woman she'd seen in town, she thought as she stud-

ied the woman in the scarlet, spangled gown. The woman who'd disappeared. The woman who had about convinced Meara she was losing her mind. Studying her now, Meara tried to understand why she seemed so blasted familiar. Her white hair was done up in a loose knot at the top of her head and one long, blue feather jutted out to the right. The deeply cut bodice of her gown displayed a fair amount of her lush, white breasts, and her well-rounded hips swayed as she came toward Meara, a wide smile on her red-painted lips.

"I've seen you before, haven't I? In town. You waved at me. Do I know you?" Meara asked, and the gray mists around her trembled slightly.

"Sure you do," the woman said with a shake of her head. "Just think about it for a minute. It's time to remember, Meara. Time to remember everything."

Remember? Meara frowned as her mind whirled and tried to settle into order again. Remember. She lifted one hand to rub her forehead between her eyes. Remember. Slowly, as if a cloth was being pulled away, her brain began to clear. Memories flooded her mind and she mentally raced to sort them all out. Her breathing quickened. She stared at the woman opposite her, and realized she did know her. This was her friend.

"Daisy?"

"Atta girl," the woman crowed, then grinned at her. "All coming back now?"

"In a tumble, I'm afraid." Meara shook her head as if to settle her splintered thoughts into place. Daisy. Gideon. The Great Chamber. Dream Weavers. Charges.

Eyes wide, she whispered, "Gideon. That's why I'm here. To hide from Gideon."

"Yep," Daisy told her and walked to her side.

"*Supposed to be here a month, remember?*"

"*Aye. Until the new moon,*" Meara said, filled with wonder at having her faculties restored.

"*But,*" Daisy went on, "*the way things were buildin' up down here, figured I'd come check on you early.*"

A Dream Weaver. That's who she was, Meara thought, nearly giddy now at having all of her questions answered. A soul in charge of guarding children's sleep. Protecting their dreams. Bringing comfort.

She smiled to herself. Now she understood Luke's dream and just how she'd managed to help the boy. She understood so much. What a relief this was, to have her mind settled and her questions answered.

"*Meara,*" another voice called to her from across the void of mists. This voice was deeper and called to her like no other ever had.

"*Conner,*" she whispered guiltily and looked toward the sound of his voice.

"*Yeah,*" Daisy said kindly, knowingly. "*Conner. Things got a little out of hand down here, huh? You should know, Gideon's not real happy about this.*"

"*Sweet Mother, Daisy,*" Meara cried, "*what am I to do?*" Now that she'd remembered who she was, she knew that there was no future with Conner. Mick Reilly wasn't the threat to their happiness. It was her own reality that would keep them apart. Soon, she'd have to return to the Dream World and leave him behind. She'd never see him again. And that knowledge slammed into her chest with the force of a crossbow's arrow.

"*What do you want to do?*" Daisy asked, and frowned slightly as Conner's voice drifted toward them again, louder this time. Insistent.

"*'Tisn't as if I have a choice,*" Meara said. How

infuriating this was. Only a moment before, she'd been thrilled to have the return of her memories. Now, she'd gladly have them gone again. So she could go back to being simply Meara Simon, in love with Conner James.

Odd, too, how dealing with the likes of Mick Reilly seemed like nothing. If only their problem was really that simple.

Conner called out once more, and his voice tore at Meara's soul.

Daisy however, was less moved. She turned and shouted, "Keep your shirt on, Conner!"

Silence.

Meara gave her a halfhearted smile.

"There's always a choice, Meara," the woman said and pushed her breasts a bit higher.

"Not for me," she countered. "I can't love the man. I'm not alive anymore. I can't stay with him."

"But do you love him?" Daisy asked, her sharp blue eyes fixed on Meara.

She hesitated only a moment. 'Twas useless to deny it to her friend. "Aye, I do. With all my heart. More than I ever thought it possible to love a man."

Daisy grinned and winked at her. "Where there's love," she said, "there's hope."

"Hope," Meara repeated. "What hope have I? I can't stay here, and Gideon is—" She shot Daisy a questioning look. "Is Gideon still furious with me?"

Daisy shrugged, and her dress threatened to spill her breasts free. "He ain't as hoppin' mad as he used to be, but he's still feelin' pretty nasty."

Meara groaned.

"Don't you worry about Gideon, hon," Daisy said, and patted her shoulder affectionately. "You got another week or so here. I'll work on him."

"What can you do?"

"Dead or alive, Gideon's a man," Daisy *winked again.* "And, honey, the one thing I know how to do is handle a man."

Meara *nodded absently. A bit more than a week with Conner. Could she stand being here that much longer, knowing that it was all going to end? Knowing that she would have to leave him before either of them was ready for it?*

"Who's there with Meara?" Conner *shouted from a distance.*

"Lord, that boy's got a mouth on him," Daisy *muttered.*

"I don't know," Meara *said softly,* "maybe 'tis a bad idea, me stayin' here any longer. Perhaps I should just go back to the Great Chamber and face Gideon now."

"Now why'd you want to do that?" Daisy *demanded.*

"Because I don't know if I can stand being here. With Conner, knowing it's all going to end."

Daisy *shook her head, then reached up to smooth her top knot unnecessarily.* "It ain't how much time together you get hon', it's how you spend that time that counts."

Meara *wrapped her arms around herself and turned toward the sound of Conner's voice, still calling her name.* "But 'tis such a short time, Daisy. So pitifully short."

"Honey," *the other woman said and took* Meara *into her embrace briefly,* "you can live a lifetime in a few days, if you spend your time wisely."

A lifetime. The lifetime she would never have with Conner. Was she really willing to walk away from him before she absolutely had to? Wasn't Daisy right? Wasn't it better to take everything life had to offer while you could?

She would have an eternity to miss him. To think

of him and remember every moment they'd shared. Wouldn't it be easier, if she had a lot of moments to recall when the loneliness was at its bleakest?

Meara nodded to herself as she made her decision. She would stay. She would continue on as she had been. The only difference now was that she would know she was only pretending to be human. Pretending to be building a life for herself and those she loved.

"I'll stay," she said softly, already moving in Conner's direction.

"You do that, hon," Daisy said as she began to fade into the surrounding mists. "I'll take care of Gideon—you take care of Conner."

"I will," Meara said, and before her friend disappeared altogether, she added, "And thank you for sending me here to hide, Daisy. I'll be forever grateful."

"No, Meara," the other woman replied with a gentle smile. "Thank you."

Then she was gone and Meara turned back to face Conner as he raced up to her, his eyes wild as he searched the mists around them like a madman. "Where is she?" he demanded.

"She who?" Meara asked, thinking it better not to tell him about her friend if she could avoid it.

"She was here," Conner said flatly and grabbed Meara's shoulders in a firm grip. "I heard her. I'd know that voice anywhere, dammit! Now, where is my mother?"

CHAPTER SIXTEEN

The dream shattered around them and Meara woke up gasping for air. A heartbeat later, Conner shot into a sitting position beside her.

Viciously, he rubbed both hands across his face before turning his head to look at the stunned woman clutching a sheet to her chest like an ancient shield. He'd blown out the lamps in the room before they fell asleep and now he wished he hadn't. The dim light provided by the moon seemed altogether too intimate, too private for how he was feeling at the moment. But he was too agitated to strike a match.

When he spoke, he somehow remembered to keep his voice down, even though he felt like shouting.

"That was my mother's voice I heard," he said tightly. "What in the hell are you doing dreaming about *my* mother?"

Meara pushed her hair back from her face with one hand and looked at him in confusion. "Your mother?" she repeated. "Are you sure?"

That ridiculous question set off an explosive charge inside him. He jumped off the mattress and started pacing wildly around the room. "Am I *sure*? Of course I'm sure. A man knows what his mother sounds like, doesn't he?"

"I suppose so," she admitted, her gaze following his progress around the room. "But if it's true, why wouldn't she have told me?"

"Told you?" He stopped dead in a puddle of moonlight and looked at her, eyes narrowed. "You've dreamed about this woman before?"

Her gaze dropped to her lap where her fingers plucked nervously at the sheet covering her.

Something heavy and tight settled in Conner's chest as he waited. There was something he didn't know. Something beyond the fact that she had dreamed about his mother. The minutes ticked by slowly. His pounding heartbeat marked the passage of time. While he studied her, he remembered running through the grayness, searching for Meara. Knowing that, once again, he would find her in his dreams.

He still didn't know how it happened. Didn't even know if it mattered to him or not.

But then he'd heard his mother's voice shouting at him and realized there was more going on than just two people linked together by destiny. There was a secret. One he wasn't privy to. And that knowledge jabbed at him like a knife point.

"Meara, damn it, how could you know my mother?" he finally ground out, unable to keep still another moment. "She died over twenty years ago in a spot in the road down in Texas. You couldn't have known her. So why in hell would you be dreaming about her?"

Meara heard the tamped-down anger in his voice and couldn't blame him, really. She shot a quick look at him from beneath lowered lashes, and her breath nearly stopped. He looked like a warrior of old.

Bathed in moonlight, his hard, muscled body was defined by light and shadow. From the sculpted planes of his chest to the long, hard lines of his legs. But it was his eyes that drew her. As they always had. From the first, she'd seen magic in his Kerry-blue eyes. And now, despite the fact that temper glittered in their depths, the magic was still there.

But what could she say?

Her gaze lowered again to her hands on her lap. Her body still warm from his touch, she ached to be held in the circle of his arms again. To feel that sense of safety and peace that she had had only a while ago.

And yet, now that she knew the truth about herself, peace would be a hard thing to find. How could she have forgotten? she asked herself. How could she have not known that she was a Dream Weaver?

In a flash, images raced through her mind. From the Dream World and from long ago, when she had lived as a poor peasant girl in Ireland.

She'd died in that life, alone, unloved by a man. Not until more than a century after her death had she found a love she'd always longed for. Tears swam in her eyes as she wondered why she had found the love of her life now, when she was long past the chance at keeping it.

"Meara, damn it, answer me," he demanded.

"I don't know what to say to you," she finally whispered into the darkness, her words swallowed by the lingering shadows.

"The truth," he said. "Why don't you try the truth."

Lifting her gaze to look at him again, she shook her head sadly. "Truth isn't always for the best, Conner."

He stalked forward and stopped at the foot of the bed, staring down at her as though he didn't even know her. As, she thought, he really didn't.

"It's a simple question, Meara. How could you know my mother?"

His mother. Why hadn't Daisy told her that she was Conner's mother? Meara had thought she and the other woman were friends. Yet Daisy had sent her here, to this place, to her *son*—and left her in darkness. With no memories. No one to turn to. Her breath caught. For the first time, Meara considered the possibility that her *friend* was also somehow responsible for the memory loss she'd suffered until tonight.

But why?

"Meara?" Impatience colored his voice.

She sighed, letting all of her questions go unanswered, for the moment. Just now, 'twas Conner's questions that needed to be attended to. "I met her in the Dream World."

He frowned, lines gathering between his eyes. "You mean like you and I meet in our dreams?"

"No."

Conner shoved both hands through his hair, holding onto his scalp as though expecting his head to explode unless he had a firm grip on it. Her heart went out to him. And yet it was clear he didn't want her sympathy.

"Explain," he said shortly.

"You won't believe me."

"Try anyway."

She inhaled sharply, blew the air out of her lungs in a rush, then blurted the words out, knowing even as she said them, that the truth would only push Conner further from her. "I'm a Dream Weaver."

His scowl deepened, casting his familiar features into darker shadows than the ones that surrounded them both. "Am I supposed to understand that?"

Feeling at a disadvantage with him staring down at her, Meara slipped from the bed, drawing the sheet with her. Once on her own two feet, she wrapped the cotton fabric around her like a toga and kicked at the puddle of material at her feet. She tossed her hair back behind her shoulders and met his gaze evenly as she said, "I guard children's dreams. Protect them from nightmares. Offer comfort and love where there's none."

When she stopped talking, the silence in the room seemed to grow and blossom into a monstrous beast that stood between them, fangs bared.

"A Dream Weaver," he said, shaking his head.

"That's right." Her job was a proud one and she wouldn't apologize for it. Nothing she'd ever done had given her the pleasure she found when bringing peace to a troubled child. Not even for Conner's sake would she pretend different.

"And my mother?"

"She too, is a Weaver," Meara said, watching the disbelief etch itself into his face. Absently, she wondered if she was breaking another of Gideon's rules. But then how could there be a law against telling a mortal about Dream Weavers? She was sure the situation had never presented itself before. So, casting her fate to the winds, she added, "She's been a Dream Weaver since she died. That's when I met her."

Once the words had left her mouth, she braced herself, half expecting a lightning bolt to strike her down. But none came and the moment passed.

"*After* she died." He crossed his arms over his chest and braced his bare feet wide apart.

The tone of his voice carried the sting of sarcasm. He didn't believe her. But that was no surprise. Hadn't she told him that he wouldn't? Still and all, it was to his tone she responded.

"Of *course* after she died," Meara snapped quietly. "I couldn't very well have known her before, could I? Bein' dead an' all myself."

He laughed shortly. But that bark of laughter held no humor in it. Instead, it brought a chill of dread to Meara's spine.

"Well, sure," he agreed, "if you were dead, how *could* you meet her?"

Meara had never seen him this distant before. 'Twas as if he'd already dismissed her. Even after what they'd shared, he was closing his heart to her. She felt the chill of separation despite standing so close to him.

"I told ya you wouldn't believe me," she reminded him.

"So you did." He nodded slowly, his gaze never releasing hers. "You were right."

"Why would I make this up?"

"That I don't know yet," he conceded, then said, "So, you're saying I just spent the night making love to a dead woman."

She frowned and tightened her sheet around her. "Aye, I suppose so."

"You seemed alive enough to me."

"For now. While I'm here," she said.

"Uh-huh. Well, if you don't mind my asking, how did you die? I mean"—he waved one hand at her—"you seem to be in pretty good health. No scars. No blood."

" 'Twas a long time ago, Conner," she said.

"How long?"

"A bit more than a hundred years."

That piece of news hit him between the eyes. But in an instant, the shocked expression was gone, hidden behind a mask of indifference. "A hundred . . ." He shook his head. "All right, then. How, Meara? How did you die?"

His question dredged up memories of a time she'd near forgotten over the last century. 'Twas useless to dwell on the how and why of one's death, once the deed was done. But for Conner's sake and in the hope of convincing him of the truth of her words, she recounted it now.

" 'Twas in Ireland," she started, and in her mind's eye saw again the small patch of rocky earth she and her family had worked so diligently to try and scratch a living from. "We had a farm," she said, a soft smile of remembrance curving her lips. "Not so grand as this place of yours, but 'twas ours. Or so we thought of it."

"What do you mean?"

She flicked him a quick glance and shrugged. "All the land was owned by an English earl, but he gave it no care, save to collect his rents and hie himself off back to London." Meara scowled to herself at the old sting of injustice. " 'Twas we Irish, who lived on the land and worked it ceaselessly, who really owned it, or were owned by it, body and soul." She wrapped her arms around her middle and squeezed. "Me father was late with the rents—'twas a hard summer. And his lordship summoned his soldiers to put us off our land." She closed her eyes against the questions in his and lost herself in the tide of memories. "I can still hear the thunder of their horses pounding across the fields, their great hooves tearing up the grass and scattering the few grazing sheep. We stood in front of the wee house, me father, two brothers, and I. Da wanted to talk to his lordship. Ask his pardon and leave to stay. But there was no talkin' that day. The earl stayed on the crest of a low mound while his men in their blood-red tunics charged their animals at us. When Da saw there was nothing to be done, he yelled at us to run, but 'twas too late. A hail of arrows took us down and there we died. Together."

When the tale was done, she inhaled deeply as if cleansing herself and waited for his reaction. His expression was unreadable. 'Twas as if he'd closed a door into his soul to keep her from seeing what he was feeling.

Still she told herself, surely he would believe.

Several long moments passed before he spoke. His voice issued from his throat in a harsh rasp. "So, you died in Ireland a hundred years ago."

She nodded.

"And you can't be married to Mick Reilly if you're dead."

She nodded again, more hopefully this time.

"Well, hell, why didn't you just say so before?" He threw his hands wide and let them fall to his sides.

"I didn't remember, Conner. Not until this very night."

"No," he said with a shake of his head. "I'll tell you why you didn't say any of this before. Because this is horse shit, Meara."

She gasped on a sudden sharp stab of pain. Pain at his

disbelief. Pain that ripped at her with every glare from his glittering blue eyes.

He took a step closer to her and bent low until their eyes were on the same level and he could stare accusingly into hers with ease. "All of it. Horse shit. A hundred-year-old woman dropping through my roof. Arrows from English earls. Dream Weavers! Dead people wandering in and out of dreams?" He shook his head fiercely as if he could shake loose the story she'd only just told him.

Meara stiffened, preparing for the fight she knew was coming. She should have known that he wouldn't accept her story. And yet, she'd so hoped he would. " 'Tis the truth," she answered simply.

A short, hard bark of laughter shot from him. "Lady, you wouldn't know the truth if it walked through the door shouting 'Howdy'!"

Meara's face flushed with anger of her own. She couldn't help what she was and wouldn't have changed it if she could. She'd given him what he wanted. The truth. Even knowing that this is exactly what would happen. "Didn't I say you wouldn't believe me?"

"You surely did," he countered, and bent down lower to snatch up his pants. "And that at least was true."

"Well, how else do ya explain you and I meeting in our dreams? How do you explain me knowing about Luke and what his father had done to him?"

His features tightened even further. "I can't explain it."

"But I've just given you the explanation."

"I can't believe that, either."

"Ya mean ya won't."

He whipped around to look at her. "I mean I can't. Dead people don't wander in and out of our dreams. When you're dead, you're dead. Over. Finished. There's no angels playing golden harps. There's no forgiving God waiting to welcome you with open arms and there sure as hell are no Dream Weavers!"

"Conner," she said as he yanked his jeans on and up his legs, "how else would I know your mother?"

"I don't know that you do," he grumbled, reaching for his shirt. "I probably just imagined hearing her voice."

"Her name is Daisy."

The entire world went quiet.

He stilled briefly, straightened up and looked at her through cold, hard eyes. After a moment though, he shrugged that piece of information off and said, "Grub could have told you."

"She has lovely white hair that she wears tucked up with a blue feather in it."

A muscle in his jaw twitched violently. "He could have told you that, too."

"But he didn't."

"And I should believe you."

" 'Tis the truth, you great stubborn man."

He laughed shortly. "You stick to a story that wild and *I'm* stubborn?"

" 'Tis the only story I've got, because it's the true one. I remember it now. I remember everything." Meara reached out to him, but he evaded her. This man, who had known her so intimately, now recoiled from the touch of her hand? A cold fist tightened around her heart. And still, she tried to make him hear. "I know who I am. Why I'm here—"

He sent her a quelling look. "Ah. Now, you *remember*. Well, that's convenient. All right, I'll ask. Why *are* you here?"

"I was in trouble," she started to say.

"That at least, I believe."

She glared him into silence. "Daisy thought it best if I stayed away from Gideon awhile. *She* sent me here."

"My mother sent you to me?"

"Aye," she whispered. "I don't know why. But she did."

"And you remember all of this."

Meara wrapped her arms around her middle again and held on tight. How could such a glorious night end so badly? Visions of the time they'd just spent together rose up in her mind and she wanted to weep at the loss. She wanted the hours back. She wanted *him* back. For however long she had left in this place, she wanted Conner beside her, building memories that would carry her through the lonely eternity stretching out ahead of her.

"I *do* remember, Conner," she whispered. "I almost wish I didn't."

"You know something, Meara?" he asked and moved toward the door, his boots clutched in one hand. "So do I."

Two days later, things were no better between them. They hardly spoke and passed each other in the house like two ghosts, each unaware of the other's presence. It tore at Meara's heart, this distance between them. She'd tried at first to bridge the chasm dividing them, but Conner had closed himself off to her, and there was no getting through to him.

She tightened her grip on the reins and concentrated on the road in front of her. Perhaps she should have left right away—as soon as she'd remembered who she was. But even as she thought that, she realized she wasn't ready to leave Conner yet, even in the face of his hurt and anger. Besides, she couldn't very well leave, knowing that because of her, he could lose the home he loved so much.

No, she had to do something. Had to try and right whatever wrongs had been done to him and assure herself that he would keep his ranch. And the only way to do that was to find out why Mick Reilly was lying about her—claiming her as wife. If she could prove Reilly a liar, then the townspeople would welcome Conner's business again. Then, she could return to the Dream World where she belonged and there would be no more ugly rumors about Conner James.

He and his home would be safe.

And she would spend an eternity missing him.

As she entered the town, Meara steered her horse toward the Mercantile, the one place she knew was open to her. She lifted her chin and prepared herself mentally for the snubs of the people wandering back and forth across the narrow street. They shunned her because they thought her a loose woman and Conner a man who would keep another's wife. What would they think, she wondered if they knew the truth? The *real* truth?

Of course, she told herself wryly, they were all partly right, now. Oh, she wasn't a married woman. But she *had* given herself freely to Conner—an act she would never regret no matter how he may feel about it now.

Tying the reins to the brake handle, she climbed down from the bench seat, balanced herself briefly on the wheel hub, then jumped to the ground, landing smack in the path of a man stepping down off the boardwalk.

"Ma'am," he said quietly as he stepped around her, giving her a brief tip of his hat.

Surprised, Meara stared after him, telling herself that the man must be a stranger in town and unaware of her stained reputation. Still and all, if felt good to be acknowledged, and the small courtesy lifted her spirits slightly.

She clung tightly to that kindness as she took the few steps up to the boardwalk and crossed to the Mercantile's door. It swung wide before she reached it as a woman leaving the store stepped outside. Prepared for a haughty reception, Meara was caught flatfooted as the woman gave her a very small smile and a muttered, "Good morning," before sailing past her to continue on down the walk.

Stunned to her shoes, Meara stared after the woman for a long minute. What was happening? Two people wishing her a good morning in a town where only a few days ago, people had closed their doors in her face?

Shaking her head, Meara finally tore her gaze from the retreating figure and yanked open the door to the Mercantile. Hopefully, she would find some answers from the Higginses. The comforting sound of the welcoming bell rattled around her as she entered. She paused briefly to relish the now-familiar scents hanging in the still air and found yet another thing she would miss when she returned to the Dream World. Then she hurriedly crossed the scarred wooden floor to the counter.

"Well, look here, Eli," Dora Higgins exclaimed. "It's Meara."

"I got eyes, don't I?" her husband muttered from his chair.

Meara shot the too-thin man a quick smile. She'd grown used to his complaints and knew she'd miss them, too, when she was gone. Then Eli Higgins gave her her third surprise of the morning as he smiled back at her— though it was more a baring of teeth than an actual smile.

Something very strange was happening here.

"Oh, Meara, I'm so glad you came in," Dora was saying as she bustled to the counter and held out both hands toward her.

"What's happened?" Meara asked, slipping her hands into the other woman's.

Dora gave her hands a quick squeeze, then released her. "Quite a bit," she said with a grin.

"Durn women," Eli commented. "Start the trouble, then when they stop it, they all want a big yahoo."

"You hush, Eli," Dora snapped. "I'll tell her."

"Then get to it."

Meara waited impatiently and was rewarded a moment later.

"The other day," Dora started, "when you took Luke

out of school and told the other children to go home and tell their folks about that *teacher?*"

"How did you know about . . ." Meara asked.

"It's all over town," Dora interrupted. "Those kids did just like you told 'em," she said with a hard nod. "And when they did, the fur started flying."

"Flying fur?" Rather than clearing things up, Dora's story was only making Meara more confused. What did any of this have to do with the odd reception she was receiving in town? "What are you talkin' about?"

"Seems that fella was whalin' the tar outa those kids," Eli put in while Dora was taking a breath.

Meara inhaled sharply, horrified.

"Didn't I say I was going to tell her?" Dora shot her husband a dirty look, then turned back to Meara. "Those poor kids was all scared to death of the old stick," she said. "Until you went in there and gave him what for. Seems the *teacher* told the kids if they was to tell their folks about what went on in school, they'd get it twice as bad."

Disgusted, Meara remembered now her first visit to the schoolhouse when she'd noted the children all with their gazes locked on their teacher and how Meara had thought he must be a fine man indeed to command such dedication. Why hadn't she noticed it was more fear than appreciation that dictated their attentiveness?

Suddenly furious at the man who had frightened so many children, Meara demanded, "And what's happened to himself? The teacher?"

Eli snorted a laugh. "Hell, he's gone."

"Durn you, Eli," Dora snapped, glaring at him.

"Gone where?" Meara demanded.

"To the devil, no doubt," Dora threw in before her husband could interrupt again. "Where he came from in the first place."

"So many folks was chasin' that fella, all you could see was the soles of his feet and a cloud of dust," Eli said, his entire body shaking with suppressed laughter. "Hell, he's prob'ly still runnin'."

Well then, Meara told herself. She'd accomplished *something* during her stay here, at any rate. No more would the children of High Timber be afraid to go to school.

"And, Meara," Dora added in a quieter voice, "folks around here are real grateful to you for finding that man out."

"Ah . . ." She nodded slowly. Now she understood why she'd received a more friendly reception.

"Everybody's thinkin' maybe they was wrong to act so harsh to you and Conner just because of what that Reilly had to say." Dora folded her hands primly at her waist. "They're thinkin' that maybe they shouldn't take a stranger's word against one of our own."

"Yeah," Eli said. "Especially since Reilly ain't been sober since he hit town."

Dora sniffed. "Not the point, old man. Point is, folks are startin' to take Conner's side in all this. And yours, too, Meara."

"Point is, old woman," Eli huffed, "it's the durn women around here that started all this and now they're feelin' ashamed, as well they ought."

That was all well and good, Meara thought, but it still didn't explain why Mick Reilly had lied. And unless she could *prove* that he had, the townspeople might turn on Conner again. Especially with Robert Carlisle ready to cast the first and last stones.

Conner stood in the center of the corral, blindly watching one of the mares being put through her paces. But his heart wasn't in it. Only a few short weeks ago, nothing could have diverted his attention from the horses that were the future of his ranch.

Now, he couldn't keep his mind from straying to

Meara. Despite the ridiculous story she'd told him the other night.

Dream Weavers.

Hell, if she was going to lie to him, why couldn't she at least have come up with a good one?

Grumbling under his breath, he reached up and pulled the brim of his hat down low on his forehead. Squinting into the morning sun, he tried to concentrate on the mare. Though with the way things were in town, he had little hope of selling any of his horses now.

Damn it, he should have gone with Meara to town. She shouldn't be facing all those condemning stares alone. But they'd been as strangers for two days now, and he'd convinced himself she wouldn't have wanted his company, anyway.

Blast it, how had everything between them gone so bad so quickly?

A horse raced into the ranch yard just then and Conner turned toward it. Tommy, the youngest of his ranch hands, rode low over the horse's neck and dismounted before the animal had come to a complete stop. Walking up to his boss, reins in one tight fist, the kid took off his hat and said, "Tucker sent me to tell you Reilly's still at the saloon."

Reilly. Hell, Conner'd been so wrapped up in his own misery, he hadn't given Reilly near enough thought. Now that Conner knew without a doubt that Meara was a virgin—whatever else she was besides—he had to ask himself why Mick Reilly would claim a wife he didn't have.

He still had Tucker Hanks and Tommy keeping an eye on the man, hoping to find out what he was up to. But so far, Reilly had led them to nothing.

"He meet with anybody?" Conner asked, forcing himself to concentrate.

"Not that we've seen." Tommy shook his head and shrugged. " 'Course, you told us to stay out of sight, so we're outside, lookin' through a window, and we can't be sure.

Conner sighed heavily. "You have to stay out of sight. I don't want him knowin' he's being watched."

Tommy snorted. "Hell, he's so drunk all the time, I don't reckon he'd notice if we sat down at his table with him."

"Maybe. But you stay where you are."

"Whatever you say, boss. Anyhow, he ain't come out of the saloon at all. Just drinks all night and sleeps most of the day."

"What the hell's he up to, then?" Conner wondered aloud. They'd heard nothing from the sheriff that Reilly had threatened them with. So what was the man planning?

"I heard him arguin' with somebody," another voice piped up, and Conner half turned to look at Luke.

"You heard him? When?"

The boy ducked his head, then lifted it and squinted against the morning sun. "The other day. When Meara come and got me out of that durn school."

Well, why the hell hadn't the kid said anything? Conner wondered. "Where was this?" he asked, trying to keep the ring of impatience out of his voice.

Luke rubbed the tip of his nose with the back of his hand. "I was sneakin' around behind the saloon and I heard two men arguin' in the storeroom."

"You sure it was Reilly?"

"Not at first, but the more I thought about it, yeah." Luke nodded again for emphasis. "His voice sounds funny, like Meara's."

Funny. The Irish accent, Conner told himself. "Who was he talkin' to?"

"I don't know," Luke admitted. "I was gonna go closer, but then Meara found me and hauled me off to school, so I couldn't."

He would have wished for a bit more information, but

this at least was something. Now he knew that Reilly did know someone in town. Someone he argued with.

Conner was grateful to have something to concentrate on besides the confusion of his feelings for Meara. Mick Reilly was alive. And here. And lying through his teeth. *This* kind of problem Conner knew how to deal with.

"I shoulda told you before, huh?" the boy said softly.

"It's all right, Luke. You did fine." He smiled and hoped the kid wouldn't notice that the action was forced. "You found out more than we did."

Luke grinned at him.

That smile tugged at his heart, and Conner realized how easy it was to care for people. To love a child. But he also realized that without Meara, he might never have discovered that. "Why don't you go on to the barn and start forkin' some hay into the horses?" he said.

"Yessir."

As soon as the boy was out of earshot, Conner turned to Tommy. "Reilly's a stranger in town. If he's arguin' with somebody, I want to know who. You and Tucker keep a sharp eye out, and one of you stay close to the storeroom where you can hear good."

Tommy gave him a brief nod, then climbed back into the saddle.

"Tell Tucker I'll be in later myself. Hell. Maybe it's time I had a long 'talk' with Mick Reilly."

The kid nodded, wheeled his horse around, and rode out of the yard at a hard gallop. As the dust settled back down in his wake, Conner still stood there, rooted to the spot. His hands fisted at his sides, he acknowledged that he should have done this in the first place. Just have it out with Reilly himself.

He'd get the answers he needed. One way or the other.

CHAPTER SEVENTEEN

"Do you see what's happening?" Gideon demanded.

"A few problems," Daisy said with a shrug.

The Great Hall was empty, and their voices echoed in the vast stillness. Every other Dream Weaver had been making a point of steering clear of Gideon lately. Daisy, of course, having lived through Comanche raids, flash floods and the slings and arrows of "decent" women, wasn't going to let a cranky Dream Master scare her off.

"Problems?" Gideon shook his head, then glared at her. "I never should have listened to you."

"Take it easy, Gid," Daisy said, laying one hand on the Dream Master's forearm. "Everything is going to work out fine. Just like I told ya."

"You told me that your son would fall in love with Meara," he reminded, looming over her like a vulture over a fresh kill. "You told me that if Meara loved him in return, I'd be able to send her back to Earth to live so she could stop making my Eternity miserable with her little 'revolutions.'"

"And it's workin' out just like I said," Daisy muttered, wondering, not for the first time, how men always seemed to be put in charge of things *despite the fact they had so little vision.*

Gideon's black eyes glittered dangerously. A lesser woman might have known when to back off. But Daisy was a woman determined to see her plan through.

From the moment she'd met Meara Simon in the Dream World, Daisy had known that this was the woman for her son. As soon as she'd discovered that the Dream Master had the power to return the souls in his charge to the mortal world, everything else had fallen into place.

All she'd had to do was wait enough Earth years for Conner to grow up and realize that he needed a woman. After that, she'd needed an excuse to place Meara in Conner's path. That part had been easy enough, though. With the knack Meara had for causing trouble, all Daisy had had to do was wait for a good time and convince the girl she had to hide from Gideon.

Although convincing Gideon of the plan's rightness had taken a bit more effort. Still, Daisy thought with a private smile, she always had had a way with men.

Dead or alive.

"Nothing is working out," Gideon grumbled angrily. "Your son now thinks her a liar, and Meara is so miserable, she'll cause even more trouble than usual when she returns."

Daisy smoothed her hands down the shadow of her narrow waist, then back up to push her magnificent breasts higher in her low-cut gown. As she'd hoped, Gideon was distracted long enough for her to say, "The game ain't over yet, Gideon honey. And there's more than one way to skin a man—I mean, a cat."

Since she seemed to be less a pariah than she had been a few days ago, Meara lingered in town. There was no reason to rush back to the ranch. Heaven knew Conner wouldn't be happy to see her. In fact, she was beginning to suspect he would be greatly relieved to never have to see her again.

His cold expression when he looked at her and the careful distance he kept between them now tore at her and constantly made her rethink her decision to stay. Perhaps it would be best if she left now, when he would be more relieved than hurt at her departure.

But she couldn't bring herself to go. Not yet. Not when there was a chance for even a few more days here. How she'd grown to love this place and so many of the people. Grub, Luke, Dora Higgins, and even her husband Eli, had each claimed a piece of her heart. And of course, Conner. The man who had shown her what she had missed when last she had lived. The man who made her wish for mortality. The man she never should have met. The man she would love for eternity and miss for even longer.

She shivered slightly despite the warmth of the fall sun and stepped off the boardwalk into the street. A horse-drawn wagon lumbered toward her, and she paused, waiting for it to pass. From the end of the street came the strident tones of the blacksmith's hammer ringing against an anvil. A chill wind swept in off the lake, bringing the cool reminder that winter was on its way. Meara half turned and looked up at the ridge of mountains marking the rear of High Timber. She imagined this place she'd come to love covered in snow, and wished she could be there to see it.

But she would be gone before the first snow fell, and after a time, she'd be nothing but a dim memory to the people she'd met. Perhaps Luke would miss her longer than most, but children grow and put pain behind them. Even Conner would go on with his life, filling any emptiness her absence created with new things. New people. New loves. Not that he had loved her, mind you. She wouldn't fool—or torture—herself with that notion. But he had been fond of her. And when she was gone, he would find someone else to care for. Marry. Have children with.

How she would have loved to carry his child and hold it in her arms.

Meara winced at the pain that thought brought and closed her mind to the impossibilities of daydreams. Better she should spend what time she had remaining on earth trying to right a wrong. For that, she needed to find Mick Reilly and discover why it was he'd lied about her.

With renewed determination, she crossed the street and headed for the saloon—a spot she instinctively knew was the first place to start searching for an Irishman.

Meara waved one hand in front of her face to clear away the swirling dust left in the wake of the big wagon. She climbed the steps to the boardwalk, nodded absently to a woman she distinctly recalled snubbing her only a few days ago and kept walking, her gaze now locked on her destination.

Her heels clattered busily on the wooden planks beneath her feet as her mind whirled, looking for just the right thing to say to Mick Reilly. As she drew nearer to the saloon though, her steps slowed as she noticed, ahead of her, the Carlisle family gathered around a carriage. A man she didn't recognize was strapping leather bags to the back of the buggy while Hester Carlisle helped her daughter climb inside.

The heavyset woman then snapped her husband a sharp nod, muttered something that slapped at Robert Carlisle like a blow, then settled herself inside the buggy beside the little girl. The driver then snapped the reins over the horse's back and the carriage jerked into motion. One hand lifted to hold her bonnet in place, Hester Carlisle gave Meara one hard look before the buggy jostled past and continued on down the street.

The man left standing alone on the boardwalk still

hadn't noticed her and that was fine with Meara. She was in no mood to be confronting a man who'd already named her a whore. Pausing quietly in one spot, she thought to slip past him unseen once he was on his way again. But as the carriage carrying his family rolled down the street, Carlisle looked furtively around him, as if checking to see who had witnessed the odd farewell.

Meara felt a sting of discomfort as his black eyes fixed on her.

She fought down the urge to hurriedly cross the street. After all, unpleasant as he was, he didn't own the town. She'd every right to walk where she chose. She'd simply ignore him and hope he had the good grace to do the same. Lifting her chin bravely, Meara started walking again, determined to sail by him as though she couldn't see him a'tall.

She should have known the man wouldn't be ignored.

He grabbed her upper arm and swung her around to face him. This close to him, Meara nearly gasped at the changes she saw in the man. 'Twas more than his clothes, which looked rumpled enough to have been slept in. His once neatly combed hair looked dirty and untended. Salt-and-pepper whisker stubble covered his jaws, and deep violet shadows lay beneath his eyes. Eyes that bored into hers with a depth of hatred she'd never experienced before.

"You saw, didn't you?" he asked and the stench of stale whiskey breath fanned the air.

"Saw?" she asked, trying unsuccessfully to take a step back from him.

His grip on her tightened, his fingers digging into the flesh of her upper arm. "She left. Took my daughter and left."

She'd suspected as much from the amount of luggage accompanying the pair. And looking at him now, Meara wasn't surprised that Hester had fled with her child. She'd never thought of herself as easily frightened, but there was something disquieting about the odd glitter in his eyes. He stared at her, as if waiting for her to speak. To acknowledge his loss.

"*Me!*" he said in a harsh, tight groan. "I'm the only fool her father could bribe into marrying her, and *she* leaves *me*?"

So it wasn't for love of Hester that he mourned her passing, but as a blow to the man's too-high opinion of himself.

Meara glanced around her quickly, covertly. There was no one nearby. Odd, for the street had seemed so crowded only moments ago. Now, she and the man who'd set himself up to blacken her name and ruin Conner were as alone as if they stood in the middle of a field.

Hoping for a way to blunt his anger, she said, "I'm sorry," and knew it for a mistake the minute the words left her mouth.

"Sorry?" He spat the word back at her. Thrusting his face closer to hers, he said, "It's *your* fault she's gone. Yours and that bastard who stole my house."

A flame of anger burst into life in the pit of her stomach and did battle with the curl of fear already entwined there. The man had maligned her. Nearly cost Conner his home. Lost his wife and children and had decided to take the blame for none of it?

Meara tugged against his grip, but his fingers curled into her arm like a hawk's talons around a freshly caught rabbit. Clearly, there would be no getting away. Not until he'd had his say. And if that was the case, she told herself, then fear or no, she, too, would speak her mind.

"Conner didn't steal your ranch," Meara said, even knowing he would never see the truth in it. She yanked her arm in a more desperate attempt to free herself, and when she failed, heard herself say, "As for the other, I'd nothing to do with your wife leavin' ya, as well ya know."

A fat man in a checked suit, with a bowler hat perched

absurdly on his bald head came out of nowhere, strolled past them and Carlisle tugged her back on the walkway, out of the stranger's path.

"Sir," Meara called, but Carlisle gave her a shake that rattled her teeth, so she fell silent again quickly. The man kept walking, his steps, if anything, a bit more hurried than before.

She knew if she screamed loudly enough, dozens of people would come streaming from their shops to see what was the matter. And with help that close by, she was in no real danger, so she kept quiet. She wanted to handle this herself if she could. The townspeople had only just decided that perhaps she wasn't so evil as they'd thought, and she'd do nothing now that might change that opinion and harm Conner's future here.

Besides, more than a century ago, her brothers had taught her a few handy tricks designed to waylay a man out to maul her. And she remembered them all. Most importantly, she wasn't above using them if need be.

"The fools in this town," Carlisle said, with a quick, venom-filled glance at the nearly deserted street just a few feet from them, "are ready to forget what you are. Forgive your sins. All because of that damned teacher." His gaze snapped back to hers, and she noticed that spittle had formed at the corners of his mouth.

Meara inched backward and lifted her right foot, just in case it came down to her kicking him.

"But I know you for what you are," he went on, his voice low, hard. "No better than a whore."

"I'll not stand for that," she said, despite his fingers digging into her skin.

"If not for you, Conner James would have given up." Carlisle gave her another shake to emphasize his words. "He would have left when the town stopped doing business with him. And the ranch would have been mine again."

How little the man knew about Conner, she thought, if he truly believed what he was saying.

"Ya know nothing about the man ya claim to hate so," she said.

"I know all I need to know," he snapped. "He put a whore in my wife's place."

"No," Meara said flatly. "*You* did that, when you wagered your wife's home and lost it."

He sucked in a gulp of air and swung his free hand back in a wide arc. But before he could deliver the slap he clearly intended, Meara drew her right foot back and slammed her heel into his knee. There were other, more sensitive spots she might have aimed for, she knew. Her brothers had taught her well. But if this blow was enough to free her from the situation, Meara would leave it at that.

Carlisle's eyes widened. He yelped in pain, released her and staggered backward a step or two, crashing into the man who'd rushed up behind him. Then the haggard Carlisle fell to the boardwalk and lay between Meara and her would-be rescuer.

She nearly sighed in relief when she recognized Tucker Hanks.

"You all right, Miss Meara?" Conner's foreman asked, glancing down at the injured man. Moaning, Carlisle lay curled up on one side, clutching at his leg.

"Aye, Tucker, I am," she said, taking her first easy breath since running into Robert Carlisle.

Tucker grinned at her. "Tommy saw what was goin' on and I run down here, fixin' to teach this fella some manners." He scowled down at him before looking up at Meara again. "But, I reckon you don't need rescuin', do you?"

"Not any more, but I do appreciate the thought."

As if a storm had passed and it was now safe to come outside again, townspeople once more dotted the street.

But Meara ignored their curious stares as she rubbed her now-aching upper arm.

Tucker nodded, dusted his palms together, then offered Meara his arm. "Ma'am," he said, "can I escort you back to the ranch?"

She thought about that for a long minute before deciding that she was in just the right mood now to take on Mick Reilly and demand some answers.

"No," she said and Tucker looked at her, surprised. "But you *could* escort me to the saloon. There's a man I need to be talkin' to."

"Miss Meara," Tucker said with a shake of his head. "You can't go in there."

"And why's that?" she asked and stepped across Robert Carlisle to continue on to the saloon she'd started for earlier.

"It just ain't done, ma'am," Tucker said, keeping step with her. "Ladies ain't welcome. There's some real rough men in yonder. Usin' coarse language and such."

A soft scrabble of sound from behind her caused Meara to glance around quickly, in time to see Robert Carlisle limping hurriedly away. At least she wouldn't have him to worry about as well.

"It ain't respectable at all," Tucker finished earnestly.

"Then that's just the place I'll be findin' Mick Reilly."

"Reilly?" Tucker looked at her, stunned. "Does the boss know what you're up to?"

" 'Tis no business of his what I do."

"Maybe not," he said and stopped beside her when she paused outside the batwing doors. "But, ma'am, I don't figure the boss is gonna be one bit happy about this."

Taking pity on the man, Meara reached out and patted his arm briefly. "Then we won't tell him, will we?"

"Ma'am?" He looked at her blankly.

"As me mother used to say, 'A silent mouth is sweet

to hear.' " She peeked over the top of the twin doors into the shadowy interior of the smoky saloon.

"Miss Meara," Tucker told her firmly, "you go in there and we won't have to tell him. The whole town'll be talkin' about it."

The younger ranch hand, Tommy, appeared from the mouth of the alley beside the saloon and threw in his opinion as well. "It'd be a for-sure scandal, ma'am."

She slanted him a look. There was that. Hadn't she only just decided to not cause a scene with Carlisle because she didn't want the townspeople to turn on her—and so, Conner—again? Biting back an oath of frustration, Meara admitted silently that Tucker and Tommy were right. She couldn't very well go into the blasted saloon without sending the local gossips into a frenzy of whispered conversations.

"Miss Meara," Tucker said quietly, "you really ought to let me see you home now."

Sighing, she went up on her toes again for one last look into the saloon.

"He's right. Go home, Meara."

Meara gasped at the sound of Conner's voice and lost her balance. She caught herself by grabbing onto the tops of the swinging doors and instantly swung forward in a slow fall she couldn't seem to stop. The floor rushed toward her and Meara closed her eyes.

But Conner grabbed her around the waist and hauled her back against him. When she found her breath again, she lifted her gaze to look at him. "Conner," she said with a false note of brightness. "When did you get here?"

"Apparently just in time," he countered, and couldn't quite bring himself to release her. The past two days had seemed like forever to him. He'd hungered for the scent and the taste of her. His hands itched to touch her again. His body clamored for the peace he'd found deep within her.

The connection that they'd discovered together was the

main reason he was in town now. No matter what else lay between him and Meara, he owed it to both of them to find out what the hell Mick Reilly was up to. He remembered all too clearly the rush of pain and panic he'd felt the day the Irishman had shown up trying to claim Meara. He remembered the emptiness he'd felt at the thought of losing her.

And now he *had* lost her. Not to Reilly. But to the lies she'd told him to avoid having to say she didn't love him. A woman desperate enough to make up the wild tales she had was a woman ready to leave.

On that black realization, he released her abruptly. Conner stared into the green eyes he knew would haunt him forever and damned her for ever coming to his ranch.

And damn her twice for wanting to leave him.

CHAPTER EIGHTEEN

What are you doin' here?" Meara asked, splintering his thoughts.

Conner felt Tucker Hanks's interested stare and idly noticed that one or two of the townspeople had just "happened" to stroll slowly past them. But he ignored everything but Meara. As he had since the moment she'd entered his life.

"Keeping you from going into that saloon," he ground out.

She shook her head, and he deliberately avoided watching the way her hair swung and swayed about her face with the movement. " 'Tis my right—" she started to say, then corrected herself. "No. 'Tis my *duty* to discover the truth here."

A buzz of conversation swarmed around them, but neither took any notice. Conner's gaze was locked on her and she gave him back stare for stare. Then her eyes softened slightly, and he knew he was in trouble.

"What the hell do you think you can do that I can't?" he demanded, his voice deliberately harsh.

He watched her stiffen at his tone and thought it for the best. At least if she was mad at him, she wouldn't be giving him dewy-eyed looks that would melt his insides.

"I think," she said, tilting her chin defiantly, "I'll ask

Mick Reilly a few questions." She sniffed, jerked her head sharply, then spun around and started for the doors again.

Conner reached out, snagged the limp bow at the back of her dress and yanked her right back. Meara swung one hand behind her and smacked at his hand, but he didn't let go. From the corner of his eye, he noted several faces appearing above the batwing doors as a few of the saloon's customers took a peek at the commotion brewing.

"You're not goin' in there," Conner said flatly.

"And who's goin' to stop me?" she demanded.

He tugged at the bow again, drew her closer, then turned her dismissively into Tucker Hanks's arms. "I am," Conner said, then told his foreman, "Hold onto her even if you have to sit on her."

Tucker grinned, caught a heated glance from Meara, and immediately looked more fearful than pleased at his latest assignment.

Tommy stepped up behind the foreman and then shrunk back, obviously hoping his employer wouldn't put him, too, in charge of the small woman already trying to twist her way out of Tucker's grip.

"Conner James," Meara grumbled, seeming to notice for the first time the knot of curious people beginning to crowd around them. "I've just as much right as you to find out why the man lied about me."

She swung her hair out of her eyes, and the wild tangle of red danced around her head and shoulders in a shower of curls that made him want to snake his fingers through them. As he had before. Damn it.

He swallowed back that urge and lowered his voice as he leaned in closer to her. "It may be your right, Meara, but it's not your place."

"My *place* is it?" she practically snarled. "And who might you be to be tellin' me my *place?*"

"The man who's goin' to see to it that you stay out of

trouble for once." Someone closeby chuckled, but Conner ignored it. "Take her home," he told Tucker, and straightened up.

"I'll not leave," Meara warned him, and something in her green eyes let him know that she meant it.

Blast her, he needed to be able to concentrate on Reilly. He *didn't* need to be hearing her screams and shouts of outrage while he did it.

Sparing a quick glance at the interested faces of the growing mob of bystanders, Conner muttered, "Fine. Stay, then. But, Hanks . . . you keep her out of the way."

Then before she could say another word, Conner pushed through the doors, sending the curious customers flying off to either side of him. The room was cool and dim compared to the bright sunshine outside. A thin layer of blue-tinged smoke hung in the air and twisted with the puff of breeze he'd sent rushing ahead of him.

The saloon reeked of stale sweat, bad whiskey, and broken dreams. In a rush of memories, Conner recalled the nights of his youth and the hundreds of saloons just like this one that he and his father had lingered in. The only good thing that had ever happened to him in a saloon was winning his ranch in a game of poker. But one lucky hand wasn't enough to remove the ugliness he felt whenever he stepped inside a barroom.

But to get this settled, to clear up the lies, he would have been willing to walk into the mouth of hell.

Conner took a moment to let his eyes adjust to the shadows, then slowly turned his head until he found the man he'd come looking for. Slumped over a table, his bearded face resting on one outflung arm, Mick Reilly watched him approach through red-rimmed, whiskey-glazed eyes.

"Get up," Conner said when he stopped alongside the other man's table.

"Go 'way," Reilly muttered and turned his head aside. Around the room, Conner heard the half dozen or so morning customers move to form a wide half circle around the two men. The bartender leaned on his bar and crossed massive arms in front of him, clearly intending to stay out of whatever was about to happen.

Good. He wouldn't have stood for interference. And he sure as hell didn't need any help dealing with the likes of Mick Reilly.

Conner stared down at the drunk who'd been the start of all the problems between he and Meara—and the cause of the gossip that could have destroyed him. Angrily, he kicked at the man's chair leg and, drunk or not, Reilly reacted quickly.

He jumped up, steadied himself, then lifted one huge fist and shook it at Conner. "If it's a fight ya want, boyo, I'm the man to give it to ya."

Conner didn't think so. The other man was swaying slightly, and the slurred tone of his voice was testament to the amount of liquor he'd put away. As much as he wanted to pound his own fist into that florid, whiskey-soaked face, Conner doubted the man would even feel it in his condition.

As if to prove it, Reilly swung at him. Conner stepped to one side and the man's heavy body followed his fist's momentum, falling to the floor with a crash that set the glasses on the bar tinkling.

"He took the first swing," somebody said from the far corner. "I seen it, young fella. You go ahead on and tear into him."

"Tear into him?" someone else said. "Hell, he'd have to scrape him off the floor, first."

"I'll hold him for ya," yet another voice offered.

Conner flicked a glance at the last man. "I'm not going to hit him."

"Well, hell, boy," the first man said on a lusty sigh. "What'd you come in here for then? Gettin' everybody all primed for a good fight for nothin'?"

Conner bent over, reached down and grabbed the front

of Reilly's shirt, dragging the heavier man up until he stood swaying on his own two feet.

"Leave go," the drunk complained, swiping at Conner's hands ineffectually.

"Not until you do some talkin'," Conner told him. "I want to know why you lied about being married to Meara."

"Lied?" one of the men asked his neighbor. "Why would a man *want* to be hitched?"

"Heck, boy," another voice answered. "You seen that gal?"

"I have," a quieter voice said. "And no woman looks like that'd marry that fella."

"That's the lie the big man's talkin' about."

Conner inhaled sharply and sent a glare around the room, silencing the gossiping men. Then he slowly focused his attention on Reilly again. "Let's have it," he said, voice tight.

"Don't know what you're talkin' about," Reilly said with a snort.

"Yeah you do," Conner prompted, allowing his rising temper to color his voice. "You lied about Meara and then spread your story all over town."

From outside, came a rumble of conversations followed by Meara, warning, "Hush!" He shook his head slightly and hoped that all of the *good* citizens of High Timber were getting an earful. With so many witnesses gathered round, all he had to do now was get Reilly to confess.

"My head hurts," the man whined and lifted one hand to his forehead. "Can't think. Need a drink."

"Sweet Saint Bridget," Meara said from the doorway. "Need a drink. And himself already near to fallin' down."

Conner's teeth ground together, but he forced himself to concentrate on Reilly. "Well, you're not getting a drink. Not yet."

"Mother of Saint Patrick, Conner," Meara cried, louder this time, "he's not so drunk he can't answer a question or two."

"I know that," he shouted, frustrated now by more than the uncooperative man in front of him.

"Well, then," she yelled back, "ask him some, for pity's sake!"

"Hanks!" Conner shouted, glancing back over his shoulder. "Can't you keep her away from the damn door?"

"I'm tryin', boss," that man called, "but she ain't an easy female to hold onto."

One or two people outside laughed, then came the sound of a loud thump followed by a grunt of pain and Hanks's voice saying, "That hurt, ma'am."

"Nothing about Meara's easy," Conner muttered, tightening his grip on his opponent's dirty shirtfront. He gave the man a hard shake and demanded, "Why? Why'd you do it?"

The Irishman shook his head as if to clear some of the liquor-induced haze, then cocked his head to one side as he looked at him. "Fella paid me to."

"Who?" Conner asked, despite the gut-deep certainty of just which man was behind all of this.

"What's it worth to ya?" Reilly demanded, swayed backward and staggered fitfully to regain his balance.

"Don't you be givin' the likes of him any money!" Meara called out, her voice loud and clear.

"Shut up, ya harpy, ya!" Reilly yelled at her.

More laughter bubbled up from outside, and Conner shook his head, knowing Meara wouldn't be quiet now.

"Harpy, is it?" Her outraged tone rang out a moment later, and as she continued, her voice crept up several notches. "Why, ya no-good, drunken son of a fishmonger's dog . . ."

Someone laughed, and even Conner was almost willing to see the humor in the situation. Almost.

"I ask ya," Reilly said with a wave of his hand toward the doorway, "what man would want to settle himself with the likes of that screechin' banshee of a woman?"

"And what woman would be havin' *you*, I'm askin'?" Meara yelled right back, her voice carrying over the rising laughter. "Let me go, Tucker an' so help me Saint Patrick, I'll show that spalpeen a thing or two . . ."

Conner's chin hit his chest briefly as he sighed.

"Spalpeen, is it?" Reilly countered, then glanced at Conner. "Why would ya be wanting that female, mister? Are ya light in the head?"

He looked up into Reilly's confused eyes and nodded shortly. "Maybe I am."

"Pity, that."

"Enough," Conner said, his calm, even tone dispensing with the remaining chuckles around him. "I'll give you two full bottles and a train ride out of the territory for the name of the man who paid you."

"Done," Reilly snapped. "And glad I'll be to see the last of this miserable, cold place."

"Well, hell," the old man in the corner muttered darkly. "Looks like there ain't gonna be a fight after all."

"Give me a name," Conner said quietly, and noted with grim pleasure the silence that now filled the room. Good. He wanted everyone to hear so there would be no doubts left in anyone's mind.

Reilly shot an uncomfortable glance at the unsmiling men ringing him, then took a breath and said clearly, "Carlisle."

A few hisses of surprise issued from the assorted onlookers until it sounded like someone had stepped into a nest of rattlesnakes. This gave way to silence until one voice spoke up.

"I wish I'd known that a bit ago," Meara commented from the door. "I'd have kicked him a good deal harder, I would."

Conner half turned to look at her. "Kicked him?" he

demanded, wondering when she'd had time to confront that man and how he'd missed hearing about it. "When did you see Carlisle?"

"Hey, young fella!" the old man in the corner called out. "Watch out!"

Conner turned back around in time to see Mick Reilly's fist flying at his face. He ducked his head and instinctively threw a short, hard jab of a punch into his opponent's stomach. Reilly groaned loudly and dropped like a sack of potatoes to the sawdust strewn floor.

"Nearly got ya, young fella."

"Nah," someone else said, "a clear miss."

"Isn't it like me da always said," Meara observed, and Conner slowly turned to look at her. Only her mop of red hair and the clear green of her eyes were visible over the edge of the door.

Shaking his head, Conner couldn't keep himself from asking, "What's that?"

She lifted her gaze from the fallen Reilly to stare directly at Conner as she said solemnly, " 'Drink is the curse of the land. It makes you fight with your neighbor. It makes you shoot at your landlord—and it makes you miss him.' "

In spite of everything, Conner smiled then. Damn, she was a hard woman to ignore. And he didn't even want to think about what his life without her would be like. On that thought, he turned his back on the fallen drunk and dug into his pocket. Drawing out some money, he laid it on the closest table and told the bartender, "When he wakes up, see that he gets to the train with his two bottles."

"You bet," the other man muttered as Conner marched across the floor toward the doorway.

Meara backed up, forcing the others behind her to move as well. When he stepped out of the saloon, she lifted her gaze to meet his. "Where are you going now?"

she asked, although knowing Conner as she did, she knew what he would do next.

He looked away from her to stare briefly at the people surrounding them. "I'm going to have a talk with Carlisle."

"I seen him," someone offered. "He was headed to the livery."

As Conner nodded and turned, Meara fell into step beside him. "I'll come along, shall I?"

He stopped dead in his tracks and several of their followers bumped into each other. "No, this time, I go alone."

"You'll not," she argued, determined to see this through to the bitter end. She wasn't about to let Conner go and face down the man behind all of his troubles. She'd already seen Carlisle that morning and knew him to be a man on the edge of a madness large enough to swallow him down. Who knew what a man in that condition was capable of?

"Dammit, Meara," Conner said, and two or three of the interested bystanders sucked in gulps of air. Clearly frustrated, he drew her to one side and leaned down so that she and she alone could hear him. "I don't want you near him, do you understand? I don't want you hurt."

Looking into those Kerry-blue eyes of his, Meara felt her heartbeat stagger. He cared for her, and that knowledge should have made her happy. Instead, it tore at her, knowing as she did that there was no future for them. She'd been a fool to remain after her memory had returned. Needlessly torturing the both of them with her presence, she was only driving the hurt deeper, making it that harder to recover from.

In that moment, she realized that as soon as this last piece of business was finished, she would go. Leave Conner, Luke, and all she cared about to return to the Dream World forever. But until she left, she would be with him.

"Ah, Conner," she said softly, laying one hand on his forearm. "The man can't hurt me."

"You don't know that."

"Aye, I do." She pulled in a shuddering breath and reminded him, "I died long ago, Conner. He can't hurt me now."

His features tightened and his blue eyes narrowed until she could no longer read his feelings in their depths. "Stay out of this, Meara," he said simply. "Please." Looking behind her, he added, "Hanks . . ."

"Yessir, boss," came the reluctant reply.

Then Conner started for the livery, the now-sizable crowd of onlookers right behind him. Women lifted the hems of their skirts to hurry after the men's longer strides. Meara shook her head and made to follow when Tucker Hanks took hold of her arm.

"Miss Meara . . ." he started to say.

Meara drew her right foot back and warned, "I'll kick you again, Tucker, though I've no wish to . . ."

Immediately, he released her, took a half step back, and lifted both hands. "I ain't gonna stop you," he said, clearly disgusted with her and himself.

She nodded, jumped off the boardwalk, and ran after the man she loved and the others, Tucker hot on her heels.

Conner ran into the livery stable, his gaze flicking from one shadowed stall to the next. Absently, he noted the blacksmith had wandered in to see what all the commotion was about, but he paid no more attention to him than he did to the people following him, waiting for a confrontation they'd been expecting between Carlisle and Conner James for far too long.

Carlisle had spread his venom about Conner months before Meara had come to stay. Ever since losing his ranch, the man had been bound and determined to make sure Conner never knew a moment's peace on the place.

Meara's arrival had only fueled a fire that had long been smoldering. With a few well-aimed sparks from Carlisle, the town had erupted into a bubbling pot of gossip and lies. Well, now it was time for the finish.

Conner'd tried to be patient. He hadn't wanted an enemy. Hell, if he hadn't won Carlisle's ranch, someone else would have. All he'd wanted was a home of his own. A place to put down roots. A chance to build a future. Then later, he'd wanted Meara to join him there. To be a part of a life he'd never before imagined having.

But Carlisle, like so many men who authored their own destruction, couldn't bear to accept the responsibility for it himself.

Today, Conner would see that he did.

"Carlisle," he shouted, and the name seemed to echo over and over again in the dimly lit structure. The horses penned in individual stalls moved restively. Heavy, iron-shod hooves pounded against the earth like a chorus of heartbeats.

A gunshot sounded out suddenly, and the bite of a bullet slamming into the beam beside him had Conner crouching low instantly. Surprised shrieks rose up and were quickly silenced as the men in his audience swiftly hustled the women to safety, just outside the livery. Hopefully, Meara was among them.

"Shooting me won't do you a damn sight of good," Conner shouted, his gaze moving over every square inch of the damned building, searching for Carlisle. "I talked to Reilly," he called. "Everybody knows you paid him to lie."

Carlisle laughed giddily, the sound scratching the air. It wasn't the reaction Conner expected.

"Doesn't matter anymore," the other man said finally.

Conner shifted his gaze to a stall just to his right. The horse stabled there pranced nervously in the tight enclosure, and Conner was sure he saw another shadow ducking behind the big animal's body.

"It's all your fault," Carlisle yelled, and again that horse shifted wildly, arching its back and rearing its head.

Another bullet exploded from Carlisle's gun, this shot going wide of Conner's position. Apparently the man couldn't get off a clean shot, what with the horse continuing to change position and constantly ruining his aim. Keeping low, Conner started for the stall.

"Damn you!" Carlisle shouted. "I didn't mean to lose my ranch!"

"You put the bet on the table," Conner reminded him before he could think better of it.

"A gentleman wouldn't have taken the bet."

Gentleman. For months, Carlisle had done nothing but point out just how far from a gentleman Conner was. The man was a fool if he'd really believed anyone would return a ranch fairly won and desperately wanted.

"You've said yourself that I'm just a gambler's son," Conner said, inching still closer to where the man hid.

"A gambler and a whore," Carlisle screamed. "Just like the whore you've taken up with!"

Conner gritted his teeth and shuffled closer. Behind him, he heard the townspeople muttering and could only hope that Tucker had succeeded in keeping Meara back.

"You made me do this, James!" Carlisle yelled furiously. "You! All you had to do was quit. Give up the ranch and go away. You humiliated me. You took everything from me. You made my wife leave me."

The frightened horse's breathing strained the air and frantic hooves pounded against the stall door.

"Carlisle," Conner told him as he got closer, "get on out of there and we'll settle this. Just the two of us." Why the hell he cared if the man was crushed by the panicked animal, Conner didn't know.

Another gunshot, and the horse reared up on its hind legs, whinnying desperately.

"You cost me everything," Carlisle screamed. "You left me with *nothing*! Nothing!"

Another gunshot and the horse went crazy. Clamoring back and forth against the stall doors. Rearing up and down, its hooves slicing the air. Eyes rolling, mane flying, the animal snorted and screeched in fear, and then another scream, a man's scream, tore through the air and was cut, abruptly and finally, off.

Moving quickly, Conner reached for the latch. Before the terrified animal could bolt, he grabbed its bridle and held on tight, easing the horse out of the stall, all the while whispering soothing noises and running his hands over its black coat.

As the people began to crowd through the door, Conner saw Meara push her way to the forefront and hurry to his side. He glanced into the stall long enough to note Carlisle's wide, staring eyes and the odd twist to his neck. Then he looked away, instinctively searching out the cool green eyes that held the peace he'd always searched for.

"It's over," he said, and held her when she leaned into him.

Meara's gaze rested briefly on the body of the man who had caused so much grief. Then she determinedly turned away, looking at the small crowd of people thronging around them. Whispered comments rustled the air like dead leaves swirling in the wind.

"Got himself killed."

"No more than he deserved."

"Poor Hester . . . it's a blessing she left before this happened."

Conner released the still-agitated horse into the blacksmith's care, then draped one arm around Meara's shoulders. Together, they started for the wide double doors. The knot of people split apart to allow them passage.

A few hesitant smiles were offered them as they walked. And one woman even went so far as to reach out and touch Meara's arm briefly, as if offering apology and friendship all at once.

They stepped out of the shadowed barn into the warm

sunshine, and Meara lifted her face to its heat. It would be all right now. Conner would be all right. He would be able to keep his ranch, and maybe, one day, he would find a woman to share his life with him.

"C'mon," he said, and gave her shoulders a squeeze.

Meara looked up at him.

"This is finished," he said, his gaze locked on her. "What's between us isn't. Let's go home and sort the rest of this out."

She nodded, not trusting herself to speak. But Conner was wrong. What was between them was just as finished as the confrontation with Carlisle. All that remained was the final goodbye. Then she would go back where she came from and spend the rest of eternity mourning the loss of him.

CHAPTER NINETEEN

Once back at the ranch, Conner was swept up into an emergency of a different kind. His prize mare had gone into labor. Meara looked at the timing of the event as a blessing. She'd no wish to spend the last of her days with Conner fighting. And she'd no doubt that's exactly what they would be doing at this very moment if they'd had a chance to sit and talk as he'd wanted.

Now, hours after leaving town, she walked into Luke's bedroom and blew out all but one of the burning lamps. Outside the window, night crouched close, kept at bay only by the glow of the moon and the circle of lamplight at the head of the wide bed.

Sitting gently on the edge of the mattress, Meara drew the blankets up close under Luke's chin, then smoothed his hair back from his forehead. The boy lay nestled in a puddle of golden lamplight, his still-damp, clean hair lying soft on the linen pillowcase beneath his head. Just looking at him, safe and warm and loved, brought a happiness to Meara's heart that was tinged slightly with the regret she felt at knowing she would soon be leaving him.

"Everything's all right now, ain't it?" Luke asked quietly.

"Oh, aye," she said, forcing a calm she didn't feel into her voice. "Everything's grand."

The boy nodded sleepily. "Conner says all the trouble's over."

"I know, darlin'."

"An' he says I can help train the new foal when its born, too." A small smile curved his lips as he drifted closer to the Dream World.

"That's wonderful," Meara told him and felt the sting of tears behind her eyes. Tears she dare not let the child see, because once he did, he would ask questions she didn't have the heart to answer.

"He says the ranch is *my* home now," Luke said, and the words came out like a prayer.

"Of course 'tis," Meara said, running the tips of her fingers along his cheek.

"An' I don't never have to leave?"

"Never." Conner's voice, deep and soft, came from the doorway. Meara's heart shot into her throat as she swivelled her head to look at him.

"Is it a boy or a girl?" Luke asked on a tired sigh.

Conner smiled briefly. "It's a colt. Almost bigger than you already."

Luke's eyelids fluttered half open. "He's part mine, huh? 'Cause this is my home."

Amazing, he thought as he walked quietly to the foot of Luke's bed and stared down at his peaceful expression. Amazing how a boy's pleasure could light up a man's soul. "That's right," he assured him. "Just like it's my home. And Grub's and Hanks'."

"And Meara?" Luke asked sleepily. "Is it her home, too?"

That question tugged at his insides. He slanted a glance at Meara, and when she ducked her head to avoid his gaze, his heart ached. But Conner wasn't going to be the one to tell this kid that she was leaving—as he knew she would. He wouldn't make it easy on her. He would let Meara herself break the boy's heart.

"It's her home, too," he said, and wished it were true.

Luke smiled softly again and this time, took that smile with him into his dreams.

Reluctantly, Meara stood up from the bed and followed Conner from the room. Once Luke's door was closed, she crossed the hall and went into her own bedroom. When she heard Conner come in behind her, she wasn't surprised.

"You're leaving, aren't you?" he asked and shut her door soundlessly.

"Aye. I have to get back."

"When?"

She sucked in a gulp of air that did nothing to quiet the clamoring inside her. "By the new moon."

Only a week or so away, he thought, horrified at the hollow sensation that realization opened up inside him. To disguise the pain he felt at the mention of her leaving, he barked a short burst of laughter that scratched his throat as well as the silence staining the room.

"New moon?" he asked with a shake of his head. "How do you get to this Dream World of yours? On a broomstick?"

"I'm not a witch," she snapped.

"Don't be too sure." At least that might explain what she'd done to his mind and heart. How she'd ruined him for any other woman. How she'd made *him* of all people start thinking about the future. About the two of them together. About children. About wild, crazy notions that were never going to come true.

Earlier today, they'd faced down an entire town together. They'd put rumors and gossip to rest and had returned triumphantly to the ranch. Together.

Now it was as though a wall stood between them. A wall he couldn't see over or around. A wall he had no idea how to breech.

Damn her for making him want things he'd never wanted before and then ruining the dream before it beame real enough to touch.

"Conner, will ya go on punishin' me for who I am?"

"Will you go on lying about dreams and being a hundred years old?"

" 'Tis no lie," she said sadly.

"It has to be," he said, giving into the frustration welling within him. "It makes no sense. None of it!"

"Why must you be so stubborn?"

"Why can't you be honest?" he shot right back.

"I have been."

"No." He reached out and grabbed her. His hands tightened around her upper arms as he pulled her close enough that she had to tip her head back so their eyes could meet.

Were her eyes an even darker green tonight than usual? Or was it simply that her face had lost all color? The splash of freckles across her nose stood out in sharp relief against the milk-white creaminess of her features. And those eyes of hers seemed to widen even as he watched her.

How had this happened? How had he allowed himself to fall in love? His gaze moved over her face, desperate now to etch this memory onto his brain.

Jesus, he loved her.

Conner James, in love.

He never would have believed it. Hell, he'd never even been interested in the possibility until she fell into his life. And he'd been right to avoid this feeling, he told himself. Because as sweet as the love was, losing it was killing him.

It took every ounce of will power he possessed to keep from throwing her onto her bed and making love to her until both of them died of exhaustion.

But that still wouldn't be enough to make her stay and he knew it. Not if she was so frantic to get away from him that she made up ridiculous stories about Dream Weavers and meeting his dead mother in some kind of strange Heaven where people worked rather than sitting around playing golden harps.

"Conner." She said his name softly, and it slipped inside him like a double-edged blade.

"Why are you doing this?" he demanded roughly, giving her a shake that sent her long, curly hair into a shimmer of movement.

A sheen of water filmed her eyes, and he cursed himself for causing her tears even while damning her for using a woman's ultimate weapon against him.

"Conner, love," she whispered, and his mind flashed back to those hours in her bed, when she'd held him and called him her love.

"Don't say that."

"Love?" she asked.

Moonlight flooded the room through the shining windowpanes, bathing her in a silvery glow that made her look as though she did belong to another world. As though she was already slipping away from him. To a place he would never be able to reach her. She looked beautiful and sad, and Conner knew that he would be haunted by this image of her until the day he died.

Giving into an impulse too strong to deny, Conner pulled her to him and bent his head to claim her mouth as if he had the right. As if there wasn't already a good-bye hanging in the air between them.

His tongue parted her lips. He was shaken to his bones at the rightness of it. A sweet sense of homecoming swept through him as his tongue stroked hers. She leaned into him, giving him more than he could have taken. Her breath brushed across his cheek, and he told himself to remember. Remember the feel of her in his arms, the scent of her hair, the taste of her lips.

Because she was already leaving him.

Because soon, all he would have were the memories of this woman, empty dreams and a shattered, dark future.

When he drew back at last, he held her face between

his palms for a long minute. His gaze moved over her features. He tried to tell himself he would survive her loss, but he knew that just the thought of her leaving was already tearing at his soul.

But he wouldn't tell her of his love. That final bit of humiliation he would keep to himself. Because through all of this, he was sure of one thing. She didn't love him as he did her. If she had, she couldn't leave. Wouldn't leave. And he'd be damned if he'd give her the satisfaction of knowing that she'd won a love he hadn't known he possessed.

He released her abruptly and took a half step backward. "Enough of this, Meara," he said, and she winced at his tone. "No more. If you're going, go now. The hell with this 'new moon' notion. Do all of us a favor and just go."

"Ah, Conner," she said and reached out one hand toward him.

He shook his head and moved toward the door, stepping past her as if she was already invisible to him. "I mean it." He stopped and grabbed hold of the cut-glass knob. Turning to look at her over his shoulder, he added, "Don't drag this out another week. If you're so damned anxious to leave us . . . *me*, then get out. Tonight."

Her features stricken, she said, "I've no choice, man. Can ya not see that?"

"No, I can't. We all have choices, Meara. And I guess you just made yours."

He walked out of her room, and she was alone in the pale light of a fading moon. She moved to the window and stared blindly out at the night. Her heart broken, her chest tight, she struggled for breath past the tight hand closed around her throat. He was right. Meara closed her eyes at the memory of the pain glittering in Conner's blue-eyed gaze. She couldn't bear to spend the next week with him, seeing that pain, knowing that she was the cause of it.

He loved her. Though he hadn't said the words, she knew it to be true. A man didn't feel such pain without a deep, abiding love being at the root of it.

Wrapping her arms around her middle, Meara turned her back on the window, walked to her bed, sat down, and rocked silently. All of this because she had been hiding from Gideon's wrath. 'Twas fitting somehow that the torture she'd found in hiding was far worse than anything the Dream Master might have done to her.

Now, there was nothing left for her here. She had to go back where she belonged and try to pick up the threads of eternity.

Meara smoothed Luke's hair back from his forehead, leaned down, and brushed a goodbye kiss against his temple. The boy smiled in his sleep and snuggled deeper into his pillow. His dreams peaceful now, he was lost in the countless pleasures awaiting a nine-year-old boy in the Dream World.

Standing up, she covered him with the quilt, tucked it in around his small body, and took one last, loving look at him. How she would miss watching this boy grow up. Meara knew he would miss her when he woke to find her gone, but it was better this way. She wouldn't be able to look at him and explain why she had to leave or even where she was going.

'Twas because of her cowardice, too, that she wouldn't stop for a last look at Conner. She didn't have the strength for it.

On that thought, she turned to leave, stopping at Luke's bedroom door for one last look at a tousled blond head and the smile of a child she'd grown to love as her own.

Then she closed her eyes, concentrated and returned to the world she'd come from.

Gray mist shivered around her and Meara strode deeper into it. A sense of familiarity welcomed her, and she felt, rather than saw, other Dream Weavers close by.

Lost in her own misery, she blinked back the tears born on Earth and carried into this place that knew neither love nor pain.

"Meara!" Conner's voice rang out, and she turned abruptly to stare into the encroaching mists.

He was dreaming of her. Searching for her.

Did he regret asking her to leave? Was he as steeped in melancholy as she?

Meara looked over her shoulder, in the direction of the Great Chamber, then back again toward the man she loved, and made her decision. Even if only this one last time, she would go to Conner and be with him the only way she could.

In his dreams.

Conner searched everywhere for her.

He had to find her. Hold her.

Time was running out.

He felt it, knew it instinctively. There was no waiting until the new moon. She'd done as he'd foolishly demanded and left him too soon.

Tonight.

He ran as fast as he could, but still he hardly moved. It was as if his boots were nailed to the mist covering the ground. The taste of fear, sharp and bitter, settled on his tongue. Panic welled up inside him. What if he was too late? What if he never found her again?

Conner's eyes narrowed as he squinted into the filmy barrier. But there was nothing. No sign of her. He shouted her name again, fighting against the invisible bonds that held him to this place— kept him from reaching her.

He'd lived a lifetime alone and that had always been enough. Until now. Now, when she was lost to him, he knew that life without Meara would be meaningless.

But it wasn't this fog keeping her from him. And he couldn't believe her stories about dreamers and guardians. She simply didn't love him, and he didn't know how to fight that.

Then she was there, running out of the grayness directly into his arms. Relief coursed through him. Her features joyous, he let himself believe that perhaps he'd been wrong. Maybe she did love him. Maybe there was still hope. Otherwise why would she still come to him in his dreams?

Her long red hair flew out behind her in a waving flag of color amid all of the nothingness, and when she was close enough, he swept her into his arms. They clung to each other, hands and mouths groping, seeking. He held her tighter, molding her body to his, as if he'd never let her go. He buried his face in the curve of her neck and inhaled her scent, taking it deeply within him.

Nothing he'd said to her mattered at all. He didn't care anymore if she loved him. It was enough that he loved her. More than his next breath.

He felt her hands running up and down his back, smoothing over his bare flesh and up into his hair as she pulled his mouth down harder on hers. He devoured her, his mouth moving on hers even as his hands explored her body with familiar sureness.

"Stay with me, Meara," he whispered when he tore his mouth from hers long enough to drag air into screaming lungs. Looking down at her, he said the three words he'd never thought he'd have occasion to say. The words he'd held from her, wanting her to feel the same pain he did. "I love you."

"Ah, Conner," she told him, heartbreak in her voice, "I love you, too. More than you could know."

He looked long and deeply into her eyes and saw the truth. A truth that nearly brought him to his knees. She did love him. And yet, his heart told him he would still lose her.

"Stay, damn it!" He entwined his fingers through her hair, pulling her head back until she was forced to look into his eyes. "Stay with me."

" 'Tis not up to me, love," she said, reaching up to cup his cheek in the palm of her hand.

But he didn't want to hear her say she wouldn't stay. Not now. He tasted the skin at the base of her throat and felt her tremble in his arms. He tightened his hold on her, even though his own body shook with the force of his response to her.

He couldn't lose this. Couldn't give her up. He needed her. Like air and water and food, he needed her. Without her, there was nothing beyond a dark emptiness that seemed to stretch out in front of him like an immense, yawning blackness threatening to envelop him.

Conner drew her down with him, and the gray mist around them rose up and settled over them like a fine, soft blanket. Alone in the quiet, they came together. In an explosion of desire, lips and tongues mated as their bodies did, wildly, hungrily, with frenzied strokes and silent promises.

Poised over her, weight braced on his palms, Conner pushed himself home, sheathing his body deeply inside hers, glorying in the sweetness of her body cradling his. He drove harder against her. Closer. Tighter. He wanted to touch her heart. Brand her soul. And she lifted her hips against him, welcoming his powerful thrusts, moving with him, pulling him farther inside until he no longer knew where his body ended and hers began. They fit together as if made for each other.

She loved him. The words filled his mind and heart.

He bent his head to taste her breasts, one after the other. His tongue stroked her flesh with long, hot sweeps of passion, tasting, sucking. He drew the edges of his teeth across their sensitive tips and nipped at her gently.

Meara moaned, lifted her legs and locked them around his middle. Holding onto his head, she guided him from one rigid nipple to the other, urging him silently to take more. Give more.

He moved against her in a timeless rhythm, his body thrusting and retreating, her soft sighs and breathless anticipation feeding his desire until it became an inferno, swallowing him in its flames.

"I love you," he whispered, relishing saying the words again, and wishing he had a lifetime to repeat them.

Her hands moved over him, and he felt the heat of her touch warm him to his soul and beyond. This woman. Only this woman, he thought. He suckled her, his tongue working the sensitive tip of her nipple relentlessly until she groaned aloud, arching into him, demanding everything he had and more.

And he gave it to her.

A fever built within him. The raging heat engulfed him, and he pulled her into the flames with him. One last, powerful thrust and together they jumped into the bottomless chasm that cradled lovers on the fall to oblivion.

Moments later, a deep, angry voice seethed through the enshrouding mist. Distant and yet demanding in its intensity, that voice shouted, "Meara!" and shattered their sweet interlude.

"Sweet Saint Bridget," she muttered frantically, " 'tis Gideon!"

"Gideon?" Conner asked as he stood up beside

her. "Who in the hell is this Gideon and what's he doing in my dream?"

All around them, the mists were changing. The gray brightened to silver and shimmering streaks of gold moved through it, like patterns of lightning bolts in a summer storm.

"What's going on, Meara?"

"I have to go," she whispered urgently.

"I won't let you," he said firmly and took a step closer.

"Conner, go back," she told him, one hand on his chest. "You must wake up now. Go back to your world and leave me to mine."

"My world? Yours?" He grabbed her and pulled her tightly to him. "What about our world? This is crazy, Meara."

"No," she said, with a quick glance over her shoulder. " 'Tis the Dream World. Where I belong and you do not."

"Meara!"

That voice came again and even the mists seemed to tremble with its thundering power.

"Go, Conner," she said. "Go quickly."

"Gideon," he demanded instead, refusing to be run out of anyplace until he was good and ready to go. "You mentioned him before. Who is he? Why's he here?"

"Gideon is the Dream Master," Meara told him. "And I think he's here to deliver my punishment."

Conner straightened up and turned his gaze on the surrounding fog. He'd be damned before he stood by and watched anybody punish Meara.

"This is loco," he said, more to himself than to her. It was the strangest dream he'd ever had. And yet it all felt so real. Loving Meara. The silvery mists. Gideon's big mouth. "Why would this Dream Master want to punish you?" he asked, then added, "Not that he's going to get the chance."

"I've done something no other Dream Weaver has ever done," she confessed, taking a long, last look into his eyes. "I've fallen in love with a mortal."

Conner's heart nearly burst from his chest. "Say it again."

"I love ya, ya stubborn man," she said, a reminder of her temper leaping into her voice. "Have ya not been listening to me?"

Before Conner could enjoy the sensation of knowing she loved him, the spell between them was broken.

A tall, lean man with long dark hair and eyes the color of midnight joined them suddenly and Meara took a step away from Conner. He grabbed her arm and pulled her behind him, instinctively moving to protect her. With his life, if necessary.

"Meara," Gideon said, locking his gaze on the human who dared to defy him. "Tell your mortal goodbye."

"Goodbye, Conner love," she said, and Conner whipped around to discover that she was gone. Only her words were left behind, echoing softly in the mist. "Be well. Be happy."

A deep, rumbling growl rolled up from his chest and roared through the Dream World as he turned back to face the so-called Dream Master.

But Gideon, too, was gone.

And he was alone in the now cold, still, gray world.

Conner woke abruptly, gasping for breath.

He jerked into a sitting position and stared blankly around him at the surrounding darkness. Still alone, he stared at the shadowed corners of his bedroom as if he'd never seen it before. Heart pounding, he threw his legs off the side of the bed, stood up, then stalked to the window. Throwing up the sash, he breathed deeply, drawing the cool, night air into his straining lungs.

Conner's body felt depleted, drained, and he knew that what he'd just experienced was real.

It didn't matter that it made no sense.

He felt the truth in his bones. It had all happened.

Then another truth reared up inside him.

Meara was gone.

Damn it, the one time she actually *listened* to him was the one time when he'd made no sense. What kind of fool tells the woman he loves to get out? Snatching up his jeans from the chair he'd tossed them on earlier, he pulled them on, then marched barefoot out of his room and across the hall. He threw open her door and stared helplessly at the empty bedroom.

The bed hadn't been slept in. There was no light burning. She was gone as if she'd never been. He suddenly felt cold all over. How would he stand it? How could he continue to live in a place that so definitely carried her stamp on it?

Conner's fist slammed into the doorjamb. The aching sting in his knuckles was nothing compared to the gaping hole in his heart. He bit back a groan as his empty future opened up in front of him. He would have to face that kitchen every morning. He would stare at the splotchy yellow walls and remember Meara's pride. Her pleasure in making his house a home.

Every room in the ranch house would hold memories just waiting for their chance to ambush him. Living there would be torture, he realized. Yet at the same time, he couldn't leave.

Living without Meara will be hard enough, he told himself. And the constant reminders of what he'd had for too short a time would be more than painful. But it would be worse to live in a place where he couldn't even imagine her spirit wandering through the house with him.

Somehow, he had allowed the woman who had made his life worth living to disappear forever.

Silently, Conner walked back to his own room and strode to the window again. He looked out at the wide, star-splattered sky overhead as if he could see past the brilliant points of light to worlds he couldn't even imagine. To one particular world that he'd had all too brief a glimpse of.

It was all real.

He felt it.

Dream Weavers. His mother. An existence beyond death. And Meara was a part of it all.

The woman he loved was as unreachable now as the very stars.

"Ma," he whispered fervently, his grip on the windowsill tightening until his knuckles stood out white in the darkness. "If there's anyway you can do it . . . send her back to me."

"Where's Meara?" Luke asked as he ran into the kitchen and skidded to a stop beside Grub.

"Don't know, boy," the man said, shaking his head slowly. "Ain't seen hide nor hair of her this morning."

Luke frowned thoughtfully. Usually, Meara was in the kitchen now, fixing up some special treat for breakfast. Every morning when he woke up, he would lie in bed, listening for her. The sounds of her quick footsteps in the hall, snatches of songs she sang softly to herself. Just knowing she was there was enough to let him know everything was all right. But this morning, he hadn't heard a thing.

Worry curled up tight in his stomach, making him feel all sick and strange like he had a couple of months back after eating six sour apples. Idly, he rubbed his belly, hoping to ease the ache building up there. But it didn't help.

"You reckon she went to town?" he asked quietly.

Grub glanced away from his mixing bowl to look at him briefly. "Maybe," he allowed cautiously. "But none of the horses're missin', and I don't think she would have tried walkin' to town again."

No she wouldn't, Luke thought. Meara herself had told him that trying to walk in this up-and-down country was a lesson in patience she'd no wish to learn again.

So if she wasn't in town and she wasn't in the house . . . where *was* she?

"I'll go look for her outside," he said suddenly, breaking for the back door, his shoes clattering loudly on the floor.

"I already did, boy," Grub said, and the note of kindness in his voice tightened Luke's stomach even further.

He looked over his shoulder at the older man who had become his friend. Sweeping his long hair out of his eyes, Luke said, "I'll look again. And I'll find her. I'll bring her here. For breakfast."

Eyes filled with sadness and regret, Grub nodded.

Luke shouted at him and heard fear in his voice. Fear that was rising in his chest, threatening to choke him. "I *will* find her. You'll see. You'll see!"

Then he was out the door, slamming it behind him.

Grub walked to the window, pulled back the curtains and looked after the boy. Luke raced to the barn and after only a few moments, ran back out again. His head turning this way and that, he looked frantically for signs of the woman he loved so desperately. Then he took off again, running for the corral and after that, the stable.

Grub had thought better of Meara. He hadn't thought she would just up and go . . . hurting the boy this way.

The older man stood silently at the window, feeling every one of his sixty-eight years. His eyes filmed with a sheen of tears, and he reached up to wipe them away.

He wished he could spare the boy this, but he knew that Luke had to discover for himself the truth that Grub had already reluctantly accepted.

Meara was gone.

And nothing would ever be the same again.

Late that night, Conner left Luke's bedroom and walked along the hall toward the stairs. The boy had finally fallen asleep, tears still staining his cheeks. All Conner had been able to do for him was hold him and let him cry. He couldn't give the child the one thing he needed— an assurance that Meara would come home.

All day, despite everything, despite knowing deep in his bones that Meara was gone for good, Conner hadn't been able to keep from looking for her. A part of him had expected her to run out of the house, calling him to supper.

And when she didn't, another piece of his soul died.

Now, the house lay in darkness.

But it was more than simply a lack of light.

With Meara gone, Conner knew the darkness would never completely lift.

He walked down the stairs, turned and headed for his office. Unable to sleep, he'd decided to get up and try to keep his mind off Meara by studying the figures in the accounts ledgers.

He took a seat behind the desk, struck a match, and held the wavering flame to the wick of the oil lamp. As he set the chimney back in place, dancing patterns of light filled the room. Conner's gaze moved over the familiar place again and again before he realized that he was looking for something in particular.

And it wasn't there.

Gritting his teeth, he pushed up from the chair, marched out of the office, down the hall and into the shadow-filled main room. Conner knew where it was. He'd put it there himself a day or two ago. He crossed the floor with determined strides, his narrowed gaze piercing the darkness, until he came to the small table set just behind the sofa.

And there it was.

The white china ivy pot, just where he'd left it.

His chest tightened uncomfortably, and he fought down a wave of frustrated fury and heartrending regret. Meara wasn't there to play the game anymore.

She would never be with him again.

Conner reached down and gently rubbed one of the shiny, dark green ivy leaves between his thumb and forefinger. A soft, sad smile curved his mouth briefly as he recalled the first day she'd potted the silly plant.

Slowly then, his smile faded and after a long, thoughtful moment, he picked up the china bowl and carried it to his office.

CHAPTER TWENTY

Conner was miserable.

For a week now, he'd spent his days working himself to exhaustion so that he'd be able to sleep. And then in his dreams, he searched restlessly for Meara.

But he couldn't find her.

For the first time since meeting her, his dreams were empty. Colorless. Lifeless. And he was more alone now than he had ever been.

Stepping out of the kitchen, he squinted against the morning sun and turned his head to look over the ranch yard. A couple of the men were already in the corral working one of the stallions. Another, he knew, was in the stable, looking after the mare and the foal born the night Meara left.

Hanks was out on the range somewhere, and Hobart was up in the high timber. Since Grub was in the kitchen banging pots and pans, that left only one person to be accounted for.

Conner shifted his gaze to the wrought-iron gate that arched over the drive leading into the ranch. As he'd expected, Luke was there.

Every day, from sun up to sun down, leaving only long enough to take care of his chores, Luke was at that gate, waiting. The kid's gaze never strayed from the long road leading from the ranch to town.

Conner wasn't the only one suffering Meara's loss.

He stepped off the porch and walked to where the boy sat, his back braced against the gate. Luke turned his head slightly as Conner approached, yet still managed to keep his gaze trained on the road.

Going down on one knee in the dirt, Conner looked at the boy and shook his head sadly. "Luke, you got to stop this."

"She'll be back," he said.

Conner sucked in a gulp of air and forced himself to say the words he'd been trying not to even think about for a week. "Meara's gone, Luke. And she won't be back, son."

"She wouldn't go away forever," Luke insisted, and Conner saw a single tear roll from the corner of the boy's eye down his cheek. "She wouldn't."

"Luke . . ." He laid one hand on the child's arm, but he pulled away, shrugging off Conner's touch.

"You shoulda made her stay," the boy muttered thickly, emotion clogging his throat. "You shoulda told her that we need her."

"I did," Conner said through gritted teeth. "I did tell her." When it was too late, he admitted silently. When all that was left of her was the dream image, *then* he had finally admitted to loving her. Needing her. Would things have been different if he'd spoken up earlier? He frowned to himself. Another question he would never know the answer to. "I miss her, too, Luke."

He waited for the length of several heartbeats before the child slowly turned to look at him. Misery etched into his small features, tears swam in his pale blue eyes as he chewed frantically at his lower lip in a futile attempt to hold the tears back.

A tight fist grabbed Conner's heart and squeezed painfully. Chest tight and aching, he reached out for the boy and pulled him into his arms. Luke buried his face in the curve of Conner's neck and he felt the dampness of the boy's tears on his skin.

Rubbing Luke's narrow back with long, measured strokes, he held the boy gently while heartbreaking sobs tore through the child's throat. Shuddering with the force of his grief, Luke clung to Conner as though he was a sturdy tree standing in the midst of a flood.

Conner stared off down the road for a moment, wishing that he could see Meara striding toward them, red hair flying wild, a grin on her face, and one of her mother's favorite sayings on her lips. But finally, he closed his eyes and concentrated on comforting a boy who'd learned too young that happy endings only happened in fairy stories.

"This is your fault," Gideon thundered, jabbing his index finger toward Daisy. "I hold you entirely responsible for this—this—" He shook his head, muttering, "Words fail me." He shot the woman a look that had been known to send archangels scurrying for cover. Daisy didn't even blink.

But she did keep quiet. An unusual occurrence of itself.

At last, Gideon turned his furious glare on Meara. He shoved himself up from a silver high-backed chair and began stalking around the perimeter of the Great Chamber. Muttering to himself, he punctuated his words with an occasional shout that seemed to rattle the very heavens. "A simple thing," he said. "Punish Meara for ignoring the rules. A simple punishment was in order. Perhaps a year or two of guarding the dreams of cockroaches." He looked up, glared at the two women across the room from him, and shook his finger at Daisy again. "But no," he shouted. "I had to listen to her! 'Send Meara to Earth,' Daisy said. 'Send her to Conner. He'll take care of her,' she said."

Meara turned to look up at her friend.

Daisy shrugged, smiling.

" 'It's the answer to your problems,' she said," Gideon went on, his deep voice rising and falling like thunder. " 'Meara is out of your way for a month and my son is happy,' she said."

Gideon paused in his pacing and shot another look at Daisy. "Have you seen your son lately?" he demanded. "Does he look happy to you?"

"Oh, stop roarin' like an old bear," Daisy told him, then deliberately pushed her breasts higher.

Gideon shook his head and forced himself to look away.

"Gideon," Meara said quietly, hoping to break the cords of tension strung between the other two spirits. "I'm back now. Conner will learn to forget me. Everything can go back to normal."

Gideon stared at her blankly for a moment, then turned to stare at Daisy. "She doesn't realize yet, does she?"

"No," the woman said with a glance at Meara. "I wouldn't have known either if you hadn't seen it right off."

"I'm only surprised no one else has noticed yet," he said.

"Noticed what?" Meara asked, looking from one of them to the other.

Nodding briskly, Gideon turned to face Meara. "Nothing around here is normal now. Or will be. You can't stay here."

"I don't understand."

"It's simply unheard of," Gideon went on as if she knew what he was talking about. "One soul carrying another soul? It can't be done. And even if it could, we have no facilities here for such a thing."

"One soul carrying another?" Meara asked as a faint hint of a monumental realization began to take root in her mind. But it wasn't possible. Was it? "Are you saying . . . ?"

"You're carrying the soul of a mortal's child," Gideon said in a bit kinder tone than he had been using.

"I'm pregnant?" she asked, her hands moving instinctively to cover her abdomen protectively.

"Barely," he said. "No more than a week or so."

"But . . ." Meara glanced down at her flat belly as if expecting to see the evidence of Gideon's statement. "How is this possible?"

"It isn't possible!" the Dream Master shouted.

Ignoring him, Daisy said simply, "With love, Meara, anything's possible."

"Possible or not, it doesn't matter now," Gideon announced. "What does matter, is that you can't stay here now. You'll have to go back."

"Back?" Meara asked, almost afraid to believe what they were saying. "To Conner?"

"Of course not," Gideon said flatly, dashing the hopes that had only just begun to bloom within her.

"Now, Gid . . ."

"Daisy, she has to return to the time of her original life. Those are the rules. I've explained this to you before."

Meara looked at the Dream Master. Go back to Ireland? To the time of her death? And then what? Her family had been killed along with her. She'd have no one. And no where to go. And worst of all, she would be alive with one hundred years separating her from Conner.

"Now, Gideon honey," Daisy said softly, insistently, "you're the one who makes the rules . . ."

"He told her to go, remember?" Gideon said flatly, clearly refusing to discuss this further. "Your son told Meara to leave. He doesn't want her there."

Meara blinked back a sheen of tears that seemed to be always near these days. Conner had told her to leave. But later, in his dreams, he'd proclaimed his love for her and begged her to stay. Didn't that mean anything?

"My boy's just like every other man," Daisy said. "Don't know what he wants half the time and don't appreciate it when he does get it till it's gone."

"Be that as it may . . ." Gideon shook his head solemnly, muttering darkly to himself.

A baby, Meara thought, hugging the knowledge to her like the precious gift it was. If only things were different. If only there had been a way for she and Conner to be together. If only . . .

"I'm sorry it's come to this, Meara," Gideon said. "But perhaps it's for the best." Then he turned and left the Great Chamber, still grumbling furiously to himself about why it was no other Celestial Department Head had the same kind of troubles that seemed to plague him.

"Oh, Daisy . . ."

"Now, don't you fret, girl," her friend said. "I'll think of something."

"But there's nothing we can do. Gideon was right. Conner did tell me to leave."

"Doesn't mean a thing."

Meara wished she could believe. But the facts were too clear. Too strong to be denied. She was going to have Conner's baby, and he would never even know about it. "I hurt him," she said softly, wishing it wasn't so.

"Hogwash."

Meara looked at her. "Pardon?"

"I said, hogwash." Daisy stood up and smoothed

*her hands down the front of her red spangled gown.
"You hurt each other. When you love deep and
hard, too. Love ain't easy, Meara. But it makes all
the difference."*

"I know." Just the thought of a lifetime spent
without Conner beside her was enough to bring a
cold chill to her heart.

"So," Daisy said, commanding Meara's complete
attention with the strength of that one word. "Do
we give up and let Gideon call the shots here? Or
do we do what women have been doin' for centuries?"

Meara found herself smiling in spite of the heaviness settled in her chest. "Which is what, exactly?"

"Why," Daisy said with a wink and a grin,
"straightenin' up the messes men leave wherever
they go." Her smile softened as she leaned closer.
"What do you say, Meara? Do we show Gideon a
thing or two?"

Meara laid one hand on her unborn child and
reached out the other to the best friend she'd ever
known. Even if there was only one chance in a
thousand that she and Conner might be reunited
. . . wasn't it a chance worth fighting for? "Aye,
Daisy. We do indeed."

"Atta girl!"

As he had for a week, Conner fell into a restless sleep
and immediately began his battle against the gray nothingness that hid Meara from him. Surrounded on all
sides, he called her name over and over until his throat
was raw, but there was no answer. Only his own voice
echoing around him in the vast, gray world.

Every night it was the same. He was no closer to finding her. And yet he refused to give up. If it meant spending every sleeping moment for the rest of his life, he
would continue to rail against whatever barriers Heaven

devised. He *would* find Meara. Even if the cost was his sanity. Or his life.

"*You are a sore disappointment to me, boy.*"

That voice. Conner turned in a quick circle, letting his gaze slide across the filmy gray shroud hovering around him. He knew that voice. And if she was here . . . then Meara might be close by, too. "Ma?"

The mist shivered, then sighed apart like cobwebs dissolving in the wind. And then she was there, wearing the same expression she used to give him when she'd found out he'd played hooky to go fishing. "Ma!" Conner raced forward, picked her up, and swung her around in a wild, crazy circle.

"Put me down," she ordered, slapping him gently on the shoulders. "We got no time for this."

"But," Conner said as he set her on her feet, "it's been so long."

"I know," she said, smiling at him. "But I've been keepin' an eye on you all the same." She frowned suddenly. "That's why I sent you Meara."

"Meara," he whispered her name reverently. "She's why I'm here. I've been trying to find her, but this damn mist is always in the way."

"It won't be now," Daisy said, stepping back into the grayness. "Go to her, Conner," she told him. "Before it's too late. It all rests with you now, boy."

Horrified, he watched his mother's form disappearing into the fog. "Too late?" he demanded. "What do you mean too late? And I've been trying to find her for a week. Don't go! Where is she?"

"Follow your heart, Conner," Daisy said, and her voice now was no more substantial than the mist writhing around him. "Trust your love for her and hers for you. Hurry."

Then she was gone. Follow his heart? His heart

was with Meara. Conner paused at the thought and smiled to himself. Maybe that's just what she meant. Closing his eyes, he concentrated on Meara. Her face. Her voice. Her warmth. A calm, sure awareness settled over him, and an instant later, he was racing through the mist. Barriers fell before him, and for the first time since she'd left him, Conner felt Meara's presence. So close, he could almost touch her.

Dream Weavers gathered around the high podium, all eyes fixed on Gideon and the woman standing directly in front of him.

"Meara Simon," Gideon's voice thundered "you may no longer stay in the Dream World."

A few strangled gasps were heard from the crowd, but Meara didn't flinch. If anything, she defiantly lifted her chin another notch and squared her shoulders as if awaiting a blow.

"You, along with the soul you carry, will return to Earth to live out mortal lives."

Meara nodded and flicked a quick glance at Daisy, who seemed to be focusing her gaze on the far wall and the wide double doors that marked the entrance to the chamber. Apparently, the woman couldn't bear to watch the end to her schemes. Meara swallowed back a stab of disappointment. She'd so hoped that whatever Daisy had been planning would work.

"Meara," Gideon intoned, his voice as deep and dark as his eyes, "you will be returned to the year one thousand seven hundred and—"

A crashing clamor of sound startled every soul in the room into silence as the great doors swung open and slammed into the marble walls of the chamber. Gideon broke off abruptly and turned a steely glare on the intruder.

"Where is she?" Conner demanded as he rushed forward, pushing his way through the hundreds of Dream Weavers standing between him and Gideon. "Meara!"

She whirled around, hope and shock trembling in her breast. She went up on her toes in a vain effort to see over the heads of her fellow Weavers. But in moments, that effort wasn't necessary as the crowd slowly fell back, creating a path down which Conner strode like a man possessed.

Her heart in her throat, she looked her fill of him and knew she could never look enough. His worn boots and faded jeans struck an odd chord in the celestial chamber, but she didn't care. All that mattered was that he was here. Somehow, he had found his way to her and they would have one more moment together before being separated forever.

As he drew near, she bolted toward him. He swept her up into his arms and held her so tightly, it was as if he was defying Heaven to try to tear her from him.

"Meara," he whispered, unmindful of the hundreds of pairs of eyes locked on them both. His gaze moved over her, as if rediscovering a long-lost treasure. His hands cupped her face and drew her lips up to meet his.

When he kissed her, Meara sagged against him, lost in the wonder of finding something she'd thought lost to her forever. She wrapped her arms around his neck and held on to him as though he meant her life. As indeed, he did.

"If you don't mind . . ." Gideon spoke up then, his voice tight with barely leashed anger.

Reluctantly, it seemed, Conner broke the kiss and lifted his head to glare at the Dream Master. But he kept one arm around Meara, pinning her close to his side.

"Just how did you get here?" Gideon demanded, with one quick, sidelong look at Daisy, who shrugged innocently.

Conner, too, glanced at his mother before saying simply, "I followed my heart."

Was this the plan, then? Meara wondered. Had Daisy counted on Conner arriving at the very last moment? But even if she had, what could he do to prevent their separation?

Several of the female Dream Weavers in their audience sighed lustily, and Gideon frowned at them. "You have no voice in this place, mortal. Leave now."

"Not without Meara," he said.

"Impossible."

"Then get used to seein' me, mister," Conner told him. "Because now that I know the way past those damn walls of yours, I'm figurin' to be here real often."

Clearly, Gideon was furious. And if Conner's arm around her hadn't been quite so tight, Meara might have joined her fellow Weavers in taking a few hesitant steps backward. As it was, she stood her ground beside the man she loved and waited for the terrible retribution that was no doubt headed their way.

"Now, Gideon hon," Daisy said softly, "nothin's impossible."

Gideon faced her impatiently. "Your son is a man of too many moods. He wants her now, but only days ago, he told her to leave him."

"I didn't mean that," Conner interrupted.

"Now, Conner love," Meara said with a shake of her head, "you must admit, at the time, you did mean it."

He turned his head to look at her. "I'll never say it again," he swore. "When you left, you took my *heart, Meara. I discovered that I'm nothing without you. And the world without you in it is an empty place."*

More sighs from the crowded room.

Conner shifted his gaze back to Gideon and prepared for the fight of his life. "You want to send her back to Earth," he said. "I heard you when I came in. Send her back to me." He pushed Meara behind him, braced his feet in a fighting stance and added, "I love her and I won't let her go."

"And what about the child?" Gideon asked. "Do you love it as well?"

"Child?" Conner felt as though someone had sent a hard fist to the pit of his stomach. Turning, he held Meara's shoulders and looked down into her green eyes. "A baby?"

"Aye," she said with a smile. " 'Tis why I can't stay in the Dream World."

"But, this is impossible," he said, letting his gaze slip to her still flat belly. "Isn't it?"

"Just like I said, Gideon," Daisy spoke up clearly. "Nothin's impossible if there's enough love."

"Hmmm . . ."

Conner turned again to look up at the Dream Master. Now it was more than just he and Meara at stake. Now it was their child. Their baby. The family they could have together. And he'd be damned before he'd give all of that up.

"Who gave you the right to separate people who love each other?" Conner demanded hotly.

Gideon's eyebrows lifted into high, black arches. "I should think that would be fairly obvious," he said.

Conner blanched slightly as he realized just who Gideon's Boss must be. But his hesitation lasted only a second. "Fine. Take me to Him. Let Him tell me love doesn't matter."

"Conner!" Meara whispered, astonished at the very notion.

Daisy chuckled, and Gideon's frown deepened further.

"That won't be necessary," the Dream Master said finally. "If you can prove your love for Meara and the child, I might reconsider."

"Prove it? How? I'm here, aren't I? I found my way to her despite your efforts to keep me out." Conner released her and took a couple of steps closer to the podium. "And if you still try to keep me from her, I'll find a way to fight Heaven itself to find her again."

Gideon nodded thoughtfully, then glanced at Daisy. He gave her a small, secret smile before shifting his gaze back to the couple in front of him. "Very well," he said, his voice again thundering throughout the room. "Do you swear by all you hold holy, to love and care for Meara and the children you create together?"

Conner, stunned at the Dream Master's abrupt change of heart, glanced quickly at Meara, grabbed her hand and said in a loud, clear voice, "I do."

"And you, Meara Simon," Gideon announced, "do you relinquish your title of Dream Weaver to once again take up the mantle of mortality? Do you swear to love and care for the human and the children you are blessed with?"

Meara stepped in close to Conner, tilted her head back to look him in the eye and said, "Aye, Gideon. I do indeed."

"Then it is done," Gideon finished.

From despair, to hope, to joy in a matter of just a few minutes. Meara threw herself at Conner, then looked over her shoulder to smile a farewell at her *dearest friend. As if he was thinking the same thing, she heard Conner say, "Thanks Ma, for Meara. For everything."*

As the mists rose up around them, Daisy's voice reached them. "Be happy, you two, and make me lots of grandchildren to look after."

And then they were gone, and the Great Chamber echoed with the hum of conversations resumed. With the others occupied, Gideon slowly walked to Daisy's side.

"I told ya it'd work out fine, didn't I?" she said with a satisfied smile.

"So you did, my dear," Gideon acknowledged and leaned in close to seal the successful closure of their scheme with a kiss.

When the mists lifted, they stood locked together, on the road just beyond the ranch.

"We're back," Conner said, his voice filled with wonder as he stared around at the familiar, sunwashed landscape. He'd fallen asleep the night before, a man desperately lost. Now in the light of a new day, he was a man reborn and even the air tasted sweeter than it had before.

"Ah, Conner love," Meara said and wrapped her arms tighter around his neck. "I'd thought to never see ya again."

He pressed his fingertips to her lips and shook his head. "Don't even think that, much less say it out loud. We were meant to be together, Meara. Always."

"Always." Releasing him, she stepped back a pace and looked at him cautiously. "But, Conner, are ya happy about the baby?"

He reached up, tore his hat off and flung it into the air before grabbing her to him for a fierce hug. "Happy isn't a big enough word, Meara." Then it was his turn to release her, abruptly. A worried expression crossed his face

as he said suddenly, "C'mon. We've got to get you home.
So you can rest."

"I don't need a rest, Conner love," she told him. "I've
never known a better feeling in me life. *Either* life."

He smiled, but wasn't convinced. "*I'll* feel better when
you're safe at home."

"Home," Meara repeated, tasting the lush feel of the
word on her tongue. " 'Tis a lovely thing, is it not?"

"It is now," he said and bent his head for another kiss.
Silently, Conner sent a prayer of thanks Heavenward for
this chance at loving the woman who'd tumbled into his
life.

"*Meara!*"

Startled, they broke apart and, as one, turned toward
the shout. Luke leaped from his post on the pile of rocks
and raced down the road at a speed so fast his shirttail
flew out behind him like a cape.

Instantly, Meara dropped to one knee and caught the
crying boy as he hurled himself into her arms. She staggered slightly under the impact, but a more welcome
weight she'd never felt.

"You did come back," the boy muttered thickly, his
face buried in the curve of her throat. "I knew you
would. I knew it."

"You sure did," Conner said gruffly, his throat tight
with the emotions strangling him.

"Ah, love, 'tis all right now," she whispered, stroking
his back and smoothing the mop of blond hair. "I'll never
leave ya again. I promise."

"But where were ya, Meara? You were gone a long
time."

Catching her eye, Conner answered the boy's question.
"She was far away for awhile, but she came home as
quick as she could."

Meara stood up then, kept one hand on Luke's shoulder and with the other, caught Conner's right hand in a
tight grip. Smiling up at him, she said, "Aye, I was far

away. But it's as me mother always used to say . . ."

Conner threw his head back and laughed out loud. When he caught his breath again, he looked deeply into her green eyes and asked, "What could she possibly have to say about a situation like this?"

Meara's lips twitched, then she surrendered to the smiles bubbling within her as she calmly announced, " 'Twas her favorite saying, if ya must know." She looked fondly at each of them in turn before saying, " 'The longest road out is the shortest road home.' "

Conner reached out and pulled her close. "You know something? I think it's my favorite saying, too."

KATHLEEN KANE

"[HAS] REMARKABLE TALENT FOR UNUSUAL,
POIGNANT PLOTS AND CAPTIVATING
CHARACTERS."

—*PUBLISHERS WEEKLY*

A Pocketful of Paradise

A spirit whose job it was to usher souls into the afterlife, Zach
had angered the powers that be. Sent to Earth to live as a
human for a month, Zach never expected the beautiful Rebecca
to ignite in him such earthly emotions.

0-312-96090-5 _____ $5.99 U.S. _____ $7.99 Can.

This Time for Keeps

After eight disastrous lives, Tracy Hill is determined to get it
right. But Heaven's "Resettlement Committee" has other
plans—to send her to a 19th century cattle ranch, where a
rugged cowboy makes her wonder if the ninth time is *finally* the
charm.

0-312-96509-5 _____ $5.99 U.S. _____ $7.99 Can.

Still Close to Heaven

No man stood a ghost of a chance in Rachel Morgan's heart, for
the man she loved was an angel who she hadn't seen in fifteen
years. Jackson Tate has one more chance at heaven—if he finds
a good husband for Rachel…and makes her forget a love that
he himself still holds dear.

0-312-96268-1 _____ $5.99 U.S. _____ $7.99 Can.

Publishers Book and Audio Mailing Service
P.O. Box 070059, Staten Island, NY 10307
Please send me the book(s) I have checked above. I am enclosing $_____ (please add
$1.50 for the first book, and $.50 for each additional book to cover postage and handling.
Send check or money order only—no CODs) or charge my VISA, MASTERCARD,
DISCOVER or AMERICAN EXPRESS card.

Card Number_____

Expiration date_____Signature_____

Name_____

Address_____

City_____State/Zip _____
Please allow six weeks for delivery. Prices subject to change without notice. Payment in
U.S. funds only. New York residents add applicable sales tax.

KANE 9/98

LET AWARD-WINNING AUTHOR

JILL JONES

SWEEP YOU AWAY...

"Jill Jones is one of the top new writing talents of the day."
—*Affaire de Coeur*

THE SCOTTISH ROSE
TV host Taylor Kincaid works on a top-rated series that debunks the supernatural. But her beliefs are challenged when she travels to Scotland, in search of Mary Queen of Scots' jeweled chalice, The Scottish Rose. For there she meets Duncan Fraser, a man who helps her to find what she seeks—and to understand the magic of love.
0-312-96099-9___$5.99 U.S.___$7.99 Can.

MY LADY CAROLINE
During a séance, Alison Cunningham encounters the spirit of Lady Caroline Lamb, a troubled apparition whose liaison with Lord Byron ended bitterly. Compelled by the spirit, Alison purchases the London manor where Byron's secret memoirs are hidden. But Alison isn't the only one searching—so too is a sexy, arrogant antiques dealer whose presence elicits not only Alison's anger, but the fiery sparks of attraction.
0-312-95836-6___$5.99 U.S.___$6.99 Can.

EMILY'S SECRET
Handsome American professor Alex Hightower has always been fascinated by Emily Brontë and her secrets. Alex journeys to Haworth, the village where the young writer lived and died, to discover more about her. But while there, he discovers another mystery—a beautiful gypsy woman named Selena who also ignites in him a passionate curiosity.
0-312-95576-6___$4.99 U.S.___$5.99 Can.

Publishers Book and Audio Mailing Service
P.O. Box 070059, Staten Island, NY 10307
Please send me the book(s) I have checked above. I am enclosing $_____ (please add $1.50 for the first book, and $.50 for each additional book to cover postage and handling. Send check or money order only—no CODs) or charge my VISA, MASTERCARD, DISCOVER or AMERICAN EXPRESS card.

Card Number_____

Expiration date_____Signature_____

Name_____

Address_____

City_____State/Zip_____
Please allow six weeks for delivery. Prices subject to change without notice. Payment in U.S. funds only. New York residents add applicable sales tax.   JONES 8/98

Let bestselling author
ANTOINETTE STOCKENBERG
sweep you away... -

A CHARMED PLACE

In a charming town on Cape Cod, professor Maddie Regan and correspondent Dan Hawke team up to solve the mystery of Maddie's father's death. And what they discover are old secrets, long-buried lies—and an intense, altogether unexpected passion.
0-312-96597-4 ___$5.99 U.S.___$7.99 Can.

DREAM A LITTLE DREAM

Years ago, an eccentric millionaire decided to transport an old English castle—stone by stone—to America. Today his lovely heiress Elinor lives there—and so do the mansion's ghosts, intent on reclaiming their ancestral home. Now Elinor must battle a force stronger than herself—and, when a handsome nobleman enters the picture, the power of her own heart.

0-312-96168-5___$5.99 U.S.___$7.99 Can.

BEYOND MIDNIGHT

Ghosts and witches are a thing of the past for modern day Salem, Massachusetts—but Helen Evett, single mother, is beginning to wonder if this is entirely true. A strange power surrounds the man with whom she is falling in love—is it the ghost of his dead wife trying to tell her something?

0-312-95976-1___$5.99 U.S.___$6.99 Can.

Publishers Book and Audio Mailing Service
P.O. Box 070059, Staten Island, NY 10307
Please send me the book(s) I have checked above. I am enclosing $_____ (please add $1.50 for the first book, and $.50 for each additional book to cover postage and handling. Send check or money order only—no CODs) or charge my VISA, MASTERCARD, DISCOVER or AMERICAN EXPRESS card.

Card Number_____

Expiration date_____Signature_____

Name_____

Address_____

City_____State/Zip _____
Please allow six weeks for delivery. Prices subject to change without notice. Payment in U.S. funds only. New York residents add applicable sales tax.   STOCK 3/98

It only takes a second filled with the scream of twisting metal and shattering glass—and Chris Copestakes' young life is ending before it really began.

Then, against all odds, Chris wakes up in the hospital and discovers she's been given a second chance. But there's a catch. She's been returned to earth in the body of another woman—Hallie DiBarto, the selfish and beautiful socialite wife of a wealthy California resort-owner.

Suddenly, Chris is thrust into a world of prestige and secrets. As she struggles to hide her identity and make a new life for herself, she learns the terrible truth about Hallie DiBarto. And when she finds herself falling for Jamie DiBarto—a man both husband and stranger—she discovers that miracles really *can* happen.

ON THE WAY TO HEAVEN

TINA WAINSCOTT

ON THE WAY TO HEAVEN
Tina Wainscott
_____ 95417-4 $5.50 U.S./$6.50 Can.

Publishers Book and Audio Mailing Service
P.O. Box 070059, Staten Island, NY 10307
Please send me the book(s) I have checked above. I am enclosing $_____ (please add $1.50 for the first book, and $.50 for each additional book to cover postage and handling. Send check or money order only—no CODs) or charge my VISA, MASTERCARD, DISCOVER or AMERICAN EXPRESS card.

Card Number_____

Expiration date_____Signature_____

Name _____

Address_____

City_____State/Zip_____
Please allow six weeks for delivery. Prices subject to change without notice. Payment in U.S. funds only. New York residents add applicable sales tax.   HEAVEN 9/98